## *"What do you want from me?"*

He slowly smiled.

"Bastard," she whispered.

"Not even close, love."

The quirt dangled loosely from his wrist as his mouth took hers. The tremor that moved through her settled inside him and, without conscious thought, he deepened the kiss with a single sweep of his tongue.

Her legs parted slightly, inviting him. He heard her soft moan.

He didn't know if control had ever been his but restraint escaped his grasp when her tongue met his. Pushing his kiss deeper still, she ravished his mouth.

Then his hands tightened in her hair, abruptly breaking contact between his mouth and hers. She blinked up at him.

He shouldn't be ravishing her on the stairway in this house, yet something about her challenged his needs, tested his self-control.

"You're mad," she whispered against his lips.

He'd been called far worse . . .

## Other AVON ROMANCES

# Melody Thomas

## Passion And Pleasure In London

**AVON**

*An Imprint of HarperCollinsPublishers*

This is a work of fiction. Names, characters, places, and incidents are drawn from the author's imagination or are used fictitiously and are not to be construed as real. Any resemblance to actual events, locales, organizations, or persons, living or dead, is entirely coincidental.

AVON BOOKS
*An Imprint of* HarperCollins*Publishers*
10 East 53rd Street
New York, New York 10022-5299

First Avon Books paperback printing: September 2008

Printed in the U.S.A.

10  9  8  7  6  5  4  3  2  1

*For my wonderful editor, Erika Tsang,*
*with great respect and admiration*
*for all that you do.*
*Thank you for giving me*
*the opportunity to find a place at Avon.*

# Passion And Pleasure In London

# Chapter 1

*Outside London*
*Summer 1877*

**T**emptation came in many forms. The shine of a gold coin, the taste of fine whiskey. A fine woman with eyes the color of expensive dark chocolate.

Rory Jameson knew temptation. And he liked chocolate.

What he could see of the woman's hair beneath the voluminous hood of her cloak was as dark as her exotic eyes. He'd felt her gaze pause on him as she'd squeezed into the crowded taproom, then made her way toward the long oaken bar with an ease born of familiarity.

Buried in the smoke and noise surrounding him, Rory watched her, intrigued by the womanly shape her cloak failed to hide. Everything about her brought to mind a night of sin. Over the rim of a shot glass of smooth Irish whiskey, a smile slowly tugged at his mouth. He had finally found something worthy of his interest in this backwoods hamlet.

Rory was a man who enjoyed his vices. He'd lived hard, but unlike many of his peers, he hadn't died young. And he had no intention of doing so. At least not tonight.

Indeed, at two and thirty, he'd managed to live longer

than most ever expected. A combination of luck and forti-
tude got him this far in a profession that fed its young into
the gristmill just to see what came out on the other side.
He'd seen much of the world in one fashion or another and
intended to see the rest before old age or a bullet took him
off the playing field forever.

He feared little, except perhaps missing his niece's birthday and disappointing his sister, which in the end had been
what brought him to this part of England on this sleepy
summer's eve. The letter she'd received a month earlier
from their estranged grandfather burned more than a hole
in his pocket, and, more than once, he'd wondered how Lord
Granbury had found them.

He relegated those thoughts to the back of his mind as
he relaxed in his chair and felt it creak beneath his weight.
He sat in the shadows near the open window, his legs casually crossed at the ankles. Soft leather riding boots hugged
his calves. He drank as he continued to watch the dark-eyed
beauty's progress across the room as she stopped to talk to the
barkeep. Her hood slipped slightly to her shoulders revealing
her profile and he wondered for a moment at her age.

His eyes narrowed as he watched her, her gloveless hands
animated as she spoke, the movement of her lips drawing his
eyes to her mouth.

Arousal pressed against the fine black wool of his trousers, which he found damn hard to ignore. His mind noted
that everything about her seemed out of place in this crowded
public room filled with a medley of drunken men, footpads,
and slatterns, yet no one accosted her. In fact, the burly barkeep currently eyed Rory, something of which he had just
became aware. The oaf's silent warning seemed to overtake
other patrons as well for they too turned to peer toward

where Rory sat, as if he'd trespassed in forbidden territory. The air around him grew chilled. Recognizing the type of men here, he suspected the only reason he'd not been challenged yet was that his manner and clothing warned them he would prove to be something more than a casual mark.

Amused by his interest in the local entertainment, Rory tipped back the shot of whiskey, liberating his conscience as he set the glass on the scarred table next to the half-empty bottle. He stood, removed a coin from his pocket, and flipped it into his shot glass. At two inches over six feet, he had to duck his head to avoid bumping the low-hanging gas lamp. He didn't look back at the girl, though he could feel her eyes on him now. The sensation was as physically arousing as if she'd put her hands all over him. And it was as novel as it was discomfiting. Perhaps even more so because she'd left him with a curiosity. He wanted to know who she was.

Winter Ashburn's hand paused on the frayed edge of the curtain separating her from the crowded taproom, her gaze lingering on the door through which the tall, dark-haired stranger in black had just passed. The mammoth rack of antlers above the oaken door seemed to frame the quiet drama of his exit in her mind as she stood hidden within the confining shadows of the storage room. She dropped the curtain, shocked as awareness of him shimmied through her veins like an electrical current. The man was a stranger, an outsider yet there had been something familiar about his lazy smile.

And the race of her heart had nothing to do with the frantic reason that had brought her to this inn tonight.

A solid thud of the door sounded behind Winter, and she turned to greet the older woman who stepped into the room.

A soiled apron clung to Mrs. Derwood's ample bosom where her hands now made use of the apron skirt as if it were a towel.

Mrs. Derwood's massively built son, the Stag & Huntsman's proprietor and barkeep who had directed Winter into this storage area, was also the sheriff. He had once been the overseer for Winter's father's stable of horses at Everleigh Hall, and his mother a cook while they'd lived there. Winter had known both Derwoods her entire life, and always felt safe inside the walls of this inn.

"I would have been here sooner," Winter said, holding out the scrap of paper in her hand. "But I only just received your note."

Mrs. Derwood's brown eyes softened as she approached. "Fie on that rascal brother of yers for not tellin' ye we found yer mam. She is with Mrs. Smythe."

Last month, Winter's mam had been making nightly treks to the cemetery where Winter's father was buried. Father Flannigan had found her asleep atop the grave. Tonight was worse, though—Winter hadn't even known Mam was missing until she'd received Mrs. Derwood's message. She'd been looking for her errant brother the entire evening.

Winter scraped a hand through her unbound hair. Tears suddenly filled her eyes. "I'm sorry to put you through this again." Suddenly tired, for these incidents had become too common this past year, she looked away. She disliked showing emotions and took great care to keep them walled most of the time. But tonight had been too close a call. "I just don't know what I'd do if something happened to her."

"Leave her be. Mrs. Smythe could do with the company as her husband just recently passed. Besides, ye take too much on yerself." Mrs. Derwood patted her like a babe and Winter laughed at the incongruous thought that it would be perfectly natural to burp. "Now, that's a good girl."

Wiping the moisture from her cheeks with her fingertips, Winter drew away. "Thank goodness the baron is in London. He would be none too pleased to learn of Mam's latest escapade."

Not that Winter cared what the bastard thought, but his money gave him the power to destroy their lives. And he would, too, if he learned that in addition to Mam's illness, she had now taken it upon herself to wander about the night. The baron would lock Mam away.

"Your uncle should be the one brought to shame, lass." Mrs. Derwood took Winter's hands, her concern mitigating the sternness of her expression. "You should be with them in London for the Season."

"Goodness, no." Winter withdrew her hands. "I don't care about such frivolity and nonsense."

"Nonsense. Your uncle don't want you with him because you outshine that snippety daughter of his, lass. It is you what should be weddin' Granbury's heir—"

"Mrs. Derwood." Winter pulled the hood of her cloak over her hair. "It's late. Please, I need to be getting back to Perry before he and Robert get into their usual mischief."

"I'll have Old Ben fetch the cart and take you back."

"I have no need to worry about ghouls, ghosts, or wild dogs surprising us in the woods. Perry and Robert are in full character tonight."

"If you would wait a minute, I've something for them in the kitchen."

Mrs. Derwood bustled out of the room. The noise filtering

through the curtained barrier from the taproom eased over the silence that followed the elderly woman's departure.

Barrels and crates filled the airless storage room. The smell of yeast and a hint of the night's smoked boar teased Winter's senses. She touched a barrel as if it were an old friend. This place had been like a second home to her since her father died.

Though on paper, Winter Ashburn might be the great-granddaughter of a duke, she never let herself think anymore about how things used to be when her father was alive. She focused these days on how to keep her life running as smoothly as possible. As long as she did nothing to draw her uncle's attention, he ignored her, which was just as she wanted it to remain.

Baron Richly was the husband of her father's older sister, and had entered Winter's life just before her father's death left the family without funds to pay their debts. In a matter of months, Winter had gone from society's prevailing darling to someone her father's once staid friends pitied. Not a single high-minded elitist stepped forward to stop the baron from taking her beloved Everleigh. The only people who had aided her during those awful years were the estate's tenants and many of the villagers. They were Winter's family now.

Winter held no love for the baron's world and no allegiance to an establishment that made paupers out of other men's souls as well as their purses. In her mind, aristocrats and nabobs—aristocrat wannabes—were notoriously worthless, and a wealthy reprobate might find his pockets considerably lighter before leaving the boundaries of this hamlet.

And just that fast, her thoughts returned to the dark-haired stranger whose eyes had boldly assessed her in the pub.

Maybe it was the music coming from the other room as the fiddler took up his bow and a jaunty tune drifted back to her.

Like the shadow of a great bird slowly spreading its wings, the stranger began to fill her thoughts. Or maybe he had been at the back of her mind all along. In persona, he embodied every aristocratic attribute she despised, but somehow she sensed he was not like the other *gentlemen* of her narrow acquaintance. Despite his languid sprawl, he'd exuded danger—along with his palpable sexuality and arrogance. She couldn't place where she might have seen him before. But there was something familiar about him.

Winter walked to the small window that looked out over the livery where she'd left her brother. But it wasn't for Perry whom her eyes searched.

Idly folding her arms beneath her cloak, she narrowed her attention to the white-washed livery and surrounding paddock. A full moon picked out the mist rising silently from the ground and the fleeting shadow of a spotted hound.

*Had the stranger already ridden out of the yard?* An odd sense of loss fell over her.

Mrs. Derwood returned carrying a basket filled with goodies. "Here ye be, mum. Don't be shy about eatin' some of these victuals yourself. They're fer sharing. Ye tell Master Perry and that scamp, Robert, I said so, mum."

"I will." Winter thanked the woman, not only for the basket but also for helping take care of Mam.

Mrs. Derwood opened the back door to the crisp night air. "Now run along and give that sweet potato pie to those two young pirates outside. Then hie yerself home. No good ever comes on a night with a full moon."

* * *

Once outside the Stag & Huntsman, and despite Mrs. Derwood's ominous full-moon superstitions, Winter found herself in better spirits than she had been inside. She followed the familiar sound of laugher and discovered her brother with his friend behind the livery. Perry loved caring for the horses, his father's son to be sure. He had been too young when their father died to remember the celebrated Ashburn stables.

Her brother turned at her approach. Wearing a pirate's eye patch, Perry still managed to see the white basket in her hand first. He and his friend Robert were dressed in their swashbuckling costumes. They liked to leap from trees and terrorize the unsuspecting at the most inopportune time, sending animals and people screaming.

Her errant brother already had to make restitution to Mrs. Peabody for scaring her nearly to death, but mucking stables for a week wasn't enough. Just last week, he'd nearly broken his neck after constructing wings from bed sheets and leaping off the stable roof on the assumption he could fly.

Perry ran to her and, with the instinct of a growing eleven-year-old, ferreted out the pie. The two boys tussled over who would get first bite until Winter thought they'd resort to fisticuffs.

"Perry! Robert!" she admonished just as the two dropped the pie on the ground between them.

Fortunately, Mrs. Derwood had wrapped it. But then what was a little dirt to two rambunctious boys dressed up like Blackbeard and Henry Morgan? "You can both eat that pie at home. It's getting late."

Robert ignored her and unwrapped the pie, replying for Perry, who was the younger and shyer of the pair. "We can't go yet, mum."

"Show her what the gent gave ye," her brother mumbled excitedly over a mouthful of crust.

Robert displayed a coin. "I earned a shilling."

"It's part mine, too." Perry shoved the battered wig off his brow.

"You weren't begging coins from people?" Winter demanded.

"Nah!" The two boys snickered, then Robert said, "A tall, highbrow gent come ridin' in earlier and tells Old Ben to keep 'is mount in the stable away from them other nags in the corral."

Winter flinched at Robert's annihilation of the King's English. She had been teaching both boys their letters and had taught Robert especially to speak with better syntax and less verbiage. As if reading her mind, and ever conscious of her approval, Robert swallowed. "Away from them other *horses*," he corrected. "The gent's a regular toff, 'e 'is," the urchin forged onward with a lowered voice. "Butter won't melt in 'is mouth, mum. Gisette offered to tup him for less than six pence and the chap turned her down flat."

"Robert!"

His eyes widened in distress. "Ye shoulda 'eard what Gisette said."

Perry laughed, completely unaware that such a topic could not possibly be proper. Suddenly the two boys were best friends again, planning how to spend their newly acquired wealth, her presence entirely forgotten in their gluttonous orgy as they discovered the roasted chicken in the basket. Perry acted as if he hadn't eaten in a week.

"You said the man was tall?" Winter asked. "Was he dressed nicely? Black leather boots?" *Tailored riding clothes as impeccable as the body they draped?* "Woolen jacket? Dark hair?"

Tucking away the coin, Robert considered her question. "He were tall. Don't know 'bout the boots, but he *was* wearin' a silver watch."

"Dark hair," Perry confirmed.

"He ain't like the others, what come through here, mum, who just come to . . . you know." Robert swallowed his mouthful and didn't say the word "tup." "He wanted to know which road went to Granbury Court."

"Granbury Court?"

"I told 'im, and that's when 'e gave me my shilling."

Winter looked around the mist-shrouded yard. The old Marquess of Granbury's estate sitting amid thirty thousand acres had been owned by the Jameson family since before the English civil war. Anyone who had grown up within a hundred miles of London would know how to find Granbury Court, which meant the man who had inquired was not from this part of England. But for the exception of anyone visiting Lord Granbury's rakehell grand-nephew, who was currently in London, the cantankerous marquess rarely had visitors anymore.

"The man who asked, is he still here?"

Robert shrugged a shoulder toward the back entry of the stable. "The toff's stallion is still 'ere, cause I'm guardin' it."

Caught by the sudden inexplicable flutter in her stomach, she glanced toward the stable. "Start home," she told the boys. "I'll catch up—"

"But we have to stay, Miss Winter."

"I'll ask Old Ben to keep an eye on the horse. It is late. I want you both to start home. I'll catch up to you."

Winter left her brother and Robert grumbling, but they packed up the basket. When she turned in the doorway of the stable, she saw them walking toward the woods. She was not one to chase after the identity of any man, but neither was she content to live with a curiosity burning through her mind.

Adjusting the hood of her cloak, she entered the stable. A horse snorted. The pungent smell of straw, aged leather, and manure touched her senses. Oil lanterns hung from a post at each end provided dim light. She peered up and down the narrow aisle, listening, but heard no one present.

Moving toward a bay stallion in the last stall, she kept to the shadows. Quietly stopping, she picked an apple from the barrel next to one of the stalls, keeping her ears alert for any noise that told her she wasn't alone as she approached the stall.

The horse was a beauty with long legs, a full chest and glossy coat, a thoroughbred of stellar bloodstock.

Whoever the stranger was, he knew horseflesh. This stud was worth more than most common people would ever see in a lifetime. The bridle and saddle boasted the highest craftsmanship. Wanting to get near the valise attached to the cantle, Winter eased cautiously into the stall all the while crooning softly. She held out the apple and powerful jaws crunched down on the sweet morsel.

If she could but learn the name of the dark-haired stranger, she could settle the matter of his identity.

*Liar,* her wicked self whispered.

Even as something about him warned her to be wary of her initial reaction when she'd seen him in the pub, a flicker of long-repressed femininity focused her memory on the touch of his gaze. Men undressed her with their eyes all the time, but no one had ever made her body tingle. Her reaction had both alarmed and intrigued her, for at the base of it all was an unfamiliar sense of awareness.

She saw no identifying marks or initials emblazoned on the saddle or on the valise. She struggled with the clasp before noting it needed a key. The horse stirred and Winter slid her palm gently across its powerful shoulder.

"His name is Apollo."

Winter whirled, horrified to find the voice's owner lounging against the stall door, his smile flashing white in the lamplight. "Mine is Rory," he added. "In case you were wondering the name of the man you were attempting to rob."

"I wasn't! Robbing you, that is . . ." She brought her hand to her chest as she really looked at him. *Good heavens.*

Up close, this man was beautiful. Hair nearly blue-black in the low light enhanced the dark stubble shading his jaw. Eyes not quite blue but silver, like the ornate braided chain dangling from the watch pocket on his vest. Eyes that were not nearly as friendly as his voice.

"You startled me." She pressed against the horse like some urchin caught in the act of stealing bread. Mentally chiding herself for her lack of aplomb, she adjusted her hood and straightened. "This isn't what you think."

"It never is." His crisp white linen shirt beneath his jacket opened slightly at the neck with the subtle shift of his body. "Maybe all I'm thinking is that there are easier ways to earn your money tonight, love. Especially since there is nothing in that valise worth your life."

Her heart leapt. Did he mean to slay her where she stood? The horse shifted and tossed its head.

"I would like to come out," she said with more brevity than calm and reached for the stall latch.

His gloved hand reached it first, and she jerked back. The corners of his mouth twitched. The beauty of his features juxtaposed against the harsh shadows cast by the lamp behind him made him look both dramatic and dangerous, and resentment that she should find the bounder attractive flared within her. "Step aside," she warned.

He relaxed against the stall, preventing her escape. "I thought you people were more circumspect and practiced in your crimes."

Having been caught trying to go through his things, crying innocent would do no good, but his having a low opinion of her bothered her. Perhaps not because he thought her a thief, but because he considered her a bad one. "I wasn't trying to steal from you."

He laughed, clearly at ease with his boorish behavior, more so than she with her indefensible stupidity for stepping into the stall with a horse that could be dangerous. "I would like to come out now. Please."

"Now this is the first hint of intelligence I've seen from you tonight. You *should* be afraid," he said softly.

*Of you or your horse?* The fact that he thought she should be afraid made her determined to prove she wasn't.

Rory unlatched the stall and Winter slid out, hesitating when he did not seem inclined to move.

She squeezed out of the stall, her body forced to touch every inch of his. A faintly exotic scent overlay the hint of whiskey she smelled. A suggestion of patchouli struck her nostrils as if he'd washed his hair in exotic soap. The gate clicked shut behind her.

"I will reiterate. You are a bastard."

She started to move around him when he pressed his palm against the stall and blocked her escape. Her breath caught in her chest for the second time in as many minutes. A flame-hot rush of awareness burned through her, electric in intensity, and she fought to resist the intoxicating sensations that seemed to begin in the pit of her stomach and radiate outward.

"Tell me your name," he commanded softly.

"No," she returned his whisper.

"Or maybe I should inform the sheriff I caught you trying to steal from me."

Propriety demanded her immediate withdrawal. But ten cannons wouldn't dislodge her at this point. "Blackmail?" she scoffed in rebuke, doubting he would resort to such tactics. "Talk to the sheriff. He won't believe you."

"Do you always make it a habit to go through a man's belongings then? Or am I special?"

Every female instinct warned her to caution, and it required much effort on her part not to press her palms to his chest and push him away. Yet beneath it all was born a sense of familiarity with this man. She had seen him before. Though she knew it impossible. She did not travel outside Granbury or in his circle.

Perhaps he'd once visited her father's stable. "I was merely admiring your horse," she said in a half-truth. "I have rarely seen such a fine animal. From which stable did you purchase it?"

He took a step to his side and leaned against one of the wooden posts at his back, folding his arms. "Apollo was a gift from a corrupt Bashaw in Tangiers who owed me a favor."

Her lips parted slightly in shock before she could speak. "What does a man do to earn a tyrant's favor?"

A wolfish smile appeared on his handsome face. "I didn't sleep with his Circassian lover. He thanked me for it."

Heat crawled into her face. Taking issue with her own unworldly reaction as well as his humor, she stared at him. "Is that a fact?"

"That is a fact."

His gaze lowered to her lips, and she held her breath.

He'd been right about her going into Apollo's stall. A stallion's temperament should never be taken for granted. But at the moment she was in more danger from the man than she had been from his horse.

"Trevor Jameson is not in residence at Granbury Court," she blurted out, "if that is why you are going there."

A shadow momentarily eclipsed the light in his eyes.

"My brother and his friend told me you had inquired about directions," she explained. "You do not look like Lord Granbury's solicitor, so I assume you are here to see Mr. Jameson?"

"I'm not." He peered down the length of the stable as if his senses touched on something hers had not. "No doubt this entire town is in collaboration in some form of vice or another," he surmised. "But I should warn you, your brethren will not like what happens if I even get a whiff of communal chicanery tonight."

A niggling worry probed her. "If I wanted to steal from you, I would have set someone up at the entrance to warn me of your approach, sir." Winter took a step around him. With no warning, a leather-booted leg blocked her escape before she could draw a breath and her hip collided with it. Apprehension surging, she stepped backward, her heart hammering. She shot a look to his face. "I could scream," she said.

A hint of the humor in his eyes touched his mouth. "How old are you?"

"Fourteen," she said without hesitation, and resisted a momentary swell of superiority as her lie swiped the smirk off his face.

His eyes narrowing, he gave her a lengthy inspection. "Is that a fact?" he said, pleasantly mimicking her earlier remark. "I like that you are a liar as well."

Still feeling an odd lingering heat between them despite her alarm, she lifted her chin. "Why?"

With aristocratic indifference to her shock, he replied in the lowest of tones, "Because I no longer feel guilty for wanting to do to you exactly what I've had on my mind since you walked into that pub, madam."

Winter felt the heat burn all the way from her décolletage into her cheeks. "Of all the—"

"As I said"—again, he braced his hand against the stall at her back. And there it was again. The exotic smell of him. Soap, whiskey, leather—"there are easier ways for you to earn your coin tonight."

She'd been holding her breath against inhaling the summer warmth of him but had not realized it until his gloved hand produced a florin. "We can start with your first name. I told you mine."

The dolt was far too sure of himself and of her.

"A kiss then. It's less personal perhaps."

Tension knotted in her stomach. What was wrong with her that she did not put this man in his place? That she should not feel insulted by his assertion that she was a local bawd, and that her heart was racing with something akin to devilish excitement. "I won't be forced."

"I am not in the practice of abusing women," he said in a whisper that caressed her senses. "If you don't want me to kiss you, all you have to do is step away, or say no. Or scream. I'm sure my life would be imperiled should you choose to raise your voice an octave."

His presence alone kept her pinned against the stall,

not quite threatening, but neither had he made an effort to move anymore than she'd made an effort to escape. She wet her lips against the dare in his eyes and the desire to put him in his place. "Does money buy you everything you want?"

"I don't know. Will it?"

The tone of his words told her she was merely a night's gamely diversion for him. He didn't *care* anything about her, but he would not coerce a woman to do his bidding. If she moved away this time, she suspected he would allow her to leave and would feel no loss at her defection. That he could so easily dismiss her produced an unprecedented response, for it made her feel inadequate and somehow less than she was.

Men with money thought they held all the power. Her life was managed by such a man—a bastard who wanted unfettered control. Who had already hurt her more than most people knew. The thought angered Winter.

Sometimes a woman could hold power, too, and to be less than memorable was to be dead.

Boldly pushing back her hood and letting it fall about her shoulders, she lifted her chin until she met his gaze. "You're a libertine," she accused, though in the back of her mind she remembered he did not choose to tup Gisette.

She felt the momentary weight of his eyes. "A moralist's term," he said with a restrained timbre, his gloved hand rising to cup her chin. "You're a thief."

Her hands fell lightly against his chest, and her heart pounded. She *was* a thief, more than he knew.

And she felt more alive than she had in years. Something about this man challenged a dormant part of her. She stared back at him. "Then on the whole, you find morality inconvenient. Hence, you are willing to overlook most faults in people. Even lies."

His eyes grazed her hair, touched her lips, and met her own gaze. "Lie with me," he whispered.

Her mouth trembled as he leaned to kiss her.

Anxiety surged, resurfacing to pool in her stomach along with everything else, none of which she could define. "No," she said, her face a breath away, and she found herself bracing her fingers against his chest, closing the distance between their lips on her own terms, not his.

She had only *willingly* kissed one other man in her life. No one ever made her hot and shivery, and so she imbibed as if he were a glass of whiskey. Cautious of the taste, wary of the burn, and fully conscious of the danger as she forced herself to center on the texture of his mouth, not the heat in her blood. If she wasn't careful, she would end up giving him more than a kiss. He knew it, too. His hands went to her waist.

It was that overconfidence that subdued her and ruined her at once, as she forced herself to remain focused. But her head was swimming as she continued to press her advantage, stirring restlessly.

Distantly, she felt as if he were holding back almost like an observer perfectly comfortable allowing her to take the lead. Sinking deeper into her kiss, she rose on her toes, wanting something more, yet unsure what. Her palms smoothed across the contoured planes of his chest. Her knuckles skimmed along the inside of his jacket and hit something cold and metallic in a leather sheath beneath his shoulder.

Startled she pulled back. "Is it *loaded*?"

His hands went to her face, his fingers slid into her hair,

his eyes half-lowered and intent on hers. "My gun is always loaded, love." His mouth claimed hers, taking the initiative from her, and making her previous kiss feel like a childish peck on the cheek.

*Oh my.*

His legs parted and he stepped against her, slow deliberate movements as his hand angled back her head. His tongue swept between her lips with perfect boldness, deepening the contact. She found her back against the stall door, while every female sense reacted to the press of masculinity against her layers of bulky skirts. Slowly his hands traveled down her spine piling sensation down upon new sensation as every notion she'd ever held about kissing a man crumbled to her feet.

Her body hummed. Try as she might, she could not pull away, but she lacked his carnal sophistication and could not follow his lead. She felt trapped by her response. Everything was happening too fast. Panicked by the surge of need he roused within her, so much so, she tore her mouth away from his.

"Loose me," she found the voice to say. "Now . . ."

His hands framed her face as he pulled away, his eyes now dark and unnerving. She shivered slightly. For a heartbeat, only their breathing touched the heavy silence between them.

"You are either a virgin," he rasped against the heat of her lips, "or the worst kisser in the world." Amusement laced his tone. "In either case, you are no strumpet, love."

The thought that her reaction to him could be so enormous while his toward her was naught but a frivolous passing sent a maddening feeling of humiliation straight to the core of her. "Get away from me!"

"No more games, madam. Who are you exactly? Why were you trying to go through my valise?"

His eyes were no longer laughing at her, but deadly serious. Yet for just a brief instance after he'd kissed her there had been something else in that silver gaze that went deeper than the surface, something that frightened her because it touched her on a deeper level as well.

Winter caught herself retreating and stopped. "I wanted to know who you are. You are familiar to me."

He used his fingertips to tilt up her chin. "Which part of me?"

Her brother's voice startled her. "Winter?"

Perry and Robert stood in the doorway. Dressed like pirates as they were, in their wigs and dragging their cutlasses, they looked like two highwaymen of lore.

*Good lord.* They were supposed to be halfway home by now. "I thought I told you to leave, Perry."

Her brother's usually friendly eyes peered watchfully at the man whose height and size dwarfed them all. "We were waiting for you, Winter."

"Perry," she quietly warned when he failed to leave. "Start home. I'll be right behind you. I promise."

For once, he did as he was told.

"You have a protector," the stranger said after the boys left.

"Do you find that extraordinary?"

Unlike his touch, his stare was casual. "No more than your name. Winter? I might have guessed you'd have an unusual name."

Disliking the intimate sound of it on his lips, she yanked up the hood of her cloak. Her eyes went to his face. Dangerous in the shadows.

"Will I see you again?" he asked.

Perhaps one day in purgatory, she mused, stepping away from him, an involuntary reaction as much from his words as it was from something deep inside that still wanted to wrap itself around him. "You and I will never walk in the same circle."

"No." The slide of his eyes over her body made it clear to her *walking* was not what he had on his mind. "But that doesn't mean we can't entertain ourselves."

She calmly adjusted the hood of her cloak. "Try not to break your arrogant neck on the road tonight. We would all weep inconsolably for your family's loss."

A black-gloved hand grabbed her arm as she swept past the man who was no longer quite a stranger and who still held electric sway over her response to him. His eyes, glittering with a dark mystery, continued to wreak havoc on her senses as he pulled her in.

"What are you doing?" she said.

He slid the coin he'd held up earlier down her bodice, the intimacy of his touch making her gasp. "Assuring you that this evening has been worth every bit of what that coin purchased, Miss Winter."

Ignoring his quiet, confident laughter, she spun on her heel, confident that before the evening was gone, his lordship would know he'd overpaid.

Her mouth suddenly curving at the corners into its own secret smile, she wondered how long it would take before he discovered the entire contents of his pockets had been pilfered.

Unfortunately, the arrogant toff would never know he'd just made a substantial contribution to Father Flannigan's poorhouse fund.

# Chapter 2

R ory folded his arms over his chest and leaned against the doorframe, watching the little vixen's stride take her across the stable yard. He was both fascinated and tantalized by the sway of her woolen cloak that framed soft, womanly curves as she moved. Try as he might, Rory could not reconcile her lack of experience with her bold behavior.

He felt no censure for kissing her, only regret for allowing her to escape so easily, especially after he'd caught her attempting to go through his things. Yet that mattered less than watching her leave.

The low ground mist began to swallow her image, but he could hear her steps sounding hollow against the planked low bridge that spanned the stream. Despite his reasons for being here, he doubted he'd see her again as he intended this trip to be short. His trunk would arrive at Granbury Court tomorrow, and he had just enough to remain a week. Above him, the wide sweep of black sky glittered with stars and drew his gaze. A full moon hung suspended at the tops of the trees. When he looked toward the thick edge of woods again, the girl was gone.

Behind him, a voice chuckled. "Count yourself lucky, guv'nor."

Rory unfolded his arms and turned into the stable. The owner of the voice stood inside a stall, just left of the door. It was the hostler.

"She'd have shot most men what kissed her jest as you did. I figure, she's a grown-up woman what knows her own mind, though. So it's not my place to say anything."

Winter was grown up all right, Rory considered. He lifted a brow and approached the stall where the hostler stood. He didn't bother asking the impertinent eavesdropper how much of the conversation he'd overheard. Undoubtedly, the old man had heard most everything.

His cheek bulging with tobacco, the hostler rested his elbows on the gate. His gaze traveled up Rory's black boots, over his tailored black trousers, his white shirt, and black jacket. "She couldn't place ye, but I do. You're the old marquess's grandson. She's probably seen that old portrait hangin' in that fancy 'ouse of his lordship's. Ye look like yer father did when he was yer age."

Rory's amusement faded. "You have a good memory, considering my father has been absent for more than thirty years."

The old man turned his head and spat a dark stream into a spittoon sitting just outside the stall. "Nigh on sixty years' worth of memories, guv'nor. Some of them not so good. Beggin' yer pardon, guv'nor. I 'spect a gent like yerself 'as better things to do than to be talking to an old man like me."

Rory leaned a shoulder against a stall wall, taking a few seconds to study the hostler. "What do they call you?"

He returned his gaze to his hands where he was braiding strips of leather. "Old Ben, if someone is interested in callin' me anything other than hostler. Only Miss Winter calls me Mr. Brown. Now she's a lady."

Wondering if they were speaking of the same woman, Rory raised an amused brow at the man's heartfelt avowal, "And does Miss Winter always confront strangers in stables and kiss them?"

Old Ben chuckled. "I've known that snippet all twenty-one years of her life since she were born at Everleigh. I can assure ye she ain't the kissin' type. The blokes 'round here stay clear. 'Sides the fact she'd likely skewer them, she's under Sheriff Derwood's protection. He be the proprietor of the Stag & Huntsman."

Why was he not surprised, Rory thought. "I see."

"Don't get me wrong. Miss Winter can handle herself. She's been takin' care of her mam and Master Perry and most of the tenants at Everleigh Hall fer nigh on five years." He hesitated for the briefest moment. "Despite what ye may think, guv'nor, Miss Winter Ashburn be a lady. Don't dismiss her as below ye. She ain't below no man."

Mere moments earlier, Rory had been thinking of Miss Winter Ashburn in that very position. What he now had trouble dismissing was her passion and his desire to own it. His mood, always capricious, had changed from bored to a single-minded awareness of her the moment his lips had touched hers.

Rory was suddenly more interested in who the woman was. "Everleigh Hall is her home?"

"Everleigh Hall *was* her home," Ben supplied, his veined hands hesitating over the hooks on the wall. He turned and lowered his voice. "Most folk think I'm a half-blind old rummy. But I've eyes an' ears in my head. I can tell ye tales about the goings-on in that place since her uncle took over." The man's rheumy eyes narrowed. "And I'm thinkin' to meself just now, the chap expectin' ter inherit yer grandfather's estate don't know 'bout ye." He peered shrewdly at Rory as if to discern the truth of his birth, which Rory had no intention of discussing. "Trevor Jameson is already in London spending his inheritance and the marquess ain't even in his grave yet."

Old Ben began gathering up the strips of leather he'd been braiding. "Ye can slap me down fer sayin' these words, but 'at rascal's been short of charity fer anyone but hisself of late." He sniffed as he let himself out of the stall. "Exceptin' Miss Winter. Only it ain't charity he feels toward her. The two of 'em growed up together, her bein' from Everleigh Hall and all. I 'spect she thinks she's in love with the dandy."

A fleshy fellow with curly white hair walked into the stable just then and stopped. His red-rimmed eyes pondered Rory dispassionately before telling the hostler to get outside to look at a lame horse. Since Rory was as prudent with his acquaintance as he was with his observations, he refrained from comment, telling himself it was none of his business how Old Ben's patrons treated the old man. The hostler dropped the leather strips and hurriedly latched the stall gate, his relaxed demeanor gone.

"You best be leaving now, my lord." Without a backward glance, Old Ben left the stable.

Rory stepped out of the lantern light and watched as Old Ben hurried out of sight behind the paddock to where a powerful-looking gray mare stood. The other man leaned an elbow against the faded, weather-beaten fence. Low conversation, indiscernible to Rory's ear, passed between them as Old Ben knelt to study the mare's left forelock.

A gaunt black-and-white spotted hound entered the stable just then and, spying Rory, stopped abruptly as if wary of strangers.

Rory knelt on his haunches and held out his hand. "What's your name, boy?" The dog approached and sat, its tail thumping against the straw-covered floor. "Hmm?" Rory rubbed its ears, his black-gloved hands stark against the hound's white ears.

Annoyed at himself, Rory shook his head. He had just spent the last ten minutes in the company of an old drunk imbibing in local gossip and now he was on his knee in stable muck talking to a dog. But something in the hound's guarded brown eyes touched him, like Old Ben's had when the stranger entered the stable—like Miss Winter's eyes had when she'd inquired who he was.

The long, hard path of his life left little room for quixotic ruminations. Yet he remained hunched on the ground, petting the hound, aware of the growing silence around him, mixed with the lack of desire to continue on to Granbury Court tonight. He was restless and mildly morose, a mood he had not felt in a long while.

His thoughts turned to his distant cousin, Trevor Jameson. Rory had never met the man, but more than once tonight he'd heard an undertone concerning his cousin's claim on Granbury. Trevor was the grandson of the Marquess of Granbury's youngest brother. Rory knew a little about the Jameson family history, but had never cared to learn more.

Nor did he give a fig about his grandfather's title or estates. He did not intend to stay long enough to get himself caught up in family politics. His purpose for being in Granbury was more benign than reclaiming his father's place in his grandfather's world. His grandfather had wanted nothing to do with Rory's life until now.

And *now* was too late.

Yet, without conscious direction for what he was doing,

he stood and reached his hand into his jacket pocket for the leather casing containing the letter from his grandfather. Finding the pocket empty, he checked the other side of the jacket. Nothing.

A cold chill went over him.

He shoved his hand into each pocket again.

*What the hell?*

The slim wallet containing his bank notes and the letter from his grandfather was gone. His thoughts stumbled backward over the last few hours, from when he'd first entered the pub and then, finally, landing on the kiss.

But not to the one he'd given Winter Ashburn. Instead, he was remembering the first one. The kiss she had given *him*, when her hands had been beneath his jacket, when he'd been too scorched by her touch to note anything else she might have been doing with those hands.

*Bloody hell.*

He patted his pockets again, realizing the little sneak-thief had fleeced him. While he'd so generously parted with a florin, the chit had robbed him blind.

He slowly smiled. Miss Winter Ashburn was more skilled at playing the ingénue than most. He liked that discovery, his initial fury at being so blatantly robbed eclipsed by something inexplicable. Not only had she dared steal from him, she'd done so beneath his very nose.

Hell, for that alone, she deserved the bloody five hundred pounds in that casing. He might even have let her go with her prize had she not taken, along with those banknotes, that letter—or if he suddenly didn't find himself challenged to retrieve the billfold and teach her lesson.

This last he would do with pleasure, his objective to continue on to Granbury lost in the intriguing possibilities the

night suddenly offered—a polite term for what was causing the blood to hum in his ears. No doubt, with the sheriff
on her side, Miss Winter thought herself safe. But she'd be
wrong. Rory felt more than uncivilized.

A few minutes later, in a hollow staccato of hoofbeats,
Rory sat astride Apollo and they were crossing the low,
planked bridge. He slowed the horse to a walk at the edge
of the woods, searching for tracks just past the bridge where
Winter Ashburn had vanished.

Moonlight barely penetrated the oaks, beeches, and twisty
hornbeams laying down no visible path. Apollo pulled at the
reins, snorting and prancing in a circle, but Rory brought the
stallion back around. Despite his immense desire to catch
Winter, he did not want to injure his horse or find himself
unseated by a low branch while riding blind into the woods.
He couldn't see a path.

Something darted through the bushes next to him. Rory
tightened his grip on the reins as a hound bounded past
Apollo, wagging its tail clearly ready for an adventure.
"Easy lad," Rory murmured to his high-strung horse.

Though Rory was in no mood to pick up a cur, he changed
his mind when the dog found the trail hidden in the shadows. Then Rory was riding out of town and into the night
following a dog.

The trail was no more than a footpath that wound along
a shadowy stretch for half a mile. Rory finally reined in
Apollo at the top of a rocky rise overlooking a narrow spit
of meadowland. That was when he saw her. His stomach
pitched oddly, the sensation without reason or cause except
that he was a man who loved the chase.

In a moment, Winter Ashburn would be across the glade
and sheltered in the cover of the woods again. Apollo, as if

recognizing his master's impatience, sidled in agitation, but Rory was not yet ready to relinquish his view. Moonlight suited the girl, he realized, taking a moment to savor her trek through the carpet of sleeping flowers. Then he nudged his horse, the hunt truly on.

With no clear path down the rocky slope, Rory looked for a trail that paralleled the incline. He'd just found one when two shapes dropped from the overhanging bough of the gnarled tree in front of him. "Halt!" the taller assailant yelled.

The startled Apollo reared and pranced sideways in the rock-strewn turf, nearly unseating Rory. He might have drawn his pistol, had he not recognized the two young culprits dressed in pirate regalia, complete with old-fashioned wigs and brandishing short swords he quickly realized were not real.

But their intended warning, "Stop or face death!" and "Stay away from my sister!" went no further as Rory brought Apollo under control and they were faced with his wrath. It was one thing to play youthful games but not when their antics could have endangered his horse.

Rory had just calmed Apollo when he saw them freeze, an expression of horror on their young faces. They had spied something at his back. They turned suddenly and fled. Even the hound took off barking, as if the devil were at its heels, leaving Rory to whatever fate would befall him. He turned in the saddle and saw two cowled riders blocking the path. Both men brandished pistols at his chest. In one brief glance, Rory recognized the gray mare at the stable. Disappointment pushed against him. Something told him Old Ben was involved.

Then he thought of those two boys, one of whom was

Winter's brother and wondered what their role might also be in this confrontation.

Rory had only a small purse to give them. That and his horse.

He had a bullet for them as well, he thought, crossing one hand over the other as he leaned into his saddle. *"Gentlemen,"* he said, using the term loosely.

The man on the gray mare nudged his mount into a shaft of moonlight, his gun level. Slits in the fabric revealed nothing but shadowed pits for eyes. "Keep your hands where we can see 'em, guv'nor. Get after 'em two brats, Whitey!" the blackguard said to his companion.

"Leave off." Another voice replied from the darkness, and Rory realized he faced more than two men. "They did us a favor," the voice rasped.

The bloke on the gray mare edged forward. A shaft of moonlight reflected off the barrel of the gun pointed at Rory's horse. "Get off all properlike and we'll be sparin' that valuable stud you're riding."

Rory had once served as a British cavalry officer and knew how to fight from horseback. Before the man could grab Apollo's bridle, Rory hauled back on the reins. The stallion reared and flailed his hooves. Rory brought him under control and wheeled him around, scattering the pair of riders directly in his path to prevent a flanking movement. The action gave him precious seconds to draw his gun from the leather sheath beneath his arm.

But with the moon at his back, he knew—even as he fired two shots and nailed the highwayman in front of him—that he was an easy target for the other two.

A harbinger that proved all too true a pulse beat later as a bullet struck him in the head.

* * *

*Pop, pop, pop!*

*Gunfire.* With the moon behind the clouds, the woods that surrounded Winter suddenly became a frightening place. She halted at the edge of the meadow, picked up her skirts and ran back into the field, coming to a breathless stop among the tall grass and flowers.

She had left Perry and Robert to trail after her. In a state of panic, she ran, thinking of nothing but finding her brother. *Did the shot come from poachers?*

Perry and Robert suddenly burst out of the woods ahead of her, racing in her direction. She dashed toward them. Her brother was in tears when they finally reached each other.

Robert grabbed her hand, pulling her around. "Real highwaymen, mum. Hide!"

"Were they shooting at you?"

"No, mum."

Instinctively she dropped into the long grass, pulling Robert and Perry with her. There they all remained, breathing hard, listening for any sounds that the two boys had been followed.

Winter wanted to know everything that had happened, but she kept silent, holding Perry and Robert close in an effort to still their terror—and hers. Horses approached from the upper trail, stopping at the edge of the woods from where Perry and Robert had emerged, perhaps a hundred feet from where the three of them lay hidden. The riders paused. She imagined they were studying the meadow's terrain but suspected they could see little in the ground mist. At last, they turned their mounts toward Granbury Court.

Her every sense followed the retreating sound of horse's hooves as they moved farther away. When she was satisfied

they were well and gone, Winter eased the cloak off her face
and pushed herself up on her hands and knees, her fingers
digging into the fecund soil. Heart hammering, she peered
over the long grass, glad that the moon had yet to reappear
from behind the clouds.

Her attention was drawn to Perry's quiet sobs. "We didn't
mean anything, Winter. We just wanted to scare him off a
little."

Winter looked from Robert to Perry. Neither of them was
making sense. "Scare who off? Who is back there?"

"*Him*." Perry dashed tears from his eyes with the back
of his hand.

"The *toff*," Robert said. "The one what followed ye from
the stable."

# Chapter 3

**R** ory's skull was on fire. For a moment, he thought he must be in hell. But then, his entire body hurt too much for him to be dead. More like he was in purgatory.

The woman leaning over him was surely an angel. He heard the sound of water being wrung from a rag. Something cool gently pressed against his cheek and throat, relieving him of the sticky dampness there. Featherlight fingers brushed his brow. He became aware of lying in a bed, no longer wearing his jacket or shirt. As his memory crept back, he recalled snatches of conversation, remembered being dragged into a cart, bumped and tossed about.

The scent of burning pilchard oil stuck in his throat and he thought he might throw up. Fractured images of the Cornwall coast emerged in his thoughts through a veil of thinning mist. He'd been there. Years ago. His foggy mind struggled to grasp other pieces of memory fragments: Stirling, Yorkshire . . . London, Paris, Rome . . . St. Petersburg . . .

Then his angel was pressing the cool rim of a cup against his lips. "Drink. This will help ease the pain."

*What did an angel know of pain?* he wondered idly, her words incongruent with the throbbing in his head.

Then his mouth filled with the bittersweet taste of opiates. Two sips. Three. *Christ*. He closed his fingers around her wrist. Through a sheer force of will, he shoved the cup away and opened his eyes.

She froze, her eyes locked on his. Her long unbound hair was a halo of ebony sky around her face, snagging him on the lure of her gaze. He didn't know where he was, but he was surrounded by stillness and a sultry mix of heat and shadows. A zephyr from an open window fluttered the curtains. Confusion rendered him momentarily mute.

He tried to remember why he was half naked in bed with a strange woman feeding him opiates, why he felt like a three-day hangover, but there seemed to be holes in his thinking. His hand went to the pain at his bandage-wrapped head. Then he recalled that he'd been shot. Thankfully, the bullet had missed its mark. But not by much.

His pocket colt and its shoulder holster had been removed from his body. His eyes wandered and he found the weapon lying on the nightstand.

His angel's pulse fluttered against his palm and brought his attention back to her face that now seemed paler. He could feel the resistance in her wrist, feel his own awareness of her that had not been there a heartbeat before.

He *knew* this particular angel. He'd seen her walking among the wildflowers in the meadow.

*"You,"* he rasped.

He'd kissed her in the stable, tasted her on his lips, before being fleeced and waylaid by brigands.

Indeed, she knew he remembered everything because her eyes held fear. She tried to snatch her wrist away.

His other hand closed around her throat with the threat of a man who was capable of breaking her neck, even in his weakened state. "Little . . . bloody thief."

With her free hand, she clutched at his fingers. "Let go of me!"

If the men who had tried to murder him were still around, her voice could bring them down on him. As she struck out wildly against his grip, he turned with her into the soft bedding, trapping her beneath his chest and entangling them both in her skirts. In one furious movement, he dragged both her wrists over her head, pinning them with one hand while he crushed the other against her lips. "Not on your life, love."

There was nothing sensual about his action, the movement so ingrained it was instinctual, like a wounded wolf twice as dangerous for the injuries he suffered. He pressed his thigh across her hips subduing her fight. The world spun in a circle around him before it settled again and he found himself atop her and between her legs, staring into wide brown eyes. Above the ridge of his hand, he felt her every furious breath, every rise and fall of her bosom.

With her wrists pinioned above her head, he could have shown her the true extent of what he was capable of doing.

"My angel of mercy." He said in a voice so low the words brushed her cheek. "You're a worthy adversary. But this night you and I could have had more fun in the hayloft."

She mumbled furiously against his palm and tried to bite him. "You'll force me to hurt you," he warned. Cautiously, he lifted his hand to allow her to speak. And she grabbed her breath. "Do you understand?" he asked.

She nodded, clearly comprehending that he expected her not to scream. "Who else is in this house?"

"My brother and Robert. And Mrs. Kincaid, the owner of this cottage. She is downstairs boiling more water." Her hair tangled in her face and she spit it out of her mouth. "I'm *trying* to help you. You were attacked."

"By *your* people—"

"I don't know who it was. Listen," she pleaded. "You've been unconscious for hours. We've brought you someplace safe."

"Safe?" His eyes slid over her lips. "No such place exists."

"Do you trust no one?"

He looked past her at the moonlight glinting off the thick diamond windowpanes. He returned his gaze to her. "So far this night . . . I've been robbed, attacked by pirates, shot, my horse stolen . . ." And there was still the matter of the part his angel of mercy and her unruly brother might have played in it all. "This town hasn't exactly been friendly. Has it, *Miss Ashburn*?"

She drew in a panicked breath. His mouth quirked— "Now are you ready to tell me who you are?"

"If you know my name then you must know my uncle owns Everleigh. The estate borders the Marquess of Granbury's land."

"I wouldn't know whose estate borders Granbury land. My grandfather has never been particularly enlightening about his own affairs, much less those of his neighbors."

Her eyes widened. "The Marquess of Granbury doesn't *have* a grandson."

"Tell *that* to my father," he said flatly.

"I don't believe you."

He could feel the rise and fall of her breasts against his chest. His hand tightened its grip on her wrists, but he was in no condition to argue, anymore than he'd been of a mind to foolishly dally with a local spitfire who would better serve him locked away in a gaol somewhere.

Yet, he'd been aware of her heartbeat throbbing against his chest since he'd pinned her beneath him. But now he was aware of her scent, the hint of wind and earth in her hair, and something else that reminded him of the stirring breeze that came off the summer sea. A paradox that did not fit her name. She was heat and fire.

She was alive in a way she should not be alive to him. From the first time his eyes had fallen on her in the smoke-filled tavern, he'd felt a faint stirring inside like he was waking up after a deep, long sleep.

And he saw its reflection now in her eyes, an anticipation that was bigger than her fear of him—if only for a moment—a heartbeat before she pulled it back. But he'd seen it just the same and, this time when their gazes caught, he felt the oddest sense of satisfaction, as if he had won something back from her just then, something she had stolen from him that had nothing to do with his wallet.

The florin he'd dropped between the mounds of her breasts earlier that evening had inched its way up and he plucked it from her cleavage. "This . . . you don't deserve, love."

"Oh!" Her eyes narrowed. "For a second I'd forgotten I felt sorry for you and that you *perfectly* deserved to have your pocket lifted. I am guilty of no more than thievery. Besides, I was planning to donate it all to the parish. Someplace I'm sure you've never set foot."

The corners of his lips moved ever so slightly. "I doubt even God, in all His wisdom will take your goodwill into account when judging your sins, madam. People like us spend eternity in a place a little bit warmer."

She clamped her lips shut, drawing his attention to her mouth again. The world began to spin around him once more. He told himself his irrational response to her was nothing more than the affects of blood loss. He told himself a lot of things. He was a master of lies, after all. But it wasn't the race of his pulse making him dizzy. His strength was draining from his arms at an alarming speed.

Then somewhere in the background of the rushing noise in his head, Rory heard the approach of horses. He opened his eyes. Something flashed behind Winter's stare.

She'd been waiting for the laudanum to take hold. Now, bloody hell, it had.

"Damn . . . you. How much did you give . . . me?"

"Please, this isn't what you think. It's only Old Ben returning with Father Flannigan. You can trust them."

With an oath, he turned onto his back and flung out his arm for the gun lying on the nightstand. But she had somehow leapt to her feet and positioned herself between him and the nightstand. His hand knocked a small green vial to the floor. She intercepted and grabbed his wrist.

"It must be a shock to a man like yourself to be at someone's mercy," she said so quietly that all he wanted was to sink into the abyss from which she was calling him. "But you have to believe me. If any of us wanted you to perish, we would have left you in the glade."

But his hand was already falling away from hers.

Winter came awake slowly at first. She was sitting on a spindle-back chair in the kitchen. It creaked with her movement. She lifted her head from the table and blinked in the semi-darkness of predawn. Perry and Robert were still asleep on a pallet in front of the cooking hearth. A fire smoldered, coaxing out reluctant warmth and light that did not extend far into the room. The jolt of her heart at realizing she'd fallen asleep wiped away the last dregs of grogginess.

She looked up to see the bandylegged, gray-haired father Flannigan standing at the sink. The rusty water pump squealed in protest as he worked the lever over the basin. Cold water splashed from the spout and into a large ceramic bowl, aged and chipped from use. Winter rose to her feet.

"The patient is resting as comfortably as can be expected," the priest said, vigorously scrubbing a bar of lye soap over his hands. "Mrs. Kincaid is with him."

Winter nodded, relieved that someone else had taken the responsibility for the stranger's welfare. She would rather walk barefoot on glass than go back upstairs.

She'd remembered why the man upstairs had seemed so familiar to her. Why she had seemed to know him. Was there a portrait of him in the main hall of Granbury Court? Only, that painting had been commissioned over thirty years ago. . . .

She had seen the life-size portrait once when she'd been twelve, the only time she'd ever come through the main foyer of Granbury Court with her family as a formal guest of the marquess. To a starry-eyed girl who had once dreamed of being a princess, the dashing silver-eyed man in that portrait had given her cause to believe in fairy tales. At least until she'd grown up and learned there *was* no such thing as fairy tales.

"Did the stranger say anything?" she asked after a moment.

"About what?"

*Me? About whom he believed responsible for this?* "Who he is?"

Father Flannigan plucked a rag off the countertop and wiped his hands. He peered at her, his usually warm and friendly eyes narrowing. His mouth tightened. She looked down at herself. Blood stained her bodice and skirt.

Rumored to have received his pontifical avocation while living in the rookeries of London, Father Flannigan was not a man who sidled around conflict, especially when it dealt with saving souls.

"I found this in his jacket." He tossed the familiar leather wallet onto the countertop. Winter had returned the leather casing back to the stranger's pocket earlier that evening when Mrs. Kincaid hadn't been watching. She'd returned it as if that act would cancel out all the other awful acts preceding that night's debacle. "Open it," he said. "Whoever tried to rob him left that behind. Why?"

Winter swallowed. The hand-tooled wallet was soft to the touch, not at all like the man it belonged to. Winter had not opened it when it had been in her brief possession. She hadn't had time. Reluctantly, she unfolded it. The wealth inside made her gasp. A frayed edge of a letter peeking out of the fold scraped her forefinger.

"I haven't found any other identification, but that letter is from Granbury to his grandson." The hiss of a Lucifer sounded as Father Flannigan lit the lamp. "Delivered to a woman in Scotland. Salutations are to the Earl of Huntington. Rory Jameson. That title is passed down through the Marquess Granbury's bloodline, and has been for centuries."

She dropped the wallet back onto the countertop. "Trevor is Lord Granbury's heir. If there were another heir, wouldn't we have known? Maybe someone should contact his grandfather and ask."

"What if he *is* the proper Granbury heir? Are you the one who will tell Lord Granbury his grandson is lying upstairs with a bullet wound to his head?" Father Flannigan replaced the glass globe over the flame. "Indeed, if this were a simple robbery, the robbers would not have left the wallet behind. For the moment, at least, whoever tried to kill him thinks he is dead."

Winter pressed her palm against her stomach, feeling sick, but nodded. Only she knew there had been no wallet to steal.

Father Flannigan returned his attention to the water, opening the window over the sink and dumping the large bowl's contents outside. The scent of honeysuckle briefly eclipsed that of woodsmoke. "Mrs. Kincaid said you were the one who stitched the wound," he said after a moment.

Winter nodded. She had been working side by side with Father Flannigan in the parish infirmary for years. She nursed patients through every manner of illness imaginable, but she had never drawn a needle through another man's flesh herself. Swallowing past the unexpected nausea that welled, she shrugged a shoulder. "It was not that difficult. Mrs. Kincaid helped."

A moment of silence loomed between them. "Knowing Mrs. Kincaid's scarlet past, you must have been desperate if you came to her for help."

Mrs. Kincaid might be the very last person on earth with whom she would ever talk, but Winter resented the implication that she would have allowed her personal feelings to take precedence over a man's life. "Old Ben thought it best to bring the stranger—"

"This is a fine kettle of fish stew, indeed, Winter Ashburn." He snatched the wallet back from the countertop and waggled it at her. "When are you going to explain to me what Lord Huntington was doing on Everleigh land?"

She could not avoid those piercing eyes. "We had an encounter in town. He was following me."

"I see."

"He challenged me . . . at something. I foolishly took the bait."

"And then he followed you? And your brother and Robert then leapt out of a tree wearing their pirate regalia, and while they were in the midst of that prank three highwaymen came upon him?" His eyes studied her, awaiting a nod.

Scrubbing the sudden rush of tears from her cheeks with the heel of her hand, she failed to dispute his particulars.

Turning to lean against the counter, he looked at Winter as if he could peel away the layers over her soul. "I just want to make sure the facts are straight for when we face the magistrate and explain why the grandson of one of the oldest families in England was shot on Everleigh land, and how you and your brother were involved."

To feel Father Flannigan's disappointment was like a knife thrust into Winter's heart.

"Unless there is more I should know?" he queried in the same Irish lilt he used during confession.

Wearily brushing her tangled hair from her face, she shook her head, burying herself in more deception and lies. Her throat felt raw where the stranger had wrapped his hand around her neck.

Despite what most people believed her to be, she was neither noble nor all that courageous. She had not given Father Flannigan the wallet she had pilfered from the stranger but had placed it back inside his lordship's jacket and let Father

Flannigan find it himself. Now she couldn't bring herself to tell him the truth.

Nor would she tell anyone of the kiss in the stable. Certainly, she would burn in the inferno of hell for her duplicity, but even that was preferable to facing the stranger again. Not that she feared him. Not exactly.

His very presence aroused something within her that had nothing to do with compassion for his injury or responsibility for her part in bringing him to this end. Something that had sparked in the stable when she'd turned away from his horse and seen him standing like some rakeshame against the stall—and that had ignited into flame when she'd lain beneath him in bed, his body stretched out in the most intimate way against hers. He had come out of an unconscious state like a man who knew how to fight, his instinct for survival not just heightened but lethally sharpened. She'd stared into eyes that were wild and dangerous, knowing he was capable of doing anything, and felt a strange sort of excitement that hovered somewhere between terror and bliss. An excitement he'd seen in her, too.

That perhaps was the most dangerous thing of all.

She told Father Flannigan none of this.

Nor did she mention the gun, the one she'd removed from his holster, the one he'd tried to grab and use, which was now hidden beneath his bed.

Truly, his presence in her life did not bode well for her future. Look at all the lies she'd been forced to tell.

Now she was standing in the kitchen belonging to the very woman who had abetted the collapse of Winter's and Perry's life, the woman Winter's father had been visiting the night he'd died.

She peered over her shoulder at the pale sky and the first

touch of light spreading over Angelique Kincaid's thatched, two-story stone house. Winter was exhausted and wanted desperately to go home, to sleep in the safety of her own bed and forget this night had ever happened—if only for the next few hours while she pondered how she was going to set about trying to repair this disaster.

"It's nearly dawn," she said, pushing the chair back beneath the table. "Old Ben doesn't need to take me and the boys back to the cottage. We'll walk home."

"Old Ben will take you. You need to wash up and change. Bring back any medical supplies you can find and extra food you'll need while here. You'll be at our patient's side when he awakens."

"But . . . I'm sure Mrs. Kincaid will care for—"

"Mrs. Kincaid is not a skilled nurse," he said, speaking over her. "You are. Nor will she be responsible for your upkeep while you are here. She is risking enough as it is to shelter that man upstairs."

"I can't be here." She cleared her throat, aware of the foolish way her outburst sounded. "I have Mam to—"

"I'll arrange for her to remain with Mrs. Smythe and I'll take the boys back to the rectory. I think under the circumstances that would be best."

She stared in disbelief as the priest walked to a peg on the wall and removed his jacket. "I don't fault you for the love you bear your family," he said. "But they will survive without you for a while." His eyes gentled on her. "Have you considered when this man finally comes to his senses, he could accuse Perry and Robert of complicity?"

She had indeed considered that very thing. "After you explain, he will see that they are not guilty of anything more than a childish prank. He'll believe a priest. Surely."

"Are you so sure of his character then?"

Winter had seen the affection he'd displayed for his horse. The man might be a libertine but he wasn't cold-blooded. Was he? "Maybe he will wake and remember nothing," she said offhandedly.

*One could only hope.*

Father Flannigan shoved his arms into the sleeves of his jacket. "This particular man doesn't bring to mind the type who forgets anything. Pity the poor bastards responsible for this."

"Please, Father. Don't ask me to remain."

He observed her over the beak of his nose. "Kindness is the least he deserves from the lot of us. When our patient is well enough, your brother and Robert will apologize for their part in this fiasco. Do not let yourself forget that man upstairs may be our next marquess."

Without waiting for her acquiescence, Father Flannigan looked over at the pallet in front of the kitchen hearth. Perry and Robert were now awake. "You lads be outside in five minutes."

They'd both removed their wigs and lost their wooden cutlasses somewhere. They were little boys again, very much afraid.

After the room emptied of the priest's presence, Perry climbed to his feet. Her brother hadn't been away from her for a single night since their father had died. His pale hair mussed with sleep and his clothes rumpled, he looked like a sheepherder's son, not the progeny of once-landed gentry.

"I want to go home," he whimpered.

She gathered up their wigs and pirate jerkins. "You can't."

"But, Winter!" Robert joined Perry.

Winter took them both in hand. "Hush, the both of you."

She laid each coat over their shoulders because even in June the air was nippy in the morn. She hated the wounded look on their young faces and hated even more that she did not have the mettle to be firm enough with either. "You will be allowed to return home when Father Flannigan thinks it is all right to do so. Understand?"

"Be it true what Father said 'bout the guv accusin' us of complexity, Miss Winter?" Robert asked.

"Complicity. And the answer is no. Don't even think such a wretched thing. When Lord Huntington awakens, you will apologize and it will be the end of that misunderstanding."

Why she believed this arrogant *toff* incapable of condemning two young boys, she didn't know. Her uncle, the baron, would not be so benevolent.

A moment later, the boys were gone and Winter was standing at the kitchen window watching Father Flannigan guide his horse and buggy down the weed-strewn road, finally disappearing in the morning mist. A fat fly bumped against the glass, its buzz the only sound in the room. Her gaze focused on the white picket fence and sleepy wildflowers that surrounded the yard. Purple and yellow irises grew in contented rows in the neatly kept garden, as if the rest of the surrounding world were not fraught with chaos. If Mrs. Kincaid possessed one redeeming quality, it was her ability to grow a beautiful garden.

Winter wiped at the tears that sprang into her eyes. For a moment, shame sobered her, but she was able to edge it aside and focus on an effort to right everything that had gone wrong. She was not an intentionally cruel person.

Yesterday all she'd been worried about was Mam. Now someone had tried to rob Granbury's grandson almost at her back door. Would the outcome have been different if he'd had a wallet to give them?

She knew boys younger than twelve had found their unwelcome way to Tyburn and been hanged for less than what had happened last night. Surely, the stranger would not implicate Perry and Robert.

"The guv'nor be a decent sort," Old Ben said from behind her, startling a gasp from her.

"What do you know about that man upstairs?" she asked.

Old Ben's gnarly-veined hands twisted the rim of his floppy hat. "Caused a big scandal, it did, when his Da run off and married the bastard daughter of some Scottish duke. Got hisself disowned, and Granbury never expectin' 'is youngest to spawn 'is only grandson. That toff upstairs be Lord Granbury's heir fer sure."

She glared at the timbered ceiling. Old Ben might as well have announced the stranger was in line for the throne for all the trouble she had got herself into.

"But don't ye worry, miss." Old Ben smashed his floppy hat on his grizzled head. "The guv'nor won't let nothin' happen to those tykes."

Perhaps not. But Old Ben didn't say if she would be so fortunate.

Winter climbed the stairs in Angelique Kincaid's cottage, the creak beneath her half-boots tracking her every step. She meant for this meeting with Mrs. Kincaid to go quickly and had sent Old Ben outside to wait for her in the cart.

On the landing at the top of the staircase, a walnut secretary sat just to her right. A green vase of flowers perched on it, providing an incongruous splash of cheeriness to an otherwise dim and lonely corridor. For a fleeting instant, Winter wondered when Mrs. Kincaid had had the time to gather flowers.

She hesitated, resting her hand on the rail as she drew a steadying breath. When she opened the bedroom door, she did not see Mrs. Kincaid occupying the red-tufted chair beside Lord Huntington's bed. A noise in another bedroom at the end of the narrow corridor told Winter that the woman had returned briefly to her own chambers, probably to change out of her nightdress. Winter lingered at the room's threshold like a parrot on a roost, her eyes taking in the interior.

She willed herself to calm. The stranger's jacket still hung from a spindle-back chair next to a clothes press. Lord Huntington himself lay in bed surrounded by pillows and purple sheets. His eyes were closed. Cleft between being respectable and someone she should fear, the man remained unmoving as if he had never been conscious.

She took advantage of the opportunity to observe him more closely. Wiry curls darkened his bare chest and shadowed his armpits, but he wasn't entirely naked. She knew he wore loose drawers beneath the sheet. His black hair curled over the muslin bandage wrapping his head. His stubbled face, smooth of the creases that had crinkled the corners of his eyes and framed his lips with a perpetual edge of amusement, no longer bore the portraiture of arrogance. Yet he had a chiseled wildness about him that made a lie out of his peaceful state.

She didn't want to feel the strange effect within her when she was around him, as if her world had gone topsy-turvy, as if she were drunk on ale.

All of the resentment Winter held for Father Flannigan's high-handed interference in her life bubbled to the surface.

She curled her fingers into her palm, tucked beneath her cloak. She whirled and came to an abrupt stop.

Angelique Kincaid had suddenly appeared in the doorway at the end of the corridor, her hands frozen in the act of tying a white apron around a bright blue day dress. Mrs. Kincaid was less than ten years younger than Winter's mother, but with her thick henna-dyed hair plaited in a queue that hung down her back, she looked not much older than the dark-haired stranger lying in bed.

Mrs. Kincaid pressed her palms against her apron. "I was about to brew tea. Would you care for some? You have been awake longer than I."

"I came up to tell you Old Ben is taking me back to my cottage. I'll return after I have washed and changed." Winter started to turn away, hesitated, and stopped.

"You would not be here if Old Ben had not brought you, I know," Mrs. Kincaid said.

"I would not have jeopardized your safety," Winter replied, for that much was true. "Father Flannigan thought it best I remain a few days."

"I assumed he would. I am a widow, but still it would not be . . . how does one say it? Correct?"

Winter faced the older woman fully. Winter's own father had been Angelique Kincaid's lover. Even she must know Father Flannigan's reason for ordering Winter to remain here was not so altruistic. "Neither of us are saints, Mrs. Kincaid. Perhaps we should not pretend to be so. We're each to blame for where we are *both* at today."

Angelique Kincaid's silence only seemed to underscore the cruelty beneath Winter's words.

For few had been truly kind to Angelique Kincaid even before Winter's father had died.

Once a seamstress for an infamous acting troupe out of Drury Lane in London, Mrs. Kincaid had come to Granbury six years ago and opened a boutique. She had specialized in creating gowns and unmentionable whatnots that every lady enjoyed but did not admit to wearing. That shop had been Angelique's dream for a better life.

But no one hired the woman to make a gown. She was an outsider. A woman with a questionable past. No *lady* would ever be seen with her. Winter had been among those who had shunned her. In time, Mrs. Kincaid had taken down her sign, closed her boutique, and retreated here, to the cottage.

And here she had remained, working this plot of land, despite the fact that many of the town's population treated her poorly. And still, after all of that, when Angelique Kincaid answered the door last night, she'd taken one look at Winter, put aside concerns for her own safety, and helped.

Winter didn't want to owe Mrs. Kincaid the gratitude she suddenly felt. She didn't want to feel beholden to anyone. And opening up the past that she thought she'd laid to rest years ago was like slicing open her heart and tearing away the protective scab that had formed.

Gathering her skirt in one hand, she escaped down the stairs and outside to where Old Ben waited for her in the cart.

# Chapter 4

Winter returned to her cottage. After reassuring herself no one had been to the house, she sent their only elderly servant with their horse and buggy to Mrs. Smythe's cottage to be with Winter's mother. Once in the safety of her room, Winter shut the bedroom door and leaned against the heavy oak, closing her eyes and taking a moment to grab on to her next breath. Then she pushed off the door, determined to see this unpleasant task through.

She opened the top drawer in her chest to retrieve clean undergarments. Her knuckles brushed the pewter photograph frame she kept buried beneath her unmentionables. This was where she hid all things private. No one would go through a place of such intimate apparel, and so she kept her most personal items here: a mahogany box filled with trinkets collected over the years, a locket holding her father's hair, and this photograph.

She carefully withdrew it. The picture of her sitting between a young man and her cousin had been taken years ago at the country fair outside Granbury when she'd been fifteen. The handsome man sitting to her left on the settee was two years older. She had thought Trevor Jameson, with his thick russet hair and perfect smile, the most dashing man in the land, and she'd been so deeply in love with him. The expression on her face told her she'd been happy that day. Who wouldn't have been, with the world at her feet?

For the world had indeed been at her feet, youthful though she'd been at the time. She could still taste the ginger beer and hear the merry-go-round winding down outside the A-framed tent where the photographer had worked his magic with flashing pans and silver nitrates.

The other individual sitting in the photograph was her cousin and former friend, Lavinia, the baron's beautiful daughter. She had come in from Cornwall that month to visit, something she'd done every summer for years.

Winter's father had died a year later, and it was then the baron stepped permanently into her life.

Lavinia now occupied Everleigh Hall in Winter's stead. She rode Winter's horse, lived Winter's life. And now she was betrothed to the man Winter had loved since childhood.

She wondered if Trevor suspected he had a distant cousin. Or that he was about to lose everything?

Outside, clouds smothered the sun and darkened the room. A gust of wind knocked a tree branch against the house, making the emptiness in the cottage suddenly feel ominous. Winter looked up and out the dormer window, then returned the photograph to the drawer.

She tore off her soiled gown and hurried downstairs, carrying the gown with her, angry with herself for jumping at shadows and for behaving like some maudlin waif. She didn't know why she'd kept that old picture, or what had prompted her to pull out the thing and gaze at it like some lovelorn miss wishing for a sprinkle of fairy dust powerful enough to change her life.

Yet, her mind dwelled on the photograph. Perhaps because she'd grown up with Trevor, and didn't want to see him hurt. She had once idolized him. She'd been fourteen and he sixteen when they'd made a secret pact to one day marry. That evening at the fair, he'd pulled her behind the mountebank's medicine wagon and sealed that promise with her very first kiss.

After arriving in the kitchen, Winter pumped water into the sink basin and scrubbed her face and arms, remembering that kiss, a kiss that felt nothing like the one Trevor's dark cousin had bestowed on her last night. A kiss that had left her knees wobbly like a willow weakened by a gust of wind, and had planted an odd sense of self-betrayal in her heart.

A kiss that was still a burn on her lips, a worthy reminder that injured or nay, Trevor's cousin was a rogue and a scoundrel who had stuffed a florin down her bodice.

Winter dried, then wadded her soiled dress into a ball and tossed it outside into the refuse barrel to be burned later. She had little enough clothing to spare, but she could not bear to look at that dress again.

Once upstairs, she braided the length of her dark hair to keep it off her face. She chose the first gown in the armoire. It was serviceable, dark gray in color, with long sleeves and an aged matching black mantle trimmed in crepe, which she threw over her shoulders. She then packed a valise with another gown of the same unfortunate color and grabbed Mam's black poke bonnet, tying it as she balanced the bag in one hand and walked out the door. Old Ben had returned on foot to the village, but he'd left her the horse and cart.

Climbing onto the uncomfortable wooden bench and taking the reins in hand, she turned down the drive. After a mile, she could see Everleigh Hall on the distant hill, a jewel-bedecked queen draped in ivy and clematis covered with purple blooms. She stopped as she always did when she glimpsed the house.

To her, Everleigh would always be home. Its mullioned windows caught the sunlight and reflected an iridescent glow against the partial dome of blue sky. The refaced granite façade was a testament to her father's skill as an architect when he rebuilt the crumbling manse a decade ago. Now the house was merely a monument to the baron's wealth. He did not love the house at all.

Once she arrived at Everleigh Hall's back gate, she made a line for the kitchens downstairs, and did not want to be discovered by the housekeeper, a steel-haired taskmaster who would inform on her in two heartbeats. But the kitchen staff, most of whom had known her since she was a babe in swaddling, were accustomed to seeing her in the kitchens and would never tell her uncle she made frequent visits to his pantry. If the baron only knew his bountiful larder had fed half the estate during rougher times when the crop had failed or an illness had taken its toll on a tenant's family. Today Winter absconded with medical supplies.

As Winter traveled back to Mrs. Kincaid's cottage, a stray black-and-white hound appeared suddenly from out of the woods near the meadow where she, Perry, and Robert had lain in hiding last night. The same natty mutt skulked at the stable and mooched scraps. It loped beside the cart, wagging its tail for affection, for some reason reminding Winter of her brother. Someone should be caring for it, she thought.

"Hello, boy." She slowed the cart to let the hound jump into the back. "We can both use the comp—"

The sound of thundering horses' hooves caused her to raise her head. She saw a dozen riders coming over the rise.

As they crested the hill, raising dust and debris, her hands tightened on her horse's reins.

To her chagrin, they had seen her. She identified Sheriff Derwood at the front of the pack, but that recognition did not allay the alarm rippling up her spine. In a flurry of commotion and dust, the riders reined to a halt around the cart, forcing her to set the brake lest her own horse panic and run.

A big man sitting atop a big gray mount tipped a finger against the rim of his floppy hat and pushed it back from his brow, studying her with a pass of his eyes. A beard shadowed his heavy jowls. He was the uncle of one of Everleigh's tenants. She resented his inspection. "That is Old Ben's horse and trap." He nudged his gray and rounded the cart to see inside. "What is it you have there?"

"It's a valise." She switched her attention to Sheriff Derwood. "I'm on my way to see Mrs. Smythe, who is watching Mam. If I can inquire as to why you should care how I get there? Or bother over the clothes I am bringing her?"

"We're looking for a man who was seen in the pub last night, Winter," Sheriff Derwood said, severity framing his mouth. "A stranger who left the stables shortly after you did. Where are Perry and Robert?"

Her heart gave a bump. "Why?"

Sheriff Derwood leaned against the pommel, the leather saddle creaking beneath his weight. "The man we're looking for paid them to watch his horse. It's possible this chap might be involved in an incident that took place last night."

"*Might* be?" Jowls scoffed. "The bloke's horse was recognized by everyone what saw it."

Sheriff Derwood retorted. "We don't know what he did or didn't do."

"We know me nephew was shot down last night in cold blood. You all knew Whitey. He were just a boy."

Winter's heart stuttered against her ribs. Whitey Stronghold was a skinny lad, with a chip-toothed smile, barely seventeen years old. His family was one of Everleigh's oldest tenants. "This happened last night?"

"Whitey's body was found this side of the village," the sheriff said, "on the main road. A carriage passed on the same road shortly before Whitey was found and described the horse ridden by the man they'd seen leaving the vicinity. The carriage occupant is credible."

Jowls turned to the other riders sitting on their mounts in a half-moon circle behind him. "We will find the bloody bastard responsible fer killin' me nephew." His bull-throated voice came filled with the courage of numbers. "And anyone aidin' 'im."

An angry murmur buzzed with the threat of vengeance. The sheriff met Winter's gaze. "The man will be presented to a magistrate."

"The hell you say," Jowls said. "We all know what happens when a high-falutin' toff goes afore a magistrate."

*What did happen last night?* Three shots resonated in her mind, and it dawned on her she had heard gunfire from different pistols.

Winter dared say nothing. Her knowledge of his identity would only make them suspicious of her. Clearly, this mob would harm Lord Huntington should they find him.

Sheriff Derwood quietly said, "We only want to talk to your brother and Robert, Winter."

She tightened her grip on the reins, praying no one noted her trembling hands as she lied. "They went to the fair in

Henley." She released the brake. "Last night your mam suggested they go. Father Flannigan took them."

Jowls swung his gray mount away, followed by the others. By the time this unruly pack realized they were on a fruitless chase, Winter hoped their tempers would be cooled and that she'd have had time to warn Father Flannigan.

The sheriff did not turn his horse, though, but deliberately continued to remain beside the cart as the others thundered off. His eyes intent on Winter, he started to say something, then tightened his mouth.

Winter was less reticent. Even with her multitude of sins, she drew the line at murder. "Would you let them lynch a man?"

He frowned. "What do you think?"

Her throat tightened. She watched him wheel his mount away. The hound nuzzled her hand. "I agree." She didn't know what to think either.

But she was afraid. If these men found Perry and Robert they'd find Lord Huntington. It wouldn't matter the man's identity or who his grandfather might be should an angry mob discover him.

She remembered the blood-soiled dress she'd left in the refuse barrel.

Maneuvering the cart around on the narrow path, Winter turned back toward her own cottage. The cart would leave obvious tracks. The last thing she wanted was to mark a trail directly to Mrs. Kincaid's front door.

Once back at her cottage, Winter removed the dress from the refuse barrel. She rolled it into a ball and stuffed it beneath the straw in an empty stall inside the barn. Then she unhooked the cart, saddled Old Ben's nag, packed her valise with everything she'd gathered from the house and tied it to the back of her saddle. Following the creek bed, she rode the long way to Mrs. Kincaid's cottage.

Winter stood at the upstairs window of Mrs. Kincaid's cottage and stared across the yard to the surrounding woods. Mrs. Kincaid should have returned by now. She had left hours ago to take Father Flannigan a message warning him about Winter's encounter with the sheriff.

Now the sun had nigh set, but its daytime heat had left the small bedroom stifling hot. A sheen of perspiration moistened Winter's throat. She wanted to open the window but the storm-bellied clouds she'd seen in the distance now hovered over the woods. Her eyes fixed on the clouds. They needed rain. She should not complain. But she wished it would just be done with. The night would be black enough without adding a swelter of indecision to the air. She wiped the heel of her hand across her brow, then looked down at the damp rag clutched in her hand.

Her eyes swerved to the man in the bed. Lord Huntington continued to sleep. She forced herself to keep a mental distance from him and shut her eyes to remind herself he was only a man. An outsider. An aristocrat. But there was something more to this man and its presence disturbed her.

She thought of his gun. The moment she had returned, she had gone directly to where she'd hidden it beneath the bed, pulled it to a half cock and found two chambers empty. Two of the three shots fired last night had come from this weapon. Indeed, what manner of man could not only survive an attack outnumbered, but also kill one?

She'd emptied the bullets and dropped them in her pocket, then returned the gun beneath the bed behind the rolled-up old carpet. Hardly a decent hiding place, but at least it was out of sight. If Sheriff Derwood showed up, the last thing Winter wanted was for anyone else to die.

She didn't know how long it would take the sheriff to begin checking the local farms around where Whitey's body had been found, which, thank God, wasn't anywhere near Mrs. Kincaid's cottage. Winter had to trust that Father Flannigan would know what to do in the meantime.

For now, as she drew shut the curtains and lit the lamp beside the bed, she had another, more pressing concern: Lord Huntington had been running a fever since she'd tried to awaken him that afternoon to make him drink.

She reached for the porcelain bowl filled with water and dunked the rag. Fever wasn't necessarily a harbinger of doom. But infection was. She dipped the rag in the bowl and wrung it out. Yet again, she pressed it against the stranger's neck. She did this through most of the evening. But she was not invincible against fatigue. She had eaten little and slept even less. Exhaustion finally overtook her.

A burst of thunder snapped Winter awake. Disoriented, she straightened as a flash of lightning cast a silver pall over the room. She sat on a chair next to the bed. Her hand rested on the stranger's chest. The sponge bathing and medicine had brought the fever down slightly, but not enough.

Thunder rattled the roof. How long had she been asleep? She stood and opened the curtains. Heavy rain pounded, and dawn lay in the thin thread of light on the horizon.

Alarmed, Winter checked Mrs. Kincaid's room. The bed had not been slept in. She went downstairs and found the kitchen empty as well. The ashes in the hearth had died.

Winter walked to the window and stared out across the

yard. She could not let herself worry when it was probably
the storm keeping Mrs. Kincaid away.

Instead, she made tea. Then she dished out split pea soup
from the kettle left simmering in the hearth from the day before.
Insulated in the thick iron pot, the soup remained warm.

She returned upstairs with tea and set the tray on a table
next to the nightstand. Already daylight spilled into the room.

In the pale light, she studied Lord Huntington's averted
face, his finely sculpted cheekbones showing his mouth in
stark relief, leaving her prey to softer, unwelcome emotions.
As if she had not lain beneath him with him between her
legs or he had not wrapped his hand around her throat and
fairly throttled her to kibble.

No, now he was so still. Almost as if . . .

She laid her palm on his chest to reassure herself. Her
hand yielded to a slight tremble. His flesh felt hard and well-
muscled, warm to the touch. His heart beat strongly. Measured against her own, hers beat faster.

Winter had once made an oath to herself after her father
had died that she would never again say or do anything she
would later regret or for which she would have to apologize.
Now here she was trying to save the life of a man who could
probably have her hanged.

"I'm sorry," she whispered.

Yet, strangely, she was not sorry for kissing him or for
stealing his wallet. She was sorry that she had not somehow
stopped this attack. Angry because the townsfolk were her
friends and she could not believe them capable of murder.

And now she was standing in Mrs. Kincaid's cottage, the
last place she wanted to be, wondering if the other woman
was safe and worrying about a man who had tried to choke
her to death.

If she had any regrets, it was that things once done could never be undone, and so, as she stood over this outsider, who had dared invade her life, her mourning was mostly for herself.

"This should never have come to pass," she said.

"Move your hand lower and I just might forgive you."

Winter jumped at the gravelly rasp, guilty surprise jerking her palm from his chest. His hand intercepted her wrist, freezing her hasty retreat.

Her breath expelled in a rush. "How long have you been awake?"

His fingers tightened around the fine bones of her wrist. He looked past her into the sparsely furnished room then beyond the doorway as if to verify in his mind where he was and why. She would have pried herself from his fingers but she did not want to appear weak to him.

"Let me go," she calmly said.

He turned his head. In the misty light, his liquid silver eyes held the same trace of reckless arrogance she'd seen in the stable. It made his unshaven jaw look even more disturbing to her. "How long have I been out?"

"More than thirty-six hours."

He set her hand away and with a laborious effort pushed up on his elbow, grimacing with the movement. He didn't seem to care about his state of undress or that he would probably keel over onto the floor if he tried to stand. And if he collapsed, how would she get him back to bed?

"What are you doing? You can't get up."

He tried anyway, sliding his legs over the side of the mattress, then pressing the heel of his other hand against his temple as if to still a pounding in his skull. He glowered up at her from beneath the ridge of his palm.

She took a step backward, her only concession to caution lest he grab her again. Even wounded, he reminded her of a viper she'd once seen at the terrarium in London, quick and dangerous.

Her gaze suddenly dropped to the floral sheet, imprinted with pretty violets, which barely draped his hips, a contradiction to the overwhelming masculinity of the man concealed beneath. He saw where she was looking.

"I had nothing to do with your current circumstance." The words burst from her lips as if his undressed state required explanation. "Mrs. Kincaid took your clothes. They needed to be laundered."

He lowered his hand from his brow to the bed as if to steady himself. "I'll take your word for it."

"Will you lie down? You're in no condition to be—"

"Is there a place where one can find . . . privacy? The *chamber pot*, Miss Ashburn," he said when she failed to grasp his meaning.

Blushing hotly, she pointed to the commode and wash basin against the back wall. He threw the sheet off his lap. Winter was too stunned to move. He was hardly strong enough to stand, yet somehow he did, and she watched all six feet and more of him unfurl.

"I'll wait in the corridor."

Just outside the door, she pressed against the wall and fastened her gaze on the rafters. She'd seen men perform personal ablutions before but this was somehow different. She listened for him to finish. She heard him pour water in the basin and wash his hands and face. Heard his feet scrape against the floor. He stumbled, cursed when his foot encountered something. But Winter refused to go back into the room until she knew he was either unconscious on the floor or back in bed.

When she finally stepped through the doorway, he was sitting on the edge of the mattress. He turned his head.

She cleared her throat. "Do you need anything else?" she politely asked.

"Where is my gun?"

The request startled her. She did not intend to hand over a revolver, loaded or otherwise, to him. "For your own safety, I put it away."

"Is that right?"

She refused to be bullied by him. "Such armaments are dangerous. When I think you are ready to handle your weapon, you may."

*"Christ,"* he murmured, "I've died and gone to hell."

Forcing herself to look at a place over his shoulder, she concentrated on the little purple flowers sprinkled throughout the wallpaper, the same purple as that in the sheets. Then a little gremlin on her shoulder made her say, "As you said, your gun is always loaded. I would not wish it to discharge accidentally, sir."

The silence lengthened between them. She had no idea what had prompted her to say such a wicked thing.

His mouth slowly tipped up at the corner in a smile that was not really a smile. He was so very wicked.

Even half-unconscious, he was capable of rousing and arousing her at once, challenging her at every turn, making her think carnal things no decent woman should be thinking.

"An accidental discharge would indeed be messy," he replied with sudden seriousness. "You know how to care for yourself around loaded weapons then?"

She said, her voice unfaltering. "I know enough about firearms to recognize their danger to the unsuspecting."

"Are you protecting yourself or me, Miss Ashburn?"

She certainly wasn't protecting *him*. "For the price of a half-penny mug of ale, I should leave you to fend for yourself, sir."

He lay back against the pillow and peered up at her from beneath a thick sweep of his lashes. "If you leave me I shall probably expire. In case you haven't noticed, I have a head wound."

"Count yourself fortunate you still *have* a head. You constantly challenge my goodwill," she said. "Why?"

He scoffed, but the sound terminated in a fit of coughing. Winter rushed to help adjust his pillow. He lay half-sprawled against the mattress, too distressed or in too much pain to aid her in her efforts as she rearranged the pillows.

In fact, his inaction forced her to reach across and over him to play nursemaid. His breath stirred wisps of her hair and his forearm pressed against her stomach. She raised her head to find him watching her.

Despite his odious behavior, she felt herself soften. His pallor was visible proof enough that his present exertion had cost him.

People had died from less substantial injuries than he'd suffered, and now . . . She fluffed the pillows behind him again just to keep from further considering that thought.

"Don't put me in my grave yet," he said. "When I die, it won't be wrapped in a quilt covered with little purple flowers."

Her hand went to her mouth to stifle a hysterical laugh. Some of the tension inside her eased. And she caught herself staring at his face, intrigued by the laugh lines just visible at the corners of his eyes. She wondered at such a manner of man who could be so dark in spirit and still possess the lightness of character to joke at all.

Looking away, she worked to unravel her sudden confusion, wishing she could remold her feelings back into a healthy dislike for him. Such emotions were far easier to grip than the foreign ones that danced like butterflies in her stomach. And as she seemed wary of him, something in his fever-glazed eyes told her he was equally as wary of her.

Yet his hand rose and he tested the dark curl that had escaped the coronet around her head.

She didn't understand the unexpected tenderness in that simple touch. It had been so long since she had let anyone touch her, and it burned through her resistance like a flame. She could have averted her eyes, played coy, but her reaction would only have drawn attention to his, and soon his hand fell away.

"Help me sit," he said.

Sensing his determination, she tentatively placed an arm around his back and did as he asked. Outside, the wind rose and fell like a puff of angry breath against the cottage and startled her gaze away from his to the window. Something horrible had surely happened to Mrs. Kincaid.

"Are we alone?"

She nodded. "Mrs. Kincaid left yesterday to check on the boys. She has not returned. Though in this weather that wouldn't be unusual," she said as much to convince herself as she did to answer his question.

After a moment, she poured him a cup of willow bark tea she'd made earlier and sat beside him. He didn't move to take the cup. "I propose a truce between us, sir," she offered. "I'll work hard to avail you of all manner of kindness while you are Mrs. Kincaid's guest. In trade, you must drink. See?" She sipped the tea in demonstration of her good intentions. "If I were the least feverish, I would be cured in no time."

His hands came around the cup, trapping her fingers between his palm and the cup. He brought it to his lips, causing her to lean toward him.

With a patient expression that was every bit a lie, she watched as he drank the tea, then just before he'd finished, pulled the cup away. She set the cup on the nightstand, aware he was watching her with amusement.

"How long?" he asked as she started to rise. "Our truce."

"Until you are at least strong enough to stand." She observed him prudently. "How do you feel?"

"Somewhere between stubbing my toe and being stabbed in the eye with a hot, flaming poker."

His petulant grousing made him seem more human. *It could be worse*, she thought. He could be dead.

She gave him the bowl of soup she'd brought upstairs. Rather than watch him eat, she busied straightening the little glass bottles on the nightstand. He would not be so vulnerable to her now if he were not dosed on laudanum. After a while, he returned the bowl to her and leaned back, putting his dark head against the pillow. She set the empty bowl on the tray.

"Winter." He said her name as if tasting the sound of it in his mouth. "Were you born on some frigid January day?"

Coming from him, the query sounded intimate as if he was asking if she slept on the right or left side of the bed, dressed or naked. "I was born on the summer solstice, which by happenstance that year was the hottest day in decades. My mam had a novel sense of the absurd."

Her mam had once been vivacious and filled with life. She used to play the pianoforte and sometimes Winter would listen to her for hours.

She smoothed her skirt and folded her hands in her lap. "What would you have me call you? There was a letter in your wallet addressed to Lord Huntington." She moistened her suddenly dry lips and said in a hope-laden query. "Unless you aren't the Earl of Huntington?"

"I prefer Rory." He closed his eyes. "Just . . . Rory."

"Rory is Gaelic," she pressed, remembering what Old Ben had said. "Was your mam Scots?"

"In a fashion." He contemplated her from beneath heavy-lidded lashes. "My mother's father was Scots, her mother a Romany fortune teller."

A *Gypsy*! Winter felt telltale color flood her face.

No one in his or her right mind would ever tell another he was part Gypsy.

Rain pebbled against the roof. She looked at the timbers on the ceiling and felt another kind of storm growing inside her.

As a little girl, she used to venture to the river where the Gypsies would encamp in a coppice of pines. Their fires winking like fireflies in the night invited young minds to spy. She remembered watching the dark-haired women in their scarlet skirts and loose white blouses dance for the men.

"Are you really a Gypsy . . .?" She paused.

Lord Huntington was asleep.

She placed the back of her hand against his cheek and found him still feverish. After a moment, she pulled the sheet over his chest, but did not rise.

Her eyes roved the length of him. With his dark hair curling over his nape and daylight glinting off the strong column of his neck, he looked both fascinating and forbidden, like Eden's apple. He *looked* like a Gypsy.

The kind of man a woman only glanced at when she thought no one else was watching. The kind of man a woman like her would kiss in a stable.

Yet for all of that she felt, she also remembered the tender way he'd touched her hair. She looked down at his hand, hard and strong, next to hers.

Seeing it, remembering the way his hand had felt against her cheek made her feel strange, like something was awakening inside her that she wanted to stay dead. For a moment, it hurt to breathe.

She came to her feet. And froze.

Over the roar of the rain, she'd heard the front door slam.

She rushed into the corridor and leaned over the bannister. Perry and Robert's beaming but wet faces appeared at the foot of the stairs. "Where have you been?" she cried.

"We'd of been back sooner," Perry said when she met him and Robert halfway up the stairs. "But the creek overflowed its bank last night—"

"And we had to go back," Robert finished.

Mrs. Kincaid stood below, removing her sodden cloak.

"There is hot soup in the pot," Winter told the boys.

They ran down the stairs shouting like banshees, and Winter flinched.

"Father Flannigan thought it best the boys remain here," Mrs. Kincaid said.

Winter nodded. All that was important was that Mrs. Kincaid had brought them safely back, and that she was no longer alone in this cottage.

# Chapter 5

Light pressing against Rory's eyelids convinced him he was conscious. The room smelled faintly like a confessional, that and the summer scent of lichen-infested trees. He lay still for a moment as his mind picked out the sounds in the room: the sound of chirping birds, a gentle breeze stirring the curtains, the shuffling of small feet. He slowly opened his eyes.

Two boys, one fair and one red-haired with freckles, stood at the end of the bed. Rory tried to remember if he should know these two.

"Are ye awake, mister?" the red-haired snippet asked.

Then suddenly he placed them both.

He'd given that freckled scamp a shilling to watch his horse. These two felonious urchins were the pirates who waylaid him in the glade. "You tell me. Am I?"

As if reading Rory's mind, Freckles nervously shifted. "Mrs. Kincaid be downstairs making lunch. We're 'sposed to be watching ye till she returns."

It was the first time he'd opened his eyes not to find Winter sitting in the chair beside the bed, feeding him or sponging his face. Rory turned his head toward the bright sunlight spilling into the room. A dull pain throbbed in his temple, but when his fingers touched the bandage about his head, he realized this was the first time he'd opened his eyes in days that his head had not felt like exploding.

"You've been sufferin' an ailment," Freckles said with clear authority on the matter. "Nigh on days, guv'nor. 'Is Fathership lit up the incense and prayed over ye twice. Winter doesn't take much stock in incense on accountin' of its smell, and she opened the windows. We thought you was gonna perspire."

Rory pinched the bridge of his nose because it hurt too much to do anything else. He wasn't particularly fond of children and considered them on the same level as dogs and other pets. They were entertaining enough, but he didn't want to spend too much time with them. "Make yourselves useful and bring me a glass of water," he said, anything to rid himself of the vile taste in his mouth.

The blonde scurried forward. Water sloshed into a battered tin cup that might have once belonged to a soldier's field kit.

Rory drank then lay back against the pillow, hoping if he shut his eyes long enough the pair would go away. But when his eyes opened again the two were exactly where he'd left them. Feeling like a moth pinned to a corkboard, he frowned. "What is it you both want?"

The two consulted in worried whispers. Finally, the blonde asked, "Are ye goin' to send us to Tyburn, my lord?"

Rory measured each boy in turn. It hadn't occurred to him that even if the two *had* taken a willing part in the attack on him, anyone would consider him capable of sending two children to the gallows. "I don't know. Should I?"

They shook their heads. "Miss Winter 'apends on us, your guv'norship," the redhead replied with growing melodrama in his voice. "Who would take care of her if we were smote by the hand of injustice?"

Rory's lips twitched. "Smote?"

Freckles again consulted the towheaded youth. "Smited," he reestablished, then—with a shrug of his knobby shoulder—added apprehensively, "Father Flannigan, 'e likes 'is Bible verses, yer lordship."

"Which one of you is Winter Ashburn's brother?"

"He is." The redhead pointed to the blond. "His name be Perry Ashburn."

Rory shifted his gaze from the freckled face to the taller of the pair. Though he found Winter in the dark coffee-colored eyes, nothing else about the boy resembled his sister. "And what is your partner in crime's name, Perry?"

"Robert." Perry glared at the other with narrowed eyes. "He's an orphan."

Robert's mouth tightened in sudden belligerence. "But Miss Winter would adopt me if she could. She said so."

"Where is Miss Winter?"

"Father Flannigan sent her off to bed last night," Robert said. "And no one tells 'is Fathership no, 'less they want to go straight to hell. Ain't that right, Perry?"

The blonde head nodded in vigorous agreement.

"That's why Mrs. Kincaid is hidin' us," Robert said. "Father Flannigan doesn't want the sheriff findin' Perry an' me. 'Specially after Father . . . exaggerated about Miss Winter and me and Perry accompanying Sister Margarita to the abbey in Westches— *Hmfff*—" Perry elbowed Robert in the ribs. The face behind the freckles reddened. "Ouch. What are ye doin?"

"We're not 'sposed to talk about it," Perry hissed. "Lives are in danger."

"Whose lives?" Rory asked, suddenly wondering whose life was imperiled. "Yours? Or mine?"

Robert rubbed his side and glowered at Perry.

When the boys seemed determined not to answer, with great effort Rory raised himself to a sitting position, slid his legs over the side of the bed and waited for the dizziness to pass. His fever might be gone, but with movement, every muscle in his body ached. He forced himself to stand. The pair of loose-fitting drawers tied at his waist with a string barely clung to his hips. Gripping the garment with one hand, he walked to the window and edged aside the faded yellow curtain. He looked down on bright sunlight spilling over a vegetable garden. Just on the other side of a broken-down picket fence, the branches of two large oaks cast shade across the pitched roof of an old red barn. A rope swing, suspended from one of its limbs, rocked in the breeze. His gaze touched the surrounding woods. Around him nothing moved.

In his current condition, he couldn't go anywhere. But neither did he want to be found. He wanted a brief time to consider such weighty issues as who had tried to rob him and left him for dead.

The fact that the priest didn't want the sheriff to find the boys begged the answer to more than one question. Was the sheriff somehow involved with the brigands who had attacked Rory?

He would not be surprised to learn that the sheriff might be involved in any local criminal enterprise. What astounded him was that Winter might be protecting *him*, a stranger, against her own people.

Unless, he was merely being kept hidden to ensure her own safety and that of the lads from the authorities. But then

why bother if, in the end, she worried that Rory would condemn the boys?

Dropping the edge of the curtain, he turned and peered
at the boys. "Which one of you came up with the idea to
ambush me?"

Neither spoke. Rory raised a questioning brow. They both
looked down at the floor, clearly closing ranks against him,
the little buggers.

It wasn't his place to punish the pair. But neither was receiving forgiveness an inalienable right just because someone's tender age warranted a certain degree of compassion.
Their stunt could have killed them all. Obviously someone
was now looking for them. Allowing the two to stew about
their fate might give them something to think about in the
upcoming weeks.

"How did you know I would be on that trail?" he asked.

"We'd not planned to jump from the tree and scare you,"
Perry said. "It just happened that way."

"We liked ye, honest. Especially after ye gave us that
shilling," Robert added. "But Miss Winter weren't but a
stone's throw away with no one to protect her and when ye
come down that trail, ye bein' a toff and all . . . Miss Winter
takes a lot of twaddle from the baron on account of us and
so we owed it to her to protect her."

"But we oughn't of run off and left you," Perry quietly said.

Robert studied the scuffed toe of one thin-soled shoe.
"Miss Winter says it ain't correct to leave another in need.
She says it takes more to doin' what be right than just 'tend-
ing church."

"She said all that, did she? What else does she say?"

"That we oughtn't chase the tenant's chickens," Perry said.

"Or pick apples from Lord Granbury's orchard."

"I see." He studied each face. "I'll decide what to do with you both in a few days."

"But Winter said if we apologized you wouldn't be angry with us," Perry protested. "She's never angry with us if we make an apology."

"I'm not your sister."

The rattle of dishes shifted Rory's attention to the doorway. A petite woman with henna-tinted hair entered the room, saw that he was awake, and stopped abruptly. Quickly recovering, she continued in and set the tray on a small round table next to the nightstand, then turned to the boys. "We do not wish to overly fatigue our patient. Run along now, both of you. The horse needs hay."

Their expressions already crestfallen, they lowered their eyes and left the room without argument. Turning to Rory, the woman cocked a brow. Presumably, this was the Mrs. Kincaid of whom the boys had spoken. "They have been waiting days to speak to you. Now I see you have broken their hearts." Her green eyes thoroughly assessed him and he might have wriggled in discomfort if her evaluation had been more personal. As it was, he suddenly felt eleven years old.

"My name is Angelique." She set her hands on her hips. "Mrs. Kincaid to most. This is my cottage."

"So I'm told. Perhaps I should dress for dinner?"

"I was not able to salvage all your clothes," she said. "Father Flannigan is attempting to find something suitable to fit you. For now, you will remain here."

He had to admire her pluck even if the lot of them were naïve enough to think that if he wanted to leave, a little thing like lack of wardrobe would stop him.

"You will probably want a bath later," she said.

His gaze rose from the gold wedding band on Mrs. Kincaid's left hand to her face. She was prettily plump with an appealing French accent that matched the charm in her smile. A combination of discreetly applied rice powder and henna-soaked hair made it difficult to accurately assess her age. "Is there a Mr. Kincaid?"

"My husband passed twenty-one years ago. Long before I came to Granbury. And you? Is there a Lady Huntington?"

"There is no Lady Huntington."

"Ah." She snapped open a serviette, inviting him to return to bed.

Rory distrusted the sound of that "ah." No other word held the same nuance of peril as one single "ah."

He shoved away from the window and perched on the edge of the mattress. Just the minuscule exertion tired him and he struggled to lean back on the pillow pressed against the headboard. "I can manage to eat without aid." He accepted the lentil soup with a murmured "thank you."

She smiled. "A man with manners. The mark of a true gentleman. Then I shall not worry that our safety is imperiled."

Rory observed her over his spoon. "You don't look old enough to have been a widow for twenty-one years."

"My husband was a soldier in India. He tactlessly succumbed to typhoid fever two weeks after we were wed. I was seventeen. I never remarried."

Mrs. Kincaid refilled his soup bowl twice. Afterward she brought up water, cleaned his scalp, and changed the bandage. She promised to find him a razor, but with no men in the house, she didn't think she had one. She talked just enough to take an edge off the silence yet was cognizant enough to know when he could no longer remain awake.

As she started for the door, he stopped her with a question. "Mrs Kincaid, who is the baron?"

Her expression turned briefly grave. "Winter's uncle by marriage. He was married to her father's sister. He owns Everleigh Hall." She paused. "If you are planning on staying in Granbúry, you will meet him soon enough."

The next morning, Rory stood just to the side of the bedroom window overlooking the garden below his window. If he'd been wearing more than loose-fitting underdrawers, he would have found his way downstairs to the pantry for something more substantial to eat than the soup and tasteless porridge he'd been fed for the last few days.

His gaze touched the surrounding woods. He edged the faded yellow curtain aside to see as much of the terrain as he could.

A dog barked. Then he heard her again just to the side of the house. He couldn't see her, but the sound of her voice had been what pulled him to the window. *You do know how to pull at a man's base instinct*, he thought dryly.

Winter Ashburn had come upstairs to check on him last night when she'd thought he'd been asleep, tucking the covers around him like a supplicant, which he'd thought amusing, considering how they felt about each other. With one intrepid glance at the sheet covering his hips, she'd discovered he was awake. In his opinion, had she not been looking where she shouldn't have been looking in the first place, he would never have seen her blush as hotly as she had.

When Rory awakened later that afternoon, his headache had subsided. It didn't return the next day, and neither did Miss Winter Ashburn.

But he'd long since passed the invalid stage and dragged himself out of bed. He walked to the commode.

Rory braced both his palms on the stone countertop and stared at his scruffy countenance in the glass. He doubted his own sister would recognize him. His eyes had a glassy look. Bristles filled in facial hollows and shadowed his jaw. He looked like a battle-worn orderly assigned latrine duty. But he decided, despite his aches, he would live.

After he finished washing with the hot water and sponge Mrs. Kincaid had supplied him, he began searching the room. He found his wallet on the nightstand. All the money was accounted for. He'd leave some for Mrs. Kincaid to recompense her for her troubles. The letter from his grandfather was inside. Turning it over in his hand, he pondered the salutation and address, surprised how alike his grandfather's handwriting was to his own. The thought made him frown for many reasons he did not wish to contemplate. He'd been here nearly a week. His grandfather would have received Rory's trunk by now. He'd wanted to arrive before his trunk, without fanfare.

Rory tossed everything back on the nightstand and looked around the room. It didn't take long to find his pocket revolver and leather holster. Winter had hidden both beneath the bed.

Squatting barefoot, Rory held the smooth walnut grip of his gun in his hand. The revolver was a short rimfire small caliber he'd retrieved from a Russian spy two years ago in Paris. Strange that he could remember that incident with more clarity than he could recall this past week. Though most of the last few days were like a blight on his brain, leaving patchy black holes where his memory should be, a bullet wasn't enough to wipe the kiss he'd shared with Winter from his head.

He spun the revolver's cylinder, then half cocked the weapon and flipped open the loading breech to reveal the chamber. The bullets had been removed. As he'd suspected.

With a snap of his wrist, the cylinder clicked back into place. Rory peered at the door thoughtfully, considering how he would reclaim his ammunition from his benefactor.

Why this prospect intrigued him, he couldn't say.

Perhaps it was because *she* intrigued him.

Too bad the "village saint" was a thief and charlatan. Unfortunately, for her, Rory wasn't the magnanimous type.

"Has he said anything?" Winter peered up at the cottage from the doorway of the barn. She had been gone most of the morning and only just returned.

Behind her, Mrs. Kincaid straightened from the bench where she had been repairing an old butter churn. The plunger and paddles lay on the wooden countertop. A breeze stirred the straw at her feet. "He's only been on his feet a few days," she said. "What is it you wish him to say?"

The same breeze brushed at Winter's hair. A summer storm was riding in on the wind. She could taste rain in the air. "Nothing, I suppose."

Winter removed her riding gloves. She'd been trapped here for too long. This morning she'd left the cottage to see Mam. She didn't know why she'd had the compulsion to abandon her duties here. But the well of need that had spurred Winter to ride out at dawn now seemed foolishly sentimental and frivolous.

At least in the sense that Winter thought she could share her fears or joys, or expect to be held in Mam's arms again.

"How is your mother?" Mrs. Kincaid's mouth softened at Winter's start of surprise. "It has been awhile since you have seen her, *chère*. Who else would you have visited this morning?"

"I should have told someone where I was going. It was just . . ."

Mrs. Kincaid continued to watch her with compassion-filled eyes. Winter stiffened her spine. Certainly she and Perry weren't to be pitied. "Mam is well," she replied. "Mrs. Smythe has appreciated her presence. They are both widows."

A gust of wind pushed against them. Mrs. Kincaid held a hand to her straw hat to keep it from blowing off her head. Then she went back to the butter churn. "He is stronger today," she said without looking up.

"Strong enough to leave?" Winter edged aside loose strands of hair with the back of her hand. It was one thing to come face-to-face with *Just Rory* when he was lying helplessly in bed. But on his feet, Lord Huntington was an animal of a different color entirely. "I mean . . . we don't know him. He could be . . . crazed."

"He is a gentleman."

Winter scoffed at the loosely applied term to all men who displayed even a modicum of manners. "So is my uncle."

Removing her heavy leather gloves, Mrs. Kincaid set them on the bench. "Lord Huntington has treated the boys well."

Winter glanced at Robert and Perry working or playing in the loft shoveling straw over the drop. One could not tell by their laughter. The dog was up there, too.

Every so often these last few days she had listened to Perry and Robert's laughter, envious of their ability to grab the minutest ounce of joy from the circumstances in which they lived. Nor had she heard a single grumble of discontent from their lips as they'd taken part in daily chores she would have had to force them to do at home.

Not that Angelique Kincaid had more than a rangy milk cow, a roost filled with chickens, and Old Ben Brown's horse to look after.

A surrey-top curricle sat unused and covered with dust next to a pile of straw. Looking around her at the tapestry of aged leather, yokes, harnesses, and a warped crossbeam that barely supported the roof, Winter wondered why Mrs. Kincaid did not just tear down the place and build anew.

"It is sturdier than it looks," Mrs Kincaid said. "I have learned that a thing can be saved if the foundation on which it is built is solid."

Winter scoffed at the notion. The walls looked as if they'd been built a century ago and no more durable than the roof. "I believe only my eyes."

"Perhaps that is your problem, *chère*."

Winter turned her head.

Mrs. Kincaid gave her attention to a bowl filled with rivets, lifting one into a streamer of light. "Our guest is resting. Perry and Robert helped prepare a bath for him earlier." She eyed Winter over a rusted rivet. "Your patient will be in need of tea when he awakens. Would you take it to him? I'd like to finish here."

Winter stared up at the cottage and frowned.

Once inside the house, Winter shut the door and removed her bonnet. All around her, the house was silent, but a faint rose fragrance floated in the air, the kind of scent that came from expensive hand-milled soap or that sold in little silk sachets, and was kept in drawers to make underclothes smell pretty.

She could think of only one reason for that fragrance to prevail so loudly in this house. She walked past the salon to the kitchen at the back of the house where the floral scent was strongest. An empty hip tub had been moved to the side of the hearth. Her senses still on alert, she straightened. Her left hand slid to her pocket and closed on the four bullets she'd been carrying around since she'd emptied Huntington's gun. Her pocket went with her everywhere. If he was awake after his bath, she felt some security in knowing that at least he wasn't armed.

She looked up the stairs. The thought of the masculine Lord Huntington smelling like a Parisian strumpet brought the first smile in days to her lips.

Her grin quickly turned to a frown. She refused to acknowledge him as *her* patient. She left the kitchen and took the stairs two at a time. The door to his bedchamber was closed. Careful to not creak the floorboards, she pressed her ear to the door but heard no stirring inside.

She would have to wake him to talk. She would have to do what was necessary to make some kind of a peace with him—*before* Father Flannigan arrived. She flexed her fingers to knock. But then eased her hand away from the door. First, she would make tea—then peace.

Tension diminishing within her, she made her way first to her own small room next to his to change out of her riding habit. She had no sooner tossed her gloves and bonnet on the bed, however, when the door slammed behind her.

Winter whirled, catching the bedstead to keep from falling backward.

*Just Rory* stood against the wall, one arm braced against the closed door. Loose-fitting drawers hung on the span of his lean hips and barely covered his privates, tempting her eyes to his muscled belly and the whorl of black hair that disappeared beneath the waistband, all serving to remind her that no intimate part of him was lacking.

She snapped her shocked stare back to his. He was looking at her with fierce gray eyes made more startlingly vivid by the week-old bristles that darkened his jaw. "Miss Ashburn," he said.

Suspicious, she scanned the room for anything out of place. "What are you doing here?"

He folded his arms over his bare chest, the very hallmark of vice. "I'm the model of decorum, lass." The roguish burr rolled off his tongue as naturally as if it were his own. "If I'd wanted to do ye harm, I wouldna let you gawk at me first."

He was truly a scoundrel, all the way down to his rather large feet. Nor did he look as pale and weak as Mrs. Kincaid had implied.

She narrowed her eyes, then lifted her chin, walking with stately dignity to the door and opening it, prepared to order him out. *Thud!* The door slammed shut in her face and she jumped. One of his hands braced on the wooden jamb, the other against the wall, bracketing her between his arms and pinning her to the oak door. His face came closer and she felt his breath against her temple even before she heard his soft words. "You have something I want, Miss Ashburn."

He'd left little air between her and his chest, but somehow she managed not to touch any part of him. "If this is about what happened between us in the stable—"

"Everything is about what happened in the stable."

"I've returned your wallet," she said in a rush. "What is it you think I owe you that you do not already have or cannot buy elsewhere with a florin or two?"

Winter thought he looked amused by her assumption that he wanted something more gratuitous than what she'd already shared with him in the stable. Part of her, the wicked part she kept hidden so well, the part that had driven her to press her mouth against his and kiss him, wondered if she *did* want something more.

"You tell me," he said, his voice a challenge.

"My intent when I came up here was to apologize."

When he didn't reply, she wet her lips and forged onward. "And to ask that when Father Flannigan arrives to talk to you today . . . you tell him nothing of what happened at the stable."

"Why would I do as you ask?"

She had no reply. Maybe if she had thought through her apology, she could have worded it better. But in truth, nothing she said would have mattered. She realized the apology wasn't even for herself. She could wage her own battles, but it was one of Lord Huntington's most maddening qualities that he could goad her into losing her dignity. "I can't think of a single reason why you would cede to my plea, sir, except that Father Flannigan means a great deal to me. He would be hurt if he knew the truth about me."

"Indeed." Lord Huntington shifted his palms against the wall and leaned nearer, the look in his eyes no longer as affable as the tone of his voice. "What is the going price for a thoroughbred stallion in this quaint village filled with such upstanding citizens? I make it a rule never to refuse a good offer or a bribe."

"You are entirely unprincipled. I cannot see how you have the effrontery to take me to task when your own behavior is indefensible."

"At least I don't lie to myself about whom or what I am."

Winter fairly choked. "The devil rebuking sin? Or condoning it?"

He obviously was not sorry about his part in anything. She doubted he'd apologized for anything in his life. All she felt from him was hot-corded tension brimming within him and making her feel all the things he had made her feel in the stable. Recklessness. Uncertainty. Confusion.

"What else is it you want?" she asked.

She watched the creases at his mouth deepen and his eyes narrow. No softness reflected back at her, and a different kind of silence fell between them. "Tell me why Sheriff Derwood is looking for your brother and his friend."

"I . . ." Her shoulders squared. "Who told you that?"

"Enough, Winter. I may not be in the best state of health yet, but I guarantee I am more adept at interrogation than you are."

God forbid she should ever meet him when he was up to standard.

"Who is responsible for what happened to me?"

She shook her head. "I don't know. I swear."

"Does your brother?"

She blinked back the veil of sudden tears. "Perry is guilty only of trying to protect me. You have to believe the boys had nothing to do with what happened to you."

He shoved off the door, but remained standing in front of her. Despite the appearance of strength, his stance faltered slightly. His show of weakness only reminded her that even with their differences, they were both better served on the same side—at least in this battle.

"A young man's body was found alongside the road just outside the village the morning after you were attacked," she said. "His name was Whitey Stronghold. The sheriff and the mob hunting you think you murdered him."

His brows drew together. "Why would they think that?"

"A witness placed a horse that fit your horse's description at the scene. That night at the stable, you paid Robert a shilling to watch your stallion. Sheriff Derwood thinks the boys can identify you or might know something about you. That is why he is looking for them."

"You didn't think I warranted knowledge of any of this before now?"

"Father Flannigan thought it best you didn't know until you were stronger. He was concerned you might feel unsafe here and try to leave. Despite what you think of us, we do not wish to see you lynched."

"I'm vastly relieved you are no accomplice to murder," he said.

His sarcasm was like a prod against her spine. She could not comprehend how a person could show not the slightest fear of capture or remorse over the death of someone who might have perished at his hands. Even in self-defense.

"The young man you killed was seventeen."

Anger flashed across Huntington's face. Then blankness again.

"I shouldn't have said that," she stumbled on acutely conscious of the thick rushing sound in her ears. "Clearly the men who allowed Perry and Robert to go that night in the glade did not count on one of their own being killed," she said, pressing her palm against her stomach to calm it. "After Whitey died, the other two with him must have gone back to make sure no one would . . ."

"They needed to make sure I was never found so no one could dispute their story." When she nodded, he asked, "Is your family or Mrs. Kincaid in danger from Derwood?"

The feeling in the pit of her stomach tightened. "I won't believe Sheriff Derwood would stand by and watch even *you* hang." Her voice dropped to a whisper. "I know the people of this village. They are good folk."

"Of course they are. Pillars of the shire, except when the moon is full."

This time, Winter did look away. She startled when his fingers touched her chin and turned her face back to him. "Whoever set me up cannot condemn me without first silencing those boys. Are you willing to wager Robert and Perry's life on Derwood's character?"

"Sheriff Derwood and his mother are like family to Perry and Robert."

"Are you trying to convince yourself or me?"

He had assessed her fears well. "What will you do?"

He raked his fingers through his damp hair and said lightly, "It *is* rather difficult to take action without clothes."

She didn't know if he made her want to laugh or cry. "Whatever you decide to do about me, the boys had nothing to do with what happened."

"They are undisciplined scamps, madam."

"They are only children. Have you never *been* around children?"

"Not if I could avoid it."

He leaned a palm against the door at her back. "Where are the bullets to my gun?"

She made an uneasy laugh, aware all over again of his state of undress. "We're back to your gun again?"

His eyes slid over her face, over the mess that was her hair, which she had not yet combed after removing her bonnet. Winter had the unpleasant impression he was amused with her and that their brief truce had now come to an ignoble end. "At the moment, my gun is indeed uppermost in my mind."

The power of him was a heat in the room. "Truly, you have an obsession with your weapon, sir."

"Show me a male who doesn't and I'll show you a senile old man or one that is dead."

A vast impatience consumed her. She sidestepped him, only to be brought up short as he leaned his shoulder against the doorjamb and blocked her. "I can turn you upside down and shake you until the casings drop out onto the floor, or you can reach into your pocket and give them to me."

He looked disreputable enough to carry out his threat, too. He could be a criminal for all she knew. She swallowed as he held out his hand almost as if expecting her to challenge him.

Winter shoved her hand into her pocket and retrieved the four bullets. Reluctantly she dropped each shell into his outstretched palm.

*Click. Click. Click. Click.*

His fingers closed around the metal casings. The corners of lips eased up. "I think I would have preferred that you fought."

Before she could do more than gape in outrage, he opened the door and stepped past her into the hallway.

# Chapter 6

Rory swept through his bedroom door. Winter had followed him. He could feel her standing just inside the doorway as he padded across the floor to the nightstand and removed his revolver from the drawer.

He cocked the barrel and began feeding the shells into the cylinder.

"Don't you have anyone who misses you?" she asked.

He silently laughed at the notion. With the exception of his sister and his niece, who were probably the only two people in this world he truly loved, he was a ghost. "Few even know I'm alive, love."

"Even your grandfather?"

Ignoring her question, he shoved the third casing into the cylinder. "How far are we from Granbury?"

"The town of Granbury? Or the estate?"

"Both."

"The village is two miles south of those woods. Granbury Court is another ten miles southeast. Old Ben brought you here to get you off Everleigh land. It was safer for everyone concerned that way."

"Especially for you, I imagine."

"Especially."

Her sarcasm turned his head, and his gaze paused on her. His glance took in her ghastly mouse-colored gowns. the antithesis of the high color simmering in her cheeks. And he was suddenly possessed of an irresistible urge to see her standing in front of him wrapped in red silk.

"Have you considered discharging your current seamstress?"

"You're an ass," she replied.

A corner of his mouth lifted. She'd lost her previous fear of him. Not enough to step into his bedroom, perhaps. Yet there was nothing cowardly about her, from the tilt of her chin to her dark-as-sin eyes.

She pointed her chin at the revolver in his hand. "Are you a felon as well?"

"What if I am?"

Her lips pressed into a straight line like a priggish school-marm's. "Then I would remind you that murdering me would be a violation of Mrs. Kincaid's hospitality. I trust that if you are a felon you are at least an honorable one."

"You trust?" He snapped the revolver's cylinder shut and shoved the gun back into its holster. Trust wasn't an oft-used word in his vocabulary. "If a person wanted to purchase a horse in this village, who would they see? Old Ben?"

She cleared her throat. "A horse?"

"*Cheval. Caballo*," he said in French and Spanish. "An animal with a large body and head, four long legs and a flowing tail. Larger than an ass. A steed."

"A hairy quadruped. A one-toed *ungulate* that is a relative to an African rhinoceros." She smiled prettily. "Though you have me on the Spanish and French, I've taken the boys to the London Museum and seen the zoological exhibit. Ben

Brown may be a bit odd, but if you want to know anything about horses, yes, he's the one to ask."

Again, Rory found himself pausing and reassessing his thoughts about Winter Ashburn. Only this time his scrutiny began at the tips of her scuffed boots and ended when his eyes reached the top of her mussed head where it looked as if she'd recently removed a hat. She was a ragamuffin with the carriage of a lady. Nothing about her meshed or fit into the fixed notion he'd formed of her since the moment he'd found her in Apollo's stall. What the *hell* had she been doing in that stable last week?

"How well do you know Old Ben?" he asked.

His question clearly took her aback. "He's mostly a harmless old man."

"Mostly harmless? As in occasionally perilous?"

She fidgeted with the frayed lace on her sleeve. "He's harmless as long as he doesn't fall asleep in the stable while smoking a cob."

*Christ*, Rory wasn't even going to ask what that meant.

"He's a rummy, if you must know," she said defensively.

"I don't want to know."

"Ten years ago, he accidentally burned down your grandfather's stable. He fell asleep in one of the stalls after a binge. No horses were injured. My father took him in lieu of his being carted off. When my uncle purchased Everleigh, he sold Papa's horses and dismissed Old Ben with no references and no hope of ever finding viable employment again. My uncle is a fool. There is no one better with horses than Ben. Have you any more questions?"

Before Rory could reply, the rattle of bridle and chains from an approaching buggy drew him around. Winter beat him to the window and pulled aside the drapery. Rory came up behind her and watched as a black buggy rattled around the bend in the yard.

"It's only Father Flannigan." She sighed with relief. "I thought it might be . . . "

"The sheriff?" Rory looked down at her. Her head barely topped his shoulder. She was suddenly jabbering about the weather and the condition of the roads after a rain and how likely a buggy was to leave tracks, but that Father Flannigan knew the back way through the woods.

He watched her smooth a lock of hair from her face, the gesture as articulate as anything she might say. She was frightened—or had been until she'd identified their guest. He frowned. Apparently, for all her faith in this Derwood bloke, she did not consign the boys' lives to the sheriff completely.

"Father Flannigan has been searching donations for clothes." She peered at him from over her shoulder with humor in her eyes as her gaze skimmed his face. "At the very least, he has brought you a razor. You will probably want to shave."

"At the very least."

She wasn't quite touching him, yet he felt her everywhere, like the sunlight streaming through the paned glass that warmed his chest.

She dropped the edge of the curtain. His gaze followed the movement of her fingers, then came up, settling on her mouth, and he marveled at the reckless speed at which his thoughts had raced from the danger outside to the one inside.

"Isn't someone at Everleigh missing you and your brother by now?"

Winter brushed past him to the nightstand where she checked the pitcher filled with tepid water. "My aunt passed away some years ago. My uncle and cousin, Lavinia, are in London." Without looking at him, she set the pitcher on a wicker tray along with that morning's breakfast dishes, arranging them just so as if everything had its place. Including him.

"Father Flannigan will be up shortly," she said. "He will remove your stitches and make a pronouncement about the state of your health. No doubt he will be relieved to see you so . . . robust."

"And you? Are you . . . relieved?"

She raised her head. He went still, his fingers knotted tightly around the holster. For the first time in years, Rory found himself paradoxically inclined to curiosity. Not only about her but about himself when he was around her.

Then she hefted the tray. "I'll be glad when it is safe for you to leave so I can go home."

"Why would you steal from me?" he asked softly.

*Because he'd deserved it.*

She didn't voice the words, but she knew at once he had read the defiance in her eyes. "Because I could."

Her temerity momentarily startled him. She said nothing to acquit herself, which oddly enough conferred a curious brand of honor to her actions. She puzzled him. As had her actions in the stable.

Her lips parted, as if she might say something witty to put him in his place. But she was not as socially sophisticated as she wanted him to believe, and that struggle was what finally captured him.

Why wasn't she in London with her contemporaries enjoying the Season? Clearly, she'd been educated. What kind of man was this *baron* to dress his niece in rags or care so little about her welfare that he'd allow her to traipse about the countryside unfettered like some altruistic Robin Hood?

No, he told himself, he wouldn't get involved. He'd survived the first thirty-two years of his life precisely because he'd adhered to the principled philosophy never to involve himself in someone else's plight. Unlike many of his peers who considered their work noble or patriotic, Rory considered what he did for the Crown to be neither. He went where he was told. Did what he was told. Life was fraught with less moral ambiguity when someone else was making the decisions. And he liked his life simple.

He'd deviated from the first principle of *Rory's Law* when he'd allowed his sister to talk him into coming to Granbury to make some manner of peace with his grandfather before the tyrant expired. He'd done so again when he'd taken off impulsively into the night to chase down Winter Ashburn. A third digression would only leave him floundering his way back up the slippery slope from whence few returned.

He would not make the welfare of an exotic dark-eyed thief and her two unruly charges his responsibility as he hunted those who had nearly murdered him and stolen his horse. Fools got themselves killed.

And yet . . .

There was something about her that made him want to stay just so he could strip away that self-righteous mantle she'd wrapped around herself.

"You've told me nothing about your mother." His words stopped her in the doorway and she turned.

"I can tell you she *isn't* the daughter of a Gypsy fortune teller."

His gaze briefly touched the angelic halo of tendrils framing her oval face. He smiled a slow, crooked smile. "That intrigues you, does it?"

Color heightened her cheeks. "Of course it doesn't."

But it did. He could read the thought in her eyes, just as he could read all her other thoughts when she looked at him.

Winter Ashburn was definitely no angel.

Winter awakened slowly. She stared at the cracked plaster in the ceiling. She lay in her shift atop the bed's scratchy coverlet. Her groggy mind discerned male voices in the hallway. Then the smell of hot oatcakes permeated her senses. Her mind racing, she rolled onto her stomach and looked over at the window. The sun had dropped out of the sky. It would be dark soon. She was supposed to help Mrs. Kincaid make supper.

With a groan, Winter swung her feet to the floor, hastened to the old walnut dresser and poured a pitcher of water into the ceramic basin. She vaguely remembered that after removing the dishes and tray from Lord Huntington's chambers earlier in the afternoon, Father Flannigan had asked her to make tea. But she had gone to her room to change out of her riding clothes instead, anything to delay her returning to Lord Huntington's bedroom. She'd sat on her bed, branding her thoughts traitorous, wishing with all her being that the man would just go away. And that was the last thing she remembered of the afternoon.

No, not all, she realized as she ran a brush through her hair and pinned the mass in a chignon at her nape. She had never behaved with such cowardice before, practically fleeing Huntington's room, while some invisible thread had snapped taut between them, tugging relentlessly at her will. She had to force herself to remember that he was Lord Granbury's grandson and there could never be any crossing the line between them.

The aroma of hot coffee had joined that of the oatcakes by the time she slipped on her shoes and eased open her door. Lord Huntington's door was closed. She rushed past his room and down the stairs where she could hear Mrs. Kincaid talking to someone in the kitchen. Winter took a reprieve to brush her hands down her skirts as if the movement smoothed away the kinks in her nerves as well.

She stopped in the doorway. Father Flannigan was still here. He leaned against the black-leaded range with a cup of coffee in his hands. Mrs. Kincaid sat at the table peeling potatoes.

"I'm sorry I'm late," Winter said, growing alarmed by their heavy silence. "Has something happened? Are the boys all right?"

Mrs. Kincaid returned to her task. "Perry and Robert are gathering eggs."

Winter walked to the stovetop, picked up a cooking mitten, and poured a cup of coffee. She very rarely had a chance to drink anything other than tea, yet she found herself quite unable to think about her stomach. She sipped the hot brew and peered at Father Flannigan over the cup. "Is someone going to tell me what has happened?"

Father Flannigan set down his coffee cup. "He's gone."

Winter peered over at the boot room visible behind the kitchen. Lord Huntington's tailored jacket remained hanging where she had seen it yesterday when she'd come downstairs to wash her stockings. "Someone has died?"

"Our guest has departed the cottage. Huntington has decided his needs and ours are best served if he doesn't remain here," Father Flannigan said.

Winter lowered the cup, walked to the window behind the kitchen table, and looked out the diamond-shaped panes.

Coral-tipped clouds painted the fringes of an indigo sky now speckled with stars. In the distance, she glimpsed the weather-boarded barn, its thatched roof barely visible in the fading daylight.

"How long ago did he leave?" she asked.

"Ten maybe fifteen minutes, lass. He will not be pressing charges against the boys. Nor does he want them involved in this investigation."

"*Oui.*" Mrs. Kincaid scraped potato peelings into the refuse container next to her chair. "I knew he would not wish to harm those boys."

"How can he not ask the boys to give depositions?" Winter asked. "Robert and Perry are his only witnesses."

Father Flannigan reached into his jacket pocket and withdrew a pair of spectacles, setting them on the bridge of his nose. "He would say nothing more, except he would see the horse returned here tomorrow. I have no doubt he will resolve this matter in due time, Winter. At least he will arrive at Granbury Court properly dressed."

Adjusting the spectacles, Father Flannigan leaned over the stovetop, his attention solely aimed at the oatcakes on the baking sheet. His hazel eyes took on a lusty gleam and he twined his fingers against his chest. "Are these ready to eat, Mrs. Kincaid?"

Mrs. Kincaid snapped out something about eating supper first but the rest of the dialogue was lost to Winter as she left the kitchen. She hurried out the back door, slamming it behind her. She stepped around a puddle as she caught up a handful of her skirt and sprinted across the muddy yard. The jaunt loosened the pins in her hair and part of the chignon had tumbled over her shoulders by the time she'd stumbled her way down the slope.

Breathless, she stopped outside the wide doorway as she heard her brother and Robert talking from somewhere inside the barn. Then she heard a familiar baritone reply, and she stepped into the shadows to listen. Lord Huntington was still here.

His words did not carry, but she peered over the stalls and saw Perry's and Robert's faces, their expressions glum as rain on Sunday.

Lord Huntington stood just at the edge of lantern light, his dark hair and frock coat blending with the surrounding shadows. She glimpsed his profile and part of his shoulder and arm. But no sooner had she eased into the barn, she stopped abruptly. The hound was lying on the floor next to Lord Huntington's feet, its long nose on its paws studying her. *Damn.*

The dog leapt to its feet and loped toward her. All three males turned. Pretending she hadn't been eavesdropping, Winter bent and scratched the overeager mongrel between the ears. "Supper is almost ready," she told the boys, and, when they didn't seem inclined to move, added, "Mrs. Kincaid made oatcakes. Off with the both of you now."

"We understand each other then?" Lord Huntington said to the boys, and both their faces lit up like Christmas candles.

"Yes, *sir,*" Perry snapped like a soldier.

Both boys whisked past her. "Cooeeee," Robert called over his shoulder. "He ain't sendin' us to Tyburn."

"And he said we can pick apples in Lord Granbury's orchard," Perry added on his way out, the dog yapping at his heels.

Winter frowned. Lord Granbury would as soon tar and feather any person who entered his orchard. She remained in the doorway until the boys disappeared over the rise. Then she turned.

But the scolding she'd wanted to direct at her adversary died in her throat. Lord Huntington had come up beside her.

One black-gloved hand holding the reins of the horse, he wore tall boots over black trousers, his shirt wristbands turned out over the coat sleeves. He stood in the spill of the lantern light coming from a post behind her. She had not seen him all week without a shadow rimming his jaw or the bandage on his head. Dressed as he was, he looked less the scoundrel, more like a gentleman farmer—until she stared into his eyes, and something hot raced through her.

"Miss Ashburn," he said.

"Why are you leaving?"

He made no outward reply, and Winter found her attention drawn to the wound still partially visible on his scalp. "That . . . that mare"—she waved her hand over Old Ben's aged horse—"may not make it to Granbury Court."

He arched a brow. "I thought you'd be playing the fife and drums as I rode off into the sunset."

"Someone should be going with you to protect you. Father Flannigan has his buggy . . ."

His deepening amusement stopped her diatribe. Yet his eyes were not alight with mockery as they lifted from her mouth to settle on her eyes.

"It's only that you are unfamiliar with these woods," she explained. "And it's almost dark. Can you find your way out of these woods?"

"The good Father instructed me to go south two miles and take the first left past the grove of beeches. I'll find my way to Granbury Court."

"You need the boys' depositions."

His hand reached over her shoulder and dimmed the lamp. "We can agree I should not involve the boys more than they already are. Nor do I want anyone knowing where I've been this past week. I will deal with this my own way. Savvy, love?"

He was giving her what she wanted. A reprieve for the boys. If only she still did not feel worried for him.

Nodding, she looked out across the mist-enshrouded meadow. The sun had set since she'd left the cottage.

Yet all at once, she was no longer thinking about anything or anyone outside the walls of this barn. "Thank you," she murmured.

His quiet laughter tugged her attention back to his face. "You cannot allow that I would feel grateful?" she asked, offended.

"I'm thinking it isn't gratitude I want from you, love. And you're still a thief."

Narrowing her eyes, she questioned how she could have thought him honorable for a single moment. No matter how contrite she behaved, he found a way to mortify her.

Then his hand was beneath her chin, tipping her face and he was suddenly pressing his lips against hers. She heard her own gasp, and his tongue slipped past her parted lips. His touch electrified her. Her breath faltered. She tried to be appalled at his overt boldness. Instead, she gripped his upper arms to keep from toppling backward, or from leaning into him, she was no longer sure. For even that miniscule breath of space separating them vanished as he stepped against her and the kiss deepened into something even more alluring.

As if on their own, her arms slid around his neck. She felt liquid and supple, achingly aware of his body pressed

against hers. Wildness stirred within her. A hot surging of
her blood that was as much borne of indulgence as it was
of passion and the unwelcome desire that conspired against
her. She rose up on her toes. He would be out of her life soon
enough and this moment forgotten.

His hand closed around her scalp. He pulled her away
but not so far that she couldn't still taste his breath. Her
lips felt thick and hot. He looked deeply into her eyes, passion replaced by something darker and more pensive. The
vague scent of shaving soap mixed with the pungent straw
that layered the stable's dirt floor and enveloped her senses.
His hand slid down to frame the slim column of her neck,
featherlight against her throat. Her blood drummed against
his fingertips. The corner of his mouth creased, a flash of a
smile that came then was briefly gone. She stepped backward and he let her go.

"Why did you kiss me?" she asked.

He dragged up the reins of the horse, then stepped into
the stirrup and swung his leg over the saddle. The horse
pranced sideways. Whatever tension she had felt inside him
a heartbeat ago vanished within his careless grin. "Because I
could, Miss Ashburn." He nudged his horse out of the barn.

Words failed her. She clutched a handful of her skirt and
ran into the yard tempted to pick up a rock and throw it at
him. "I would wish you to fall into a rabbit hole if I thought
it would not hurt the horse!"

Lord Huntington adjusted the reins in his hand, his movement supple as he tightened his thighs and brought the horse
around. "I'm devastated to hear it."

"Don't be. You may yet expire before you reach Granbury Court."

The horse sidestepped and pulled at the reins gripped in

Huntington's hand. "You're a tempting little baggage, Miss Ashburn. Count yourself fortunate I'm a gentleman."

She gasped at his audacity. "If you were a gentleman we wouldn't be in the spot we are in now, *sir.*"

He laughed and gave her a two-finger salute. The movement opened his jacket and briefly revealed the holster beneath his arm. The pounding of hoofbeats faded soon after the mist swallowed him.

Winter walked to the paddock fence and leaned against its sturdy support. Only then did she dare press her fingertips against her lips. She tasted him still. Coffee. Sweetened with sugar.

She didn't know how a man could taste so good when she disliked him so.

Rory reined in the horse just beneath the spread of a knotty oak at the edge of the village. The distant bark of a hound touched his ears over sounds of the woodland night. The darkness was complete tonight, but the town was not asleep. A fiddler played inside a public house at the far end of the street.

His horse sidestepped and pulled at the reins. Rory loosened his hold and, whispering soothingly, slid his gloved hand down the mare's neck. "Easy, girl," he soothed.

Granbury was like any of a dozen other hamlets he traveled through that had fallen on hard times. Brown-and-white chocolate-box establishments lined the narrow cobbled streets. Doors and windows were shut tight, many permanently by the look of weathered tax notices nailed to the doors. He came to a halt in front of the Stag & Huntsman. A wooden placard hanging from a post above the doorway swung in the evening breeze. He stared at the sign then dismounted and walked with his horse around back to the stable. There he lashed the mare's reins to the hitching post.

His presence stirred the horses in the paddock. As if sensing his mood, they huddled nervously against the far side of the pen. Rory's gaze searched for the big gray mare one of his attackers had ridden.

Not seeing it, he returned to the front entrance of the Stag & Huntsman. Pushing through the heavy door into the smoky, noisy interior, he made a survey of the room and found the behemoth of a man he'd seen the first night in Granbury behind the bar. This was the man Winter had said was the town's sheriff. Derwood saw Rory enter the establishment almost at once. So did a dozen others. Like the fall of dominoes, the voices around him began to silence as more heads turned.

He permitted himself a slight smile and, for a moment, his casual stance belied the deadly intent in his eyes. For Rory Jameson, Earl of Huntington and heir to the Granbury marquessate, had learned long ago the necessity of girding the bull by the horns. Bring it nose first into the ground so hard the bull could not easily rise again. His grandfather had taught him that much about survival, a lesson given at an early age, and one that ironically served Rory well now.

"Well, Gentlemen? Who fancies a bit of bullfighting?"

# Chapter 7

Rory glimpsed Granbury Court's castellated grandeur for the first time in the light of a pale silvery moon. For a long moment after he'd reined in his horse, he remained at the top of the wooded rise overlooking the massive estate. Until this moment, he had not imagined the opulence of it all. The palatial three-story moonlit apparition covered acres with its huge corner towers separating three wings. Lights glowing behind the windows guided him to the front doors, as if welcoming him, even if he did not care to be welcomed into this place.

And the unfamiliar sense of belonging that had briefly surged through him changed into something more recognizable to him. For Granbury Court, with all its immenseness, was nothing more than a stone prison crushing him. Yet, he would be an outright liar to deny the brief tug he'd felt from somewhere deep in his chest.

The dichotomy of his feelings did not change as the evening progressed. Even before he had dismounted on the front drive, servants began filtering out of the door. Soon he was being greeted by the housekeeper who seemed to know him, and, as word of his arrival passed through the ranks, a fanfare heralded his coming as if he were some prodigal son to be honored. His rooms were already prepared. Dinner would be brought up. A bath. Anything he needed.

And it was all Rory could do to remain polite in the wake of their greeting. "Your trunk arrived over a week ago." The housekeeper, Mrs. Casselberry, held her clasped hands to her ample bosom. "We have been waiting for you."

The moment Rory saw the portrait hanging in the main foyer, he understood why the housekeeper accepted the matter of his identity so easily, and why Winter had found him familiar. Save for the outdated garments the subject wore, the man looked remarkably like himself. Rory stopped in front of the portrait.

"Your father, my lord," Mrs. Casselberry said.

That Rory looked so much like his father nearly stole his breath. The marquess was Rory's only link to this man whose life had always been shrouded in a cloud of scandal, and was a mystery to Rory. One of the reasons he was here.

"You have the Granbury eyes," the housekeeper said.

"My grandfather?" Rory asked. "Where is he?"

But the one man Rory had traveled across the breadth of England to confront lay on his deathbed oblivious to Rory's arrival as Mrs. Casselberry took him to his grandfather's chambers. His room smelled thickly of eucalyptus oil and sickness. A lone lamp on the cluttered nightstand cast its meager light across the frail figure lying on the bed. His grandfather was alone.

Closing his eyes, Rory knew his life had suddenly grown more complicated. Nothing was as black and white as it had been when he'd left London. His purpose for coming to Granbury Court had grown diluted with ugly shades of gray. "Why is no one in here?"

"Dr. Seacomb is dining, my lord. I do not know where the attendant is."

"Bring Seacomb here."

"Yes, my lord." Mrs. Casselberry nodded to the footman standing just inside the door. After he left, she said, "When your trunks arrived . . . You should have seen him, my lord. He wanted to be well enough to stand in your presence. But the pneumonia . . ." She shook her head. "Dr. Seacomb informed us that all he can do is make his lordship's passing comfortable. That it is best this way."

Rory opened the windows. "Thank you, Mrs. Casselberry. You may leave now."

With the summer breeze spilling into the dank room, he waited for the housekeeper to go before he finally turned to look at his grandfather.

For a long time, Rory stood at the edge of the bed and did not move, his chest suddenly tight.

Rory knew what laudanum could do to a person's mind. It robbed a man of his will to fight and live. As he stood at his grandfather's bedside, Rory wanted to harden his heart against a man who had disavowed his own flesh and blood in an act that had ultimately killed Rory's proud father.

For a few moments, he could hate as he plied his thoughts and forced himself to remember. Dying peacefully in bed was too easy for a man like Granbury. But in the end, as Rory sank into the chair beside the bed, he found only confusion in the mire that separated his heart from his mind.

Winter awakened the first time just before dawn. She found herself on her side, staring out the window at the starlit sky. She felt suffocated by her thoughts wondering if Lord Huntington made it safely home, if she would ever see him again. If she cared to see him again. The thought touched her with a perplexing quickness that left her disoriented.

Punching a fist into her pillow, she turned in her bed and stared at the wall, looking forward to finally returning to her own cottage.

She must have slept, for when she awakened again the morning hours had flown. She heard Perry and Robert outside, and rose to stand at the window. Her heart gave a start. The mare on which Lord Huntington had ridden out last night had been returned to the paddock.

Winter washed and dressed. Throwing a shawl around her shoulders, she hurried out of the house and down the path toward the barn. A wind gust slammed against her. No one seemed to be around, but a ghost had not delivered the mare. So it was with consternation that she walked out of the wind and into the barn.

A lantern had been lit and hung on a peg beside the door. She looked around but could not find who had delivered the mare.

"Is someone here?" she called.

"The guv'nor told me to return the horse, Miss Winter," Old Ben said from behind her.

She whirled on her heel and saw Old Ben Brown hunched over on the three-legged stool just beyond the lantern light. He was toiling over a rusted wheel on the rundown surrey-top.

"The bill of sale be in me head, but he paid me right fair fer her. Purchased another horse and left fer Granbury Court last night."

"He made it safely then?" Winter asked, not understanding the tension that filled the barn. She walked to the door and looked outside across the meadow.

"I weren't followed, Miss Winter."

"What happened, Mr. Brown?"

Old Ben replied without looking up from the oil rag in his hand. "It be a done thing fer us all. The guv'nor, he walked into the Stag & Huntsman last night and laid down the law to Derwood. Like nothin' any of us ever seen, mum. Nothin'." The man looked up at her, wide-eyed. "He told the sheriff his-self loud enough for all to hear. 'E intends to find the miscreants what survived the attack on him. 'E said the lot of them could either stand with him or stay out of his way. That 'e would find the culprits and see 'em all 'anged right proper."

"And he survived . . . unharmed?"

Old Ben's hands returned to scrubbing at the rust caked on the wheel. "Not a one in that tavern raised a finger against 'im. Not a one." His hands stopped their rubbing and he looked up at her again. "But this morning, folks are buzzin' like a hive of 'dignant hornets what got their nest smoked. Some are thinkin' 'is lordship should be the one what should face the tribunal. Especially as 'e just about admitted to being the one what killed Whitey."

"What happened after he left the Stag & Huntsman?"

"That's when he come to the stable. The guv'nor knows, miss. He knows."

A sick feeling churning in her gut, Winter knelt beside Old Ben on the stool. "What does he know?"

Old Ben stared nervously at the toes of his tattered shoes. "He asked me where a man would take a valuable horse to sell." The old man pressed his forehead into the heels of his hands. "But 'is horse be most likely killt by now, Miss Winter. It be too rare a stud to be sold, seein' as 'ow determined the guv'nor is to find it. There ain't a stable in all England a person could hide that stud that the guv'nor won't find it, miss."

Winter placed her palm on his bony shoulders to stop his rambling—and to steady her hands. "Mr. Brown. Do you know who attacked Lord Huntington? Is that why he would ask you these questions?"

"I had no notion them two boys would get themselves involved, miss. I'd give me right foot afore I seen 'em in 'arm's way. I swear it."

Winter's heart began to race. "Ben." She gave his shoulders a firm shake. "Was Whitey Stronghold one of the men who attacked Lord Huntington?"

"Whitey, 'at fool boy. 'E comes in earlier that day looking fer a particular thoroughbred stud. I didn't know what he was talking about, miss." Old Ben stared at his palms. "Later, after 'is lordship arrives, Whitey comes back and gives me the finest bottle o' Jamaican rum a man could 'old in 'is own two hands. All I had to do was give the signal when he left the stable. But I didn't, Miss Winter. I didn't." Old Ben's rheumy eyes blinked.

"I should 'ave said something when I recognized who 'is lordship was and that he were about to be robbed, but a person only gets hisself hurt steppin' twixt him and another's affairs. Let the *swells* manage their own selves, ain't that what ye tell me, Miss Winter?"

She raised her eyes to the rafters. "Oh, Ben."

"Every man knows, miss. It be one of them *cardinal's* rules you spoke about. A few stolen horses and purses lifted from those what can afford it might nettle them fancy coxcombs, but you 'arm an aristocrat and the militia hunts you until they 'angs ye. Whitey shouldn't of done what he did. But if I'd said anything, 'is lordship would of thought me guilty. We all seen what happens to a man what's 'anged around 'ere, Miss Winter."

Indeed, they had. She lowered her arms and stood.

Was Sheriff Derwood involved? Was that why he'd been with the rabble that day looking for the boys? Had someone told him Perry and Robert had been in the glade? The larger implication suddenly became more nefarious and frightening. "You said Whitey came in earlier that day looking for the thoroughbred stallion *before* Lord Huntington arrived?"

"Aye, miss." Old Ben's fingers curled into his palms. "They were plannin' to take 'im at Oak Point Bridge."

"But that road is never used anymore. Why would they assume he would be riding over Oak Point Bridge?"

"I don't know. But 'is lordship didn't leave the stable and the big one what was with Whitey got impatient. He returns and walks into the stable, not thinkin' the guv'nor still be there."

"Lord Huntington saw you talking to this other man?"

"Aye, and 'is lordship be a crafty one. He knows the truth. The other one be that bloke what rode the gray mare."

Last week, from the back of a large gray horse, one of the riffraff with Sheriff Derwood who had confronted Winter was Whitey's uncle. He'd only just moved in with the Stronghold family some weeks before. "Was this *bloke* with Whitey big with heavy jowls?"

Old Ben nodded. And the weight in her stomach sank lower as she recalled something else that had happened at the stable. Robert had been the one to give Lord Huntington directions that night. Had Robert directed him to the road that passed over Oak Point Bridge?

The signal Old Ben had referred to was once used to warn those in wait when targets were headed toward the bridge. The rarely used ravine surrounding that notorious bridge was a narrow path bordered by trees and thick scrub. A rope across the road had unseated many a drunken swell for harmless gain and, really, a rightful balancing of accounts. Yet . . . if someone wanted to do murder, it would have been simple enough to slay a man lying stunned on the ground. A chill crept up Winter's spine.

But Lord Huntington had not done what Whitey and his cohort had expected him to do that night. Instead, when Huntington had left the tavern he'd waited for her. Then after their dubious encounter in the stable, he'd followed her into the woods. He might have survived the attack unscathed had Perry and Robert's antics not distracted him.

She drew in a shaky breath and forced herself to think this through calmly, coldly, like Huntington himself would do.

Whitey Stronghold lacked the cleverness to have planned this attack on his own. And his jowly uncle didn't seem fraught with brains, either. Yet, not only had he known in advance that Lord Huntington would be in Granbury that day, but Whitey also knew the breed of horse Lord Huntington would be riding.

Winter shoved aside the panic that urged her to rush to Granbury Court and warn Lord Huntington of her discovery, even more a despicably weak urge to plead her innocence.

But what if she were wrong? What if this was merely flawed reasoning on her part? Maybe Whitey had seen the horse in a nearby town. Maybe horse theft was his only motive, and there was no conspiracy.

But what if she weren't wrong?

As she found herself staring outside at the gathering clouds, she knew no matter what choice she made now, she doomed herself.

"Have you told anyone else this?" she asked.

Old Ben scraped a grimy palm over his head and peered earnestly at Winter. "Only the sheriff. 'E come to visit me this morn, mum. That is why I had to find you. He wanted to know 'ow 'is lordship got hisself hold of my mare. He were looking for you, Miss Winter."

Once back in the kitchen, Winter leaned against the door and forced herself to breathe in slowly.

*Lord*. She was in so much trouble.

She had more reason than most to hate the baron and the establishment he represented. But when had everything spiraled out of control?

It had been four years since that first winter after a devastating fire had destroyed the crops. People lost their farms and their livelihoods. One of Granbury's own, Nate Hollister, father of seven, had felt the burden worse than most and been driven to poach. But he never made it home.

Instead, he had died horribly when the baron's hounds caught him on Everleigh land. Later her uncle had told the magistrate that the fresh blood of a poached stag on Nate's horse had been what had driven the dogs to their bloodlust. But everyone knew the attack had been outright murder. The baron's actions had left Nate's widow alone and unable to feed her children.

The next spring a group of the townspeople began to rob the cocky London swells that came this way. Partially as punishment to the baron since most of the victims were his associates. But mostly because a way had finally been found to plump up the poorhouse fund at the baron's expense. Taking a stand had been as much a matter of principle as of revenge.

Yet, suddenly it all seemed difficult to justify. To an

outsider, like Huntington, their little band might seem like common vigilantes, but to those in Granbury, especially Winter, it has always seemed perfectly right, like nature balancing the accounts in an unfair world.

But now this. And if Winter admitted it, the "rightness" of what their band did had dulled over this past year. Something had changed, something not right had slipped in among them, like a fox or a wolf had slipped into their henhouse.

A sudden thumping noise downstairs, almost beneath her feet, jarred her from her ruminations. Mrs. Kincaid was in the cellar. After searching, Winter discovered a doorway inside the pantry. She stepped down the narrow stairs, but stopped halfway, stunned at what opened before her. A dozen sewing mannequins wearing the most beautiful silver, blue, and yellow satin costumes stood arranged against a draping gilded cloth. The swirl of colors and fabrics brought the small cold space to life, like a tableau taken directly from the drawing rooms in Versailles.

"Mrs. Kincaid?"

"Over here, *chère*."

Winter's gaze traveled toward the voice and she saw Mrs. Kincaid perched on a tall stool in front of a canvas and easel, a paintbrush in her hand. A tied red kerchief bound her hair, and a white apron covered her brown homespun gown. She peered at Winter over the top of the canvas. "I used to work in the theater," Mrs. Kincaid said. "That which I no longer sew, I paint."

Winter stepped into the cellar. "You made these?"

"Once upon a time," she said.

"I didn't know . . . The gowns are beautiful."

"But hopelessly out of fashion."

A part of Winter felt saddened that something so beautiful had never been seen by others. That same part of her realized she was partially to blame.

Water sloshed as Mrs. Kincaid swished the paintbrush in the basin. "You came down here to ask if I would keep the boys for another night?"

"I don't have a right to ask you—it was not my intent for them to remain after Lord Huntington left."

Mrs. Kincaid carefully set the paintbrush next to a dozen others on the workbench. "I have forgotten what it is like to have anyone around, especially young ones. It would please me to have the boys stay." She hesitated. "Old Ben didn't come inside for breakfast. It could only mean something is wrong."

She wasn't prepared to talk to Mrs. Kincaid, or perhaps Winter's capacity for emotion had been exhausted to the point that she no longer had the strength to maintain her guard. But for a moment, she remained immobilized by Mrs. Kincaid's kindness and by her own conflict in matters that had less to do with the moral ambiguity of her past decisions, but everything to do with the consequences of choices she had yet to make.

Winter's hand tightened on the railing. "Old Ben told me something today. I don't know what I should do."

"This concerns Lord Huntington?"

"Something happened that night before the incident in the glade, Mrs. Kincaid. Something that was partially my fault. He was there because of me."

"You did not pull the trigger, Winter."

"I know. But someone in town *did* pull that trigger. Someone I probably know, maybe even sit next to in church. And Lord Huntington still *might* be in danger." Winter felt sick. "These people are my friends. I could not have survived these last years without them."

"Who are your friends, *chère*? The ones who shot Lord Huntington?"

Winter resisted the urge to sink into a weeping blob of muslin on the stairs. "What if those involved had not set out to kill him, but just wanted his horse? What if everything that night merely escalated and this was all some tragic farce of consequential errors?"

Perhaps Winter was afraid because she was not an innocent bystander.

But with a pounding in her chest, she realized that her own guilt or innocence changed nothing. Someone knew in advance that Lord Huntington had been on his way to Granbury last week. She *had* to tell him what Old Ben had told her today.

"Winter. . ."

Mrs. Kincaid looked as if she wanted to say something else, as if she recognized Winter's distress and understood her darkest deepest secrets. Perhaps she did, for they shared more than one.

Winter let her hand fall from the rail. "Why have you never told anyone about what happened the night my father died?"

Mrs. Kincaid returned to her paintbrushes, arranging them in a row, but Winter had seen her expression before she'd looked away, and thought fleetingly, *Angelique Kincaid was in love with my father. She would not see his daughter hurt more than she had already suffered.*

"You were not to blame for his death, *chère*. Or for anything else that occurred that night."

But Winter knew that it was a lie.

She might not have caused the carriage accident that killed him that horrible rainy night years ago, but if not for her, her father wouldn't have been on the road that night.

"If something happened to Lord Huntington that I could have prevented . . . I have to go to Granbury Court," Winter quietly said.

"You will go the back way, *oui*?" Mrs. Kincaid said. "If you are seen, someone will have to explain to Sheriff Derwood why Father Flannigan told him that you and the boys are with Sister Marguerite in Westchester and not due back until next week."

"As far as I'm concerned the boys still *are* in Westchester. I don't want anyone to know they are here until Father Flannigan says it is safe."

Mrs. Kincaid nodded. Winter paused on the stairway, hesitation returning her gaze to the Frenchwoman. "Thank you," she said.

Beneath an angry sky late in the afternoon, Winter drew her reins at the top of a rise. The land surrounding Granbury had once been a place of a great battle. Stone walls that had served as bulwarks were the most visible remnants of that turbulent time and part of the world Winter saw. The palatial Granbury Court sat off on a distant knoll at the center of a two-hundred-acre parkland. All around her lay its enormous wealth of lands that snaked through the bottomlands and into the forest. Bordering Granbury's western boundary lay her beautiful Everleigh.

A gust of wind whipped at Winter's cloak and the ribbons of her bonnet. She frowned at the clouds as the first drops of rain plopped on her face.

By the time she had crossed the vale and passed through the stone gates, a deluge had thoroughly soaked her cloak. Two liveried footmen came out the door to take her horse and gaped at Winter in her drenched cloak. It was only when one of the footmen took the mare's reins that she noticed the horse favoring its left foreleg. Winter mentally groaned. She'd worried last night about Lord Huntington riding this mare so far, only to injure the horse herself.

Hesitantly, she followed the footmen into the house and wondered why even her best intentions with regard to Lord Huntington's welfare could still be met with disastrous consequences. She would have to walk back.

"Miss Winter." Granbury Court's amply bosomed housekeeper stood just inside awaiting her. "Bless ye for coming." She reached for Winter's sodden cloak, leaving Winter to wonder why Mrs. Casselberry seemed to be excepting her. "Are ye wishin' to catch your death, miss?"

"We should not complain about the weather," Winter said, shrugging out of the wet garment. "The crops are in desperate need of rain."

"Lord Granbury has taken a turn for the worse," the housekeeper said. "I knew ye'd be the first to pay your respects, seein' as how the baron is away."

Winter swallowed in nervous surprise. She should have inquired sooner about Lord Granbury's health. "Have I arrived at an inopportune time?"

"From what I see, you have arrived in the nick of time. I will take you upstairs so you can get out of those clothes and allow me to dry them."

"Mrs. Casselberry, I cannot stay long."

"Nonsense, child. You have come all this way. It would be remiss of me if I did not at least serve you tea."

Granbury Court's housekeeper was blood related to half of Everleigh's servants, so Winter was no stranger to these people. Yet, though she had not visited in years, little around her appeared to have changed. As she waited for Mrs. Casselberry to hand the cloak to another maid waiting in the wing, Winter nervously looked around at the portraits on the surrounding walls—for one portrait in particular.

The grand baroque-style staircase opened onto the second floor—and there Winter saw the oil painting she'd once glimpsed when she'd been a child.

It was the reason why she'd thought Lord Huntington familiar to her that first night she'd seen him in the Stag & Huntsman. The portrait stood six feet high. The man's silver eyes, the shape of his mouth, the color of his hair—all of it formed the dashing face she saw in Lord Huntington. Seeing it again now, she recognized why she had never really forgotten it. Even now, her body stirred.

"Lord Huntington be the image of his father," the housekeeper said. "And he's come home, lass. Lord Granbury's grandson has come home."

"He is safely in residence then?"

"Oh, yes, miss." The housekeeper's voice lowered as she guided Winter toward the double doors down the long hallway. "His trunks arrived some days ago. But he only came in last night. He be with his grandfather most of the night."

"Perhaps I have come at a bad time."

"Mr. Jameson will be glad to see you. I shall inform him you are here."

Winter followed doubtfully beside the harried gray-haired housekeeper. "Lord Granbury's grandson?"

"No, miss. The other Mr. Jameson. Lord Granbury's grandnephew."

Winter stopped the housekeeper with a hand on her arm. "Trevor . . . Er, Mr. Jameson is back from London?"

"Oh yes, mum. He returned days ago."

"Are you telling tales on me, Mrs. Casselberry?" Trevor said from the doorway.

He stood with his hand braced against its frame. His other hand held a tumbler, which he raised partway to his lips and peered at Winter over its rim. "News travels fast. Have you come to console me?"

Winter didn't move. Her heart pushed against her chest. Trevor's russet hair swept his brow and hung in his eyes. His white shirt was rumpled and he looked as if he'd slept in his clothes. She had not seen him in months. She hardly recognized him. What was he doing back from London?

"You're drunk, Trevor."

"Bravo." As he raised the glass to her, he seemed to favor his left shoulder. "I can always count on you for honesty. In fact, you are the only one in my life who has ever been honest. How did you find out so quickly?"

"You are referring to your uncle's illness or Lord Huntington's arrival?"

Trevor tipped back the glass. "Both."

His eyes dropped over her. Winter was suddenly conscious of her closely cropped riding habit and limp hair, both still damp from the rain.

"But I'm not so in my cups to know it isn't healthy for you to be standing there in wet clothes." He looked past Winter to the housekeeper. "Why don't you do something for that, Mrs. Casselberry?"

"I will prepare her a room."

"I—" Winter started to speak, but Trevor turned back into the library. She followed him. "I can't stay."

"Don't be ridiculous." He walked to the sideboard near the opened French doors that let out onto the garden veranda. "You only just arrived." He removed the crystal stopper from the decanter and sloshed whiskey into his tumbler then opened the cabinet and withdrew another glass.

"I don't want a drink, Trevor."

"Why did you come all this distance if you were only going to be here five minutes? You haven't yet offered me your condolences."

"For what? Are you upset because your grandfather is dying or because you are losing a title you never had?"

"Can't I wallow in an occasional bout of self-pity? I think I have some right."

"How long have you known that you have a cousin, Trevor?"

He cradled the glass in his hands. "I only just found out. As it was, when I received this latest summons home, I thought his lordship had heard about my antics in London and merely intended to cut my allowance again. I was wrong."

Winter didn't want to believe anything else. She couldn't. Not when he was standing in front of her and with what appeared an injured arm. "Were you in another duel? Is that why you are favoring your arm?"

Leaning a hip against the sideboard, he observed Winter standing near the tall leather chairs in front of the hearth. "I had the misfortune of defending a lady's virtue against a particular brute of a man without knowing the chap was the damsel's husband."

Winter shook her head. Did men never tire of such silly antics? Trevor was forever in trouble with someone's husband or father. "You're a betrothed man."

Laughing, Trevor set down the glass on the sideboard. "Oh, to be a fly on the wall when the baron learns his precious Lavinia is practically wed to a mere nobody, and that

Lord Granbury allowed it to happen. The baron will not be happy. He will not lose his precious hold on Granbury. Your uncle has the big fish on his hook now."

"You're speaking of Lord Huntington."

"*Coz* is about to become the most eligible bachelor in England. Unless he is wealthy beyond belief, he will have to be amenable to a profitable alliance with some rich nabob like the baron or sell the lands that aren't entailed. Granbury Court has been bleeding cash for too many years. The estate will never stand against the death taxes that will befall this place when Granbury dies."

"You sound so callous."

"Do I?" His hand fidgeted with the crystal stopper on the decanter. "I don't mean to be." He turned his back to her and braced his hands on the polished sideboard surface. "Lord Granbury thinks I haven't a brain in my head. But I know this estate inside and out. I know finances. I've even had ideas about how to make the land profitable again."

He faced Winter. "I didn't *have* to come back. I came because I thought just once Lord Granbury needed me. A foolish notion. Especially since I gave up seeking his approval years ago."

From the days Trevor had come to live at Granbury Court when he was a boy, he'd struggled for his uncle's respect. Trevor had lived for the moment Lord Granbury would publicly recognize him as a valid and vital member of the all-important Jameson family, his only surviving heir.

Winter's emotions waged the same war as they always did when she wanted to fling herself in his arms and tell him that everything would be all right. How many hours had she, Trevor, and Lavinia spent at the lake looking up at the stars and just talking? How many times in the last few years had she suppressed her feelings because she'd known as the future marquess he would one day marry Lavinia, not her? She would never have wanted to see her old dreams come true at the expense of his.

"Lord Huntington may not stay," she said.

Though Trevor scoffed, Winter knew it was not a lie.

Whatever reason he'd had for originally coming to Granbury, he held no stake in the marquess's legacy. Certainly, love for his grandfather would not keep him here. And after the incident in town, he would never ally himself with the people against the baron.

"You think I'm heartbroken?" Trevor stood directly beside her, suddenly so close her skirts touched his legs.

She startled, and his gaze fell away from hers. He dropped to the arm of the chair. "You must be concerned, or you would not have come out here."

Her hand rose and gently touched his cheek. He laid his hand over hers and held it to his face. His eyes were blue-gray—a Jameson trait she realized, and suddenly she was seeing someone else's eyes framed by dark lashes. She was feeling someone else's touch, another man's hands on her body. She lowered her palm, only to have Trevor stop her from pulling away.

"Winter." His fingers laced through hers. "If I have no title, there will be no betrothal with Lavinia. You do understand that, don't you?"

As the breeze blowing off the lake brought a faint hint of honeysuckle into the room, a thick unrelenting ache built in Winter's chest. She tried to expel it, but it remained like a knot behind her sternum. Because it wasn't Trevor who filled her thoughts.

"Perhaps this isn't the place to . . ."

Movement in the doorway made them both start and turn.

The too attractive Lord Huntington stood with one shoulder leaning against the frame. A quirt dangled from his wrist. Winter disengaged her hand from Trevor's. "My lord. I didn't see you there."

Wearing a snuff-colored riding coat, dark trousers and boots, clothes too tailored not to be his, Lord Huntington looked as if he'd only detoured here on his way to the stable. "Don't let me interrupt," he said, his handsome face bereft of its customary reckless smile. His penetrating eyes fixed on her. "Except Mrs. Casselberry informed me we had a guest and you would be staying through dinner, Miss Ashburn. I told her I would notify you that your room is ready."

Trevor looked first at her then at Huntington. "You two know one another?"

"We met in town," she said. Trevor seemed hurt she had not told him. "He was at the Stag & Huntsman. At the time I was unaware who he was."

Lord Huntington's mouth turned up at the corners. "What brings you to Granbury Court on this wretched day, Miss Ashburn?"

"She and I are old friends." Trevor placed a proprietary hand beneath her elbow, catching Winter off guard. "I would not expect her to do anything less under the circumstances. I'll take you upstairs, Winter."

But when they reached the doorway, Huntington struck his quirt across it with a snap, his challenging eyes homed in on Trevor's face. "Mrs. Casselberry is on her way downstairs. *She'll* take Miss Ashburn to her chambers."

Then he stepped aside to let Winter pass.

# Chapter 8

Rory had not expected to come downstairs this afternoon and find Winter present at Granbury Court. In fact, he had not expected to see her until he'd decided exactly what he was going to do about her and that nest of spiders in which she seemed to dwell. Nor would he be making that decision anytime soon. One reason was upstairs in bed dying and the other stood next to him.

He watched Winter's shapely form disappear around the ornately gilded bend in the corridor. Trevor started to follow her, but Rory thrust his arm across the doorway and planted his palm on the jamb, forcing the man to take a startled step backward.

Trevor straightened. "You might be the new man of consequence around here, Huntington, but stand in my way again and . . ."

"What?" Rory paused, capturing his cousin's gaze, waiting for him to complete the sentence. "You'll shoot me?"

Trevor opened his arms. "If satisfaction is what you seek, I choose swords over pistols. I am a gentleman, after all, *my lord*."

"I assure you I am not. And if it is satisfaction you think you want from me, you will not survive to enjoy it."

Trevor's smirk slipped from his mouth. His arms dropped to his sides, and, as if not quite knowing where to put his hands, he shoved them into his pockets. A lock of hair fell into his eyes.

Rory pushed away from the doorjamb. Clearly, neither of them was in the mood to banter over trivialities now anymore than they had last night when he had met Trevor for the first time just after Rory had left his grandfather's chambers to find the physician. He and Trevor might be family in some connected cousins-twice-removed way, but no bond would ever exist between them despite their shared surname.

Outside, clouds had again hidden the sun. Beyond the French doors, a lightning flash highlighted the distant woods and lake.

The last thing Rory wanted at this moment was to engage his upstart cousin in a row, verbal or otherwise. Right now, he wanted to know why Winter was at Granbury Court.

Trevor stepped in front of him. "I will save you an embarrassing confrontation and tell you to stay away from her," he said, his chin lifted in defiance, but neither was he as brave as he let on. "Mrs. Casselberry isn't the only one who would find it an egregious breach of manners should you try something untoward, *my lord*."

Rory could see that Trevor was bloody serious. The pup was clearly trying to protect Winter from him. "Aren't you betrothed to the baron's daughter?"

"You have not met Granbury Court's esteemed neighbor to the west. You should at the first opportunity, since most likely it will be *your* betrothal to the beautiful Lavinia Richland that will be announced at the Summer's Eve Ball next month rather than mine. As for me, I suffer no great loss. I am now free to marry whom I please."

"And Miss Ashburn shares your vision for her future?"

"She will when I reveal it to her."

Rory eyed his cousin's dishabille with tedium. He slapped the quirt against his calf. "How old are you?"

"Twenty-three. And capable of defending that for which I care."

Something about the younger man's idealistic defiance affected Rory in an unexpected way. Perhaps it was Trevor's copious need to hound Rory like a belligerent ten-year-old testing his boundaries, or his obvious weakness for Winter.

Or maybe Rory had briefly glimpsed the same pain in Trevor's eyes last night when his cousin had finally met him and confirmed that Lord Granbury had essentially lied to him his entire life about Rory's existence.

"I suggest you sit with Lord Granbury for a while," Rory quietly said, attempting to diffuse the conflict. "When he awakens, he will be more comfortable with someone familiar in the room."

"Don't you mean if?"

"I mean *when*."

Rory strode down the corridor. Richly furnished with fine Turkey carpets, benches along the walls dotted with embroidered cushions older than time, the processional route took him up the marble staircase to the apartments on the second floor, the *click* of his heels indicative of his foul mood.

Reaching the landing, he lingered, his gaze suddenly riveted to the portrait in front of him. For some reason, he walked to stand in front of it.

A flash of lightning lit the gallery and revealed laughing gray eyes, soot dark hair, and a mouth curled in an assessing grin, as if he had no care in the world save to stand for this portrait.

Rory remembered little about his father and knew even less about his sire's life. He'd been killed when Rory was eight. But he had never remembered his father smiling.

"It's eerie, isn't it?" Winter said.

Rory turned. She was sitting on the stairway's top tread, her knees pulled up to her chest, her chin resting on them, and he wondered how long she had been watching him. She had yet to change out of her damp clothes. Most of her thick dark hair defied the chignon at her nape and fell around her face.

"The portrait. He could be you." She smoothed one hand over the old bonnet in her lap, its only pride a wilted ostrich plume and a faded green ribbon. "How is your grandfather?" she asked.

"Dying."

"I'm sorry." She stroked the bonnet, caught herself and folded her hands. "Trevor is right, you know."

"About what, exactly?"

"The Summer's Eve ball was when his betrothal to Lavinia was to be announced. The baron will make it to your advantage to wed Lavinia. You will not be able to turn him down." She directed his gaze to the glass dome in the vaulted ceiling above the massive chandelier. Rain cascaded in rivulets down the thick glass dome. "Sound carries," she said in explanation. "I heard you speaking.

"The baron, my uncle, owns the Richland London Exchange," she continued as he approached her. "But being the great grandson of a mere tin miner from Mousehole, he will never be a peer no matter how much wealth he possesses. Since my uncle cannot overcome the unfortunate circumstance of his ancestor's birth, he will do so through his daughter. Alas for you, he has his eyes on Granbury Court."

"What are you doing here, Miss Ashburn?"

"Mrs. Casselberry is currently fetching tea while I change out of my damp clothes. I had estimated her absence would give me a twenty-minute head start to escape. But I needed to speak to you before I leave."

A gust of wind pushed at the eaves of the house. She pursed her lips at the skylight. "Which now might be delayed somewhat."

"Somewhat?"

Rory stopped in front of where she sat on the stairway. He suspected she was hiding, so no one belowstairs would see them on the landing. He squatted beside her and placed the tip of his quirt beneath her chin, lifting her face into the gray light. "Are you so anxious to pick up where we left off last night that you followed me here today?"

Her eyes narrowed. "I won't let you provoke me."

He held back the grin that wanted to crawl over his lips. "God forbid what would happen should I provoke you, love. We might end up in bed together."

"Oh!" She slapped away his hand. "You are the most arrogant, self-serving . . . *cad* I have ever met."

His eyes flicked over her, and he wondered if she knew just how beautiful she was when angry. Only dimly aware of the raging storm outside, he said, "I am waiting with bated breath for you to tell me the point of your visit, love."

"I fear your life is in peril."

"From you? Trust me, I believe it."

"I am not joking."

"I am not laughing. Merely bemused by your concern. You have gone to a great deal of trouble to inform me of something that is after the fact. Unless you are not talking about yourself."

"You know I am not." She looked around him down the stairs. "Despite what people will say, I will not believe Trevor was responsible for the attack on you."

Rory sobered. "Come again, love? I fear I am a bit slow-witted."

More than curious where she was going with this, Rory wanted to know why she thought the attack on him was something more than a case of horse thievery gone awry.

"The day you were attacked, hours before you even arrived at the Stag & Huntsman, Whitey Stronghold went into the stable looking for your horse. He knew of your coming to Granbury before you even arrived. I believe he used Robert to try to lure you to a place called Oak Point Bridge. The bridge is the least traveled route leading south in and out of Granbury."

"Those were the instructions Robert gave me to get to Granbury Court," Rory agreed.

Little she surmised thus far was news to him. Robert's part in the ordeal bothered him. But Rory didn't hang eleven-year-olds. "My grandfather could have told anyone living at Granbury Court of my coming." The servants had known.

But only *after* they had received his trunk. Had he not been ambushed he would have preceded the arrival of his trunk as planned.

"Maybe Lord Granbury did tell someone, and that some-one found out where you lived in London and spied your horse before you arrived here."

"I own no house."

"Nowhere?"

"When I am in London I sometimes stay at . . . a friend's home."

"No doubt, she has quite large . . . eyes."

Rory's mouth quirked. Somehow, he resisted letting his gaze travel down the slim curvature of her neck to that very part of the female anatomy he found so enticingly pleasant. "Do you always take so long to get to the point?"

She squared her shoulders, the prim reaction pulling at the fabric of her bodice, and he might have been more amused had he suddenly not felt as if he'd just plunged into the seven torments of hell.

"If you had no house in London for someone to watch, how would anyone at Granbury Court know the breed of horse you rode?" she asked, drawing his attention back to her words. "I think Whitey was hired to see that you did not arrive. Maybe your horse was payment."

From the beginning, Rory had not wanted to let himself believe the attack on him was more than a robbery, for it was an entirely different matter if this incident were premeditated. Until a few months ago, only his sister and his grandfather had known of *Lord Huntington's* existence. But maybe he'd erred in that conclusion.

His grandfather had found him through his sister, Eve. If someone was monitoring Granbury's posts then that someone would have learned of Rory's existence months ago when Granbury sent the letter to Scotland. All anyone would have had to do then was watch his sister's cottage and wait for Rory to show up, which he did once every few months.

As Winter said, the most obvious suspect would be Trevor, which made Rory question the trail's simplicity. Either his cousin was the biggest idiot in the world, or he wasn't guilty and someone was covering his tracks to make Trevor look like the obvious suspect should something go wrong with the plan. Something had gone wrong.

Rory did not leave the stable that night by way of Oak Point Bridge. And no one had expected him to be armed.

Miss Ashburn breathed. "You don't believe me."

"How long have you known this information?"

"I didn't know before this morning."

"Then you've spoken to Old Ben." The comment wasn't a question. Rory had approached the hostler last night just after he'd left the tavern. Old Ben was the only one who would have known the information about Whitey. And the only one who knew where to find Winter. "Is this the first time you've ever betrayed a friend?" Rory asked.

"Please don't say it that way. Old Ben's only guilt was in not telling you of his suspicions about Whitey."

"What is *your* guilt in all of this, Miss Ashburn?"

She wrapped her fingers around the rim of the bonnet crushed in her lap. "There are things in and around Granbury of which you have no ken, my lord."

"No ken? What is there not to understand about those who commit thievery and murder? Forewarned is forearmed and all that rot? Does warning me ease your conscience concerning the tawdry affairs of this village?"

Winter turned her head away but Rory would have none of her dismissal. She had had the courage to face him today; he wasn't going to allow her to cower from him now.

Rory turned her chin back to him. "Does it?"

"Yes!" Her dark eyes flashed. "Warning you eases my conscience. I have done my duty and now I am free of you."

"Liar," he said softly.

Winter rose, her back pressed to the wall. Rory followed her to her feet, one boot on the stair below, the other propped against the landing tread to prevent her escape should she elect to flee. They stood nearly eye to eye, and something hot and dangerous arced between them, something he knew she felt, too. A muscle jumped in her jaw as she clamped her teeth shut, and once again, his body was both startled and captivated by her.

But she was involved with people who had tried to kill him, and in his mind, that slight detail circumvented any good deed she might have done to keep him alive. That he was remembering both times he'd kissed her only made his current circumstance more interesting, particularly since she was going to lead him directly to his would-be murderers, whether she knew it or not.

Any more than she realized she would let him sleep with her before he returned to London.

He leaned near enough for the scent of lavender to touch his nostrils and realized it came from her hair. He schooled his voice to a shiver-soft level. "Face the truth of it, love. You came all the way to Granbury Court because you were worried about me."

Her lips brushed his cheek as she said between her teeth, "I wouldn't worry about you if you were standing naked on a cliff during an ice storm. You tempt fate, *my lord*, perched as you are on these stairs."

Rory felt his mouth shift to a scowl. "I own my own fate, Miss Ashburn, which is more than I can say for you at this moment."

A regally condemning glare came from her dark-as-sin eyes. "Do I have your permission to leave now? I consider my duty toward you finished."

"Not quite."

Her lips parted, drawing his eyes to her mouth, the desire to kiss her dragging at his will. He hadn't asked to be invited into the middle of her bloody shire politics or some long-standing feud between her lot and the baron. "I want to know how your merry little band's endeavors involve my grandfather and Granbury Court."

"Lord Granbury is not involved. He has done nothing to concern himself with our problems these past years, absolutely *nothing*, my lord."

He read the truth of her conclusions in her eyes. "And no doubt the baron would like to keep it that way. That is a serious implication, my dear," he quietly said, "particularly from the mouth of a thief."

She released the breath she was holding. But there was nowhere for her to flee. He felt her tension but her struggle was not defined only by anger. "What do you want from me?" she demanded.

He slowly smiled.

"Bastard," she whispered.

"Not even close, love."

The quirt dangled loosely from his wrist. He didn't know if she would allow him to kiss her but then his mouth took hers. Anticipation had been like a heated coil in his chest. Reality was more like a hot poker in his gut. The tremor that moved through her settled inside him, and, without conscious thought, he deepened the kiss with a single sweep of his tongue. Her legs parted slightly, inviting him. He stepped against the depression in her skirt. He heard her soft moan. Or, with his desire sharpened by the press of her body that burned white-hot against his, perhaps the sound had been his own.

He didn't know if control had ever been his but restraint escaped his grasp when her tongue met his. It forayed then withdrew, and he followed its retreat. Inviting his kiss deeper still, she ravished his mouth.

Then his hands tightened in her hair, abruptly breaking

contact between his mouth and hers. His breath as shallow as hers, he looked into her flushed face, their mouths separated by a thread of moist air.

Her hands pressed against his chest, hesitant but not pushing him away. He shouldn't be ravishing her on the stairway in this house, yet logic escaped him when he was around her. Something about her challenged his needs, tested his self-control, and made a mockery of his discipline.

"You're mad," her whisper vibrated against his lips.

He'd been called far worse. He could have told her, but conversation was the last thing on his mind. His lips slid down the fragrant column of her throat. She made a wordless sound and murmured, "I don't want this."

Rory rarely weighed the philosophical or moral ambiguity of his actions, yet he'd sensed the tremble in her voice. "What do you want?"

He felt her breath catch against the shell of his ear. "Please . . ."

The quiet plea penetrated the erotic haze engulfing him. He pulled away and studied the confused mix of emotions on her face: fear, fury, and the unmistakable flush of desire. But whether it was his conscience or physical torment that damned him, he would never know. Someone was walking down the gallery corridor toward the foyer.

He repaired her rumpled jacket. "We're soon to be discovered."

She had to have heard the foot taps as well because she wheeled away from him and stumbled up the stairs, tripping on her damp skirt. To keep her from falling, Rory grabbed her arm, his grip rougher than he meant it to be. But he wasn't about to let her flee into oblivion and break her bloody neck in the process.

"Christ." He gave her a small shake. "Are you *trying* to hurt yourself?"

Her eyes clashed furiously with his. "Don't . . . don't touch me again."

Confounded, he drew his hand back. Trevor suddenly appeared at the bottom of the stairway and halted abruptly at the sight of them.

Rory straightened. There was no mistaking Winter's pink swollen mouth and flushed skin or that Rory was responsible for her fondled dishevelment.

"Winter?" he heard Trevor ask.

Rory lifted a complacent brow at Winter. She glared back at him. At least they had returned to equal and familiar ground. "This is rather awkward, isn't it?" he said.

Trevor started up the stairs with the kind of passion that found one settling scores on a dueling field at dawn.

"Stop." Winter pinned the younger man with her eyes. "I don't need to be rescued by you or anyone."

"Your defense of her is admirable, *coz*," Rory said without looking away from her. "But she is perfectly capable of skewering us both and does not need your protection. I would advise you to remember that fact no matter how well you think you know her."

"Who are you to insult her?" Trevor demanded.

A cynical laugh formed in Rory's throat. He turned his head. "Do you truly want to fight me?"

Winter stepped between them. "Stop now, Trevor."

Her tone banked the fire in Trevor's eyes. "Why do I get the feeling you came to see him today and did not know I was in residence?"

"I thought you were in London with Lavinia. I didn't know you had returned. I'm sorry, Trevor."

The sound of someone circumspectly clearing his throat snatched Rory's attention to the foyer below. He stepped to the rail and peered down. The butler and the housekeeper, holding a tea service clutched in her hands, stood nervously on the polished parquet floor in front of a vase of yellow primroses that adorned the center table.

Rory had met thirty-two domestics last night. *Smythe.* *Smith.* The butler's name momentarily escaped his recollection. He was a man about sixty with one expression on his long face. *Smothers.* "You've found me for a reason?"

"Yes, my lord." The butler stepped forward. Rory still was unaccustomed to the title. He didn't like it.

"I apologize for interrupting, my lord." The butler's eyes skipped to Trevor. "Lord Granbury's solicitor has just arrived from London, Mr. Jameson. He has been informed of Lord Huntington's recent arrival and is asking for him."

Trevor's attention swung to Rory, but only briefly. "Does he know I'm here as well?"

"I am only conveying his request, Mr. Jameson."

Trevor nodded. "Of course. I know you are, Smothers."

"Tell the solicitor to await me in the library," Rory said after a moment.

Smothers bowed at the waist. "Yes, my lord."

Winter dragged her eyes from Trevor's and met Rory's with accusation. He could do nothing at all and she still made him feel like an ass in lion's skin.

Jogging down the stairs, he pointed his quirt at the housekeeper who remained like carved granite, the tea service still clutched in her hands. "Take Miss Ashburn to her room and help her out of those damp clothes. She doesn't leave Granbury Court tonight."

"Wait!"

Rory halted and turned, bracing one foot on the steps. Winter floated like a harried butterfly down the stairway. She stopped on the stair just above him and grabbed the bannister to prevent herself from colliding with him.

"You *can't* order me to stay. I'm not one of your minions."

He raked his gaze over her flushed cheeks and tumbled-down hair and said just quietly enough for her ears alone, "Actually, Miss Ashburn, you are."


"You've not touched your supper, miss," Mrs. Casselberry said from the doorway connecting the sitting room to Winter's adjoining bedchamber.

Wearing a pale pink wrapper belonging to Mrs. Casselberry's oldest daughter, Winter sat on the window bench, watching rivulets of rain slide down the glass. The sun had dropped out of the sky, leaving a stygian darkness blanketing the night. Distant lightning punctuated the darkness across the lake. The storm had moved past Granbury Court to expend its fury over London.

"I brought you me own brew," Mrs. Casselberry said to Winter's reflection. "The toddy will help ye sleep."

Winter peered back at Mrs. Casselberry in the glass. "You may set the mug on the dresser," she said quietly. "Thank you."

The housekeeper did as Winter asked, then retrieved the untouched dinner tray from the table. "Your gown will be dried and pressed before breakfast in the morning, lass. Good as new, it will be. Mr. Jameson wanted me to make sure you were comfortable, miss."

Winter turned on the seat. Leave it to Trevor to be the only one in her life to inquire after her well-being. "Is he all right, Mrs. Casselberry?"

"Mr. Jameson came home the moment he heard his lordship took a turn for the worse," Mrs. Casselberry said. "Then to find out Lord Granbury has a grandson all these years, and none of us knowin' the truth of it."

The housekeeper's bosom heaved. "'Tis a dreadful shame to be sure, hearin' about what happened to his grandson on his way to Granbury. Already people have begun to whisper. But the young master is not responsible, no matter what anyone thinks."

Winter lowered her eyes to her clasped hands in her lap. "You're very loyal to Mr. Jameson."

"He is not the scapegrace Lord Granbury thinks he is, miss. We've seen him in his shirtsleeves helpin' keep back the water when the river flooded its banks last year. What young man does not occasionally sow his oats? He would have settled down with Miss Lavinia."

Winter returned her gaze to the darkness outside. What man would not jump at the privilege to lie with beauty and wealth?

Mrs. Casselberry continued in a heated rush. "And I'm sayin' this to ye only because I know you can keep your counsel. But neither of those two men downstairs asked for what be brought down on them."

Winter's mind leapt to the moment on the stairway when she had seen Lord Huntington's almost vulnerable expression as he was looking up at the portrait of his father. "Do you remember Lord Huntington's father?"

"He were a wild one to be sure, miss. All the young lords were. But this one seems different."

"In what way?"

"His eyes miss. For just a moment last night when I took him in to his grandfather . . ." Her voice faded. Her passion spent, Mrs. Casselberry suddenly looked down at the tray in her hands as if she'd forgotten its presence. "Oh dear, miss." The housekeeper adjusted the tray. "Here I am jabbering like a chickadee. I will warm your plate."

"Please don't put yourself out. I'll eat what is there. It isn't that cold."

"Are ye sure, miss? T'would be no trouble."

"I'm sure." Winter rose to her feet. "Has Lord Huntington retired for the evening?"

"No, miss. But he has requested not to be disturbed."

"I see. And of course you cannot disobey his wishes."

"If it's any comfort to ye, he's arranged to see ye safely delivered to Everleigh in the morning."

"Oh, no, Mrs. Casselberry. He needn't both—"

"His lordship was most adamant with his orders. You are to return in the carriage."

Mrs. Casselberry slid the wooden chair out from beneath the table. "Would you like for me to set the serviette on your lap, miss."

The kindly housekeeper was clearly coaxing Winter to eat. She did not want to be unkind or show her irritation when it was Lord Huntington who greatly annoyed her. Lord Huntington who filled her thoughts. But once Winter took the first bite of curried pork, she had no difficulty finishing supper. She ate everything, then drank the toddy at Mrs. Casselberry's cheerful urging.

After Mrs. Casselberry cleaned up the tray and left Winter alone in her chambers, Winter walked to the door. The key was in the latch. She peered into the darkened corridor. No sound reached her from any direction. She shut the door and twisted the key.

Even if she had not felt the effect of the toddy draining

the tension from her muscles, she could not leave here tonight. Not only was her horse in no condition to travel, she was not prepared to walk miles back to Mrs. Kincaid's cottage in the rain and the darkness.

Whether she stayed or left before morning no longer mattered. A part of her already knew it was too late to fret over circumstances beyond her control.

Indeed it had been too late the moment she'd arrived at Granbury Court on some noble mission that in her mind would make up for her mistakes. It had been too late for her the instant she had returned Lord Huntington's kiss on that stairway, for it had been more than a moment of surrender. She had wanted him.

Wanted him more than she'd wanted to breathe. Wanted him so much that she had not only raised the white flag but had lowered the drawbridge over the moat inviting him into her castle.

She didn't know what bothered her the most—the realization that Lord Huntington could so easily make her lose control.

Or her lies.

So many lies and secrets that were part of her life, perhaps were even who she was as a person.

Bending forward, she blew out the lamp in the sitting room.

As she crawled into bed, she considered Lord Huntington's order to see her returned in the Granbury coach. Winter recognized that being sent back by way of the carriage would put the village on notice that no one was beyond the reach of the future Marquess of Granbury's domain, especially Everleigh's once-proud daughter. But he would soon learn hell hath a better chance of freezing over than finding her inside that coach tomorrow morning.

# Chapter 9

**A** knock at Rory's bedroom door came just after break-fast the next morning. Having anticipated it, he'd already finished his meal and dressed. Unfortunately, he had been awake most of last night, sitting next to his grandfa-ther's bed, listening to the wind and rain.

But as he caught his reflection in the glass, no one would have mistaken him for anything less than the future Mar-quess of Granbury. Rory had played so many roles in his life, playing one more should have been no different. Yet somehow, it was.

He called for Mrs. Casselberry to enter.

The housekeeper entered. "You wanted to be informed the moment Miss Ashburn slipped out of the house, my lord."

According to the groom caring for Winter's mare, the horse was still wearing a liniment poultice for a strained foreleg, the result of yesterday's excursion. So Winter would be on foot. Rory extended his arms behind him as a manser-vant helped him into his riding jacket. "How long ago?"

"Ten minutes. Do you want someone to stop her and bring her back?"

Rory would give her a half-hour start. He adjusted his

jacket, then plucked a silver watch fob from his vest pocket and popped it open. "Let her pass through the gate."

Smiling to himself, he tucked the fob back into his pocket and decided a head start was the least he could do for her. "See that I have a horse saddled."

"Certainly." Her mouth narrowed in nervous hesitation. "You aren't plannin' to do the girl harm are ye, my lord?"

"No, Mrs. Casselberry. I only intend to see that she does not walk the entire distance back to Everleigh."

"Then might I suggest you wait a bit longer? She might be more inclined to accept your hospitality were she a wee bit exhausted."

Rory fastened the button on his jacket and suppressed a grin wondering who in this town was not Miss Ashburn's champion. "That sounds like a plan, Mrs. Casselberry."

The housekeeper in her black dress and white apron puffed up like a preening penguin. "Thank you, my lord. Is there anything else?"

"Find Smothers for me," he said and the housekeeper left the room.

"Do you need anything else, sir?" the manservant who had helped him with the jacket asked.

Rory didn't and dismissed him. After he left, Rory walked to the table where his breakfast tray still sat in the adjoining sitting room. He splashed the last of the tea into his cup. Somewhere in the house, a clock struck eight.

Green velvet draperies shrouded the other windows lining the wall, and the only light in the room seeped in through the window in front of him. He pulled aside the sheers and looked across the parkland. Groves of elms covered the hillside. Weeping willows shivered in the breeze. He lifted his gaze to the horizon. The storm that had wreaked havoc over

Granbury Court last night was gone and in its place a flaw-lessly blue sky.

He strained his sight for any sign of Winter, his gaze fol-lowing the wending drive past the stone walls of Granbury Court. As he started to turn his attention in another direc-tion, he saw movement. Rory watched her vanish briefly be-neath a canopy of green to emerge on the rise. Bringing the tea to his lips, he smiled into his cup.

Another knock sounded and Rory recognized Smothers's tap.

"You wished to see me, my lord?"

Rory set down the cup on the desk next to where the solicitor had left a copy of Lord Granbury's will the night before and faced the lanky butler. Against the dark paneled walls, Smothers could have been a shadow.

"Lord Granbury has shown no sign of improvement," Rory said. "I refuse to do nothing while he dies. I want to bring in another physician to attend him."

Smothers paled. "But . . . my lord, no other doctor has attended to Lord Granbury in twenty years."

Rory was aware of that fact. Lord Granbury had ex-pressed his gratitude for the good doctor's loyalty by leaving him the cottage and plot of land where he currently lived. But Rory didn't like the man. He despised any man who could sit back and do nothing while an old man withered away and died.

"I want someone attending him who has no stake in his death. Are you familiar with Father Flannigan?"

Smothers cleared his throat. "Lord Granbury would not want a priest here. Especially that priest. It would upset him terribly, my lord."

"Why is that?"

A befuddled expression crossed the butler's face. "Father Flannigan is *Catholic*, my lord."

"Is that a fact?" So was Rory, but he did not point out that detail. "As someone whose father served as Lord Granbury's chief steward before you, I would have thought you've lived here long enough to also know that Father Flannigan happens to know medicine. I'll wager he has tended far more sick and dying than Lord Granbury's current physician who has never attended to anyone but his lordship. Send someone to bring Father Flannigan here."

Smothers cleared his throat. "Yes, my lord."

"And then have Old Ben Brown brought here."

"Y-yes, my lord. Do you still wish the carriage to be readied?"

Rory returned to the window. Winter was now a speck of black where the bright blue sky came down to touch the horizon. "That won't be necessary."

He didn't hear the butler withdraw but knew when he was alone in the room. He watched Winter until she disappeared over the last grassy knoll, but even then he could still feel her presence stirring in his blood. If he knew why, he would talk himself out of the attraction.

She possessed courage, he had to give her that, or she would not have come to Granbury Court yesterday to warn him. She was beautiful. And desirable. So were all his female acquaintances.

But Winter Ashburn was a fighter with a peculiar code of honor he understood.

Regrettably, for her, he rarely played fair.

Winter had never been more relieved to lose sight of the manor house. She drew her first real breath since slipping out of her room. Last night's rain had left the ground soft beneath her steps. The brisk wind whipped at her cloak but did not discourage her for it was summer warm and filled with the vibrant scent of wildflowers and meadow grass made more pungent by the new moisture.

She desired to put as much distance between herself and a certain unpleasant person at Granbury Court and that lent impetus to her flight.

Her trek for the next mile took her past groves of trees and grazing sheep gathered in the dips and atop the knolls of a landscape stretching as far as her eyes could see. She felt a sense of her own insignificance and solitude amidst the unspoiled grandeur surrounding her. She had stopped to pick a pebble from her boot when the faraway nicker of a horse shattered her minuscule sense of peace. She straightened.

Shading her eyes against the glare of the blue sky with her hand, she sought the source of the sound and froze. Silhouetted on the hill behind her, a man sat astride a dark horse. The rider was not looking in her direction but seemed to be studying the terrain. Her panic began small but rapidly grew.

*Lord Huntington!*

Even from a distance, she recognized him. "Bloody hell."

Lifting her skirts, she dashed down the hill to her right, into a grove of trees. Twenty minutes later, she emerged scratched and disheveled on the other side of the glade only to find her tormentor astride his horse awaiting her. He wore no hat, and the sun lightened his eyes to a wicked silvery shade. Involuntarily, her fists clenched.

"Good day, Miss Ashburn."

Seeing no sense in denying she'd attempted to escape

him, she relaxed her fists. "Are you enjoying the morning air, my lord?"

He leaned an elbow against his thigh and peered down at her. "It's Rory," he corrected. "I thought we established my name is Rory."

Casually, she picked a twig from her sleeve. "Minions do not address their lord by his Christian name, *my lord*."

"Minions obey their lord, Miss Ashburn."

"In your most cherished dream, Huntington."

He laughed, a baritone sound that had her clenching her teeth. He was a scamp and a rogue, and to the devil with her if she didn't like it.

Watching him, she understood well enough what attracted her to him. His gaze fastened on her mouth, and, from the lazy-lidded heat in his eyes, he, too, knew what she saw in him. He was dangerous and alive to her. He drove her from solitude to seek that untamed wildness she felt inside her only when he was near. Their mutual awareness sent a rush of heat through her veins, and she quickly sought to chill her reaction.

"You are an unmitigated wretch, sir," she said, disliking her predictability and that this dissolute *newcomer* to Granbury should already know her so well. "You *knew* I would escape this morning. And you let me."

"I knew it would take an act of torture to get you into the Granbury coach. As I am not a man to bypass opportunity, I considered this my chance to see the lay of the land with someone intimately acquainted with it." He held out his hand as if he fully expected her to accept it. "I'll take you back to Everleigh, Miss Ashburn."

He'd let her walk miles on purpose. She stood her ground. "I thought you'd be at your grandfather's side this morning."

"I don't intend to remain absent all day." When she made no move to take his hand, he leaned an elbow on his knee and said gently, "I propose another truce between us."

Dragging up her skirts, Winter bolted past him. "To what purpose?" she called over her shoulder.

He wheeled the horse and walked him alongside her as she slogged up the hill. "It's a long trek to Everleigh," he pointed out.

Winter ignored him.

"Do you plan to walk the entire way?"

"I enjoy walking."

She reached the crest of the hill. Lord Huntington reined his horse in front of her and blocked her path. "I'll get you to Everleigh faster my way."

He held out his gloved hand again, all deference and good breeding. But the look in his eyes made a lie of his manners. Clearly, he wasn't *asking* her to take his hand. He was ordering. "A truce implies trust between all parties involved," she said. "You and I do not trust one another."

"I'll trust you not to assault my virtue while on the back of this horse."

She smiled despite herself, before realizing that even such a minuscule reaction inadvertently granted him a victory. She frowned. "Do you *have* any virtue left to assault, my lord?"

"Do *you*?"

She refused to be baited. "Are you asking if a thief could be a virgin, my lord?" Her tone pregnant with suggestion, she lifted her chin, quite beyond any pretense of flirtation. "Does the lack of one virtue cancel out others? For I do readily admit to thievery. Does that then make me less a virgin and more a whore?"

His jaw visibly tightened, and she'd never felt more aware of her own disquietude than at this moment, awash in the intensity of his silence. "You are not the first libertine to wonder, my lord. Nor, will you be the last."

"Are you finished?"

*Yes. No,* she was about to say. But discretion wisely rejected any riposte she might have made to his parry. How could she know his game if she did not know the rules by which he sparred?

No longer shielded from her own potent sexuality, she found herself without reply, suddenly feeling inexperienced and wishing she were not. Certainly she lacked his sophistication and worldliness.

The breeze stirred her hair, the grass, and the surrounding trees. It was as if the air had come alive beneath the warm summer sunlight. The horse whickered, and Lord Huntington tightened his grip on the reins.

"Take my hand, Winter."

There was no hint of tension in the line of his jaw, no muscle working in his cheek. He removed his foot from one stirrup, leaving it open and dangling. Despite her wont to refuse him or to put him in his place, as if there was such a place for a man like him, she truly had no desire to walk another four miles to Everleigh.

She stepped into the stirrup and laid her hand in his. His long fingers closed around her wrist and with his help, she swung up behind him. The horse reacted to the move by sidling nearer to the hill's edge. She flung her arms around his waist to keep from sliding off.

"Are you on?"

She nodded but realized he couldn't see her. "Yes."

He nudged the horse into a canter. Her chest pressed

against his back. She took a steadying breath. "You aren't wearing your gun."

"I'm always wearing my gun, love. But I would be loath to have you reach around and accidentally shoot me. I'm partial to my welfare."

She felt rather than heard the restraint in his voice, and she had a vague feeling she'd made him angry.

After a while, she laid her cheek against his back. A weight settled in her stomach. He spoke to her when he needed direction. Even then, their exchange remained brief. She felt at odds with her feelings, felt cheated by this polite aloofness, by how quickly he seemed to be able to switch off his emotions, like the snuffing of a candle.

The faint smell of cloves touched her senses. The scent came from his hair. It was Granbury Court's milled soap. The same soap she'd washed with last night. But just as with the rose-smelling soap Lord Huntington had bathed in at Mrs. Kincaid's, he absorbed his milieu much like a chameleon absorbed colors and gave it his own sensual stamp.

Playing Lord Granbury's grandson was merely another role to him. He played it well enough, but it wasn't who he was inside. He barely tolerated being called "my lord" or "Lord Huntington."

Not for the first time, did she speculate about his life before he'd come to Granbury. He appeared educated and traveled. The fine cut of his cloth beneath her fingertips was *sans pareil*, like the difference between ordinary French brandy and cognac.

Last night he'd alluded to the presence of other women in his life. Winter wondered if he had a mistress. Had he bought her a house like Winter's father had purchased for Mrs. Kincaid? How did a mistress behave?

The realization that she was bothered by Lord Huntington having a life outside her existence disturbed her, for it exposed a spongy underbelly of longings she was helpless to resist. Perhaps it was merely her own helplessness that caused her to resist.

She straightened her back and tried to put distance between them, but his hand clamped on her arms and prevented her from pulling away. "Relax, Winter."

*"Relax?"* She didn't know how far she could possibly ride with her legs stretched into Chinese splits, and her breasts pressed into his back like sardines in tin. "Have you considered I may not be so hostile if you were politer, my lord?"

*"Rory."*

She laughed at his persistence. "Surely the rest of the world doesn't call you Rory."

"You've seen me as naked as most of the women I've ever slept with. I think you're entitled to speak my Christian name."

*Oh!* "I expected something base from you. Frankly I'm more shocked you held out for an entire thirty minutes into our truce."

He reined in the horse and twisted in the saddle. "Oh, you're wrong, love. I'm perfectly willing to play the gentleman if that is what you want from me. If not, we can have done with our games now and proceed to something more enjoyable."

Her blood hummed through her veins like a bow strumming the chords of a tightly strung violin. She dared not breathe for fear of touching him. And yet, she wanted to touch him.

He raised himself in the stirrups and, with very little effort on his part, slid her around and across his lap. The action caught her palms against his chest. She squirmed in mild protest against the shock of his body against hers but that only brought his arms more tightly around her. Part of her objected to his audacity even as the other part swam in the feelings he roused.

*Why am I not protesting?*

Because being with him was like nothing she had ever felt before. Because for the first time in so long someone had the power to wipe away her past and return something to her that had been ripped from her soul. Laughter. Desire.

She didn't know what it was inside Rory Jameson that drew her to him, but it was there like a slow-burning flame inviting her inside to bathe within its warmth.

"No protest, Winter?"

Her voice was a whisper. "What shall I protest?"

His mouth moved over her temple as his fingers followed the ribbons that tied her bonnet in place and his hand opened over her breast. Her startled inhalation pushed against the heat of his palm.

His eyes held hers. "This?"

He had dared challenge her to kiss him, not once but three times, had dared arouse her passions and introduce her to her own desires. He was daring her now to turn away. Even as her mind drummed a warning, she inched toward its conclusion. There was not a moment's doubt in her mind what he intended to do if she let him.

Yet even as her palm slid to the buttons on his waistcoat, she could feel the restraint coiled in him. After a pause, his hand drifted across her shoulder. "I don't normally ask, why the change of mind."

"Then why dwell on the question?"

"A *gentleman's* curiosity," he said with forbearance, his

tone even, his patience clearly gone, with something else in its place that should have frightened her.

She knew to her core, just as in the stable, if she asked him to stop, he would proceed no further, and this moment would probably be of no more significance to him than last evening's thunderstorm.

Suddenly more than anything, she needed to feel significant.

She needed to feel passion and desire. She needed to know that a man's touch could be gentle and warm like summer rain, and that her own touch could make a man want and need her equally.

"I am ready to have done with this, my lord."

A corner of his mouth turned up. "Is that right?"

Resentful of his calm, she drew in her breath. "Unless you have changed your mind."

And as she held his gaze, she wondered if he ever revealed himself to anyone, if he'd ever allowed himself to care deeply about anything. Or if his entire life was a game to be won or lost in the challenge.

Then he shifted in the saddle and, for a moment, disappointment spilled through her. Winter thought that he had suddenly changed his mind.

They had reached an old medieval gristmill, a haunted eddy of stones and vines, once the site of a great battle during the English civil war. Except for an occasional historian, even locals had long ago forgotten this place. Without speaking, he helped her dismount before he stepped out of the saddle. He walked the horse to water. Standing where he'd left her, she watched him tie the reins to a low-hanging limb. She watched his gaze travel down her body, but the distance separating them defeated her efforts to read his thoughts.

Silencing the anxious voice inside her, she removed her bonnet and shook her hair free because her hands were too unsteady to do nothing. He removed his jacket then each glove, and set them inside a leather case on the saddle. She watched his approach with an acute sense of awareness.

His hands went to the frog on her cloak. And he laid it on the grass. "I can do this without making a child between us. You do understand?"

His words sent a shiver through her. But how much was jealousy that he should be so well-studied in such things, she didn't know. "How fortunate you can manage the thing. For I cannot."

He was so much taller, forcing her to tip her chin to look up at him. He kept his expression impassive, his eyes hooded. They both stood barely touching, yet so close that had she drawn in a breath, her breasts would have touched his chest.

His thumb stroked the line of her jaw and the lazy-lidded heat in his eyes sharpened into something akin to tenderness. "We can still stop. I cannot promise it will be so easy five minutes from now."

"This is all suddenly so perfectly proper." She turned away but he grabbed her hand and brought her against him.

The pads of his thumbs pressed against the curve of her jaw, and he held his mouth to her pleasure and to his. "If you want proper, close your eyes."

Then he kissed her.

Open-mouthed and deeply.

He tasted of cloves and tea. He smelled male and dangerous.

He knew the ways to touch her with his softly rousing words, his lips, his hands. Sliding his palms over her shoulders and down her hips, he raised her skirts and boldly splayed a hand over her buttock. She arched against him, feeling the outline of him hard against her.

His lips slid down the column of her throat. He kissed her neck and shoulders. She turned her face to the side, breathing hard, her senses in tumult. And she inhaled him like a drug.

*"Christ."* He touched his forehead to her temple, his breath hot on the apple of her cheek. He still wore his shirt and waistcoat, though both draped opened as if he'd been in a brawl.

Heady with her own newfound desire, she swept her hands over his back, exploring the hardened curvature of his shoulders beneath the fine lawn of his shirt. She lifted her face seeking his mouth again. But he deprived her of the sensual contact. She pulled back, only to feel his palm close around her nape.

"What is this really about?" His breath was a harsh rasp against her lips. "Payment to me?"

She did not understand the source of his mood. But accepting this as a debt paid was far simpler than any alternative reasons she had for being here with him, in his arms. He would never understand. She did not entirely understand her reaction herself.

She kept her eyes locked on his. "Isn't payment what you have wanted from the beginning?"

Winter then made her second mistake of the day, thinking she understood a man like Rory—the first had been to climb on the back of the horse. The devil had hold of her whimsy and would not relinquish his grip. In fact, he held her arms so snugly against him, she could feel his heart beat against her palms.

"I didn't think you would be the skittish one."

"Is that what you think I am?"

Winter glanced down. Her bodice opened to her waist. Her breasts, high and full, spilled over her stays. They trembled from her breathing. She had never seen herself so wantonly displayed. The fragrant breeze touched her exposed flesh. She shuddered, trapped by strange sensations.

They extended beyond her physical barriers, and she struggled to rein them in. And she felt a moment's doubt and alarm, when her body balked and her nerves turned to dust. She couldn't do this. Yet, she could not think of anything else *but* this.

Then he moved his lips down her throat. Warm fingers unhooked her stays up the front. His forearms corded beneath her fingertips as she leaned into him. Between long, hot kisses, her dress and underclothing fell away. Her boots and much mended stockings and garters followed.

She allowed herself to be taken down to her cloak. Following her, he held his body braced above hers. Struggling to breathe evenly, she wondered if a person could die from need.

Still booted and spurred, he sat back on his calves, reached behind his back and pulled his shirt over his head. Dark hair arrowed up his abdomen and sprinkled his chest. His stomach was firm, his chest and shoulders toned with an athlete's grace. His was a body that did not balk at physical toil. Terror shot through her at the beauty of it, exhilarating yet also petrifying.

His hands swept over the buttons of his trousers as he looked down on her. She lay motionless, unable to take her eyes off his fingers. His hands paused as if he'd stopped to admire the view of her naked beneath him. An illusion of wavering light perhaps. Shade dappled the ground and moved with the sound of the wind in the trees. She had never willingly allowed herself to be so vulnerable.

But she held power, too, she realized. She saw it briefly reflected in his eyes, an elusive thing just beyond his physical grasp, like the invisible currents of wind yet substantial enough to touch him. And for just a moment, she reveled in his surrender before she realized he was watching her through heavy, slumberous eyes and knew her thoughts. He leaned over her and smiled rakishly.

"You do not have to bring me to heel, this day or any other. I've been your devoted servant since I met you."

"Oh . . ." She struggled against him.

He captured both her hands. He looked fiercely beautiful in the diffused light of the glade. Perfectly wicked.

He so easily mocked her feelings, she realized, not understanding how she could want him as she did, or that he could so easily strip away her will and control with a few words. "You are such a bas—"

His mouth closed over hers, shunting the sentiment ere it spilled from her lips.

Repeatedly, persistently, seducing, his lips foraged hers and she forgot that he could make her furious at the drop of a pin, because he also made her feel so alive.

He moved his lips down her throat, and her eyes drifted closed. Her head fell back. Her hair a wild tumble against her cloak. She gripped his shoulders. And forgot everything when his mouth found her breasts. A small cry escaped her. He laved the dark aureole around her nipples. In a heartbeat, her breathing changed.

Partially leaning on her elbows, she tried to rise but her hair caught her. "Please . . ."

But in this, he would not be controlled.

Beneath her palms, his shoulders bunched as he moved lower. His kisses flicked lower over her stomach. And while his tongue continued to do magical things to her body, her senses absorbed every sensation falling upon her—the breeze brushing her skin like the softest of touches, the cloak at her back, his silken hair against her stomach. He dipped his tongue into her navel and still lower to her hip. He'd pushed her thighs apart and raised her knees before she emerged from her sensual daze and realized what he was about.

His lips brushed her inner thigh. She should have guessed he'd do something to shock her. "Wha—What are you doing?"

She thought she felt his lips smile. This was too intimate. She wanted to cry out. But not enough to stop him.

He opened her delicately with his fingers. The sudden rush of pleasure spiking. She felt the caress of his breath as he blew on her. And then his mouth touched her in the most intimate way possible. Shattering the last invisible wall shielding her from his invasion.

His tongue and lips seared her. Her spine arched. Her hands fell away from where they had been entangled in his hair. She raised her arms above her head opening her legs to all of him. She clutched the grass still cool with rain. Her body thrummed. Waves of sensation caressed her body. He drew on her flesh, suckled and teased. She cried out. She could not stop the sound nor contain it in her chest as tremor after tremor came crashing over her.

When it was finally over, she opened her eyes and lay helplessly staring at the blue dome of sky. His body shifted and his face and shoulders appeared in front of her eyes. He gazed at her from under a dark fringe of lashes. The heat felt hot in her cheekbones. Her breasts pressed against his chest. She didn't know whose heartbeat was more thunderous.

The release had shattered her both emotionally and physically as if the broken feelings she'd dammed inside her all these years began to leak like a sieve into her soul. She could not grab them back.

Something inexplicably wicked must truly live within her as the baron had once accused her. A recklessness that now spilled over when she was around Rory, not like the gentle wash of rain on her face, but like the sweeping storm that had recently passed. Something that awakened all the other emotions she had put to bed so many years ago. Passion. Desire. Happiness. Hope.

Then the dam inside her broke in a terrible gush of confusion. She had not cried even when she had buried her father. Yet she felt the burn of tears now behind her eyes. Tears had always represented weakness to her. But something monumental was shifting inside her. For so long anger had consumed her, she was suddenly without her driving strength.

"Please forgive me," she managed in a whisper.

He leaned back on his heels. Winter sat up, pulling her knees to her chest, her hair falling over her shoulders. She'd lost all her pins, and that suddenly seemed like another disaster with which to contend. How would she repair herself? "This is not what you think."

His fingers brushed her lips, still swollen from his kisses. "Are you afraid of this? Or just of me?"

There was a darkness about Lord Huntington that *should* have frightened her, but did not. Winter didn't know what she felt. Bliss? Hunger? But not for the kind of nourishment that fed her body. No indeed, she felt like a shiny penny that had been lying in the sunlight all day. Warmed all over. Hot to the touch.

"Come here," he said, sliding the cloak around her shoulders and pulling her against him.

It had been so long since someone had held her, and she let herself relax against him even if she did not quite know how to respond. She was such a failure, as a sister, a daughter, a woman. Her sniffles clogged her nose. She couldn't even let herself be seduced by a man she wanted as much as she wanted her next breath. "I don't need you to be nice to me," she felt obligated to say.

"Of course you don't. But no one else is stepping forward to do the job."

This outsider tore at the scab of something familiar inside, and she clawed deeper inside to revel in its discovery. Today she suddenly felt less than the fabric that held her family together. She felt young and carefree again, and wanted to remain this way if only for a few more hours. After a moment, the silly urge to weep subsided and she reached for her shift to wipe her nose.

"Good God, don't use that." Lord Huntington thrust a clean handkerchief from his trouser pocket into her hand. "I'd never forgive myself."

She laughed and sniffled, and looking up at him through watery eyes, pressed the cloth to her nose. He was still holding her. One hand splayed against her back, the other against her hair, and perhaps because of the understanding and care his touch implied, she turned her head into his chest. He was undressed from the waist up. A light mat of dark hair defined the bulges and hollows, and the scent of cloves touched her senses.

She had never known anyone like him before. The man might be a scapegrace but he did not seem overset by his faults. She envied his acceptance of himself. Never before had anyone made her so aware of her own body and feelings. Or made her feel so alive and unafraid.

"Have you ever been afraid?" she asked.

"Sometimes."

"When?"

His fingers tightened in her hair, pulling her face up. His grip was not painful, but neither was it gentle, merely restrained. "Are you going to explain to me what this is about?" he asked.

Her distress and fear had already drained out of her, and all the reasons for her tears seemed ridiculously childish in the wake of her naked physical state. His eyes held hers, and even after everything, he still had the power to arouse her. She wanted to swim in his heat, paddle into the sunlight.

"I will not be a trophy," she said. "The prize for a game won between us."

"Is that what all of this is about?" he quietly asked.

"I don't know. I only know that I am all tight inside. Like I've been caught in an apple press. I can't even seduce you properly, and you're the easiest man I know."

A corner of his mouth lifted. "How many other men do you know?"

"None whom I wish to seduce."

He lifted a strand of her hair. "Tell me what happened to you, Winter."

"You happened."

*You walked into my life and nothing has been the same since.*

But she didn't say the words. Her eyes still wet, her emotions tender, she found herself on a crumbling ledge prepared to leap.

She leaned back against her cloak, her dark hair spread out

beneath her like an ebony fan. The summer breeze caressed her breasts and hardened her nipples. The wool was rough and cool against her back. Lord Huntington's eyes moved over her breasts like a slow burn, but his thoughts remained ruthlessly shuttered as his eyes touched hers. She watched him, afraid to breathe, and for a long suspended breath, Winter wondered if a woman could drown in silence.

Then he lowered his head, smothering her mouth with his lips, tilting her whole world on its axis. Her arms wrapped around his neck. She kissed him back, clinging to his lips, opened-mouthed and hungry. He pushed away, breathing heavily, his hot breath mingling with hers as if to ask her what she was doing. There was a burning place still in her belly and between her legs, a feeling so piercing, she needed him to touch her again.

"I want this," she said. "I truly do."

He pressed his lips against the rabidly beating pulse at her throat. Then as if coming to a decision rose. He removed his boots. His dark hair hung in his eyes as he yanked the buttons on his trousers. Her breathing quickened and she dropped her gaze to the grass at his feet.

He knelt and combed the hair out of her face. "Look at me, Winter."

And she did.

She resisted a moment then looked down. His sex stood erect from the concealing shadows. She felt his hand close around her wrist, drawing her hand downward over his flesh.

"You are seducing me, love." His voice was husky.

He moved his palm between her thighs and with the gentlest of skill opened her legs for him. And suddenly she could barely hear above the roaring in her ears. His hand slid around and closed around her bottom. Her eyes rose to his. It vaguely occurred to her drugged mind as he rose above her on the cloak that she was giving him exactly what he'd set out to take from her that day.

Then his lips took hers, and somewhere in that heated touch, as he seduced her mouth and tasted her lips, as he moved his body between her legs, she let him take her anyway.

And tensed at the invasion. She cried out a little, but he caught the sound with his mouth and made it his own, laying waste to her senses.

Her body accepted his until she felt him tense. Time stopped. There *had* been no virginal barrier.

His fingers entwining with hers, he reared himself up and looked down at her. Her panicked mind tried and failed to disconnect from the fact she had lied.

"Why?" The single word touched her, deep and gravelly.

Her nails digging into his hands, she shook her head. She could not tell him the truth. She could not. "I want this." More than anything, she wanted this. "Please . . ." Her body throbbed and pulsed. The fullness was an ache.

She arched and, pressing her heels into the grass, accepted all of him into her body. His shoulders lifted. With a downward force of his hips, he thrust into her again.

And his gaze burned hot, as a new hush enveloped the glade, the only sound the rasp of their breathing.

It was her final reflection before she lost herself in his fire.

# Chapter 10

W inter waded naked into the stream, the stones lining the streambed smooth and hard against her bare feet. She caught her breath as she carefully lowered herself, and the icy water fairly snatched a groan from her throat. The swirling water felt good against her most tender womanly parts. A shadow crossed over her. She looked up to see Lord Huntington standing on the bank.

Fully dressed now, he squatted, his forearm resting on his knee. He held her shift. It was a relaxed pose but she could feel the tenseness in him, and knew why.

"Are you all right?" he asked.

She sank into the stream. "I'm shivering only because the water is cold."

He studied her shift in his hand. "That is not what I am asking. And you bloody well know it." Why he might invoke some male umbrage over such matters, she didn't know. "Do you think I would have judged you harshly had you told me the truth? Or did you think I would not know?"

"Then why are we talking about this."

"Because you lied. I want to know why."

A lump lodged in her throat. She knew he was not only asking her why she had lied to him about being a virgin, but why she thought it would have mattered to him that she was not.

Averting her gaze, she sank lower in the water. Her hair floated around her shoulders. "I can't wash with you watching me."

He raised a brow and did not seem inclined to move from his place on the grassy slope. "I've already seen more of you than you've probably seen of yourself, Winter."

She looked into eyes that were wild and dangerous. He was still so much a mystery to her, part of a world she knew little about, and just staring at him she felt like a schoolgirl given a key to open the world.

A squeezing tightness grew in her chest. She owed him an explanation. But how could she speak of something she had spent five years of her life desperately trying to forget? Maybe it was the honesty that frightened her.

She forced back the hot sting of tears just as she'd forced away so many memories. "Suffice to say, my first time was not consensual, my lord." She peered at his face. "So in my heart, I was every bit a virgin until today. The first time I gave myself willingly."

His face blanched.

He wore the same look of horror she remembered seeing on her father's face when he had discovered what had happened to her. And suddenly she was remembering the same echo in time and the events that had led up to his death that stormy night when he'd climbed into the brougham prepared to defend her honor. Only to be killed that night when his carriage overturned. It was a time in her life that she had never truly recovered from. But had overcome. At least she'd thought she had.

She didn't know why his reaction should make her feel

ashamed, but it did. "Don't look at me in that way," she snapped, already feeling battered and bruised inside.

He made an impatient movement with his hand. "How the bloody hell *am* I supposed to look?"

She splashed out of the water and snatched her shift from his hand. She dropped it over her head and yanked her hair free. She could not comprehend his anger. "My debts are paid to you, my lord." She stalked past him. "I owe neither you nor any man an explanation."

His hand caught her wrist in a firm grip and stayed her from leaving. It was a curious rather than frightening gesture, and perhaps because of the understanding and care it implied, Winter found she could not fight him. Fear and anger left her as quickly as it had come and all she felt now was suddenly weary.

She dropped her gaze to the hand holding hers. Drawn to the warmth and to his presence, she raised her eyes and found him watching her.

"Tell me what happened to you, Winter?" he quietly asked.

"The incident occurred just before my father died."

"When you were sixteen? Who was it?"

This time she did not turn her face away. She faced him with dry eyes. "I'm all of a piece, my lord. The incident happened long ago and is not something upon which I dwell."

"The baron."

The heat left her face. That he could guess with such ease shocked her and shook her. She heard his muttered oath. Felt his anger on her behalf, and the heat of him through her damp shift.

"Do the townspeople know?"

"Father Flannigan knows. Mrs. Kincaid . . . She also knows." Winter swallowed over the lump in her throat. "I moved out of the main house. The baron gave me a cottage and granted me a certain modicum of independence in exchange for my silence, though such a thing would not have mattered. An accusation might hinder his political aspirations, but in the end, I would have been the one persecuted. There is only one way we ever found to fight him."

Huntington's eyes narrowed. "And we've all witnessed the success of that endeavor firsthand."

"I've told you as much of the truth as I can."

He faced her like some silver-eyed Jehovah. "One awful truth does not vanquish all the other lies between us. It doesn't clean the slate or change who you are or who I am or answer my bloody questions. Hell, it complicates everything. Why didn't you tell me this soon—?"

She pressed her fingers against his lips, cutting off his words. She tenderly held his gaze as if it were she trying to assuage him, and his temper suddenly burned out as quickly as it came.

His eyes embraced hers with compassion. "I find I do not know what to say to you."

She disengaged her hand from his but only because she knew he'd let her go. "I prefer your sarcastic wit to your pity, my lord. You are not obligated to console me." She lifted her chin. "And you needn't worry about what happened here today. I assure you I take full responsibility."

"Don't martyr yourself so quickly, love." His quiet reply held her attention. "The responsibility is all mine."

"You wouldn't have laid a finger on me had I not—"

"Are we really going to engage in another contest, Winter?"

Caught as she was in the tangled web of her emotions, she found she wanted to step into his arms and bury her face in his shirt. She wanted to know his tenderness again, the kind she felt when she was in his arms. For all of his high-brow posturing and arrogance, deep inside he was one of the most selfless people she had ever known.

But she did not move. The moment stretched interminably, for he neither spoke nor moved either. She was conscious of his warmth.

"I enjoyed today," she finally said. "Very much."

His laugh was as much self-deprecating as filled with incredulity. Shaking his head, he looked at her but made no reply. At least he had *not* made any apology, and for that, she was grateful.

"May I ask you a personal question now?" she asked.

He plowed a hand through his hair. "Christ, no."

Undeterred, she asked anyway. "Why did you really come to Granbury?"

He looked around as if her question might lie in the beauty of the countryside surrounding them. "I haven't decided why I came."

"The prodigal offspring of one of Granbury's sons does not return to the place of his father's birth driven by indecision, my lord."

"My father despised everything about Granbury Court," he said almost to himself. "I'm not sure that I'm of a different opinion."

Tenting a hand over her eyes, she joined his visual observation of the terrain. A land that she loved. She had looked out her window at Everleigh upon it most of her life. She could not imagine that for a Jameson whose family had toiled and died for these lands, he could feel no emotion, no desire to save it for his own children. She would have given anything to keep Everleigh. It was difficult to believe that Rory could not feel the same for Granbury Court.

"You wanted to see some of Granbury Court?" she said. "If you'll allow me, I'll show you."

Winter guided Lord Huntington back to Everleigh land by way of the boundary that divided Granbury Court and her old home.

They traversed gently rolling hills, rode past an abandoned weir on the river threading through the property. Thrice, they passed burned-out farmhouses, now overgrown with weeds. Naught but a crumbling skeleton of blackened stones remained to give evidence that families had once lived here. Winter had wanted him to see this.

Lord Huntington finally reined in his horse in front of a weed-infested yard. "What happened here?" he asked.

"Four years ago a fire burned this entire section of land," she said. "We had been under a severe drought. Everything went up like kindling. In less than two hours, the firestorm burned to the river and every tenant in this sector lost his farm. Four people died. As you can see, no one lives here now." She peered up at the sky. "That is why the rain these past days has not been a bad thing. This year has been terribly dry and the summer has just begun."

He looked past the dilapidated house to the fields green with hay and rolling toward the distant river. "Whose land are we on now?"

"We're still on Lord Granbury's land. Though this part of the estate is not entailed. The baron has a lease for as far as you can see. He provides Granbury Court's main source of revenue now. If this crop ever fails, the estate would suffer a terrible economic loss."

Lord Huntington gave her a considering look. "How did the fire start?"

She shrugged a shoulder. "Some say the local children playing with Chinese fireworks. Others say it was started on purpose. We could never prove anything either way."

"We?"

"Sheriff Derwood. The townspeople. Trevor. Me. We are all on the side who believes the fire was no accident."

Lord Huntington nudged the horse out of the yard. Her arms tightened around his waist. His back was warm against her cheek.

"Forgive me if I appear obtuse," he said, "but why the bloody hell would Trevor allow Richly's talons into my grandfather's estate?"

Winter pressed her chin against his shoulder. "Trevor doesn't exactly have a say in Lord Granbury's financial decisions. After the fire, I believe it was a matter of Granbury's survival to accept the baron's offer. If you want more information you will have to go to the Richland London Exchange to find it."

Everleigh Hall appeared on the horizon. She didn't want to get off the horse and leave his company, but she planned to ask him to stop when he reached the ridge.

"How involved are you with my cousin?" he asked.

"I'm not." Winter held her arms to his chest as she thought of Trevor, the way she used to see him when she was a little girl. His helmet of russet hair and smile had always been part of his boyish charm. He was the exact opposite of his darker cousin. "When I was younger, I wanted to wed him," she said. "We've rarely spoken in a year. Not since he and Lavinia became a pair."

Winter pondered that reality and Trevor's change of circumstances. She did not want to admit that a moment had passed in the library yesterday when she had suspected him of trying to kill Lord Huntington. "Everyone in upper circles had expected Lord Granbury to make the formal proclamation naming Trevor his heir years ago," she said quietly. "You must allow him some disappointment. How would you feel if you were in his place?"

"You might be shocked at my answer."

"Nothing about you shocks me," she scoffed. "You think you do not want this title or the responsibility. But it is not your choice to make."

He halted the horse. But before he could turn the force of his glare on her, she slid from the animal's rump, bounced onto her feet, and took a hopping step backward, grateful her legs held her weight after an hour on horseback. "Thank you for the ride. But I'd prefer if you came no farther."

He didn't argue. He merely looked down at her from the height of his saddle, the customary humor in his eyes absent. If she expected him to say good-bye, he did not. Pride stopped her from any maudlin reply, for what did one say to a man who knew her in every intimate way possible?

"I hope your grandfather recovers," she said.

She felt a moment's sadness for Lord Huntington. Perhaps because he was an outsider thrown into a circumstance he didn't want by a man he didn't know. Despite every facet of his persona that told her he led an exciting life, Lord Huntington still felt inherently alone to her. She knew more about his family than he did.

She looked up at the cloudless sky. The sun blazed and she tented a hand over her eyes. "Did you know a great battle was fought on these lands four hundred years ago?" she said.

Some of the softness returned to his mouth. "No, I had not been apprised of that fact."

He was probably thinking there was not a square inch of real estate on this ancient island that had not had a battle fought over it at some time or another in history. "A person can still find artifacts and an occasional tunnel," she said. "Trevor and I used to play in some of them when we were children. They snake through this entire area, though most have been boarded up and sealed."

She found his eyes on her face, casually possessive in tone, and she felt warmed by their touch. The wind fluttered the ribbons on her bonnet and she peered off into the distance toward the verdant fields shimmering in the breeze.

"The first Marquess of Granbury led the fight defeating the Lancastrian rebels that eventually put a Tudor king on the throne."

His palm rested on his thigh. "Your point?"

"The point is there is more to your family history than that of your father or your grandfather. One day you will have the opportunity to make your own legacy to pass down to your children. This is all theirs as much as it is yours."

A moment passed in silence. Her heart thrusting heavily in her chest, she brushed at the wrinkles on her skirts. She had come to the end with him.

"Good-bye, my lord."

She swept past the horse and scampered down the incline, letting the wind bat at her cloak and skirt. She reached a grove of ash and elms and, grabbing her bonnet on her head, turned to look back at the hill. Lord Huntington still sat atop his horse. A pair of jackdaws crossed the sky, one squawking at the other. Her gaze followed their noisy trek to the trees behind her. When she shaded her eyes and looked back at the grassy knoll, Lord Huntington was gone.

# Chapter 11

"**B**ut we want to go fishing," Perry protested.

"We found poles in the barn," Robert said with equal mutiny in his voice. "Mrs. Kincaid told us if we fixed them, they would be ours."

Their enthusiastic desire to remain at the cottage did not take Winter by surprise. Looking over her shoulder at Mrs. Kincaid who had stepped outside into her garden, Winter moved away from the opened window and sat down at the table where the boys were finishing breakfast.

Three days ago, the barn had needed a coat of whitewash, and they had each made two shillings. Yesterday it had been weeding. This morning, they had insisted on gathering eggs for Mrs. Kincaid. Then Winter sat through breakfast with them waiting on a second batch of griddlecakes, as Mrs. Kincaid was apparently an excellent cook and Winter never served anything so inventive as fried bread soaked in golden syrup for breakfast.

She thought back to when she had discovered the boys talking to Lord Huntington in the stable, and now seeing the same earnest expressions on their faces, she wondered why she could not inspire that manner of animated loyalty. She felt the sting of jealousy.

"Don't you want to go with me to see Mam?" she asked Perry.

"We don't want to leave, Miss Winter," Robert said.

Her brother lowered his eyes to his lap. It was not his reticence that worried her. "What is it?" she asked them both. "Are you *afraid* to leave?"

Robert shook his head. "We just want to go fishin', Miss Winter."

She leaned forward, her elbows propped on the table. She had already tried to talk to Robert about the night Lord Huntington had invited him to watch his horse, and why, when asked for directions to Granbury Court, Robert had told Rory to travel over Oak Point Bridge, a route rarely used anymore by anyone.

"He just did, Winter," Perry had replied in defense of his friend.

Now she studied her brother's face. "Did Whitey or someone else ever threaten either one of you?"

"No, Miss Winter," Robert said too quickly.

Winter wanted to force Robert to open up to her, but the boy could clam up tighter than a rusted trunk lock. He'd never had cause to trust authority.

Father Flannigan had found him years ago abandoned near the padding-kens of Southwark. The metropolitan police had arrested his mam for prostitution, subsequently leaving him to fend for himself with the other mud larks who scavenged the foreshore of the river for food. Winter had met him when Father Flannigan delivered him filthy and belligerent to her classroom.

That long-ago autumn day, she'd seen a boy who was lost. Perhaps she'd recognized something of herself in his soulful brown eyes. Perhaps that was why she'd grown to care for the little carrot-top urchin. She wanted him to know that whatever his crisis, she would help. That is, *if* she was in a position to help anyone any longer.

"Lord Huntington said we should stay with Mrs. Kincaid," Perry said, displaying a sudden avid interest in the tongs of his fork.

"He said that until you con . . . con"—Robert pressed for the correct word—"consorted with a better class of people, we should remain here."

Her jaw dropped. "This is what you were discussing with him the other night in the stable?"

Perry nodded. "He said I wore the pants in the family and I was to look out for you"—when his words halted, Winter shook his arm, urging him to continue—"because you couldn't look out properly for yourself."

She barely contained her disbelief to a mere gasp. "Of all the . . ."

"Now can we go fishing?" A hank of curly red hair fell into Robert's eyes and he brushed it aside, presenting her with a sunny smile. "We won't go farther than the pond. Promise. Right, Perry?"

Perry nodded. At least she could see the pond from the house. With a quiet sigh, Winter knew both boys would have mucked the stall again if it meant staying longer. "Very well. All right."

With a bark of excitement, both boys rose and dashed past her. A long moment passed before Winter shoved away from the table and strode into the boot room. She pulled back the threadbare curtains and looked outside at the boys as they ran toward the pond, and her shoulder brushed against a jacket hanging on a wooden rod. Rory's jacket.

He had left it behind when he'd ridden out to Granbury Court.

She didn't know what bothered her more. That Rory could be a complete ass, or that he spoke the truth.

Three days had passed since he had returned her to Everleigh land. For three days and nights, he had been a constant weight in her thoughts and heart.

She laid her palm against the sleeve of his jacket, but it was that very movement that caught the corner of her eye. Her reflection looked back at her from a silvered looking-glass above the washbasin.

Winter had not seen herself in so long. Not in the way she saw herself now. She crossed the room and stood silently in front of her reflection.

The girl looking back at her was beautiful. Touching her hand to her lips, she found she did not suffer any of the emotions she expected to feel after her woodland tryst with Lord Huntington. Emotions like guilt. Shame. It seemed impossible that he could stamp her so indelibly with exactly the opposite passion. For the first time in a very long time, maybe ever, she felt as if the woman staring back at her was no longer a stranger.

She felt almost free of a burden that had haunted the preceding years, the thought nearly bittersweet.

For was it better to feel nothing at all? Or feel this budding warmth inside her, knowing she could never allow herself to lose her heart to a man like Rory Jameson. Not that she was naïve enough to do so. But when she lay in her bed at night and listened to the stirrings in her heart, she found herself wanting to believe in fairy tales. The kind that a tall silver-eyed man in a portrait inspired.

Of course, she was too old and too sensible for such

nonsensical fantasy. Still, she had taken up her watercolors again, and that said something positive about Rory Jameson's affect on her. She had not painted in years.

Smoothing her hands down her dove gray skirt, she turned her face from side to side. Another movement in the mirror startled her. Sheriff Derwood stood in the doorway. She whirled and faced him. "What are you doing here?"

"I knocked, lass."

He'd removed his floppy hat and his big hands clutched the brim. He wore a green woolen shirt, the sleeves rolled up his massive forearms. His gaze landed on the jacket, then settled on her. "This is the one place I had not thought to search. Are the boys with you?"

Heart racing, Winter gave no reply.

"I went to your cottage this morning and found your dress bloodstained in the barn behind your cottage," he said. "Is the blood Huntington's?"

She had worn the gown the night she had gone to the Stag & Huntsman looking for Mam. The night Rory had been shot. A crease appeared between his brows. "Were you ever in Westchester?"

"No."

"Good lord, lass, I've practically raised that brother of yours. Do you think I would have harmed those boys?"

She squeezed past him through the doorway and walked into the kitchen. "I don't know what to believe. You were with Stronghold, ready to lynch a man."

"I'm the sheriff. Where would you think I'd be but with that mob until they cooled their heels and dispersed?"

"Stronghold was one of the men who attempted to kill the Granbury heir. My brother and Robert were witness to that crime. Don't you think I've been scared to death that someone I know and love might be responsible? Yes, I considered you might be involved."

"Those who did this did not act on my orders. I swear it. What purpose would I have had to try and kill the man?"

"Then why is Whitey's uncle still at large? I know Lord Huntington visited the Stag & Huntsman and told you what happened that night. Why haven't you arrested Stronghold?"

"He's no longer in Granbury." Derwood's fists tightened on the hat brim. "Even if he was, I could not allow Stronghold in front of a magistrate. What do you think the baron would pay just to get back his wife's prized diamond and ruby necklace a certain masked highwayman robbed her of some years ago?"

"That necklace belonged to my grandmother," Winter said softly. "It was mine to take back. The income from those baubles kept a dozen families from going to the poorhouse after they were burned off their land. It built our parish school, from which the entire village profited." Tears filled her eyes. "Do not dare to lecture me on my moral behavior."

"And you can scream injustice all the way to Tyburn, lass. It is one thing to take back what once belonged to one of us or from those swells that deserve the loss of a quid or two. But attempted murder is different. The fact that Huntington did not die will make no difference in the passing of judgment over any of us. Can you tell me you would put our lives in Stronghold's hands? To save his bloomin' neck, he would give us all up to a magistrate. The folks in this village have families to protect."

"But what if Lord Huntington could become an ally to us? We might—"

"Did you know Huntington left Granbury Court yesterday?"

Winter's hands tightened on the back of the chair. "He left?"

"The man you are so adamantly defending from us not only discharged Granbury's physician of twenty years, but had him forcibly removed from the premises. Then he put Father Flannigan in charge. Some are accusing Huntington of hastening his grandfather's demise and Flannigan is aiding him."

"More likely they are both trying to save Lord Granbury. How could anyone believe otherwise?"

"How could anyone believe you were with Huntington at Granbury Court three days ago when you were supposed to be in Westchester? Did you think I wouldn't learn—?"

The back door swung open and Mrs. Kincaid appeared in the doorway. A blue kerchief wrapped her hair and knotted at her nape. Her eyes widened as she looked from Sheriff Derwood to Winter. A high blush colored her cheeks. Carrying a basket filled with cut flowers, she stepped inside and shut the door. "I didn't know we had guests."

"Angie," Sheriff Derwood stiffly acknowledged.

Her eyes on Winter, she said, "Is everything well?"

"Well?" Sheriff Derwood's deep voice matched his massive size. "You lied to me when I saw you at the parish last week. You knew I was searching the local farms for Huntington and looking for those two boys. You said nothing."

"You asked no question that required me to lie."

"Your very silence misspoke the truth, Angie. I did not search this farm because I trusted you."

Mrs. Kincaid set the basketful of cut flowers on the trestle table with a firm thump. "Do not raise your voice with me, Johnnie Derwood."

Winter looked from Angelique Kincaid to the sheriff. "Please." She put a stop to their argument. "Anything she said or did was at the behest of Father Flannigan to protect a man's life. If she misled you, she did it for us."

"Flannigan isn't one of us. But you and Angie are. Some think you have already betrayed us, Winter. What were you doing at Granbury Court?"

Her hands began to tremble. For she *had* already betrayed them by repeating everything Old Ben had told her to Rory.

"The girl's reasons for going to Granbury Court are her own business, Johnnie," Mrs. Kincaid quietly said. "Can you not trust her judgment?"

"Trust?" He spoke to Winter. "There is not a one of us who hasn't followed you when you've asked. But Huntington has made it clear he is after each of us. We're damned if we give him Stronghold and damned if we don't. Tell me where you stand, Winter?"

Shaking her head, she could only look away. *Did there have to be a choice?* "I would not betray any of you."

"You may leave us now, Johnnie," Mrs. Kincaid invited.

"Don't fret, Angie. I'm leaving." His eyes gentled on Winter. "There is no straddling the line with a man like Huntington. You're with us or you're on your own, lass."

Rory held his watch to the lamp to read the time. The sun had set two hours ago. He had been waiting in Lord Ware's private audience chamber for an hour. Sliding the fob back into his vest pocket, he returned his attention to the window overlooking the Thames. London in summer was rarely pleasant. But since the embankment project had been completed some years ago, this part of the city no longer smelled like a sludge pit on the hottest days.

Tonight the wind pushed ahead of a storm and brought with it the smell of rain, and he found himself looking across the ambling lights toward the hills of Granbury. He could see nothing from this distance but felt their pull nonetheless, drawn to them in a way he could not explain.

The door behind him suddenly opened and the former Lord Secretary of Foreign Affairs entered.

"My apologies for being late." Lord Ware shut the door and walked to the sideboard. "I was in another meeting. Will you have a whiskey?"

"No, my lord." Rory fought the urge to snap to attention. Ware was not so much a big man as he was a commanding presence in any room he entered, though his hair had silvered these past years and he walked a little slower. "This is not a social call."

Lord Ware peered over his spectacles. "I didn't expect to see you back so soon. Did you enjoy your sabbatical in Scotland with your sister?"

"My grandfather found me," he replied, succinct and to the point. "The only way he could have found me was through this office."

Ware hesitated as if weighing his next words carefully. "You have spoken to him? Given your estrangement, I didn't think you would."

"Perhaps I should reframe the question." He could not respond without anger in his voice. "How long have you been giving him information about me?"

"Your grandfather was high enough in this government to find out anything he wanted about you. Yes, we spoke. I thought it better that he receive his information from me than from someone else."

"Why?" Rory shook his head. "My life. My ability to do

my job effectively depends on the very secrecy this organization affords me."

"You misconstrue my hesitation on this matter." Ware leaned against the sideboard and considered the glass in his hands. "Until his retirement last year, Granbury used to be one of the League Council members who signed your orders. He had been following your life long before you joined this organization."

At a loss for words, Rory felt as if he'd just been gutpunched. How could he not know? "And you didn't think I should be informed of this?"

"It is not your right to know who sits on the council. But neither was it mine to speak about your personal life without your knowledge." Ware's voice faded. "Do you want to tell me what this is about?"

Rory dropped into one of the ornately cushioned chairs reserved for visiting dignitaries. He didn't think anything else in this world could shock him. He allowed the new information about his grandfather to seep into him.

He leaned against his hand and his fingers brushed his scalp. His hair covered what was still an injury just above his ear, so the wound was not obvious to the casual observer—only to him: the tenderness remained though the stitches were removed. A tenderness that served to remind him that someone in Granbury had tried to murder him.

"Someone tried to kill me on my way to Granbury Court," he said. "I have reason to believe it was not a random attack. I suspect someone traced my whereabouts through my grandfather's correspondence with my sister and found me."

Rory told Lord Ware about the details of the attack, including Winter's and the boys' involvement insofar as they were the ones who had found him. His decision to include their names was merely pragmatic, as Lord Ware was smart enough to conclude there was a missing week for which Rory needed to account.

"It is easy enough to monitor incoming and outgoing posts," Lord Ware said. "Do you suspect your cousin?"

"Maybe." Rory pondered the idea of Trevor's guilt and Winter's belief in his innocence, and recognized he did not want to find Trevor culpable of attempted murder. "He doesn't seem savvy enough to manage the kind of costly enterprise it would have taken to hire a hit on me. Granbury has him on a short financial leash." He sat forward and entwined his fingers in a contemplative manner. "I spent all day with Granbury's man of affairs going through my grandfather's accounts and books to see the expenditures that have gone out these past few months. I have people going over the rest of the books."

Rory brushed his thumb over the silver cuff on his shirtsleeve as he considered his next words and sat back, "Nothing I've learned today points to Trevor, and yet, something in my gut tells me he is involved in some way."

"Are you *bloody* positive the attack on you wasn't anything more than a case of highway robbery?" Ware set the glass on the sideboard. "Miss Ashburn was conveniently near to aid you when you were shot."

"She is not responsible for what happened. In fact, circumstances have proven her more the victim than am I." The thought threatened to undo him. "Are you acquainted with Granbury Court's neighbor? One Rufus Richland, Baron Richly. Winter Ashburn is his niece by marriage."

"Ah, Baron Richly," Lord Ware said unpleasantly, clearly knowledgeable. "A powerful MP in just a few years. Some claim he could be in line for prime minister one day if he can garner the right alliances and support."

"Richly planned to announce a betrothal between his daughter and my cousin next month."

"I see." Ware studied the bottom of his glass. "Your arrival would tie an unexpected knot in his plans—"

"Except he does not have to resort to murder to force an alliance with Granbury." Rory leaned back and steepled his fingers on his chest. "My grandfather has borrowed a substantial amount of money from Richly using Granbury land as collateral through the baron's bank."

"Perhaps sending for you was your grandfather's final act of desperation to save Granbury."

"Then my grandfather erred in his estimation of my authority. I wouldn't even know how to begin."

"And yet here you are asking for help. Careful, Jameson. Someone might get the impression you care."

He did care, but not in the manner Ware thought. He despised tyranny in any form. Especially when it became personal. Attempted murder was as personal as it could get. But something else had happened to him since he'd arrived in Granbury.

Without fully understanding when his sympathies had shifted to his grandfather's side or even that of the villagers, he found himself thinking of Winter.

He found he could not *stop* thinking of her.

He found himself wanting to do battle on her behalf. To raise his sword and level the playing field. Maybe it was his way to redeem his own family honor and restore Granbury Court to some of its former glory.

Or maybe it was just his way to show up the marquess by saving what the old aristocrat had inevitably lost.

*Wasn't that ironic? The devil becoming the saint?*

A transient notion that had nothing to do with the kind of man he was. The men he'd buried over the last decade of his life would laugh at his whimsy.

"I want to know how Richly acquired Everleigh Hall with the ease that he did," Rory said. "How many other *alliances* has the man forged? I believe my grandfather is a victim and crimes have been committed."

"Investigating an upstanding member of Parliament is grave business, Jameson." Ware scratched his cheek. "Not only is this *not* a matter that concerns our national sovereignty, but unless you have something more substantial than your suspicions of his character and Granbury's poor financial decisions, the council will never agree. Not with your cousin the most likely suspect."

"I'm not asking the council. I am asking you to dig deeper." Rory knew at once, he was asking Ware to cross a line. One did not abuse his powerful place in the government to spy on members of Parliament without substantial cause. A cause that usually involved treason in some form or another. Rory could not make that accusation.

But how many times had Ware asked Rory to cross lines, both moral and physical boundaries over which he'd never wanted to cross but had done so because the mission had required it of him?

"I have a man here who will do some digging and find answers," Ware said. "I use him occasionally."

A knock sounded on the door across the room. Lord Ware answered. After a moment, he turned to Rory. "Do you have a place to stay tonight?"

Rory dragged up a leather satchel and overcoat. He was finished here. Yet the weight on his shoulders had not lessened. By coming here today, he knew he had revealed more of himself than he'd intended.

"I left my horse at an inn just outside London," he said. "I've hired a hack to take me back tonight."

Lord Ware stopped him in the doorway. "Huntington."

Visibly on edge, Rory faced the man who had been as much his mentor over the years as his superior. This was the first time Ware had ever called Rory by his title. The first time Ware had ever acknowledged him as an equal.

"You've taken little enough time for yourself in the ten years I've known you. Do yourself a favor and take the time now. Go home."

Rory gave a short laugh. Even now, he had no concept of what "home" meant. "Are you relieving me of my *duty*?"

Ware placed a hand on Rory's shoulder. "Go make peace with your grandfather before it is too late, son. I promise you, in the end little else will matter but family. England will survive without you. Maybe it is time you learn to survive without her."

Rory had clenched his jaw against his first response to remind Ware that the council was more Rory's family than his grandfather ever could be.

Without another word, he turned on his heel. He strode down the stairway and out into the uneasy night, the air perceptively cooler against his face than it had been a few hours ago. Lights from barges and the spanning arc of Westminster Bridge winked against the darkness. He stopped and, flicking a match, bent his head to light a cheroot. Then his anger flared again. It remained with him all the way back to the inn near Burnham where he'd left his horse.

There wasn't a moment in the last fourteen years of his life that Rory could remember when he had not been in service to the Crown in one form or another. Before he'd gone to work for Ware, he'd been a cavalry officer. This was all he knew of home.

Rory never had a traditional family. He didn't remember much about his father. He'd died fighting two drunken aristocrats who thought they had a right to take what they wanted, which had been his mother.

His father had been twenty when he'd married the daughter of a Gypsy and gone with her family to Scotland. Rory had never understood the cruelty shown his mother by others, never understood the intolerance that was often transferred to him and his sister. Rory had been eight when his father was killed. And even that young he never forgot. *Wild ones, all of them Jameson boys.* He'd heard the whispers the day his father was buried, and Rory made sure that he'd live up to that reputation his entire life—was hell-bent on trying to kill himself ever since.

One of the two men who had killed his father died unspectacularly of the measles a few months before Rory's fourteenth birthday. The other man, Rory met a year later when he was fifteen, on a dueling field, and put a bullet through his heart. Rory never knew what it was that had saved him after that. His mother's family had taken him and his sister. They were good folk.

Then he thought of the old man who was his grandfather, who for ten years had followed Rory's life, never saying anything. Never letting Rory know he was near. He thought back to the day he had received Lord Ware's letter inviting him to join a special branch of the Foreign Service. Rory had been a lieutenant in the cavalry that year on the verge of expulsion for dishonorable conduct with the wife of his commanding officer.

But he had done one spectacularly foolish act of heroism six months before Ware's letter arrived that had resulted in saving the lives of twelve of his men.

He never knew who had put the word in Lord Ware's ear. There were other times in Rory's life before that he could not credit—his acceptance into Sandhurst, a life-altering event that had pulled him from the wastrel life he'd been living in the stews of London; his eventual commission.

Rory had no doubt that had he not entered Sandhurst, his life would have taken a far different turn. Had his grandfather seen something in Rory that Rory hadn't even seen in himself? That he still didn't see in himself? Something that Winter had also seen in him?


Rory didn't stay the night at the inn as he'd originally planned. He paid his room tab and left shortly after his arrival, compelled by an urgent need to return to Granbury. He had meant to be gone a few days, but even that small span of time suddenly seemed too long and he rode his horse through the night.

He found the house completely lit when he arrived at Granbury Court just before dawn.

Mrs. Casselberry met him at the door and took his coat, her expression harried. "My lord. I'm so glad you have returned. It's your grandfather . . ."

A sudden burst of fear pressed against him, raw and stinging his mind. It spurred Rory up the stairs two at a time to his grandfather's chambers.

Once in the sitting room the scent of flowers overwhelmed him. To him, nothing on earth represented a more tragic dichotomy of life and death than watching a flower in full bloom wither and perish.

Without stopping, he crossed the sitting room into his grandfather's private chamber. Unable to move farther, he remained unobserved in the doorway. His feet had stopped. Trevor sat in the chair next to Lord Granbury's bed, his head lowered as he stared at his hands. Father Flannigan stood in the shadows of the tester. And for a dragging moment, the expression on the priest's face deprived Rory of the power of thought. Then Flannigan lifted a lamp from the nightstand.

"He's awake, my lord," he said.

Rory's gaze shot to the frail figure on the bed. His grandfather's eyes were opened and watching him.

"Trevor," Granbury wheezed, "give me a word alone with my grandson."

Trevor's head swiveled around to Rory. But he did not argue as he slowly stood and slipped past Rory into the sitting room. Rory was not at first aware that he was finally alone in the room. But suddenly the door shut behind him and even Father Flannigan was gone.

Silence fell down upon him.

The old man's eyes welled with tears. "Come into the light, son, allow me to see you."

Rory dropped into the chair Trevor had vacated. A breeze entered through the opened window across the room. Until his arrival in Granbury, he had been perfectly content with never knowing this man. He had been content with many things, most especially his own lot in life. Everything had suddenly changed, and he didn't quite understand why.

"You've finally come home, son."

Had he? Finally, come home?

What did a man say to another to whom he had never spoken? Yet a man who had been with him most of his life.

"Why didn't you tell me?" Rory found himself asking,

buried beneath feelings he did not comprehend. "Why didn't you tell me who you were?"

"You've been to see Ware." Granbury sank into the pillow and coughed. "I have watched you and your sister always, Rory. You were not ready to know."

His grandfather's assertion was correct. But Rory's entire world had just shifted on its axis and he didn't quite know how he felt about it. "You are a bastard," he said quietly but with no real force or venom, "sir."

Rory looked down to see that his grandfather held out a thickly veined hand to him. Despite a surge of unfamiliar emotions or perhaps because of it, Rory wrapped that hand in both of his.

Lord Granbury's fingers closed around his—and suddenly . . . it was as if thirty-two empty years between them had vanished.

# Chapter 12

"**M**y lord." Smothers voice pulled Rory's head out of the ledger. "Lord Granbury has a visitor."

Rory sat in the green writing room across from his grandfather's private chambers. Papers were spread over the desk, cost sheets covered in red ink.

Two weeks had passed since Lord Granbury's recovery, much to the dismay of the legion of solicitors who had congregated downstairs, and had only just returned to London. But no one had been more surprised than Rory. His grandfather lived a miracle just by continuing to breathe.

But the real miracle was that Rory cared.

He cared enough to ride over the estate every morning before breakfast, cared enough to pull out every billing and accounting statement detailing Granbury Court's finances. He cared enough to stay.

Smothers presented Rory a card and whispered in a low tone, "The Honorable Rufus Richland, Baron Richly, is here to see Lord Granbury."

Rory rose. He'd been waiting for the baron's return. The man couldn't have been back for more than a day. "Where is he?"

"In the library. He has requested Mrs. Casselberry bring tea and scones."

"Has he?" Rory flicked his forefinger over the edge of the card. He looked up to see the housekeeper standing behind Smothers. "Belay the order," he said walking past her. "The baron won't be remaining long."

Rory entered the library a few moments later unannounced. His eyes landed on two men engaged in casual conversation with a third man sitting in the high-back maroon chair in front of the mahogany desk. At Rory's entry the two stood.

The third came to his feet slowly. "I requested an audience with Lord Granbury."

Richly was a man of medium height and age, in his late thirties, his hair neither blond nor brown, a man of complete physical mediocrity, yet there was something about him that put Rory on edge and brought to mind a carnivore. He didn't know the baron, but he'd known men like him through the years. He'd worked for some . . . and buried even more.

Bile rose at the thought of Winter in this bastard's hands.

"My grandfather is not accepting visitors."

"Lord Huntington, I presume?"

"Baron Richly."

Richly surveyed him with interest. "You must forgive me that I have not made my acquaintance to you sooner. My daughter and I have been some time in London. I am relieved I've not arrived here to give you condolences instead." The baron started to sit and hesitated.

Rory remained standing, knowing even Richly would not dare sit until Rory had taken his own chair behind the desk. It was one thing to use subtle intimidation tactics on his grandfather but another to outright insult a man of greater social standing in his own house.

Rory walked around the desk but did not sit. "Why are you here?"

"We share mutual interests, my lord. I am here to see to those interests. Perhaps you are not familiar yet with certain business arrangements our families have between us."

Rory settled himself into the chair. "Which contract? The one denoting your daughter's betrothal to my cousin or the lease and mortgage you own on twenty thousand acres of my grandfather's land?"

"Oh, but I am Granbury's most loyal tenant," Richly said effusively. "Whether my bank holds the mortgage makes no difference in who leases the land. Each contract profits us both financially. The terms are legal, my lord, and the contracts themselves cost me substantial funds, of which your grandfather willingly took all. I am here today to reassure myself that all my interests are protected.

"If you will allow me." A snap of his fingers brought the man standing to his left forward. Rory was presented with a copy of the various contracts he had read earlier in his grandfather's private papers.

"The betrothal contract signed by Granbury is for a wedding that will take place between my daughter and the Granbury heir. As it turns out, you, and not Trevor Jameson, are that heir. And the Summer's Eve ball is but four weeks away. Unless you are also taking it upon yourself to cancel the affair."

Rory stretched out his legs. He had not put a single thought into the ball, since his grandfather's recovery had been keeping his mind occupied with other matters. But his grandfather had not been so remiss, and Rory knew from Father Flannigan that the old marquess had never been as fervent about a thing as he was about that ball. Lord Granbury intended to introduce his grandson to Society.

"I would not blame you if you did cancel the event," Richly replied, taking his own seat. "The devil knows the marquess cannot afford such an extravagant spectacle."

"Your concern is riveting, Richly."

"This estate is in debt," he said, his tone less than friendly. With a nod to the second man on Richly's right, a box filled with yet more documents appeared. The man laid the box on Rory's desk. "I know exactly how much as my bank owns those past-due debts."

He wasn't about to engage Richly in a point-counterpoint session when his own solicitors had already apprised Rory of the debt owed by this estate to the baron.

"However," Richly continued, "if your grandfather chooses not to honor our betrothal contract, I will accept the land I am currently leasing to grow my crops in return for the mortgage my bank holds on it. The twenty thousand acres is not part of your entailment and as such is subject by law to confiscation if I should pursue the matter in front of the bench."

He opened his arms expansively. "Your other choice, sir, is to stay to the terms of our contract, marry my daughter, and keep your land intact. You have my word that on your wedding day, I will sever the leases between us and relinquish the mortgage on all of it."

Richly's word was less than nothing to Rory, and it took everything in Rory's power not to respond in a way that could prove detrimental to Winter or Lord Granbury. He felt filthy just sharing the same air with the man.

"I'll consider your offer," Rory lied and pulled the cord behind the desk. "Now, if you don't mind," he drawled, "my valet is pouring my bath and I'd prefer it not to become tepid in my absence."

Rory's actions startled Richly, who came slowly to his feet as a footman entered to escort him out.

Richly applied his hat to his head. "We're going to be neighbors for a long time, Huntington. I trust we can come to some mutually beneficial arrangement."

*Trust?* He leaned forward on his elbows. "Your family is from Mousehole. That is a fishing village, is it not?"

"My family once owned the tin mine in that area."

"A place like Everleigh must be quite a change from Cornwall for someone like you."

Something ugly slid over Richly's eyes. He said pleasantly, "Not as much as Granbury Court is a change for the grandson of a Gypsy whore, *my lord.*"

Rory watched the bastard go. When his temper finally eased into something he could manage, he turned in the chair and stared out the window. A moment later Smothers entered. "My lord. Did you ring?"

"Who has the guest list for the Summer's Eve ball?" Rory asked without turning.

"Lord Granbury's secretary, my lord. He is currently with his lordship. Would you like for me—"

"No." Rory rose. "I'll talk to him myself."

The smell of flowers struck Rory as he entered his grandfather's chambers. Flowers filled the withdrawing room, exploding from corner tables and windowsills in a melodrama of color and scent. Yet despite the floral spectacle that clashed unmercifully with Italian Baroque furniture and Chinese wallpaper, his grandfather had insisted on his flowers. Who would have thought Granbury was a sentimental old codger?

Rory picked a bloom on his way into his grandfather's chambers, a hothouse yellow rose, and, for some reason as he held it to his nose, it brought to mind sunlight and blue skies beside a gristmill pond, and the woman who had not left his mind since.

On her hands and knees in the watercress section of Mam's vegetable garden, Winter shoved the small hand spade into the roots of another invasive weed. Many people found the very nature of gardening a balm to the soul. Mrs. Kincaid for instance seemed to thrive among her vegetables and flowers. Winter wilted. A large straw hat tied at her chin shaded her face, but already the sun was hot against her back. Still she labored as if working herself day after day could cure the sleepless nights that plagued her. Yesterday the baron had returned. She knew it was not Lord Granbury's recovery that brought her uncle home.

She swiped the back of her hand against her brow and started to toss the weed aside, but paused as her gaze came to rest on the hound beside her. Its tail thumped eagerly, as if it waited for her to throw the weed.

She looked around for the first time since she had started weeding and her mouth dropped open. The garden looked as if a family of groundhogs had taken root. She had been so caught up in her thoughts she'd paid no attention to anything else. Everywhere she had dug out weeds, the dog had followed. Winter glared at the hound. For some unknown reason the nameless mutt had followed her home last week from Mrs. Kincaid's cottage.

"Why didn't you stay with the boys?" she demanded, but

felt too softhearted toward the homeless creature to put much force behind the reprimand. For in the darkness of night, she had appreciated the hound's companionship, especially now with the baron back. "I have no idea why you thought you'd have more fun with me."

"Maybe he likes your company."

Winter jerked her head toward the voice. Rory stood inside the yard, looking dashing in a black riding jacket with gilt buttons, black trousers, and tall riding boots. "As do I," he said.

The dog loped over to him. Rory squatted on his haunches and, murmuring something in dog-speak, scrubbed the hound behind the ears with both gloved hands. Watching the playful exchange, Winter came to her feet. The dog crouched and barked, then took off after a stick Rory tossed over the fence. But a rabbit must have caught its attention for the dog ran into the woods barking.

She laughed. "I should have thought of doing that earlier." Her gaze settled on her visitor, his forearm resting across his knee as he peered up at her.

Seeing him in her yard was the very last thing she would have ever expected, and the smile faded from her lips. "My lord."

"How have you been, Winter?"

"You know where I live."

He made no effort to rise. "Are you uncomfortable with this visit?" he asked. "I can go."

"No." She hesitated, then removed her gloves. "It is only that . . . well, I don't usually receive male visitors." Except she'd already "received" him in the most intimate way possible. "What I mean—"

"I know what you mean."

She remained ensconced in his presence. He pulled his eyes from hers and stared up at the stone cottage behind her. Sunlight glinted off mullioned windows. With its bright green and yellow shutters, the cottage always looked cheerful amidst the shadows of the woodland glade. This place had been her refuge for so long. As much as Rory made her pulse race, she was not sure how she felt about him entering her sanctuary.

"Why aren't you staying with Mrs. Kincaid?" he asked.

"Because this is where I live. Because I prefer not to be dependent on another's charity. My independence is the last thing I truly own."

"This cottage is on Everleigh land. How independent can you be with Richly two miles away?"

"My father lies buried near here. Unlike you, my lord, this is the only place Perry and I have ever known. Where would we go? In five years, the baron has never stepped foot near this cottage."

He rose and her breath left her chest. "Where are the boys and your mother?" he asked.

Winter walked to the water pump and worked the lever until cooling water poured over her hands. "Mam lives with an old childhood friend." She kept her voice casual and did not tell him that Father Flannigan thought the arrangement best. "The cottage is not far from here. The boys are staying with Mrs. Kincaid."

He came nearer. Her chin snapped up as his tall lean body cast a shadow across her. "After all, you told them that until I consort with a better class of people, they should remain with Mrs. Kincaid."

"You do consort with the wrong—"

"And that I couldn't look out properly for myself. And

that Perry wears the pants in the family. Even if he is only eleven years old."

Rory's eyes softened with amusement. "If I'm not mistaken, he still wears the pants." His bold gaze dropped to her ankles visible just above her pattens. "Unless you are wearing something beneath that skirt, other than red stockings, garters, and drawers."

He tipped her chin and the warmth of the sunlight touched her face. Or perhaps it was the heat from his intense gaze. She edged aside his arm and said in the lightest of tones. "I have never known a person to touch as much as you do, my lord."

"And I have never known a woman who needs to be touched as much as you do."

Even as her heart drummed a tattoo against her ribs, she allowed herself to be backed into the stone wall behind her, awash with fragrant vines of ivy. He caged her between his arms. If his intent wasn't clear in his eyes, all she needed to do was look lower and find it pressed against his trousers. He smelled of cloves and sunlight and feral heat. And she longed for him to kiss her.

"Are you going to invite me in for tea?" he asked

"You wish to go inside?"

He raised his brows. "You can't very well make a pot out here."

Lowering one arm, he waited for her to move. She slipped past him, her old wooden pattens clicking on the stepping stones. She left the cottage door ajar behind her and heard him enter as she removed her gardening apron and hat and hung both on a peg. She resisted the urge to check her reflection in the looking glass and walked past the sideboard and plate racks, into the kitchen.

This kitchen was usually the domain of their only servant, but currently she was helping Mrs. Smythe with Mam. The sink was made of brown glazed stoneware and sat beneath a window overlooking the yard. She filled the teakettle with water from the pump and lit the stove. She could hear the clip of his boots on the floor tiles as he took a turn around the small room. She found him a few minutes later in the family parlor looking at the watercolors on the wall. She stood in the doorway watching as his eyes touched everything that belonged to her, bits and pieces of her life, an act as intimate to her as the one they had already shared.

Only she didn't want him touching her possessions, imprinting himself in this house. "Has anyone ever told you it isn't polite to wander about a person's home?"

Without replying, he squatted and picked up the drawing tablet beside the old worn brocade chair. He flipped opened the book. The top page displayed a landscape of the medieval gristmill where they'd had their tryst. So did the second page. The third drawing was of him. But before he could turn the page and see himself as she saw him, she stepped forward and removed the tablet from his hands. "Are you always this meddlesome, my lord?"

He rose to his feet and, like a sleek black cat on the prowl, returned his attention to the watercolors on the wall. "Did you paint these?"

She peered at the colorful landscapes drawn from various stoops and hills overlooking Everleigh. "Yes, when I was younger. Mam had insisted they be displayed."

A grin creased his mouth. "And the tablet?"

"Nothing inside is worthy." She sidestepped him, but he was quicker and snatched the tablet from her arms. The small scuffle knocked a curio table to the side. "Give it back, my lord."

But he raised the tablet out of her reach and flipped the pages. His grin stated he was being willfully obtuse about his actions. At the drawing of him, he stopped.

Her eyes rose to his half-naked image staring down at her. She'd drawn his hair slightly longer than in reality. The tanned sinews of his throat were exposed above the vee of a shirt that opened to his waist. She had sketched him wild and shameless, the way her mind had captured him as she'd sat alone in this room at night with her charcoal and tablet. Now she wished the ground would swallow her.

"You've seen it. Give it back."

She waited for him to say something and be done with it.

"You think about me a lot, do you?"

*Always.*

He peered at her over his shoulder, held her gaze then surprisingly, before she could respond, he handed the tablet to her. "I hope you keep that private."

The teakettle began to whistle and she hurried out of the room to remove the pot from the fire. She pulled out her best teapot from a Wedgwood setting that belonged to Mam and set tea in a strainer. She turned around to speak to him and found him standing inside the doorway.

Struggling for something to displace her restlessness, she strived for dialogue. "I understand Old Ben is now working for Granbury Court."

Humor reasserted itself in the features of his face. "It seemed to be the wisest course of action. At least there I can keep an eye on him."

They were gravitating toward familiar ground again, she thought as he reminded her of her many foibles and that cur-

rent circumstances had not hindered his goal to find his attackers and his much-loved Apollo. But keeping Old Ben
under foot also gave the hostler a more secure place to live.
For that she was grateful and told him so.

"Your approval warms my heart, Miss Ashburn."

She eyed him shrewdly. For Lord Huntington was not as
heartless as he wanted people to think. All she had to do
was recall how he'd done everything in his power to keep his
grandfather alive to know that. "And yours mine, my lord."
She dipped into a lofty curtsey to find his eyes fraught with
more than amusement when she rose. Heat stirred in their
liquid depths.

He reached into his shirt and withdrew a gold-embossed
invitation. "I was not sure where to send this," he said. "You
have no idea how I had to pry this out of the hands of my
grandfather's secretary."

Her hands began to tremble and she tucked them in her
skirts. The Summer's Eve ball had been the talk of Granbury for weeks.

Initially organized to celebrate the harvest in September, the ball had become a Granbury Court tradition since
the third Marquess of Granbury had chosen his bride from
among the attendees two centuries ago. Three days of soirées and games held for the shire at Granbury Court marked
the celebration. But only those who received their gold-
embossed invitation attended the ball itself. Winter had
never received an invitation.

"It will most likely be an abominable crush." He joked
but there was a hint of seriousness behind his eyes. When
she didn't step forward to take the invitation, he set it on the
table. "Do you have a ball gown?"

Ball gown indeed. "Of course." She tried to keep her voice level. "All Granbury minions have ball gowns."

She had not meant for the words to come out as sharp as they had. He took a step nearer and gently chucked her chin with his knuckle. "You're industrious, love. You can always steal one."

She followed him out into the yard to where his horse was tied to a post. "For your information, I don't steal anymore," she called to him.

Stepping into the stirrup, he looked over at her. The roan pranced sideways. "Pity," he said with a grin.

He nudged his horse into motion and cleared the ditch at the edge of the yard in a graceful arc as he continued down the road. Pity, indeed, as she thought of the invitation inside.

She'd chosen the wrong time to give up thieving for a life of honest poverty.

Winter meandered down an earthen path hardened by the footsteps of many feet. Pushing the bonnet brim a little higher on her forehead, she peered at the landscape of busy activity stretching for as far as the eye could see. A dandy in green-striped trousers and a yellow coat sauntered past her with his fashionable ladybird draped on his arm.

The riverside town of Henley in late July was always crowded as Londoners fled the heat and stench in the city to enjoy an occasional illicit tryst and swill country ale. Mrs. Kincaid kept a booth here on Wednesdays and Fridays where she sold her paintings. Today, Winter had grabbed her watercolors and charcoals and come to sit in the booth with her, but had taken a break as she set out with her white basket to secure supper. To that end, she had found no culinary dish beyond her discernment, and she'd purchased roasted turkey legs, strawberry tarts, and pulled taffy.

Winter reached Mrs. Kincaid's booth set within an exotic Moorish tent, and looking like something out of a Marrakech marketplace. Patrons gave her coins to sketch their portraitures against the painted backdrop inside. Winter was considering asking Mrs. Kincaid if she might join her in the enterprise as a way to earn extra income to subsidize her teaching wages. Winter was not above selling her skills in trade if it brought in a legitimate income.

She had barely stepped into the tent when Perry and Robert raided the basket, then swept past her with a brief good-bye.

"Boys, wait . . ." She hurried outside, but lost sight of them in the parade of tumblers and rope dancers wending through the busy aisles.

"They need to run, *chère*." Mrs. Kincaid came up behind her. She wiped paint from her hands on a white apron. "I have given them instructions to return after the fireworks."

Mrs. Kincaid was right, but it did not allay Winter's apprehension.

"For you as well." She plunked a weighted purse in Winter's hand. "Purchase something. Explore the grounds. Enjoy yourself."

"I cannot take your money, Mrs. Kincaid."

She pressed Winter's fingers over the leather purse. "Do not argue. You sold three of my paintings today. Now go. Be frivolous."

Still holding the purse, Winter suddenly found herself standing alone in the arched canvas doorway. Hesitantly, she turned and looked across the fairground. The last thing she wanted to do was be frivolous. But all around her, colorful striped canvas tents with fringed awnings shaded tables of wares from crockery and spices to fripperies. In the fading late-afternoon light, the rushlights dotting the riverbank blinked like fireflies. All of it invited her to explore. But with an audible sigh, she started to turn back into the tent when something caught her attention.

And that was when she saw Rory just beyond the painted beer tent astride a horse. He was bent over the saddle talking to someone. She had not seen him since the morning he had brought her the invitation.

From behind her, the setting sun gilded him in gold and for one suspended moment, the music and the drunken laughter and all the noises around her faded as she focused only on him.

The future Lord Granbury, or the devil lord as the townsfolk were apt to describe him these days. Even wearing simple garments, he exuded the kind of authority that made one hesitate and take notice.

As if the entire village of Granbury could take more notice than they already had these past weeks. He'd wasted no time since Lord Granbury's recovery, making it clear to all that he still hunted the men who had attacked him and would not stop until they had been brought to justice. He had accomplished in a few short weeks what the baron in all his tight-fisted malice had not done in five years. There hadn't been so much as a pocket picked for almost the entire first half of July.

Winter had thought to warn Rory that he needed the shire on his side. But she wasn't about to involve herself more than she already had—not this time—not after the last time she'd gone to Granbury Court. And since his unexpected visit to her cottage, she had chosen to stay as far away from him as she could and mind her own business.

Not that her newfound conformity prevented her from listening to gossip at the rectory while tending to the elderly women who took part in the Monday quilting circle with Mam, or at Mrs. Peabody's reading group, or at Sunday-morning breakfast served in the parish hall.

He would inherit a debt-ridden estate, crumbling at its foundation. No one expected Granbury Court to be restored to its former glory without substantial help. And much ado had been made about the new lord's questionable character after he'd only last week discharged his grandfather's solicitors for utter incompetence.

In addition, any man who'd spent time on a prison barge was no gentleman, as Mrs. Peabody, clearly having read the gossip column in the *Times* three days ago, had informed the reading group in a knowing whisper. Prison was the only explanation for his absence all these years. Last week he'd been in London hobnobbing with the rich and was rumored to have been seen with a beautiful countess on his arm. Winter had listened to all of it in utter silence.

Now as she watched Rory's progress toward the river, all vows forgotten, she wondered what had brought the infamous Lord Huntington to the Henley fair.

She tucked the purse Mrs. Kincaid had given her inside her pocket and emptied the basket of food. "I'll be back in a few hours," she called over her shoulder to Mrs. Kincaid, and ventured into the crowd.

# Chapter 13

Winter kept herself to higher ground, pausing every once in a while to purchase something—a ribbon for Mam's hair, a platoon of toy soldiers for Perry and Robert, all the while keeping an eye on Rory. He stopped to talk to someone at the paddock, looking over the horses people had brought from all over England to sell and buy in the auction at the end of the week. He was looking for his stallion, always looking for his horse.

She would not wish to be connected to the men who had assaulted him and stolen his beloved Apollo.

She waited until he left the livestock area before stepping out into the open. Chinese lanterns lit the path he followed. He walked as if he had a destination in mind, and she could not keep up with him. A sign stuck in the dirt told her that for a guinea, she could have her fortune read, so she followed the crowd down the path. A fire burned ahead and she could hear drums and violins. At last, she glimpsed him across an encampment of Gypsy wagons.

She stopped in front of a mountebank's wagon and idled over the nostrums and other health remedies laid out on the tailgate, at the same time furtively peering around the wagon. Rory was talking to three rough-looking men, drinking a pint, and he looked anything but civilized standing beside them in conversation. As Winter watched, he tilted his head back and laughed.

The world froze. For a moment, she was back in the glade again, his touch a hot burn against her body.

Her breath stuck in her throat, as if it were a dry piece of toast that wouldn't go down. Or a noose around her neck.

Up until that moment, she had considered herself free of any deep feelings for him. No matter the physical intimacies she'd shared with him, she was not, after all, some naïve schoolgirl who suffered crushes. Yet, her brain evidently had failed to inform her heart of her resolve.

Just then, he turned his head. Winter quickly stepped behind the mountebank's wagon and collided with a woman huffing up the hill in her path. Mrs. Derwood, her arms laden with packages wrapped in brown paper, juggled and failed to hold on to her bundles.

"Winter!" she gasped breathlessly.

She dropped to her knees and began gathering up the packages. "I'm sorry, Mrs. Derwood. I didn't see you."

"Of course you didn't or you would not have run into me. Where are you off to in such a rush?"

"Nowhere." From her position on the ground, Winter peered beneath the wagon. Rory no longer stood by the wagon, nor could she spy him anywhere. Balancing her basket on one forearm and holding the packages against her chest, Winter stood. "Are you here alone?"

"Heavens, no. My son brought me." Mrs. Derwood fanned a hand in front of her heated face. "Though I have no idea where he has got himself off to. I can't carry these packages to the buggy. I'm not as young as I used to be."

Winter offered to help her. "I don't mind," she said.

"Please, that would be lovely." The older woman handed the rest of the bundles over to Winter. "Where have you been keeping yourself these days, child?" Together, they set off toward the mews. "You haven't brought the boys into town in weeks. Are they here tonight?"

All Winter could move was her chin and she aimed it toward the red striped Moorish tent on the distant hill. "We've been helping Mrs. Kincaid in her booth. She comes to Henley to sell her paintings."

Mrs. Derwood clucked her tongue. "I'm surprised at you, cavorting with . . ." she lowered her voice. "Her ilk. I don't mean to sound cruel and it isn't like me to speak ill of others, but what would your mam say?"

"Please, Mrs. Derwood." Winter knew that she herself was responsible for much of the gossip years ago concerning the Frenchwoman. She wished she had the power to take it back. "Mam has been ill for years. She is not capable of saying anything."

When they reached the buggy sometime later, Winter loaded the packages in the boot. She faced Mrs. Derwood as the older woman climbed onto the buggy seat. "Mrs. Kincaid is adopting Robert."

"Oh my. I see."

Winter tucked a woolen shawl around Mrs. Derwood's legs, as the evening air had grown cold. They spoke trivialities after that, but Winter's heart wasn't in the conversation. She left the mews to return to the fairground along a less traveled footpath through the trees that would return her to the fairground unseen. The approaching evening made the pathway dim, but Winter picked her way along. Something made her look up and she stopped abruptly.

Rory stood at the end of the path. His shoulder leaned

against a post, his arms folded over his chest. Light from a nearby torch darkened the shadows on his face, but even from this distance, she could feel his eyes on her.

Holding her basket closer against her stomach, she approached him. "My lord."

"Good evening, Miss Winter."

The scent of horse manure, straw, and other animal odors wafted over them from the makeshift stalls behind her. "You are out for a stroll of fresh air?" she inquired pleasantly, wondering how he always seemed to find her.

"It looks as if I am forever plagued with having to chase you down dark paths. With whom are you here, love?"

"I might ask the same of you, sir."

A sudden flash of white appeared. "If you want to spy on me, I can arrange a better place than at a fairground to accomplish your goal. One I will see that you enjoy more."

She scoffed at his arrogance. "There is a name for that which you suffer."

He laid a thumb on her collarbone, tipping her chin with the gloved knuckles of his hand. "Conceit?"

Despite herself she laughed. Clearly to make her laugh had been his goal. She stepped back just enough that he could no longer touch her, but not so far it would signal a retreat. "I should not laugh. For you do suffer conceit."

The corner of his mouth creased. "Some sins are too irresistible, love."

Truly he was wicked, and she was more so for all that she had allowed him to do to her. For all that she was thinking of it now and remembering more than his hands on her body.

She changed the direction of her thoughts. "Those men you were with." They were Gypsies and she was curious. "Are they your friends?"

"They are helping me search for my horse. Very clandestine business. Auctions bring in horseflesh from all over England."

"If your appointment was meant to be secret, I doubt you would have conspired to meet in such a public place," she said offhandedly.

"If you believe that, love, you know little about subterfuge."

Her smile fell. He was wrong of course. "I know a great deal about subterfuge. Possibly more than you do."

His eyes gentled. "Why do you think that?"

Whatever reasons she'd had for her deceptions had been born out of desperation. But she had never considered his past might have shaped him in the same way. She had been so quick in her suspicions of him, when she had been the one lying and stealing. For her entire life, she'd been judgmental, thinking she had a right to her feelings, even at the expense of others.

"I didn't mean to follow you," she said.

"Then you accidentally followed me?"

The breeze snatched a lock of her hair, and she tucked it behind her ear. "I saw you and I wanted to know why you were in Henley."

"This is hardly a private affair, and not so far from Granbury. I've noted many familiar faces here tonight. Including your sheriff. It must be novel for him to be out on a full moon and not pillaging the countryside."

Ignoring his sarcasm, she neither refuted nor agreed with his assessment of Sheriff Derwood, but found her gaze straying to the Moorish tent in the distance. "I think he has a *tendre* for Mrs. Kincaid."

"Not tonight. He's been staring into a pint of ale for most of the evening over in that beer tent."

"Oh." Her brows rose. "You've been spying on him?"

"Accidentally. Of course."

"Of course."

Winter moved beside him, her shoulder nearly touching his. Let him spy on whomever he wished if it made him feel as if he were doing something rather than waiting around helplessly for fate to dictate the terms of his life.

The river breeze cooled her face like a gentle whisper. She looked across the fairgrounds to the river, the moon above it limning the currents in silver light.

"I believe this is a perfect night, my lord."

A silence fell between them. And she looked up at him.

He lifted a strand of her hair. "I want to see you again, Winter."

She tried to mold her response into some indelible form of nonchalance but her pounding heart ruined the effort. He'd seen her at the cottage. "Why?"

His gaze rose from the curl in his hand to touch her eyes. "Because the next time I see you naked beneath me, it will have nothing to do with debts or deals between us. No games. No challenges. It will be because we enjoy the pleasure of each other's company."

*Oh God.* She stood on shaky legs. "You are to the point, my lord."

"Maybe it's time for a modicum of honesty between us."

"Are you asking for an affair, my lord?"

He pulled his hand back and folded his arms. But for all of his masculine arrogance, his hands did not seem steady. "I'm asking."

Winter didn't know how to respond. Was he offering her a compliment or an insult? Did she care? She knew she ought to show some degree of shock to her female sensibilities, but what would be the point?

"What about your countess?"

"You spend too much time reading gossip, love."

But his tone was not nearly as conciliatory as the amusement in his eyes implied, and she looked away. "I . . . I don't even know you." She'd known him even less weeks ago. But he didn't bring up that skew in her logic.

"Ask me a question. I'll tell you anything you want to know about me."

"One question? That is hardly enough, my lord."

"Ah, but if I tell you my entire life story, I'll become a bore."

"A bore? I doubt it." She narrowed her eyes pensively. "Then we will be honest with one another?"

"I will answer any question. Save one area. Don't ask me about my relationship to my grandfather or my feelings about Granbury Court. I am not prepared to talk about either, as I have not figured out those answers myself."

She remembered the night she'd seen him standing in the hallway at Granbury Court staring up at his father's portrait. But whatever vulnerability she'd glimpsed in his face then did not lend itself to interpretation now. His pain might go bone deep, but he'd never show it to her.

She worried her lower lip, aware to what she was agreeing. "All right." Winter pondered her question.

Of all the questions in the world to ask him, where would she begin? She studied his face as she considered.

Where had he been living before he came to Granbury, had he ever been married? It was not unheard of that a man his age might already be widowed.

Had he traveled, why did he carry a gun, was he planning to remain in Granbury? Had he been in prison?

Why didn't he want her to ask about his relationship to his grandfather?

But would answering that question tell her who he was inside? The kind of man he was. Perhaps. Perhaps not.

Clearing his throat, he dipped two fingers into his fob pocket and withdrew a watch. "Did I fail to mention a five-minute grace period?"

"You seem very adept at taking care of yourself. You are not like any typical aristocrat I've ever met."

He laughed. "Is there a question in that statement someplace?"

Clearly, he knew her statement was a two-part inquiry. How did he learn to take care of himself so well? And if he had not been raised an aristocrat then where had he been living all these years? So in effect, she'd imbedded a slew of questions into her statement, which she surmised he suspected.

"Those rough-looking men you saw me with? I grew up with two of them. Traveling all over England and Scotland following fairs. One learned to defend oneself if one wished to live past the age of ten."

She couldn't quite hide her reaction. He'd told her once his mam was half-Gypsy. "Those men to whom you were speaking. They are your family?"

"Try not to look so tragic, *gadji*. They are my friends."

There was a tautness in his eyes that made a lie out of the indifference in his voice. For one tiny moment before his expression changed, she'd seen vulnerability and what he must have been like as a boy. Proud, defiant, a boy who had grown into a man with the deepest of convictions, who could be an integral part of his grandfather's life.

"I'm not." She stepped against him, against his lingering warmth and cupped his jaw with her palm. "Truly. It's only that I've never known a Gypsy."

"I'd say you more than know me, love," he said quietly.

Behind her, an explosion of Chinese fireworks suddenly lit the sky in a burst of red and gold waterfalls. Winter looked out across the fairground, caught by the excitement of the night, a little afraid of her feelings. She was cognizant of the heavy thudding of her heart. Then he was turning her slowly in his arms. As if in slow motion, he lowered his head and covered her mouth with his own. She felt the taut muscles of his chest beneath the slide of her palms. Her hands found purchase against his shoulder.

Then he was framing her face with his palms and they were both deepening the kiss. Her skirts enfolded his legs. Her arms slipped around his neck, until she stood on her toes, her breasts crushed against his chest, giving, even as she took. Too soon, his lips retreated. Silence fell between them again, and, as his eyes passed over her mouth in that way of his that made her feel ravished, she thought he might begin their affair here and now.

People were coming up the incline now, their merry laughter carried to her on the breeze. Her face warm, Winter picked up her basket and whirled on her heel, letting gravity carry her down the hill at a pace faster than was safe.

Would she awaken tomorrow and wonder what she'd been thinking to agree to Lord Huntington's proposition? Daylight would surely reveal the flaw of her logic. She could already see the cracks and crevices much clearer.

She also recognized the shiny lure that was Rory Jameson.

\* \* \*

When Rory looked at the clock on the mantel across the room, a half hour had passed since he'd had his morning tea and the sun had gone behind the clouds. He sat behind the desk in the library, leaning his forehead against his fingers woolgathering.

His hand fidgeted with a letter that had arrived from London. It smelled of Parisian perfume. He had not opened it. Instead, he put it in his pocket.

Smothers entered the room before Rory knew he was there and looked up when the man spoke. "My lord, your appointment, a Mr. Gerard, is here."

Rory had been expecting the man's arrival since yesterday. He rose and walked to the sideboard where he poured himself a liberal splash of brandy. Lord Ware had Gerard do some of the investigation Rory had wanted. The man entered, and Rory directed him to one of the chairs that fronted the desk.

Gerard's face was flat, his features coarse. He looked exactly like Rory imagined the grandson of a Bow Street runner should look. They didn't waste time with trivialities. They were both professionals.

Adjusting his bulk in the seat, Gerard set his black leather satchel on the floor and removed his papers. "I apologize this investigation took longer than anticipated," he said. "I'll begin with your cousin's whereabouts . . ." He shuffled through his papers, "on the night of June seventh. I believe that is the day you said you arrived in Granbury."

Nodding, Rory waited for the man to get to the point of this meeting. "Proceed."

"He was recovering from a duel that left a wound on his shoulder. I spoke to the physician who knew what happened firsthand, through the account of the unfortunate young

woman who was involved. It seems there was a misunderstanding. Mr. Jameson did not know she was married."

"Did you meet the woman to whom the physician
spoke?"

"She never gave her name. And I could not discover it.
She left London soon after the incident."

"What else?"

"I have an itinerary of Mr. Jameson's activities these
past weeks. He lets a townhouse on the West End where he
spends most of his time." Gerard shuffled his papers and
started to stand. But Rory was already walking over to him
and took the itinerary. "Mr. Jameson has met with his solicitors. I believe he may be conducting his own investigation
on you, my lord."

Amused, if not a little impressed, Rory peered at Gerard
from over the top of the papers. "Really?"

Maybe dear *coz* didn't know as much about Rory as Rory
thought he did.

"What have you discovered about Richly's acquisition of
Everleigh?"

"It was a result of the simple fact that he paid the death
taxes on the estate after Mr. Ashburn passed. His daughter
swore that Baron Richly embezzled her father's money, but
there was never any proof or records to prove any of her accusations. She was sixteen. No one listened."

Rory stared into his tumbler a moment, not allowing his
thoughts to travel where they naturally wanted to go.

"Afterward, she moved into the dower cottage. The baron
is her brother's guardian. Her mother is also his custodial
ward. Richly has allowed the family to remain together."

"Why?"

But the question was more rhetorical and Rory did not

expect an answer. They spoke awhile longer. But even after Gerard followed Mrs. Casselberry to the kitchens for a bite to eat before returning to London, Rory remained at the desk.

He thought about what he knew about Trevor, about the report Gerard had just given him, about the letter in his pocket and knowing he needed to go to London and deal with certain issues in his life. Already he was feeling confined by responsibilities he did not want.

Yet always Winter burned just at the back of his mind.

As Rory had taken his horse from the groom that morning and swung into the saddle, he knew he was violating his own rule never to allow his personal life to interfere with business. Now as he reined in his horse and stared up at what had once been Winter's home, he found himself pulled nearer into the epicenter of her life, without fully understanding all that drove him there.

Unlike Granbury Court, which suffered the rigors of age and neglect, Everleigh Hall was much like that yellow bloom Rory had plucked from the vase of flowers in his grandfather's chambers. The house was a fairy-tale structure of refaced granite and lead windows caught in the afternoon sunlight, an implicit testimonial to the baron's prosperity, and to the architect that had built the home.

The entire pictorial scene spread before him was so incongruous with reality that Rory found himself momentarily lost in his thoughts as he nudged his horse.

He looked up just in time to find himself on a collision course with a fast-approaching barouche. He yanked the reins and barely missed colliding with the conveyance as it veered to the right and into a manicured hedgerow. A shriek of outrage met his ears, but after deciding the female carriage occupants were unharmed, he started to check on the welfare of the two horses.

A shrill voice stopped him. "How dare you care more for those horses than for someone you are responsible for injuring? *Oaf!* I shall have Papa . . ." Her eyes fell on Rory's face, and her tone diminished in intensity. "Papa will not be happy to think I could have been injured."

The woman was a pretty blonde with coiffed hair and silken attire the height of Parisian fashion. She was Winter's age, perhaps younger. "My apologies," he offered, for good manners required him to do so, "but had your driver been on the correct side of the drive, this mishap would not have occurred."

Eyes the color of violets snapped back at Rory. "This is *my* drive," she replied as if her wishes and desires were the only consideration. "You are the only interloper, Mr . . ."

"*Lord* Huntington. You are the baron's daughter, I assume?"

He saw momentary shock in her widened eyes, but she quickly recovered her mien as one of an injured party. "He will be away until evening. Perhaps if you had taken the courtesy to send a note of your intended visit he could have been here to greet you."

*Lavinia Richland.* Baron Richly's daughter's opinion of Rory Jameson's character was less than incidental. But if he had ever held the slightest doubt that his grandfather had been coerced into signing a betrothal contract for this woman, Miss Richland erased it.

He let his mouth ease into the artificial smile he was very good at assuming when desired. "I believe you are supposed to be my intended bride?"

Her face took on the pale hue of her white gown. But her discomposure lasted only as long as it took to draw in her next breath. "Papa says I will be the next Granbury marchioness."

"Does Papa always get what he wants?"

Rory saw a flicker of doubt pass over her expression. "He does. But he did not tell me I would have to put up with boorish behavior. You would be wise to remember your manners. I have other offers from which I could choose."

Her words and tone eliminated the last dregs of sympathy Rory might have summoned for her plight. "Then I consider myself duly forewarned, madam." He high-stepped the gelding across the walk and around the barouche. "Give my regards to your papa, Miss Richland."


"'Tis not the done thing, Miss Winter," Mrs. Peabody replied. "I can't be takin' those from ye, not when they mean so much to ye."

The Emporium shopkeeper stood in front of the glass countertop where Winter had laid out a miniature wild animal menagerie she'd brought from home. Made of glass with ruby eyes, they were extremely valuable, enough to purchase the silver lamé gown she had seen in the display room. The gown was as beautiful as spun moonlight—the perfect ball gown. Winter didn't care if the gown had been worn before.

Mrs. Peabody had acquired it from a fashionable upscale shop in London as she did with all the gowns in the back room. It was not unheard of that such gowns were returned for resale, especially after a season when costly items were either cast off or returned to recoup revenue spent. With the ball a mere week away, Winter had come to town today desperate to find anything. She'd never dreamed she'd find such a beautiful dress.

"My father is gone, Mrs. Peabody. He'll never know." The bell on the door tinkled as someone else came into the shop and Winter lowered her voice. "Surely there is something I can do, Mrs. Peabody."

The old woman laid a hand across Winter's. "You sat with my son for three days when he suffered the influenza. You will take the gown," she said quietly. "And pay me when you can. It is not every day one of our own receives an invitation to the ball. It is about time, I say."

Her throat tight, Winter began to gather up her glass pieces and to wrap each one. "Thank you, Mrs. Peabody."

The shopkeeper hurried off to the back room. All around Winter, the women shopping in the Emporium chatted over fashion plates, the newest colors from Paris, and if Lord Huntington's eyes were blue or gray.

The ball had been all the talk wherever Winter went these days. In the beginning she had not planned to attend. Now, it was all she thought about. Everyone had been surprised that Lord Granbury had agreed to continue with the festivities in light of his illness.

But Lord Granbury had said only yesterday when she had gone out to Granbury Court with Father Flannigan that tradition must continue. Winter had never seen him so animated, almost childlike in his excitement, even as Father Flannigan trounced him over a game of chess.

Rory had not been present at Granbury Court yesterday. Indeed, Winter had not seen him since the fair over a week ago. He'd abruptly quit Granbury to attend to business in London, and until she'd visited Granbury Court and seen Lord Granbury, she'd been afraid Rory would not be back.

The rustle of a petticoat stirred the air. Winter's eyes widened. Lavinia stood at the end of the cabinet. Her peacock blue silk trimmed in pleated blond lace was as out of place here as a sapphire among a barrel of stones.

She and Lavinia had never been enemies. There had even been a summer before Winter's father died when Lavinia had tagged along everywhere Winter and Trevor went, wanting so much to be friends.

Until the baron had learned of Lavinia's indiscretions as he'd called them. Winter had not known for sure what he'd done to his daughter, but Lavinia no longer ventured anywhere with them. Now, they were merely polite strangers.

"Papa is the only person this side of London who did not receive an invitation to the ball," Lavinia said, her eyes downcast.

Winter cast a quick glance around her to make sure no one was listening. "I don't understand."

"I managed to *mismanage* my first meeting with Lord Huntington last week. But I have *never* acquainted myself with anyone so boorish." Lavinia sniffled. "Papa has attempted to see Lord Granbury but has been prevented from doing so on Lord Huntington's orders. Papa only wants to make things right, Winter. But Lord Huntington is preventing him from doing so. Last night I heard Papa talking to his solicitors." She dabbed a silk handkerchief against each eye. "But how will that get us an invitation?"

"Why was he speaking with his solicitors?"

"Lord Granbury apparently owes Papa a great deal of money. Papa was the only one who would loan Lord Granbury anything years ago at great risk to himself. Now Lord Granbury publicly snubs him. Why would he do such thing? I'll never see Trevor again."

What had Rory done? One did not publicly humiliate someone like Baron Richly. "Have you considered the invitation could be lost in the post?"

Hope fostered Lavinia's response. "Perhaps *you* received it by mistake."

"I doubt my cottage would be mistaken for Everleigh."

Her distraught cousin looked away. "That sounded boorish of me. It is just that I am overset. I cannot get Trevor a message . . ."

"You care about him, don't you?"

"Papa wants me to be the next marchioness, but I would not have agreed to marry Trevor if I did not have feelings, Winter. And Trevor does not keep a mistress tucked away in London. I would not wish to wed Lord Huntington for any title. He can keep his countess. He is a dark horse just as Papa says, and they are the worst lot of them all."

Winter's fingers tightened in the folds of her skirts. "How would you know anything about Lord Huntington's private life?"

"Truly you cannot be so naïve. Everyone knows Huntington keeps a mistress in London. They have been together for two years. Lady Mildred heard the countess tell everyone that very thing at the Wiltshire tea last week." Lavinia's face fell. "Even Lady Mildred received an invitation to the ball. How will I ever be able to face that nosy parker again?"

Winter held her hand to the countertop. "'Tis gossip, Lavinia."

"'Tis far more than gossip. Where do you think he went this week?"

Mrs. Peabody returned, her cheeks flushed. "Come." She took Winter's hand. "See what you think?"

Winter did not want to go to the back room. Not now. She wanted only to return home. But she allowed Mrs. Peabody to take her to the back room anyway where she had arranged the silver gown on a dummy complete with slippers and gloves and beautiful beads for Winter's hair. She had even found a glass sapphire necklace and earrings. Everything was a vision. Mrs. Peabody's thoughtfulness and utter kindness rendered Winter speechless. Not so Lavinia.

Her cousin gasped as if a spider had dropped from the ceiling. "That is the gown I wore two seasons ago at Lord Margrave's ball. Wherever did you *get* that old thing?" Then she burst out laughing as if such a reaction would not hurt Mrs. Peabody who had put together the ensemble with the most heartfelt intentions.

In the stunned silence that followed, Lavinia's glance went across the other gowns lining the wall to Winter. "You aren't considering *wearing* it? Even if that gown were not mine, lamé is so passé this season."

Mrs. Peabody's chest puffed in offense. But her voice faded. Not because she agreed with Lavinia's assertion but because she suddenly realized with whom she was about to engage in an argument.

"The gown is beautiful, Mrs. Peabody." To Lavinia, she was not so kind. "You should not take the gifts you've received so for granted."

And Winter took the gown.

# Chapter 14

Two days after Father Flannigan delivered a message to Granbury Court for Trevor, Lavinia received her precious invitation to the ball. The day of the ball, Winter found herself walking the well-beaten path to Mrs. Kincaid's where she had taken the gown to be altered.

Winter no longer cared if the gown had once belonged to Lavinia or if the style was now passé. The dress was beautiful and it was hers.

Nor did she wake up in the night any longer thinking of Rory with his fingers caressing another woman's hair, his slow kisses on another woman's mouth, and his dark head lying pillowed on another woman's breasts. He had not forced Winter into an act of intimacy or made promises.

She hadn't chosen to attend the ball for him; she wanted to go for herself. She wanted to dance.

Just once in her life, she wanted to waltz and to remember what it used to be like. Even if she never saw Rory again after this night, she could live with the choices she had made.

As she reached the cottage, the boys greeted her on their way to the barn to gather eggs. Laughing over some secret, they told her Mrs. Kincaid was awaiting her in the cellar.

Once inside, Winter removed her cloak and bonnet and

hung both on the peg beside the door. The room smelled of hot, scented roses and she knew Mrs. Kincaid had prepared a bath for her. Winter looked at the old regulator clock on the wall and saw that Father Flannigan would be here in two hours to fetch her in his cart. He would also be attending the ball, but not so much as a guest as to keep an eye on Lord Granbury and make sure the old marquess did not overexert himself.

Winter opened the cellar door and peered downstairs.

"Is that you, *chère*?" Mrs. Kincaid called up to her, appearing at the bottom of the stairs and out of breath. "You are late." She joined Winter on the landing. "Now, off with your attire and take a bath. I will need to repair your hair."

Winter submitted to Angelique Kincaid's pampering with humbleness, some humor, and finally with deep, abiding affection for the French woman. Angelique made her close her eyes as she slipped on the gown and dressed Winter. When she had finally been placed in front of a long looking glass, Angelique told her to open her eyes.

Winter took a breath. And opened her eyes.

The mirror reflected back a beautiful young woman with raven-dark hair piled in curls atop her head and wearing a gown that looked as if it had fallen from the nighttime sky. She laughed. *"Oh my heavens."*

Frothy white organdy overlaying the silver lamé beneath had transformed the gown from something merely beautiful into an ethereal creation of silvery gold glitter that belonged in the heavens among the other stars.

Winter dabbed a finger at the corner of one eye and smiled at Angelique in the glass. "Truly, I do not know what to say. I have never had a gown made of starlight." She had never been so beautiful.

"He will not be able to resist you, *chère*."

"Oh, Angelique," Winter whispered. "What if Lord Huntington has forgotten he gave me the invitation? What am I doing? What am I thinking?"

Angelique placed her palms on Winter's shoulders and turned her. "Are you in love with Lord Huntington?"

Winter raised her eyes and met Angelique's softly beseeching gaze. "I have told myself I am not. I thought he cared for me as well. Maybe it is better that he does not."

"You do not believe you are good enough for him. Do you have so little faith in yourself that you cannot *see* what *he* might see?"

"I am a thief."

"You are a *lady* . . . of strong convictions."

Winter laughed and pressed her fingertip against the corner of one eye. "Truly a character trait that is more my downfall than something to be revered."

"Lord Huntington is not the local vicar's son. If you should wed, the baron would not have an easy time seeking an annulment."

"Wed?" Winter shook her head at the ludicrous notion. "He doesn't wish to wed me. Even if such a thing were possible, it won't happen. The baron is Perry's guardian and he is Mam's legal steward. My uncle holds the power to take them both away from me if I should try to leave here. Not even Lord Huntington is immune from the law. I would lose them, Angelique."

"Why hasn't the baron already taken them?"

"He doesn't care about us. All he cares about is power and maintaining his name, making alliances. If I should *involve* myself publicly with Lord Huntington, I guarantee the baron would find a way to use that to his advantage."

Then suddenly Winter was remembering everything Lavinia had told her. "Truly, I am full of myself. Rory Jameson is naught but a silver-tongued rogue." She laughed in an attempt at indignation. "I am not even sure it is anything other than finding his attackers and his horse that is keeping him in Granbury. He is a singularly focused man."

"He is a man of great passions. He does not do anything halfway, *oui*?" Then Mrs. Kincaid, her father's former mistress and now her dearest friend, brought Winter's hands to her cheeks and kissed them as a mother would do. "Neither do you." Together they walked arm-in-arm into the front room. "Or the rest of the shire."

Angelique opened the door. Winter looked out into the warm faces of three dozen or so townspeople gathered expectantly around the old dilapidated surrey-top wagon that Winter had once seen in Mrs. Kincaid's barn. The wheels had been cleaned and polished, the tears in the seats repaired. Old Ben, hat in hand, stood at the step next to Father Flannigan who looked dapper in his pressed attire. Perry and Robert all scrubbed clean beamed up at her. They had all been waiting for her to appear. The only person not present was Sheriff Derwood.

Tears blurring her eyes, Winter stared at them all.

"It took us awhile to get the surrey cleaned," Angelique said as if she had to possibly apologize. "Perhaps 'tis not as fashionable as a coach and four—"

"Oh, Angelique." She flung her arms around the older woman. Then she greeted Old Ben and many of the others who pressed around her as she went to inspect the surrey. Finally, she turned toward Angelique. "It is the most beautiful carriage I have ever seen."

"Come"—Angelique herded her toward Father Flannigan—"it is time for you to go to your ball."

An hour and a half later, Winter walked into the Great Hall from the west front and water terraces, where the Granbury coat of arms was on vivid display, and where a long receiving line climbed the stairs and followed a corridor down to another set of marble stairs that led into the ballroom. She could hear the strings of a waltz floating over the low din of voices. "Well," Father Flannigan announced when he saw the line, "This is where I leave you, my child."

Abandoning her for the servant's entrance, he left her standing between a prune-faced matron and a gentleman towing his five giggling daughters behind him. Winter would gladly have gone with Father Flannigan and told him so when she caught up to him. He returned her to the receiving line and ordered her to remain and enter the proper way. "The people of this town didn't go to all this trouble to see you enter Granbury Court as a servant, Winter."

The ball was already another hour into the night by the time Winter finally reached the end of the receiving line. From the gilt-edged balcony, overlooking the ballroom, she gazed down upon the shifting rainbow of colors as couples danced across the polished floor, the shimmering silks and satins of beautiful gowns vying with a thousand candles glittering against the glass and blending with the reflection cast by the gaslight chandeliers. Winter had never imagined that such a place as this existed in all of England much less Granbury.

The old marquess himself sat in a wheeled chair at the bottom of a long, curving white marble staircase to receive his guests as they filtered down into the ballroom. Rory stood next him. And Winter's breath stopped as he looked up from where he was politely bent over the hand of a young woman. His eyes found hers as if he had been waiting for her and watching her for some time.

Seeing him for the first time since he had kissed her under the cover of darkness at the fair was like walking into a room that was too hot and too bright.

Incredibly handsome, he wore a black formal swallowtail coat and neatly tied cravat, his gloves the palest white. He stood beside his grandfather, ever polite, greeting each guest with an open easy smile, though something in his expression hinted at his reserve. A beautiful dark-haired woman stood next to him. Winter could only glimpse her profile, but her heart pitched against her chest as she wondered who the woman was. Trevor was not present.

And for a moment, as Winter approached Lord Granbury, the absurdity of her presence here hit her like a wall of stone. For the first time since she had decided to embark upon this journey tonight, she considered fleeing. She didn't belong here. Truly, she'd been insane.

Then the majordomo took her invitation and she was formally announced to the room.

She noticed the sudden hush as people standing around her turned to look upon the ever-reclusive Baron Richly's niece. But she could not know how she looked to them, a vision in glittering white standing in the diamond-bright light of the overhead chandelier.

"Good evening, young lady," Lord Granbury intoned, snapping her attention to the receiving line and, all at once, the world settled around her.

She was not entirely out of her element here. "You are a

vision, Miss Ashburn." Granbury's gray eyes twinkled dev-
ilishly. "Flannigan said you had grown into a beauty. For
once I shall agree with that old Irishman."

Winter didn't remind Lord Granbury that she had only
seen his lordship a week prior when she had come out with
Father Flannigan and the two of them had played chess. "I
will tell him you said so, my lord."

"Pah, then I will never find an ounce of peace. He is here
tonight?"

"Yes, my lord. I imagine he is at the Faro table attempting
to take advantage of your generosity . . . for the poorhouse
fund, of course."

Lord Granbury chuckled. Their twenty seconds at an end,
and with her heart racing, he introduced her to Rory.

Her gaze finally rose. "Miss Winter," he said her name
and a frisson of sensuality caressed her.

"Lord Huntington."

But before she could curtsey in the way she had practiced all week in front of her mirror, he scooped up her
gloved hand with a flourish. His tailored clothes did naught
to refine the wildness he exuded. "You look"—his voice
paused with drama and his lips tilted with his come-hither
smile—"beautiful."

She narrowed her eyes. Rory was causing her to plug up
the line. "You needn't sound so shocked."

Still holding her hand, he leaned toward her. "But you
would allow I have cause to note you clean up rather nicely."
His gaze lowered and caressed her bosom. "Perhaps I will
see more of you later."

"Have you been equally complimentary of all your minions, my lord?" she managed in a voice of suppressed emotion. "Or am I special?"

"Only one minion interests me," he said in an equally low voice that made her shiver, and she forgot the other five hundred people present in the room. "Have you missed me?" he asked.

With a start, she cast a surreptitious glance at the woman standing beside him, unduly interested in their exchange. "My sister," Rory replied with magnanimity. "Mrs. Evelyn Macgruder."

"Oh." Winter smiled and dipped her head. *Oh.*

Mrs. Macgruder smiled in return. "Miss Ashburn."

Her black hair wrapped in a thick coronet around her head and wearing a celestial blue velvet gown, Evelyn Macgruder was beautiful in the Romney fashion with a hint of an exotic tilt to her blue eyes. But for the color of her eyes, there was no mistaking her relationship to Rory.

"My brother has spoken of you."

Winter's eyes touched Rory's. "You did?"

"Such things slip out when one is traveling together for days," Eve said. "He trekked all the way to the lowlands of Scotland just to bring my daughter and me here for the festivities. He is a good baby brother. Bless his kind heart."

Eve patted Rory's arm with sisterly affection and Winter was captured by their obvious kinship. Perhaps because it did something to civilize Rory. Unsure what to say, Winter politely stole one last glance at Rory. His eyes touched hers, and, for a heartbeat, before she turned away, she borrowed from his warmth.

Then he was once again the attentive rakish lord as he bowed over the next lady's gloved hand.

But Winter had not forgotten that departing look as she went in search of Trevor.

Nor did she see Rory look up as she walked into the crush, a slow smile on his face, awareness of her touch lingering on his palm where he had held her hand. Rory closed then flexed his fingers.

She had accepted his invitation, and he hadn't been certain until the moment he'd glimpsed her on the stairs that she would attend. She wore a gown to rival that of the most fashionable present.

But then Rory had never doubted her skills to accomplish any of those things.

He looked up at the long receiving line. "Patience, brother," Eve said from beside him just loud enough for him to hear the reprimand in her voice. "You'll break the girl's heart soon enough without rushing things along."

Rory turned his head and looked at his sister.

"She's so young. Whatever are you thinking?" Eve whispered.

He leaned over and kissed her lightly on the cheek. "I'm not asking for your approval, Eve."

Then the majordomo's words rang out, *"The Honorable Rufus Richland, Baron Richly, and his daughter, Miss Lavinia Richland."*

Rory turned his head and met Richly's cold gaze, just as Lord Granbury claimed the man's attention with a brisk greeting. An icy chill ran down Rory's spine, then pure cold hate. Rory felt Eve's hand tighten on his sleeve as the man spoke to their grandfather.

"I am surprised to see you looking so well, Granbury," Richly said, "considering I have been denied the privilege of paying my respects to you for reasons of your health."

"Don't put me in my grave yet." Granbury sniffed. "My health has never been better."

Then the baron was standing in front of Rory touting an air of dominance like some noble lord who expected by right to be here at this ball, when he should not have been. "Huntington," Richly said. "May I present my daughter?"

Lavinia curtsied. "We've met, Daddy."

Richly frowned down at his daughter. "Not properly."

"Baron," Eve acknowledged. "Miss Richland. Do enjoy yourselves tonight," she said in the wake of Rory's silence.

His shuttered gaze followed the baron's departure. He did not see Winter. And now he also searched for Trevor.

An hour later, Winter still had yet to find Trevor, and soon she quit looking as she stopped to watch the beautiful swirl of colors on the dance floor and to listen to the lively music. Enthralled by the magic of it all, she tapped her foot in time to the beat.

She had not danced a waltz since her last lesson when she was sixteen. But she had practiced in her kitchen all week and knew she was up to the challenge. Lavinia, wearing chartreuse satin trimmed in blond with a glimpse of matching slippers, strolled toward her with a handsome gentleman on the way to the floor. They saw each other at the same time.

Winter had been in the ballroom when she had heard the majordomo announce Lavinia and her father. But Winter had already made up her mind that it was time she stopped spending her life running from the baron. She had known he'd be here tonight.

She smiled tentatively at her cousin in greeting. But Lavinia passed her with only a subtle nod on the way to the dance floor. Behind her, someone tittered. Winter turned. A group of young ladies stood at the buffet table. At once, they raised their fans and looked busy.

Winter knew them from the days of old when she had attended soirées as a young debutant, though she had not seen any of them for years. Certainly, they had never called upon her. But two of them had once been her friends.

Summoning her nerve, she approached the group, only to hear someone mutter something about Lavinia's poor relation as they disbanded like chickadees leaving Winter alone at the table. She had not expected the snub.

She turned to look around and glimpsed another young woman from her past. The daughter of a viscount. The girl was wearing pink satin and stood among a lively crowd of other women. Their gazes briefly touched and Winter started to raise her hand in greeting. But she too turned away.

Curling her fingers into her palm, Winter lowered her hand and pretended interest in the plate of strawberries, shoving aside the rudeness of others as she contented herself with watching the crowd of beautiful dancers.

Society could be a closed and hypercritical lot regarding who they socialized with. She remembered enough of the customs and rules about etiquette to know it could be her lack of pedigree, her gown, or something else they found wrong with her. Winter no longer expected anyone to ask her to dance.

Rory had been standing unobserved at the entrance to the ballroom before shouldering through the crush toward where Winter took a seat alone near the back of the room. He had seen enough in the last half hour as she'd made her way around the ballroom to find adequate reason to dislike his peers.

He had yet to officially join the party since he had taken his grandfather upstairs and left him with Eve, and suddenly those standing around him noted his presence.

Upon his entrance, the music came to a sudden halt. People turned to speak to him. His temper showed faintly in his eyes as a viscountess stopped him with a hand on his arm and invited him for champagne. Politely ignoring the woman's request, he disengaged her hand, and a path seemed to open up between him and Winter. For one look at his face was sufficient to inform even the least perceptive that the woman dressed in a cascade of iridescent white, reminiscent of her name, was his intended target.

Winter saw his approach and rose slowly to her feet, dipping into a curtsey as he stopped in front of her.

"I believe this waltz is mine, madam?"

She stared at his gloved hand aware that others were watching her, aware that he watched her. Their fingers touched and then she placed her palm on his hand and let him escort her onto the floor. "Are you *trying* to cause a scandal on purpose?" she whispered.

It was a dangerous premise. But not out of his character. "Everything I do has purpose. You should know that by now, love."

He pulled her around into his arms and raised his hand to the minstrel's gallery as if they were committing some conspiracy together on a glittering ballroom floor in front of the world. Her eyes sparkled. She understood him, he realized, perhaps more than he understood himself.

His hand tightened on her waist as the orchestra launched into a lively waltz. Winter's hand trembled slightly against his arm. "I should warn you—"

"Follow my lead, Winter."

And she did. Beautifully. He swept her past gilt-framed mirrors and beneath glittering chandeliers, and he pulled her nearer as they stepped in perfect time to the music. Soon other couples were on the floor and they were no longer dancing alone. Though in his mind, he had eyes only for her. His gaze fell on her flushed cheeks, and then a little lower over the slenderness of her neck, before he raised his eyes and found her watching him. Ruled by instinct as much as caution, he presented her with a smile.

"I'm impressed," he said, because he could no longer maintain the air of needed sobriety around her. "You haven't peered at your feet once."

"Or tripped you." She smiled. "Thank you," she said.

"For what?"

"For making me appear less an outcast. I had forgotten how quickly they can close ranks against an outsider. I must appear somewhat backward to them."

"Don't attach noble intentions to my motives, Winter. I'm dancing with you because I get to put my hands on you."

Before she could protest his comment, his arm tightened around her waist, and he gathered her closer. "You are beautiful. Have I told you so yet?"

A glimmer of a smile lifted the corners of his mouth. She clearly knew it was on the tip of his tongue to ask her how many purses she had lifted to afford the gown she wore.

She saved him the query. "Mrs. Kincaid made most of the gown for me," she said. "Mrs. Peabody, she is the shopkeeper, supplied the skirt and bodice and the shoes. Old Ben and some of the townspeople cleaned up the old surrey, and Father Flannigan was my escort tonight."

He studied her with interest. "Will you turn into a pumpkin at midnight?"

She laughed, and Rory could only stare in awe at the shine in her eyes. "I believe it is the carriage that turns into a pumpkin at midnight. Do you not read fairy tales?"

"So this is what you've been doing during my absence."

She suddenly looked away and he was sorry to see her smile fade. "Were you gone, my lord? I had not noticed."

He laughed. "Do I detect censure in your tone, love?"

She said pleasantly, "I am not your love."

"Oh, but you are," he said in the quietest of tones.

There fingers twined like lovers, and he leisurely swung her around in his arms, his gaze holding hers, conscious of her heat and the perplexing covetousness he felt toward her. Tonight she smelled like roses. He leaned in nearer to her until his cheek was nearly pressed to her hair.

"Do you know many of the people here?" she asked.

From over her head, he studied the crowd of dancers. "Some," he replied. "I'm not a novice to this particular social scene if that is what you are wondering."

"Why wasn't Trevor in the receiving line?"

"*Coz* chose not to be there."

She looked up at him. "Why do you dislike him so?"

This time he felt himself squirming beneath her regard. Rory had tried to cultivate some positive opinion about his younger male relative, but had yet to find one, especially when he'd learned from Smothers moments ago that over Rory's explicit instructions, Trevor had sent an invitation to the baron for this event.

"Richly is here."

"I know." Her eyes sharpened on his. "You shouldn't have attempted to exclude him from an event such as this. You are only courting trouble."

His brow cocked. "Don't tell me how to handle the man. He isn't welcome at Granbury Court."

"I don't want to be the one responsible—"

"This has nothing to do with you, Winter."

Rory wasn't exactly truthful in that regard, but the baron had sufficiently pillaged a seventy-eight-year-old man, and Rory had developed his own opinions regarding Richly. "I'm not going to kowtow to the bastard simply because people are afraid of him. I've dealt with men like him most of my life. If you turn the other cheek, he'll only strike that one as well. And harder."

Winter seemed to consider this. "Then choosing me as your first dancing partner of the evening is your way of making a public statement to him? You do understand that this dance should have gone to Lavinia?"

Her conclusion about his reasons for choosing her was only partially the truth. A truth he was only now coming to realize. And for a flashing moment, he felt contentious and predatory in his possession of her.

"I don't mind," she surprised him by saying. "I rather like that you did."

He found his pulse raced oddly. Acutely aware of the brush of her skirts, her very nearness, he regretted hearing the music coming to its inevitable end.

"I imagine we should not dance twice," he said.

People were watching them. Dancing more than one waltz with the same woman would only raise speculations and cause tongues to wag. What he wanted between them, he wanted to keep as private as possible.

"I understand," she said.

Doubting she did, for he was loath to leave her, he bowed

over her hand. "You won't be ignored any more tonight, love."

Rory did not ask her to dance again, but it didn't matter. Winter waltzed twice with Trevor, who found her shortly after she left the floor with Rory, and later with two other gentlemen to whom Trevor introduced her. Rory danced with other women as well and his sister twice. But always, she was aware of him.

After a while, he left the ballroom, and Winter found a quiet room away from the music and the low din of voices.

Wineglass in hand, she walked to the window, the thrill of excitement now faded but not extinguished as her mind moved in time to the faint music. She stared at the moonshine on the sill, her complexion in the glass as coolly colored as marble. She was happy, yet, a hollowness weighted her stomach, its source somewhere else in this house.

Movement behind her lifted her gaze. She looked in the glass and saw the baron's face. He stood directly behind her. She whirled to face him, nearly dropping the glass in her hand.

"Winter."

The only lamp in the room burned near the door. The surrounding shadows were sufficient to hide his expression from her as he stepped forward.

The last time she had stood this close to the baron, he had been standing outside her cottage on a "mission of peace" as he'd called his attempts to woo her back to Everleigh. She had calmly held her father's old Webley revolver and pointed it at his chest. She had been perfectly polite but quite definite when she had told him that she would shoot him if he ever violated the terms of their agreement and approached her again. Until now, he had kept his word.

"What are you doing in here?" she demanded.

"I've been watching you all night, hoping for a chance to talk to you." He raised his hand to touch her hair. "You have grown up from the little waif I left at your cottage all those years ago."

Winter sidestepped him. A chair blocked her escape. His eyes startled as if he had not realized what he was doing, his fingers curling into his gloved palm.

"We have nothing to say to one another," she said. "How could you think we would?"

His eyes slid over her gown. "Who is the lucky chap keeping you? Huntington?"

"No one is *keeping* me. The gown is a gift made for me by friends."

"And which of your *friends* put your name on the guest list for this event?"

"I made sure she was on the guest list," Trevor said from the doorway. "It is my right to see whom I want invited."

The baron turned. A chill dropped over his eyes. "That is a deuced brave act for one who has been reduced to the poor Granbury relation. But I imagine your circumstance does give the two of you something in common. Misery loves its own company and all that hash."

Then he turned and smiled at Winter with the supreme confidence of his position. "You may look the part of a high-born lady tonight, but underneath the cheap fabric and glass jewels, you are merely common. A sparrow wearing the mask of a swan. You are not fooling anyone. They are laughing at you."

He still had the power to hurt her. Yet, remarkably, Winter had expected no less from him, and it was to her credit that she did not pick up the vase beside her and throw it at his head. That such a beautiful piece of art might be destroyed over someone like him had been what stopped her.

"I suggest you leave this room." Trevor's quiet voice burned.

The baron walked to where he stood just inside the doorway. "Stay away from my daughter, Jameson. She is not for the likes of you."

"Clearly she is not for the likes of Huntington either, baron."

For a moment, Winter feared for Trevor's life. Then the baron turned on the heel of a shiny black shoe and quit the room.

Trevor's gaze lifted to hers as if to check her state. Winter drew in a breath. "You should not have said that."

He walked over to her and slipped the glass from her numb fingers. He set it on the table beside the chair. "Let's take a walk to the lake."

He led her outside the French doors. The moon shone brightly. The scent of honeysuckle touched her nostrils. He pulled her down the stone steps and across the yard, her slippers sinking into the thick grass and her skirts billowing around her like a church bell. She was breathless as Trevor pulled her up in front of him and stopped.

"Thank you," she said.

"I should have followed my cousin's lead and kept the bastard off the guest list. I'm sorry that he said those things to you."

"Everything he said was true, Trevor."

She did not belong here. But with the moonlight washing

over her, she felt otherworldly and no longer interested in facing the reality of her circumstances as she stared up at the beautiful sky and listened to the music drifting across the lawn. "But I don't care. I'm still glad I came."

"I could kiss you, Winter," Trevor said.

Shocked, she found herself looking from the sky and into his face, and then he pressed his lips to hers.

She raised her hands to push him away then changed her mind. His lips were warm and dry. She didn't open her mouth, though she felt him prying to get inside. She squeezed shut her eyes and thought of Rory's mouth and hands on her and how different his touch made her feel.

Finally, she pressed her hands against Trevor's shoulders and stepped away. They were both breathing harder. "We shouldn't have done that."

"Then why did you allow me?"

"For the same reason you wanted to kiss me. We are both looking for a way to go back to a world that no longer exists for either of us."

For so many years, she'd been looking for the path that would vanquish the last five years. The glory of the moonlight, the stars shining down on her, and the beautiful gown were merely props to foster the illusion. There was a danger in believing that the fantasy could transform her life. But she didn't need the fantasy to be happy. She had also proven that to herself tonight.

She drew in a measured breath and pulled away. He took her hand. "Don't feel as if you betrayed Huntington, Winter. He is not the saint you think he is."

Winter sighed. She didn't want to hear anything more about Rory's wretched vices. "Are any of us saints, Trevor? Are you? I certainly am not."

"I've been doing an investigation into him."

Poor Trevor. She would probably behave no differently in his place. She closed her hand around his. "Why weren't you in that receiving line?"

"Why should I be? Lord Granbury doesn't need me around anymore."

She sighed. "Come." This time it was Winter who tugged his hand. "Ask me to waltz."

Too soon it would be time for her to go home.


Rory was leaning a shoulder against the windowsill, watching Winter from the blue room overlooking the lake. His mouth tightened, and feeling predatory as his gaze landed on Trevor walking beside her, he continued to track the two across the moonlit lawn.

Behind Rory, his sister's velvet skirts made a *shushing* sound with each step as she spoke with ceaseless melodrama reminiscent of their childhood when it had only been just the two of them. She stopped to readjust her spectacles as she peered at their grandfather puffing on a pipe like a billowing chimney. "You do not bully me, Grandfather," she said. "One only has to watch you in the orangery talking to your flowers to know you are all bluster and no bite. This discussion is not about me."

His grandfather *humphed*. "It is against the law of nature for a woman to smoke."

One hand on her hip, Eve peered over her gold spectacle rims at Rory. "Have you been listening?"

Indeed, he had not. His mind still on the scene outside, he continued to watch Winter, only to raise his eyes in the glass as Eve stopped behind him, clearly expecting him not only to respond but to take her side.

"What does Rory care if I smoke a pipe? Men understand these things. We *are* in the smoking room."

Eve, who was enjoying her own pipe, peered at Father Flannigan comfortably ensconced in a fat velvet chair also smoking a cob. "I told him it was not healthy for his lungs," he agreed. "But does he listen to anything?"

Rory thought they were all quite round the bend, the argument ludicrous, but typical of his sister's verbal exchanges with their grandfather. Clearly, they suffered a fondness for each other. Eve only argued with those for whom she cared, and his grandfather thrived on debate. Spare them all when those two shared the same room.

But his stubborn grandfather did look paler tonight and Eve had a point. She had not wanted him to remain in the reception line for as long as he had.

Clearly noting Rory's scrutiny, Granbury glared from Eve to him. "Why aren't the two of you down with our guests? What will they think, having all of us disappear at once?"

Rory walked over to Lord Granbury and removed the pipe from his mouth. He tapped out the tobacco in a tray beside the chessboard.

"Some vices are worth the consequences, sir," he told his shocked grandfather. "This is not one."

# Chapter 15

**W**inter returned to her cottage just after midnight. Mrs. Kincaid had helped her remove her dress and pack it away, and Old Ben brought her home. She waved to him, then ran up the drive and across the yard. She hung her cloak on the post beside the door. She leaned for a moment against the wall and closed her eyes. The rout itself would continue well into the morning but for her it was over. She had danced the entire night, not only with Trevor, but with others as well. If she'd had a dance card, it would have been filled. But she had not danced with Rory again.

She lit the lamp sitting on the kitchen table and walked into the kitchen where she lit the stove and boiled water for tea, too restless to sleep just yet. After putting tea in the strainer, she took the lamp and walked upstairs to change. Hers was the only room where the door was not closed. At the doorway she stopped.

Rory's dark jacket lay across the white painted bedstead. Her chest tightened. Expecting to see him at the window or sitting in a chair, she strode into the room. But he was not there. She set the lamp on the nightstand.

She touched his jacket, laying her palm against the cloth

still warm from his body heat as if he had just removed it. Then something made her turn.

Rory stood leaning against the wall behind the door, the starched white collar of his shirt opened and the light in his eyes. Those eyes held hers. And when they dipped downward, she felt branded by their burn. "I wracked my brain for every conceivable argument not to come here," he said. "And yet, here I am."

She could scarcely breathe.

"Am I welcome here, Winter?"

He didn't so much as ease her away from any trepidation she might have had, as he conquered them in one fell swoop.

Wild longing raced like a hot wind through her blood. And suddenly for the first time in years since she had so foolishly destroyed her life, something wonderful and powerful stirred inside, and threatened to stay. She nodded and for a long moment, they stared at each other in silence.

His arm rose and he shut the door.

There was no doubt where this moment would lead. No doubts at all as Rory twisted the key in the lock and said something about not trusting unlocked doors, or perhaps it was merely the opened door at his back he didn't like or his fear that she might change her mind. The notion was silly considering she was exactly where she wanted to be.

She stepped into his arms and into his kiss. His mouth slid down her throat and her senses erupted. "Winter." He brought his mouth back to hers. Heat became sensation. "I didn't like seeing you with other men tonight. With Trevor."

He sounded jealous. Proprietary, as if he had a right to his feelings. And even that did not bother her. His tongue swept her lower lip, and his mouth possessed hers. She mewed softly against his lips, heated and low. Her urgency matching his.

She rose on her toes and stretched her arms around his neck. Reveled in the hardness of his body. She wanted to blurt out what was in her mind and her heart, that she had felt so beautiful tonight in his arms dancing the waltz.

"I must wash first," she murmured against his warm lips, pulling herself back from the sensual brink. "There is tea downstairs."

His mouth smiled against hers. "You want to wash in tea?"

"Tea?" She breathed the word and pulled back with soft laughter. "No, you goose, the tea is for your enjoyment while I clean up and change my clothes."

"My enjoyment"—his hands cupped her face, his eyes bore into hers—"is here. I'm only going to take your clothes off anyway." He made good on his promise as his hands worked the tiny silver buttons on her bodice.

Winter stepped away to finish the job herself. Her hands unsteady, she worked the ties on her skirt.

After a moment, Rory began to remove his own clothing, starting with his gun. He set both the weapon and its holster on her dresser.

He wondered if there would ever be a time in his life when he would feel safe without a firearm, as its presence briefly reminded him who and what he was. And what he was not. For a moment, as the mask slipped, he didn't know why he was here in this room with Winter, taking what he knew he should not be taking from her. And yet here he was weighed down by his desire. By the primal need to make her his. Seeing her with Trevor tonight had done something to him.

He and Winter both were silent as they attended to the task of disrobing, the only sound in the room the rasp of their clothing, pooling around their feet. Still wearing her shift, Winter raised her head, her lips faintly swollen from his kisses, and her eyes fell on his body.

All of him.

Closing the space between them, he framed her face in his hands and lowered his mouth to hers. Her shiver revealed her vulnerability and he didn't kiss her. "Tell me what you want, Winter."

She did not look away and he could not. He sensed that she knew she'd off-balanced him. Tentatively her fingers splayed his chest. "I want this, my lord."

He kissed her deeply, seducing a groan from her throat. "Tell me what you want," he repeated.

"You. I want you."

He brought her hand to his hardness and wrapped her fingers around it. "Feel," he said huskily, "what you do to me."

"Oh," she mouthed. Her hand slid lower and encompassed all of him from staff to bollocks in her sweeping touch. "Yes . . ."

Nearly undone, he pressed his smile against the pulse at her throat. "Your eloquent prose is the stuff of poetry, love," his uneven words rasped.

"You are the stuff of poetry, my lord."

The force behind her reply flowed like a current into him. She stretched against him. The shape of her mouth changed, meeting the hard slant of his. Her hair swung loosely over her shoulder and he brushed it away from her breasts. Their movements were nearly synchronized like the steps of their waltz. She drew him across the wooden floor that was cool against his bare feet. Where she led, he followed. Then he stopped and looked down at the mattress behind her.

Her bed was narrow and would be a tight fit for him from crown to toes. She raised dark brown eyes to his, a crease settling between her arched brows, clearly an expression of concern. "I imagine you are used to bigger."

He would have laughed if the sound of his amusement would not have injured her pride, even if it was himself with whom he found humor. He liked her simplicity, the way it extended to everything around her, including him. She simply was who she was. Her bedroom might be modest compared to some in which he'd been, but *she* lacked nothing.

Despite himself, he did smile. "Before we even hit that mattress neither of us will notice where we are."

He eased her down to the bed, flesh to flesh, spilling her luxurious hair across her pillow. Its rose fragrance came to him as he caught himself above her and he brushed his face against it. He inhaled her heady scent, moved his fingers along the insides of her naked thighs, until he reached her softness. A hunger born of abstinence these past weeks controlled the tempo of his need. She was a banquet to his starving senses. His kiss was hard and impatient. She moaned a little at the pressure of his lips and his touch as he pushed a finger inside her.

"You're hot, love," he whispered against her ear and gently cupped her sex. "And wet." Like a hot mouth.

She murmured what sounded like his name, pulling his mouth down to hers. His tongue thrust into her mouth, the same even cadence that controlled his hand as he caressed her and stroked her intimate places. Her hands roamed his back. Then her thighs opened and she was eagerly offering herself to him and he was lifting her bottom with one hand, while with his other he guided himself to her sweetness. He pushed into her and took her lips open-mouthed, trapping her groan with a kiss so demanding that all she could do was match him.

Earthy sounds came from her throat, sounds that moved him to restless abandon as easily as her innocent touch. All thought narrowed to the feel of her surrounding him.

"God," he rasped. "You're so . . . tight."

He rode her hard, his thrusts shoving his head against the headboard. The sheet entangled his legs. His heels smacked the footboard. An oath followed. Dimly, he was aware of the desire to kick against the footboard to be rid of the hindrance.

Then with a low growl, he stopped, his heart pounding violently. Their gazes touched and locked briefly. Her eyes questioned.

"Hold on," he choked out. "I'm going to turn us."

He clasped her bottom against him as he rolled her over on top of him, placing them face-to-face, mouth-to-mouth. Her musky scent came up to him and filled his senses. He pushed her thighs wide, reached between them and placed her on his erection. Her weight forced her down.

Her head fell back, exposing her silken throat and giving him her perfect breasts. He suckled her breasts like a babe. "Please, my lord—"

"Rory," he rasped. "Call me Rory."

His hands gripped her hips. Then he was a part of her, lost in the rocking rhythm of her body. The old rope springs beneath them screeched and groaned and the wooden bedstead knocked against the wall. As if she embraced the same violent emotions he felt, her fingers dug into his biceps. Her kiss only grew hungrier, immersing him in a sensual feast that only left him famished for more.

Somewhere a part of his mind told him she needed to slow down and he forced her back from his mouth.

"Do *not* move . . ." he said through clenched teeth.

Her eyes locked on his, she arched, her labored breathing the only sound between them. Pressure mounted low in his belly, her body convulsed around him. With a groan that was her name, he crushed her lips to his and caught her outcry, his own breath fracturing against her mouth.

*Bloody hell.*

His hands grabbed her waist. He remembered at the last minute. "I have to pull out, Winter. Now."

He did, lifting her and dropping her back against the pillows as he caught himself against his palms above her.

His heartbeat eventually slowed, he opened his eyes and found her eyes wide on his, a flicker of concern—or was it amusement?—in her gaze. And a sticky mess between them.

"Are you all right?" she asked.

Hell no, he wasn't all right. Then he realized he hadn't been *more* right in a very long time. He cleaned her stomach with the edge of the sheet and collapsed to his elbows, careful not to crush her beneath him. "What part of *don't move*, did you not understand?"

She smiled, stretching like a feline beneath him. And for a long suspended breath, he stared down at her. Then she smiled wickedly. "If we're going to do this again, me thinks we'll need a longer bed."


Winter awoke to the scent of him on her pillow. She lay on the floor in her bedroom atop the coverlet she'd pulled from the bed, and wrapped in sheets that also smelled like him. She drew in her breath, inhaling a measure of his presence and turned on her side only to find the space beside her empty. But for the flame from a single lamp burning on her nightstand, the room was still dark. She pushed herself up on her elbows and thought Rory had gone, but then she heard the rasp of cloth against cloth.

He sat on the faded purple chair beneath the window, one ankle resting on his knee, his elbow perched on the chair arm as he leaned his chin against his hand watching her from the shadows. Winter had the notion he'd been staring at her for some time now. His hair was slightly damp from a wash. She looked past him out the window.

"How long have I been asleep?"

He sat forward partially into the light. He was fully dressed. "A few hours."

"I see." Even after the incredibly intimate things they'd shared many times over, she suddenly felt shy in her nakedness. She pulled the sheet to her neck. "Are you leaving now?"

"If you haven't looked outside, the sun will be up shortly. I have guests to return to at Granbury Court."

She wasn't sure if he was amused by her reaction or if he was merely accustomed to this routine.

"I didn't want to leave without talking to you first. I made tea, when you are ready." He rose to his feet.

"You made tea?" But her tone said, *"You actually know how?"*

He turned in the doorway, and his masculine presence seemed to dominate the room. "The penalties for remaining a bachelor so long. I have learned to boil water." His eyes softened on hers. "There is a basin on the stand for you to wash."

She noted the ceramic bowl and pitcher next to the chair. A rag lay folded next to a bar of soap. He'd thought of everything.

After he left, Winter dropped back to the pillow. Her entire body throbbed. Rory had done things to her that even now made her blush. She buried her face in her hands and forced herself to breathe calmly and slowly, telling herself this was merely an affair and it would be a mark of her inexperience in these matters to allow herself to feel more than a physical attachment. Falling in love with the future Marquess of Granbury opened the door to a disconcerting landscape.

Winter quickly collected herself. She gathered up the sheets and tossed them into the corner of the room. The water in the pitcher was cold and she sucked in her breath sharply at the feel of it as she completed her ablutions, working as quickly as she could, worried Rory would tire of waiting for her and go.

But when she descended the stairs, he hadn't left. He was sitting at the kitchen table contemplating the cup of tea in his hands when she swept through the doorway, her face flushed from her exertions, her hair loosely bound in a thick knot at her nape. She'd donned her favorite dress: a bright yellow muslin with white lace cuffs. The fashion might not have been up to Parisian standards, but the dress itself was only two years old. He came slowly to his feet.

Her glance rose to the wooden beam just above his head. "If you were any taller, my lord, you would need to duck when you walk."

His mouth crooked. "I have found it prudent on occasion to duck anyway, even when not on foot."

"Yes." Her heart took a hard thud. "You said you had

tea?" she asked, steering the question away from that which she had no desire to discuss.

"I was told the baron approached you at the ball."

Winter was surprised he would know this. But this was also a topic she did not wish to discuss. "He did. And then he left the room. He did not touch me."

His gaze took in the room. "Why has the baron left you alone here?"

Folding one hand over the other, she lifted her chin. "I told you we have an agreement. If I am not mistaken, he's more interested in you at the moment, my lord, than me." She looked past him to the window. "Perhaps the time for tea has passed. It will be light by the time you return to Granbury Court. People will wonder where you've been."

His silence forced her attention back to him. "Why are we behaving like polite strangers?" he asked.

"We *are* strangers."

"The hell we are."

He turned his head away, his jaw set at a hard-edged angle. His eyes took in the row of painted teacups hanging from hooks beneath the cupboards, her grandmother's collection of porcelain thimbles lined neatly on a curio shelf, the miniature wild animal menagerie her father purchased for her from the London museum, and other pieces of her life she'd taken from Everleigh when she'd left.

Rory picked up a giraffe and peered at her from over its brown and white neck. "And you just became complicated," he said.

"No more so than you, my lord."

"Have you ever considered that marrying the right man might alleviate some of your circumstance?"

She laughed. "Are you proposing to sacrifice yourself?"

He set down the giraffe and considered her. "I haven't the faintest notion what I'm proposing."

"I imagine you do but are too polite to tell me." The last thing she wanted was for him to pity her circumstances and offer to pay for her services. "I am not so desperate yet that I choose to wed someone in this shire for circumstance alone. Pardon me for thinking as a romantic, but I believe a woman should be in love with her husband. There is no one in this village with whom I am in love."

They stood across from each other, the table between them, the small kitchen resonating with suppressed energy. "And here I was under the impression marriage has little to do with love."

"In time that will prove true in my case, but I think you would marry for nothing less, my lord. Whether that would be love for Granbury Court or something else, only time will tell."

She had the minutest impression that her words annoyed him. To what degree she didn't understand, but the fact that she could move him should have lent her some degree of satisfaction. It did not.

He reached into his jacket for his riding gloves. "I can make your life a great deal more comfortable here, if you'll let me, Winter."

She stiffened. "What I give you, I give freely. Don't take that away from me by offering to pay for my services. I'm your lover. Not your mistress."

"Please Lord"—he cast his eyes to the heavens—"tell me the difference."

She clenched her jaw. "The difference is you do not own me. Would you shame me now by making me feel like a whore?"

"Dammit, Winter."

She skittered away from him. He glared at her as if he wanted to say something more, and they stood like two enemy combatants in the silence surging between them. "You're right. I should leave," he said.

Winter followed Rory to the stable where he'd put his horse the night before and watched as he saddled the roan. The sun rose while he was inside the stall, and the rooster crowed. She'd turned to watch the sunrise paint the sky with color when, suddenly, Rory was beside her, his gloved hand holding the horse's reins. She looked up into his eyes and forged a smile even as she did not feel much like smiling.

"You would enjoy being my mistress."

"I enjoy being your lover," she said. "Can we not leave it with that?"

He stepped a boot into the stirrup and mounted the gelding, reining it around until he faced her. The roan sidestepped as if held in place by Rory's will alone. "As you wish, love."

He rode out of the yard, scattering the chickens that pecked at the ground. Winter picked up a handful of her skirts and, darting out of the stable yard, hurried past the clearing in the front of the cottage. She climbed the hill that looked out over the road.

By the time she reached the top, she was too late to see him. He was gone. Then, just as she started to turn away, a man astride a horse appeared at the edge of the woods and Winter's breath caught. The horse pranced sideways. She could feel it when Rory found her standing on the hill. Suddenly the horse charged forward and galloped back up the road toward the cottage.

She tensed, but only for a minute. She whirled on her heel and managed to traipse through the brush in her slippers and long skirts and back down the hill to the road as he crested the drive.

He halted in front of her, and she stood there stupidly searching for something relevant to say when he leaned over in the saddle and picked a twig out of her fallen hair. "I was thinking that I had not yet had breakfast," he said.

"Breakfast would be wonderful."

He lifted her into the saddle and she kissed him. It wasn't until the forest had settled back into silence that he finally raised his mouth from hers. But Winter's mind was already skipping to thoughts of another kind of nourishment as he urged the horse back to the cottage.

He slept afterward with her wrapped tightly in his arms. Winter did not sleep and finally climbed from bed. The sun had touched the tops of the trees as she drew on her robe and went down to the kitchen to wash; she was surprised when she returned to the bedroom to dress and looked at him in her small bed, at how soundly he slept. He slept on his belly, cradling his ebony head on his forearm, his dark lashes like smudges on his bristled cheek. His back was bare to the waist where the coverlet twisted around his hips. In sleep, he seemed younger and more innocent, not the aggressive male who took her without abandon.

For Winter, what had started as a kiss in a stable between her and the Granbury heir had evolved into something far more personal.

She did not know how to define what it was between them or if it was merely her lack of worldliness showing. But if the wild longing in her blood was any proof against her heart, she was in love with a man driven by an intensity she was beginning to realize was an integral and dangerous part of who he was.

She wanted to understand him, why he had come back to her that morning, but always he was just beyond her ken, like smoke she could not grasp.

Winter gathered up eggs in the yard and tended to his horse. She finished the final touches on a basket she planned to bring Mam. It was filled with items from the garden, jam that Mrs. Kincaid had given her, a new book Father Flannigan had let her borrow last week. She was halfway to Mrs. Smythe's cottage when she heard hoofbeats and turned to see Rory approaching.

He reined in beside her, stirring up dust with his abrupt stop. Delicately fanning away the cloud, Winter smiled up at him. "Good morning, my lord. I thought you would have returned to Granbury Court."

He was without a jacket and wore his shirtsleeves rolled to his forearms, the stark white of the cloth in contrast to his damp hair and the shadow on his jaw. His irritation was evident in the taut grip he held on the reins. She knew that part of the source of his irritation had to do with his being unaccustomed to sleeping away the morning, but she did not understand the rest.

"You should have awakened me before you left."

She ignored his surly mood. "Why? Clearly, you needed the rest."

Lines drawn around his mouth, he peered around her as if he attempted to see through the thick curtain of elms and sycamores to discern where they were. "What are you doing out here?"

"I'm visiting Mam. Then I will be making my rounds to

check on some of the tenants. Father Flannigan usually does this, but he is with your grandfather."

"I thought the tenants at Everleigh were no longer your responsibility."

"Just because I no longer live in my house does not mean I have stopped caring about the people who live on these lands." She eyed his horse. "You are welcome to join me. Unless you have something else to do."

Rory did join her, astonishing even himself. He found himself more than a little gratified to see that he had also stunned her, as she had clearly expected him to decline. Halfway into the afternoon, it occurred to him that she made him do things he never expected he'd do. Remaining in Granbury was one, though he had his separate reasons for doing so. Leaving his sister to deal with their grandfather's guests was a sure sign he suffered another ailment of the brain.

Thinking about Winter incessantly was another. Actually acting on his desires, something else entirely, yet he did it all just the same.

And now he followed her about and met many of Everleigh's tenants as well as Granbury Court's remaining tenants as she checked on their needs.

He'd met Winter's mother and the woman caring for her. Mrs. Smythe had invited him inside her humble residence.

Winter was neither shamed by her mother's condition nor embarrassed to introduce him to her. Rory had been surprised at how incredibly fragile Mrs. Ashburn was. Mrs. Smythe had told him she'd suffered some manner of seizure some years ago when Perry had been born. She could not speak well and most of the time did not know who Winter was. Yet, Rory was not surprised by Winter's complete devotion to her.

"Miss Winter visits us everyday," Mrs. Smythe declared over tea and hot crumpets as Rory sat outside in the garden, his legs stretched in front of him watching Winter and her mother stroll arm in arm around the garden.

"Some days her mother recalls everything," Mrs. Smythe reminisced. "Other days she cannot remember where she is. It helps that we are childhood friends. Winter quit bringing Perry here some weeks ago. The visits were too hard on the boy."

"Why isn't Richly providing for her care?"

"That would never do," Mrs. Smythe said. "Miss Winter takes care of us."

Rory understood far more than Mrs. Smythe did about how Winter had been taking care of them. But then again, as he'd studied the woman's profile beneath the black bonnet brim, he decided Mrs. Smythe might not be as ignorant of certain matters as he supposed.

For an entire day afterward, Rory didn't think about the life he had outside of Granbury or his plans to return to it when he finished his business here. Or the whole bloody other world that dwelled just beneath the surface surrounding him, a darker less pleasant one than what he glimpsed now in the daylight.

He saw only Winter, felt only her in his arms, inhaled the flower scent of her hair as she sat in the saddle in front of him. But, as his hands tightened on the reins he'd also come to realize that if Winter had brought him to these places to see these people's lives, she had done so with a greater purpose.

He considered that purpose later when he returned home the next evening.

*Home.*

Men like him didn't belong to old estates or ruminate over a dark-eyed provincial miss.

Deep inside, he knew she didn't fit into his circle. She was as far removed from everything that was familiar to him as she could be. That quality was what drew him to her and now troubled him. They were like moonlight and sunlight that shared the same sky only at dusk and dawn. He didn't want her vulnerable to ridicule. Or to change for him. Yet, strangely, he knew she fit into his grandfather's world here at Granbury Court far better than he did.

He rode into the stable as the moon touched the tops of the trees. Not all the guests had gone. Old Ben hurried out to meet Rory as he dismounted.

"My lord, they be lookin' all over for ye," Old Ben said. "Somethin' terrible be goin' on at the house. Yer grandfather . . ."

Rory turned on his heel. He dashed across the stretch of yard leading to the house. The door flung open and a footman appeared telling him he was needed in Lord Granbury's chambers at once.

Rory pushed through the crowd of servants and guests gathered in the hallway and outside the door.

Trevor sat by the bed, Lord Granbury's limp hand clasped within his. His sister sat on the other side next to Father Flannigan. Eve stood. "Lord Granbury succumbed to a heart stroke just before supper," he heard Father Flannigan say.

Heard the words, but did not comprehend. Trevor rose. "He's dead, *my lord*." He shoved past Rory, leaving him to stare down at the ashen face of his grandfather, understanding nothing when his grandfather had been improving.

Father Flannigan said, "His heart gave out, my son."

How ironic that Rory would have found his own heart,

as his grandfather's had stopped, and an awful sense of savagery struck him at the injustice of it all.

He had not said good-bye, or any of another hundred things he should have said but had not.

"Should we send word to toll the bells, my lord?" Smothers inquired.

Grief welling inside him, Rory nodded, telling Father Flannigan to get everyone out and away from Granbury Court. "Eve and I need to be alone."

# Chapter 16

Winter stood at the top of the hill overlooking Granbury Court's family cemetery. Wrapping her shawl across her shoulders against the late-afternoon chill, she knew she shouldn't linger, but she couldn't seem to make her legs walk away.

His lone figure was silhouetted against the gray marble of a crypt. For all that, he looked splendid and tall in an overcoat and hat, he also looked alone. She saw his face only in profile. He'd been standing in the same place for a half hour. She had not seen him in three weeks.

She'd been at the stable talking to Old Ben when his carriage had rumbled through the gates. She'd remained hidden in the barn's doorway, watching as Rory descended the steps, left the yard, and disappeared into the woods near the chapel.

The last time she'd stood on this hill had been when Rory had buried his grandfather. For all the pomp and circumstance that had followed Lord Granbury's passing while he lay in state, the funeral itself had been relatively private. Rory had been present, along with a dozen people, including his sister and a small child at Rory's side Winter had later learned was his niece. He'd returned to London for an investiture ceremony and to do whatever it was peers did when they inherited their little kingdoms with all their responsibility.

He was now the new Marquess of Granbury.

Without wishing to be seen, she took a step backward then turned away only to stop abruptly.

Trevor stood before her. Shadows lay like smudges below his eyes. He had not attended the private funeral service. Strangely, she had not even thought of him and, for a moment, guilt assailed her.

"I saw Old Ben at the stable," he said. "He said you were here."

"Old Ben has been keeping Mrs. Kincaid's mare this summer. The horse is finally healed enough for me to take back."

Winter strode past him, but Trevor drew her up. "Walk with me to the gazebo by the lake. I need someone with whom to talk."

"Where have you been, Trevor?"

He shoved his hands in his pockets. His jacket opened over his rumpled shirt. "I remained in London," he said. "It isn't as if my presence was missed. Walk with me."

"Trevor." She swallowed a sigh. "I can't. Old Ben is waiting for me. I need to fetch the mare. It's late."

She stepped around him to the gravel path that made a neat border around the estate, but he moved in front of her. "Or would you rather it just not be me standing here talking with you?"

The remark chastened her. Winter opened her mouth but barely found the words to reply. "Why would you say that?"

"Because I've been watching you for ten minutes. You

didn't even know anyone else was standing behind you, so intent were you watching *him*. Why would you follow him to this place?"

Winter bristled. That Trevor had spied her in a vulnerable moment did more than merely anger her. It revealed her own carelessness.

But before she could ask him to stand aside, she knew they were suddenly not alone. She knew an instant before Trevor's eyes darted to a spot over her shoulder. Rory was here. He had come up over the hill.

Everything inside her seemed to give way and she was certain her knees would collapse. But they did not. She turned to greet him. He was so tall he had to bend beneath the oak branch just above his head. He looked every bit the aristocrat as he stopped in front of her, the pale linen of his shirt stark against the caped coat worn in a negligent fashion over his shoulders.

His eyes held hers and never more than at this moment had she felt something inside her shift and move, like a monumental earth tremor. Maybe it was the way he looked at her. Maybe it was the powerful chemistry they shared even now as they faced each other.

She dipped in a brief curtsey. "My lord."

"Miss Ashburn."

"I didn't mean to intrude," she felt compelled to say as his eyes moved from hers to home in on Trevor. "I was at the stable when I saw your carriage—"

"You didn't. Intrude," he said.

"Please accept my condolences on your grandfather's passing," she said after a moment. She felt the growing tension between the three of them. "I should go." She dipped again before she could stop herself.

*Good heavens,* she cringed. *What is wrong with me? Behaving like a child's jack-in-the-box.*

"I'll walk you to the stable," Trevor said.

But Rory stepped between them and grasped her elbow, a possessive gesture she felt through the layer of her sleeve. Startled, Winter dropped her attention to her arm. Trevor's fingers wrapped around Rory's forearm.

Rory tightened his grip on Winter's elbow. "That isn't necessary," he said. "I'll accompany her to the stable."

"I think it is necessary," Trevor said. "Unless it is your want to ruin her? Haven't you already done enough?"

Her heart knocked against her ribs. "Trevor!"

He pulled his gaze from Rory's and looked pointedly at her. "After listening to the rumors flying around here, the last person you need to be seen with is him."

She cast an imploring look at Trevor. "Please. Are you planning to challenge him with pistols at dawn? This is absurd."

Rory peeled Trevor's fingers from his jacket. "I believe he prefers swords."

"Do you want to know what I've been doing in London these past weeks, my lord?" Trevor asked. "While you have been doing your inquiry of me, I've been doing my own inquiry of you. I found some of Lord Granbury's private papers. Do you want to know what I've discovered?"

"Do tell, Trevor," his cousin said dispassionately.

Winter pulled her elbow free of Rory's grip, but like walking into a wall, his arm prevented her from stepping between him and Trevor. "Cease this. Both of you."

Trevor gazed at her as if it were her he had to convince. "He killed a man when he was fifteen, an incident that was mysteriously swept beneath the rug. His reputation at Sandhurst was abominable. He should have been thrown out on his arse long before he was drummed out of the dragoon guard for behavior unbecoming an officer."

Fury burned in Trevor's words as he continued. "Then he vanishes for years. Where? Prison? Where else would someone like him go? Only to miraculously reappear just as Lord Granbury is about to expire. Discharging the physician. Everyone knows what my cousin tried to do and why he did it. It's the talk in London. Now he is finally the marquess."

Winter held her breath. But Rory laughed, actually laughed. "All acts of a blackguard to be sure. But then I've never claimed to be of the noble sort."

"Bastard. You ruined my life! You didn't even care about him. And now you have everything. He died asking for *you*. And where were you?"

For an awful moment, taut silence filled the glade.

Rory stepped forward to take Winter's elbow and almost didn't see Trevor swing his fist, but he evaded the intended blow more quickly than lightning.

One moment Trevor was standing; the next he lay flat on his back, sucking in great bouts of air with sawing breaths as if he were about to die.

Winter didn't know how everything happened so fast. "Trevor!" She dropped to her knees beside him, frantically feeling for broken bones. Amazingly, she saw no blood.

He lifted his head, but it fell back against the soft mat of leaves and pine needles. He pressed his balled fists against his eyes as if to stem more than the groan that followed. Rory remained standing above Trevor, blank-faced except for the twitch of his jaw.

Winter had never seen anyone move with such lethal economy of speed. He didn't learn to fight like that living among Gypsies.

He had reacted in that same way the night he'd been shot, when he'd come out of a state of unconsciousness with his hand wrapped around her throat. A man trained to fight, perhaps even to kill. That Trevor still breathed spoke volumes to Rory's proficiency.

"You didn't *have* to hit him so hard."

Rory squatted, his coat folding around his feet as he placed an elbow on his knee. He shifted his attention to Trevor. "Would you like for me to send Smothers back with a litter, *coz*?"

Trevor lowered his hands and wiped at his nose. "Bugger off, *coz*." He pushed himself into a sitting position. "Mourning is over. It is only a matter of time before your real problems begin. Has someone thought to warn you what is about to befall you? You will be fortunate to hold on to Granbury Court. Richly owns you."

Winter tightened her grip on her shawl, but she did not look away as Rory's gaze touched briefly on hers.

"It will be dark soon, Miss Ashburn," he said. "I will see that Old Ben accompanies you back to the village."

He clearly expected her to oppose him. She did not.

"Don't come here alone again," he quietly warned. "Unless you want to spend the night. I mean it."

His glance touched Trevor, then his broad shoulders shifted beneath his coat, he stood and strode past her.

Swallowing around the thickness in her throat, she watched him walk out of the clearing until his tall form disappeared through the dense foliage. Suddenly conscious of the chill, she returned her attention to Trevor.

"God's life, Trevor Jameson. What were you thinking trying to strike him? He could have hurt you."

His fingers closed around a rock and he slung it against a tree. "That should tell you all there is to know about his character."

"Don't ever accuse him of conspiring to kill Lord Granbury again. I won't abide you besmirching his or Father Flannigan's name."

"I merely repeated what is being said."

"Well, do not. If anyone has been wronged here, it is he. Don't forget he is the man someone from Granbury tried to kill." Her voice lowered. "He'll make a difference here, Trevor. If he isn't run out first."

*Or worse.*

"Are you in love with him?"

"Don't be absurd."

Trevor grabbed her hand, halting her before she stood. "He met you in a pub, Winter. Think about that before you wonder if you could have a future with him here."

She turned her head away, but he tipped her chin. "I am sorry if I sound cruel. I don't mean to be. I'm sorry, Winter."

Because he was intent on forcing her into seeing the precarious reality of her circumstances? Or because he'd reminded her that her social status could never be more than what it was?

"You know I have always stood behind you," he said. "You believe that, don't you? I'm not as ignorant of the events around here as you think I am. People are still talking about the ball and asking where he was when Granbury died." The line of his mouth softened. "You deserve better than what he'll ever offer you, Winter."

Instead of the scorn she expected to see in his eyes, she glimpsed only compassion and knew he did not want to hurt her with his words. "Where have you been anyway?" she asked.

Trevor let loose of her hand and drew one knee to his chest. "Lavinia is in London," he said. "That is why I stayed there. This place isn't home anymore."

"Don't be ridiculous. I suggest you make peace with your circumstances and give your cousin a reason to trust you." She made a sweeping motion with her arm that encompassed the glade. "You live *here*, Trevor. You belong here as part of one of the oldest families in England. If you would cease your sulking, you would see that the new marquess is nothing like the old."

"You can stop denying it now. You definitely have a *tendre* for my cousin."

Winter studied Trevor with a shake of her head, and just gave up. So what if it was true, she thought, short of burying her head in her hands. Rory had seen her naked, touched her, made love to her on numerous occasions in numerous places. How did a woman forget that? Nothing could ever come of her feelings, but commiserating with Trevor was a little like confiding in an old friend.

And she remembered what Mrs. Casselberry had once said about Trevor. *He would have settled down with Miss Lavinia, miss.* Probably because he was in love with the girl, Winter thought. Poor Trevor.

"Aren't we just a fine pair?" she said.

"Sulking?" He threw back her previous accusation. "Is that what I've been doing?'

"Terribly."

For a moment, neither spoke.

"Can you stand?" she asked. "Where does it hurt?"

"My pride. If you count that I am now sitting on it."

She offered to help him stand and he took her hand. Trevor walked her to the stable. Suddenly they were twelve again and their old camaraderie returned as Trevor began to reminisce about old times. They had spent so many hours of their childhood at the lake, swimming and fishing and climbing trees, just being friends before he'd been sent off to Eton and Oxford, and life had changed for them both. He put his arm around her, asking if she still remembered attending the fair where he had kissed her behind the mountebank's wagon. She leaned into him, but didn't tell him she still had the picture they had taken together that day tucked in her secret whatnot drawer.

She looked up at him and studied his fair features, trying to find a little of Rory in him, and wondering what her childhood would have been like had Trevor's older cousin been around.

"I could end this absurdity for you. We could marry," Trevor said. "That would settle both our problems."

"You don't love me, Trevor. Why would you wish to wed me?"

"The way I see it, people don't marry for love. I know your income from teaching at the parish school won't be enough to sustain you indefinitely. You loved me once."

"What about Lavinia?"

He frowned. "What about her?"

"You should be asking her."

"I am asking you, Winter."

Old Ben awaited her next to the buggy, and she was relieved to see him. He had tied Mrs. Kincaid's mare to the boot. At Winter's approach, the horse pranced a sprightly jig, pulling at the reins. Winter ran her hand along the mare's satiny withers. "I didn't think she would ever be well again, Mr. Brown."

"You can thank his lordship for seeing she was properly cared for, Miss," the hostler informed her with pride as he climbed into the buggy. "He put me in charge."

Winter lifted her face to Trevor. He held a lock of her hair, his eyes contemplative as they touched hers. "I should never have let you go all those years ago."

But he *had* let her go.

He'd given her up for something he'd wanted more than he'd wanted her, she thought, aware of the slight tremble in her hand and knowing the reason was somewhere in the grand estate behind her.

"I have to leave, Trevor," she said.

Her clammy palms curled into her serviceable shale gray shawl that covered an equally serviceable black cotton dress, and she felt an unwelcome longing again to be that woman she was at the ball.

Along the inside of the stable's darkened interior, Rory propped one shoulder against a wooden brace and watched Winter leave. Trevor had said something to her just before she'd climbed into the cart and now also watched her, his elbows resting on the white paddock fence, unaware that Rory stood thirty feet behind him.

Then Trevor turned and marched off in the direction of the house with a long-legged stride. Rory abandoned his pose, only when he was sure his cousin was well and truly gone. He walked over matted straw to the doorway, stirring the blooded mares in the stalls beside him. He leaned against the doorframe. He could see Winter's buggy in the distance,

a fading speck moving along the hedgerow-lined lane that
twisted over the manicured parkland and its ancient oaks
and elms, a world that now belonged to him.

Winter Ashburn belonged to him, too. But she didn't yet
know it.

Even from this distance, he still felt her presence, so tac-
tile it was as if she had pushed her hands inside his jacket
and touched his beating heart. He watched until her buggy
turned a corner and was gone. After a moment, he shoved
away and followed in Trevor's wake to the house.

"My lord! My lord!"

He looked toward Smothers's voice and saw him huffing
and puffing like a bellows up the incline from the direction
of the cemetery. "I thought you were still at the cemetery,
my lord. Mrs. Casselberry said you had gone down there
after ye returned. But you weren't there, my lord."

"No, I'm standing here. What is it Smothers?"

"Yes, my lord." He handed Rory a note. "This came for
you earlier."

Recognizing the writing, Rory unfolded the note.

"The ruffian talked his way past three smitten maids,
my lord, before I knew he was even in the house. Said you
knew him from the old country and would be offended if we
didn't allow him inside. I found him entertaining the kitchen
staff over hot scones and jam, all the ladies tittering over his
every word." Lowering his voice as if someone might hear
them standing in the open a hundred yards from the house,
Smothers added in a properly affronted tone. "I suspect he
pocketed two place settings of silver, my lord."

A corner of Rory's mouth tilted into a grin as he stuffed
the note in his jacket pocket and glanced surreptitiously
around the courtyard for the man in question. One of the

three men Winter had seen him with at the fair in Henley that Rory had sent to keep watch over the baron. "To be sure, he probably did, Smothers."

"Baron Richly will see you now, my lord," Richly's butler said to Rory, turning on his polished heel, obviously expecting to be followed.

Rory had arrived at Everleigh just after breakfast the next morning. He had been left in the foyer for the past half hour. He followed the butler to a darkly paneled room at the end of a long corridor. It was not a pleasant room, nor was it overtly appointed with the trappings of wealth. He recognized the game Richly played, the challenge the man was making to Rory's rank and status, the complete arrogance of a man who felt safe and secure in his power to intimidate.

Rory strode past the baron's guards, his eyes landing on Richly behind the oaken desk.

"My dear Lord Granbury." Richly stood. "How pleasant to see you so soon after your return. My condolences on your loss. But your grandfather had been ill for quite some time. His death was not unexpected."

Rory sat in the chair the baron offered. "But then death is the one thing we can all eventually expect. Is it not, Richly? You can save your profane sentiments. I'm not here for your condolences."

Richly lounged back in the chair. "I assume you are here then to discuss our business arrangements? You have received the documents my bank has sent over for your signature?"

"I have my own arrangement to present to you." Rory removed the folded packet of papers from within his pocket and tossed it onto the desk. "I am severing all contracts between our two families."

Without moving to untie the string around the bundle, the baron said, "You take our business agreements lightly, my lord." His tone now less affable. "In my recent inquiries, sir, I have discovered you have no assets in any bank in England. You own no property. You are exactly as rumored. A varlet, my lord. You do not have the funds or the tenants to bring Granbury Court out of debt."

Rory kept all his assets in his sister's name in a bank in Scotland. He'd made sure no one knew where he kept his funds until he was sure when he would need them.

But what suddenly bothered him was if, months before he had come to Granbury Court, Richly had known of his existence. Why had the baron only now conducted a search into Rory's financial status?

"Since you have not honored the betrothal contract then I will expect you to hand over the twenty thousand acres you owe me."

Rory contemplated Richly. "All very aboveboard legal maneuvering. Is this how you stole Everleigh?"

"Ah." Richly nodded his head as if he were some wise sage. "Then the rumors are true about you and my niece. I was wondering what would finally get you in front of me. Now I can see I blundered in my assumption that it was Granbury Court that brought you here."

Richly crossed his legs, and allowed the full force of his attention to settle on Rory. "Have you enjoyed fucking her, Granbury?"

Rory had never been more aware of the blood rushing through his veins, the roar in his ears, the urge to kill a man. As the baron's satisfaction heated his eyes, the man had no idea how close he was to dying.

"I see, it is all you can do not to rip out my throat."

Richly said, taking pleasure in recognizing Rory knew the truth about what the baron had done to Winter. "Frankly, I could not care less what my niece does with herself and with whom. She and I reached an understanding about our . . . *family* relationship years ago. But if you think to offer her marriage"—the baron chuckled as if amused by the idea—"I can already tell you what her answer will be."

"You know a lot for someone who couldn't care less," Rory replied, his blood ice-cold in his veins.

"My niece is twenty-one," Richly replied. "But she is not as independent of me as she might have led you to believe. You will learn soon enough that she is a devious little bitch quite adept at getting what she wants. She has the entire town wrapped around her finger and doing her bidding. And I see that includes duping you, too, into fighting her battles for her. Will you kill me for her?"

Rory rose to his feet. Behind him, he heard the two men stir. Without turning, he warned, "I promise you if either of your two gossoons makes one move toward me, it will be their last. Call them off. Now."

The baron's gaze flickered uneasily to the door, and the men settled back against the wall. The malice in the baron's small dark eyes eclipsed prudence. "If you want her, my lord, you can have her. For the price of the twenty thousand acres that I lease." He opened his arms. "Granbury Court is still surrounded by ten thousand acres entailed to your estate that no one can touch. And of course"—he relaxed in the chair, as if he believed his coup complete—"you still hold the manse of crumbling stones where you currently reside."

"I still hold it all."

"But for how long?"

Rory leaned his palms on the desk. "I will offer ten thousand acres, pay off the mortgage you hold on the rest of my property, and recompense you for your crops over the next five years as per terms of your lease," he said, the swelling need to protect Winter driving his actions, to hell with consequences. "In return you will also sign over custodial guardianship of her brother and mam to me."

Richly sat back in the chair as if to gauge what he had missed in his "careful" research into Rory. "You have no such funds."

"Not in your banks. And if I have my way no one else will either."

"A threat?"

In a voice void of emotion, Rory said, "I'm no sixteen-year-old girl without recourse or means. There is nothing you can throw at me that I can't throw back harder," he said in the lowest of tones. "Take my deal or the only Granbury land you will ever see will be out your windows."

Richly rose to his feet. "I'll consider your offer. Just as you once considered mine, my lord."

"You do that, baron. And if you *ever* go near your niece again or do her harm in any way, ask yourself first," Rory's voice lowered, "just how long does it take for a man to bleed out with his throat cut?"

Richly's color darkened. "You'll only be giving me the other ten thousand in due course, Granbury. I have no doubt you'll be back."

But Rory was already walking out of the room.

# Chapter 17

**R**ory made a detour around the town, deliberately avoiding being seen by the locals. He skirted the edge of the woods. A mile outside of the village he glimpsed the glow from a cooking fire.

Rory wore no jacket. The day had been inordinately warm and he welcomed the cooler evening air against his face. He'd waited until nightfall to come here. His horse stirred dust. The ground was parched and in need of rain. The brief tempests in June had not been enough. Strange that he could look at the sky now and think only about crops on his land. A moment later, he saw the *vardo*, the Gypsy wagon of the Rom, beneath the trees. One man was in camp sitting beside the fire. Dressed in well-worn black silk trousers, an opened-neck white shirt with puffy sleeves, and a crimson velvet jacket, the man came to his feet as Rory rode into camp.

Rory had worked with Restell Ryder on and off for years. Mostly off since Ryder had been working in Cairo since seventy-five. He happened to have been in London last month, and Ware had tapped him for his services.

"I received your message yesterday," Rory said.

"There was a robbery outside town two days ago," Kestell

said. "The culprit was neither the sheriff nor your cousin. I had men on both."

"An outsider?"

Restell took the bit by the shank and ran his hand over the horse. "The couple robbed said one of them was a woman with dark hair. Both were masked."

"But not enough to hide the woman's hair color." Rory looked away, considered that and frowned. "Have you found where the townspeople meet?"

"This place had been quiet as a church for weeks."

"The baron goes nowhere without being followed," Rory said. "He especially does not go near Miss Ashburn."

"Someone is already at Everleigh watching his movements."

Rory peered around the glade. "I don't think we will have any trouble from the villagers, but I suggest you continue to stay out of sight. Unless of course someone is trespassing. Then you have my permission to bring him or her to me."

"Is it true then? Is your sister coming back to stay for a while?"

Rory narrowed his eyes and leaned into the saddle. "I think you would have learned your lesson the last time you saw her."

Restell laughed and released the bit as Rory swung the horse away.

It was the moonlight upon her face that roused Winter from a deep slumber. That, and the warm body spooned against her back. She opened her eyes to the window. Pale radiance invaded her bedchamber. She eased to her back. Rory lay beside her, his dark head sharing her pillow only inches away from her. His eyes were closed.

She had not heard him come into the room and didn't know how long he had been in her bed. She tried to move away so she could turn on her side in the crowded bed, but she found herself pulled against him. His eyes opened.

Stretched taut against the strength of his body, his arousal insinuating itself against her hip and desire explicit in his eyes, he needed her, she realized, perhaps in the same way she needed him.

His fingers wrapped in her hair and he pressed his lips to the pulse at her throat. "I've missed you."

"I didn't think you would ever come here again," she said softly.

He smoothed the hair from her face and kissed her and she felt his reply against her mouth. "I'm here now."

She wrapped her arms around his neck. "I'm so sorry about everything that has happened. I wanted to go to you so badly."

His head lowered and he kissed her. "Shh," he said into her mouth. As she responded, his mouth passionately ravaged hers.

When he finally pulled away, she slid her toes along his calf. "How is it you can get into this cottage when I take care to lock it up so well?"

"Locked doors are irrelevant," he said simply, though his gaze lacked simplicity as he moved over her. "Especially when they keep me from you."

The quiet of the room surrounded them like velvet solace. The summer air smelled of lilies from the garden below the window and the scent of cloves from his hair.

His fingers entwined with hers, pressing them into the mattress. She accepted his weight against her. He settled himself between her legs. Then he caught her mouth for another long, hard kiss. His hand caressed her waist and the curve of her hip, exploring the delicate inner area of her thighs and she stared up into his eyes, their burning brightness unmasked beneath the thick fringe of his lashes. He pushed inside her where she wanted him to be. And then he was part of her.

She slid her fingers through the tangle of his curling hair. With his breath harsh in her ear, he made love to her. Her eyes drifted shut. Soon her doubts became as irrelevant as locked doors, even those that were barred against her heart. And when she awoke in the morning, the pale sunlight had replaced the moonbeams in her bedroom and a chatty squirrel sat outside the window. Rory's eyes were open and watching her.

She smiled at him. "Why did you never once in your life visit Granbury Court?" she asked, easing a lock of hair from his brow.

For a long time he said nothing. Then he surprised her by answering. "Because my grandfather disinherited my father for disgracing him. Because he hated my sister and me for the Rom in our veins. Or at least I thought he did. The man was too proud to even compose a bloody letter and explain himself or his actions. He's dead and he still confuses the hell out of me. *You* confuse the hell out of me." His gaze encompassed hers. "Marry me, Winter."

She stared at him, her heart beating so loudly she thought he could surely hear it. Fear reared its head all over again like a seven-headed dragon that refused to die.

She sat up, spilling her hair over her shoulder. "I cannot."

"I know the baron has legal guardianship of your family, Winter. We'll find a way to protect them."

"You've been to see him?" At his silence, she clenched her jaw and looked away. "Did he accuse me of manipulating you?" she demanded to know, bringing her gaze back to his. "He must have said dreadful things to you."

"I don't care what he said."

"I hate him. I truly do. Were I a man . . . he would never have stolen Everleigh from me. I would have . . ." Her blackest thoughts froze her words.

"You can't kill him," Rory quietly said, "and I can't kill him for you."

"He can hurt you. He's responsible for trying to kill *you*."

"I don't know that he is. Do you have proof? What would he have to gain?"

"Control over Trevor. If he ever knew about us . . . Truly, Rory, if you had thought the proposal through to its conclusion, you would know my past alone precludes me from making a proper bride to a marquess." She cupped his face between her palms. "Why can't you just be satisfied with what we have?"

"Because I want more. More than this. I need a bride."

"How could you possibly consider marriage to me?"

He glared, "Hell, I don't know. Maybe I like you. Maybe you're convenient and you're saving me from having to put up with all those mewling mamas and their daughters charging my doorstep. Christ, why do people get married?"

He rolled out of bed. His mercury-quick change in demeanor struck her to near silence. Despite knowing many of his moods, she had never seen this one.

"You think you are protecting me." Her voice was a whisper. "You aren't. He'll find a way through me to destroy you."

Rory shrugged on his trousers. "Where were you two nights ago?"

Confused by the question, she answered, "Here."

"Did you know there was a robbery on the roads outside town? Tell me you did, Winter, and you'll tell me who is involved."

She stood and yanked the sheet around her. "I wouldn't keep something like that a secret."

"Then arrange a meeting between me and the leader of your people," he said as he shrugged into his shirt. "It is time we have a pertinent discussion about our combined futures."

"A meeting?" She could barely respond. "So you can throw out more accusations and carry through with your threats?"

"I want the crimes to stop. Is it Derwood to whom I need to go?" His quicksilver gaze challenged her silence. He cocked a brow. "And I thought we had moved past the lies between us and started to trust."

She swept past him to open the bedroom door, but he grabbed her wrist. She looked down at the fingers and was tugged gently to stand in front of him. "This is important to me, Winter."

"Lord"—she raised her gaze to the ceiling—"I'm in bed with the enemy. Do you know what that makes me?"

"Smart?"

Winter yanked her hand from his grip. "Mock me all you want. But that makes me a collaborator. A *spy*! I would prefer to be the lowliest thief and lie among swine than be a spy."

"Christ, Winter. Is there nothing you aren't passionate about?"

"You should leave now." She opened the door.

He slammed it shut in her face. Then he leaned his hands against the door trapping her between his arms. He did not have to touch her for her to feel his anger. The threat made her face him squarely.

"Don't you want to know my proposition to you?"

"You can't ask me to betray them to you. You cannot."

The words disappeared as they were uttered, falling like a silent echo beneath a violent sweep of sensations: the steady beat of his heart against her ear, his arms warm and strong around her, her warring emotions every time he was so near. She felt his body tense.

"All right, Winter. I won't ask you again." He pushed away from the door and walked to the bed where he began to dress.

He *didn't* understand. It was because he had every right to ask that tore her heart in two. But she needed these people. They had loved her and taken care of her family when she'd had no one. How did she reconcile her need to do what was right with protecting those she loved?

"What is the proposition?" she quietly asked.

"I can't rebuild Granbury Court alone. I need this town. I need tenants."

She shook her head wondering if he realized what he was suggesting. "The baron owns the lease on most of your land. You'd have to break the leases to rebuild the farms. My uncle would tie you up in court for years and ruin you. No one has that manner of wealth."

"Why don't you let me worry about the baron?"

She searched his eyes, seeking any hint that would tell her this was some sort of trick. Rory was about to do what she had both hoped and feared. He was about to entangle himself in Granbury's politics. He must have a substantial fortune, then, to wage a war. But whether he was doing so out of an abiding respect for Granbury Court and the legacy passed down from his grandfather or retribution against the baron for what was done to Rory's grandfather and possibly because he believed the baron was the man behind the attack on him, Winter didn't know.

But for all his courage, Rory Jameson stood alone. She only knew that if he was stepping out on a precarious limb, she could do no less.

"You can promise them the moon and it will make no difference if they do not trust you. Swear you'll let me talk to them first. Then I will arrange a place for you to meet those who wish to hear what you have to say."

"I swear, Winter."

Four nights later, Winter reined in just outside the old empty church that lay at the southernmost edge of Granbury property. Wind snatched at her hair. She looked up at the sky, hoping for rain. The grounds were too dry and the crops needed rain.

She pulled on the bridle straps of the mare she had borrowed from Mrs. Kincaid and moved toward the structure just visible through the oaks. Even above the wind, Winter could hear voices coming from the underground chamber across the old courtyard. She tied her horse near the oaks.

The guard standing outside the stairwell saw her as she approached. "Miss Winter." His youthful voice cracked as he removed his tweed cap. "What are you doing here?"

"Is the sheriff inside with the others?"

The youth moved aside. "Yes, mum."

Descending into a lichen-encrusted stairwell, Winter followed the sound of raised voices. Torchlight lit the narrow chamber. Two dozen men were inside. When she entered, the room grew silent.

"I am the one who called this meeting," she said.

Winter looked around her at all the weathered faces as the voices rose in concern. She knew each man present. They trusted her. She reminded them of that trust before she launched into the reasons she'd called this meeting. When she had finished, another murmur of discord met her ears.

"Toffs have spent centuries lobbing arrows at each other," someone said. Others voiced agreement. "It's none of our affair. If they're fighting amongst themselves then they aren't fighting us. Let them destroy each other."

"If you think to resume activities along these roads, he'll hunt the lot of you down," she told them. "I called this meeting because I want to give you a chance at another direction that he is willing to offer. Just listen to what he has to offer."

A deafening silence met her.

"And if we don't? Then what?" another demanded. "Not a one among us is not guilty of some 'angin' offense, lass. Including you."

When the men began to rise from their seats, Winter raised her voice over the growing din. "Lord Granbury is in a position to help this community."

"Because he says so, lass?" the sheriff quietly said.

"Yes. Because he said so and because I believe he can."

"What did the last lord do?" Derwood asked. "The people got their rents raised three times. Most of us don't own anything anymore. No one knows who this toff is."

She pressed her fist to her chest. "I trust him to keep his word."

Sheriff Derwood rose from the wooden trestle table at
the front of the room. The flame from a candle on the table
weighted the frown on his face. "You shouldn't have told
him about us, Winter."

"He won't harm you." He'd promised, she wanted to
shout at them all.

"He were the one what killed Whitey," one of Everleigh's
tenants replied.

"And threatened to 'ang the lot of us," someone else
said.

"If Lord Granbury had not been armed when he was attacked, he would now be the one who is dead." Winter spoke
to each of them, cowing some, emboldening others to anger.
She only knew that she was losing them. "Whoever attacked
him meant to kill him. I defy any of you to tell me a man
doesn't have a right to defend himself."

To her despair, they each began to file past her out of
the room. Suddenly the men stopped and as one collective
body backed slowly into the room. Rory suddenly stepped
beneath the low-arched doorway.

Winter barely retained the gasp in her chest. Candlelight
glanced off his dark hair. He wore a black sailor's sweater,
black trousers, and dull black leather boots so as not to re-
flect a shine. Clearly he knew how to dress in the night like a
thief. Disbelief scoured her soul. He had *followed* her.

Followed her when he had said he would not.

He let his eyes touch hers before moving over the men
standing near the stone walls, then settled on the sheriff.
"Are you all my audience then?"

The sheriff's eyes narrowed on her. "Do we have a
choice?"

"Life is filled with choices." Rory moved next to Winter.

The heat of him burned through her cloak to settle in her belly. "Do I rob, do I steal, do I fight, do I do nothing and let someone else fight for me? Do I stop hiding in shadows? I don't need to tell you to what I am referring. Am I speaking to the brain or the brawn of your little merry band of thieves and agitators?"

Color heightened Sheriff Derwood's face. His voice hesitated but only for the breath it took to say, "I am an officer of the shire."

Winter tried to step between them but both men blocked her with their arms. "This is *not* what we agreed to talk about," she said.

Rory hadn't even looked at her. But his hand held her arm.

"Some of you may not yet know who I am. I am Rory Jameson, Lord Granbury. This shire is my new home. Not one that I wanted, but nevertheless one that I have. I will be residing here for some time. Some of you also know that my first day in Granbury was not one of my best."

A man in front singled out Winter. "Is this what ye brought him here for?"

"I have no want to bring the lot of you up on charges," Rory said. "I'm interested in finding two men. I think you know who at least one of them is. He rode a gray mare and goes by the last name of Stronghold. He may be responsible for a robbery a few days ago along these roads. I want both men delivered to me. In return, I'm interested in rebuilding what belongs to all of us."

Sheriff Derwood suddenly grinned. "You have bollocks coming out here, my lord. I will give you that. Even if you are a fool." To Winter he said. "You ought not have trusted a toff to keep his word."

"She isn't responsible for leading me here—"

"Bloomin' 'ell, she ain't, m'lord," someone in the back murmured.

"Beggin' yer pardon, m'lord," a surly fellow to Winter's left replied, "but what is it yer wantin' us to do?"

"I need men to rebuild what once used to be at Granbury Court. I need masons, carpenters, and eventually tenants to farm the lands. I need people who are willing to work for wages and for a stake in what I have to offer."

"A *promise* of money?" the same surly fellow asked. "Not a one of us here hasn't already heard that promise or isn't owed something by the old marquess."

Rory's gaze met the man's squarely and without hesitation. "If anyone doubts my intentions or that I can pay you for your services"—he dropped a bag of coins onto a stone bench—"this is a start. A large sum is about to be deposited in a bank in Bisham as well as in Henley, High Wycombe, and London. Anyone who works Granbury lands will be working hard, but will find a good living to be had. You may pass the word to your friends."

"What does Richly have to say about you taking his lands?" someone asked.

"You are mistaken. He is on my lands." Rory moved his attention across each man's face as he took Winter's arm. "Think about your choices, men. Or you can find your bloody way to Tyburn without the baron's help."

The room settled into a deep silence.

"What about Miss Winter?"

"She is no longer your concern, gentlemen. Now I bid each of you good night."

Without asking her, he pulled her outside. Her jaw ached from the effort to hold back her anger. A montage of wind-whipped trees stirred the air like a cauldron fitting her mood as she strode past him and mounted her horse. He caught up to her on the road, and they rode the distance to her cottage in silence.

At her cottage, the hound greeted their arrival, distracting Rory as he stilled his agitated horse. Winter had already dismounted when he walked into the stable. "Are you going to speak to me?" he finally asked.

"You don't want to hear what I have to say to you."

She swept past him and ran across the moonlit yard to the door. Her hand fumbled in her pocket for the key as she heard him call her name. She shoved the key into the lock and swung open the door.

"Winter, wait."

She could hear his boot steps behind her, the sound consuming her with panic. She pushed her shoulder against the door and slammed it shut in his face, dropping the bolt as she saw the latch move.

"Dammit, Winter."

A wetness spilled over her cheeks and she wiped the heel of her hands over her face as she stepped away from the door. "I *trusted* you!"

Without lighting a lamp, Winter ran upstairs to her brother's room, which overlooked the stable yard. She'd left the window open to let in the summer air. She stood to the side and peered down into the yard.

Rory was backed against the white picket fence, looking up at the cottage, rubbing the knuckles of one hand as if they'd been injured against the door. She pressed her back to the wall and slid slowly to the floor beneath the window, drawing her knees to her chest. He'd used her.

Her umbrage was so fierce and blinding she saw nothing

else but that violation, not even that some of the men had responded and seemed to welcome his ideas. For her anger welled from a deeper, blacker despair. He had violated her trust. He had violated *her*. Violated.

She pressed her hands against her head. Who in this shire would ever trust her again?

"What are you doing in here?" Trevor paused in the doorway.

Rory sat sprawled in a chair before the fire in Trevor's chambers, his boots crossed at the ankles, his hands cupping a tumbler of cognac. The hour was late. No amount of drink tempered his current mood.

He peered at Trevor. "Waiting for you."

Trevor yanked off his gloves and dropped them on the ormolu side table. "You just bloody fobbed off one of the wealthiest men in England tonight. Thirty guests were at that supper to honor you—"

"And did they?" Rory raised his glass as if in toast. "Honor me?" He sipped the drink, savoring the burn.

"I told Richly you left today for Henley on business and did not make it back due to a broken carriage axle."

Rory leaned forward in the chair. "Richly can fuck himself. I don't need you to lie on my behalf. He knew I wouldn't be there tonight."

"Did you stop to consider what your actions would mean to Granbury Court? You may not care about what happens to yourself, but I care what happens to this estate and my own name."

Rory dragged a handful of folders from the other side of the chair and tossed them on the floor. They slid across the burgundy carpet, spilling financial plans, designs, and plat variances over the floor. Rory had found them in Trevor's study along with papers on crop profitability and animal husbandry.

"Are you the one who did the research in those folders?"

Trevor's jaw clenched. "I should have bloody known nothing I have is sacred in this house."

Rory propped his elbows on his knees. "How can I implement half of what I read about in those folders?"

The steam left Trevor's body. "You're interested in my ideas?"

"I don't understand all of them, but I do understand the difference between profit and bankruptcy. Why did you never talk to Granbury about your ideas?"

"I did," Trevor said. "Or that is, I tried. But we have people who manage such things. Solicitors, estate managers, bankers, and they are old school. Nothing I've proposed is inexpensive to implement. After the land was mortgaged, we would never have found anyone to invest the capital."

"If you could implement your ideas, what are the odds of this estate becoming profitable again?"

"You do understand the entailed part of the estate cannot be confiscated, not even for nonpayment of taxes. No matter what, you would still have this house and the land it sits on."

Rory understood the laws of entailment as granted by the patent of the title he now carried. He also understood that without the means to support his grandfather's precious legacy, the inheritance would bleed him dry, and, in the end, he would still lose everything. Granbury needed tenants and farms rebuilt. He needed a plan. "This house is no good to any of us if we do not have the income to support even its day-to-day expenses. A hundred people who work for their wages at Granbury Court might take exception to starving."

Trevor sank into the chair across from Rory. His eyes went to the folders on the floor. "There is the fishery on the river. It was a profitable venture at one time. Our horses are some of the best in the country and in another few years, we have a chance to bring in huge purses at the Ascot and Manning Downs. The land? We need tenants to farm and pay us rents, which necessitates rebuilding farms. All of which still takes time and enormous capital. I repeat, we won't find a bank to loan to us."

"If I offered up fifty thousand, would that be enough of a start?"

*"Fifty thousand."* Trevor slumped back in the chair. His hard stare came at Rory. "You never spent a day on any prison barge, did you?"

Rory, too, sat back and crossed his ankles. "No."

"Fifty thousand." Over steepled fingers, Trevor contemplated Rory, nervous excitement brightening his eyes. For the first time since meeting his younger cousin, Rory saw the man smile. "His lordship mortgaged this place to the hilt." Trevor considered the rest, as if he were calculating in his head. "Thirty thousand to begin. That doesn't include death taxes still owed. Fifty thousand is a solid start. Enough to temporarily circumvent the baron."

Rory would have spent his life's blood to see that the baron did not get a square inch of this estate. He stared into his tumbler a moment.

"You aren't doing all this to keep our servants from starving."

Rory's mouth twisted into something that was not quite a smile. "I've been told Granbury land has been in our family for four hundred years. Maybe I'm just sentimental and want to save what I have."

"I never believed you would remain after His Lordship passed."

Rory rose to his feet. "My goals have changed."

"Are you in love with her?" Trevor asked.

Rory's gaze fixed on his cousin's face. Then he tilted the tumbler, quaffed the last of the cognac, and set down the glass without answering. "Pay off the banknotes. Dissolve the contracts. From now on, I deal with Richly."

He said his good-nights and walked past generations of Jamesons to his own chambers in the main wing of the house.

Smothers had appointed himself Rory's personal manservant, appearing every morning at dawn and every evening before bedtime with port and cheese as he helped Rory dress for bed. Unable to fault the man's meticulous devotion to routine, Rory had not complained. But tonight he dismissed Smothers.

Standing in his shirtsleeves in front of the window, his braces hanging against his trousers, he shoved his hands into his pockets and stared up at the full moon shining down on Granbury Court.

Was he in love?

He knew nothing of love. Such sentiment was defined by bards who bayed at the moon with lovelorn sonnets on the brain. Yet, here he was, finding he wanted to believe in something that might not exist and wondering if this was where he belonged.

Indeed he might know nothing of love, but he did know longing—the longing to belong somewhere.

He looked away from the window. And at once, he knew

he could not return to the solitary world he'd built these past ten years.

His gaze fell on the table where he had taken supper and the folded sheet of paper next to the lamp. Rory picked up the drawing of himself he'd stolen from Winter's tablet. He felt no gratification looking at himself. But seeing himself through Winter's eyes made him feel . . . alive.

Tucking the drawing away in the nightstand beside his bed, he rehashed every damned thing that had occurred that night. He accepted that he had hurt her. He'd known he would when he'd followed her. He'd been right to do what he'd done. Results sometimes meant dealing with the unpleasant means to that end. Until now, logic had always insulated him. Until now.

Just before dawn, Rory rose and dressed before Smothers arrived. He felt the dearth of warmth within the old manse's walls the moment he departed his chambers. The draft eased along the darkened passageways of the old Elizabethan house. He stopped in the guardroom where his grandfather had lain in state and where hundreds of mourners filed through to pay their final respects.

At his request, little had been moved in this room since the funeral. A breastplate surrounded by various orders and badges of honor, gilt spurs of knighthood still hung on the wall. His grandfather had been a Knight of the Garter, as Rory was. One day, Rory's own life would hang on that wall, and if he had his way about the future, his children would be standing in the place he now stood. He needed only to find a way to marry their future mother.

# Chapter 18

**D**awn broke clear and bright in Winter's chambers. Opening her eyes, she stared at the cracks in the ceiling. Her heart raced and she was wondering what awakened her when she heard the soft whicker of a horse outside. The sound had come from the stable yard. Alarmed, she rose, and snatching up her wrapper on the way downstairs, she shoved her arms into the sleeves and buttoned it as she peered through the shutters.

At first, she saw nothing. The hound wasn't barking. Perhaps she had imagined the sound. But the sound came again and this time Winter hurried into the mudroom. She eased aside the shutters and peered outside.

Indeed, she *had* heard a horse. A black mare with three white stockings and a white flame on her nose stood over the trough slurping water. She wore a bridle but no saddle and dragged a pair of reins as she sauntered into the garden and began to eat the row of lettuce.

Winter flung opened the door and ran outside to rescue her plants. She grabbed the shank of the mare's bit, gently pulled the mare away, then examined her find. Truly, she was a horse of quality stock, with a shiny sleek coat and perfect proportions. Uncommon. "Where did you *come* from, sweetheart?" she asked the horse.

Sliding her hands over the mare's flanks and back, beneath the thick mane, she stepped around to peer toward the road.

Sunlight had already burned away the morning mist that usually hovered over the ground. The scent of larkspur touched her nostrils. She smelled lilac, too, and something else more elusive, mixing with the scent of dry earth.

Tobacco.

Alerted to another's presence, she whirled and saw Rory. She had missed his presence when she'd come outside. He sat with his back against the trunk of the old oak with branches that spread a canopy of shade over the cottage. He wore a light woolen coat. His white shirt beneath was unbuttoned at his collar and stark against the tanned column of his throat. His face was blank, but the corner of his mouth twitched and then he appeared to study the cheroot in his hand. He looked as if he hadn't slept last night.

"The Greeks would call her a Trojan horse," he said casually.

She didn't want to feel her heart race when she stared at him or find his statement amusing, but she had no more control of either of those emotions than she had of the sunrise. "I believe the Greeks hid *inside* the horse."

"But this particular horse really is a gift. Not a ruse to get me inside . . . your barred gate."

In another world, Winter might have let herself drown in the dark passion she saw in his eyes. In a kinder world, she would not be standing here at all, berating herself and Rory for making her heart race and for reminding her of impossible dreams and how carnal desire felt. But he had lied to her, and she could not escape the sense of betrayal.

"Please go away, my lord."

The tip of his cheroot brightened with his inhale, then faded. He stabbed it out in the dirt before he rose. She thought about running back into the house, but fleeing him a second time would only look too undignified. She schooled her features and managed to portray indifference as he stopped in front of her, casting his shadow over her face.

His long coat brushed her knee. He held his gloved hand out to the mare and offered a cube of sugar. "Her name is Flame."

"Who named her?"

His hands stroked and patted the mare's neck. "The people I bought her from at Henley."

"The Gypsies."

"Rom," he corrected without looking at her.

She lowered her eyes. "I seem to always be saying the wrong thing. You must think I am a terrible snob."

"Aren't you?"

Her face heated. He was skilled at keeping conversation moving in exactly the direction she did not want to go. "Are you referring to the reason I can't marry you?"

"Can't implies another reason that has nothing to do with whether you want to or not."

She folded her arms. "You lied to me about your intent last night. You set me up to lead you to those men. You had no right to impose your plan on me. No right to take matters into your own hands when doing so affects my life. You haven't exactly inspired me with your integrity."

He stepped backward and into the sunlight spilling through the canopy of branches overhead, looking dark and beautiful, like her drawing of him. The one he'd stolen. "Maybe it isn't my integrity that has ever interested you."

"Were you really drummed out of the cavalry ten years ago for conduct unbecoming of an officer?"

Her abrupt question and its explicit directness silenced him and lent her an instant of satisfaction. His jaw tightened. "In part. Yes."

The admission shocked her. She hadn't expected him to reply, much less reveal the truth. "Why?"

"I admit to my character flaws. There are things about me that I doubt you will ever understand."

His hand came around her cheek and tilted her face. "Accept the mare, Winter, as a gift from me. Or agree to marry me and take her as a betrothal gift. Become my partner."

Hot tears suddenly burned in her eyes. Her gaze turned to the mare. "Have you ever given another woman a horse?"

"No." He brushed his lips against hers with an unhurried, gentle inducement to open her mouth and allow him inside.

And she found herself seduced not only by him, but by the security and material comforts he could provide. Self-righteous nobility and vengeance suddenly seemed less important to her when he could see that her mam's medicines would be paid for and that Perry and Robert *both* could be attending Harrow next year together, all exclusive of the baron's support.

Her heart told her this was a silly argument. Accept his offer and his promise at face value. But her brain did not so easily capitulate when there was far more than desire that melded into the landscape of her future.

For Rory Jameson was two men. He was both the light cast by a flame and the darkness beyond the light's reach. He was the man she'd glimpsed when she'd seen him looking up at the portrait of his father and standing in the cemetery in front of his grandfather's tomb. And he was the man who would win at any cost.

He was the man who had deceived her last night and who hid another life inside the one he now lived. She didn't trust him.

Love she could learn to live without. But trust?

She'd trusted him.

Just as she'd trusted her parents to keep her and Perry safe. As she'd trusted in her father's love for her mother, yet, when his life became rough and proved to be unkind, he found shelter in another's arms. She'd believed in the goodness of her uncle's character when he had first come to visit at Everleigh and had helped her father out of debt. Her father had allowed him to purchase the beautiful gown she had worn for her debut that year. She'd been seduced by him as well, as he bore gifts for his niece, and she'd trusted in his intentions and generosity. And then one night . . .

One night the time came to repay the piper as he so eloquently put it after an evening of drinking that brought him to her room. Yes, indeed, everything she'd trusted in came with a price and eventually betrayal.

Now the only thing she truly trusted was her own judgment.

She tilted her head to look up at Rory dry-eyed. Tendrils of her dark hair shifted against her shoulders drawing his gaze. "What is it you were doing in your life before your sister received your grandfather's letter?" she quietly asked.

Looking away from her, he suddenly seemed very tired. "Nothing of import, Winter."

"A man raised by Gypsies does not amass a fortune doing

nothing of import. You were doing something of import for someone. I may have been a thief but I was an honest thief."

"A saint in the guise of a devil."

"Far better to be that than the devil in the guise of a saint. You use your honesty as a cloak. The way you took Trevor down that day near the cemetery, the gun you wear . . . I asked once if you were a criminal."

His eyes crinkling at the corners, he scratched his chin. That he should find amusement in her distress made her furious. "I hope you did not sink your fortune into Granbury Court because of me."

He laughed, but when his eyes bored into hers, she saw no humor. "I admit to leaping upon my white charger with the desire to avenge you, love. That is what you have wanted me to do all along. To fight for you? But fifty thousand pounds is a lot for any man to invest for the mere privilege of spending time with you, love. Don't carry the burden of my welfare on your shoulders. I'm here because I want to be."

Fifty *thousand pounds?*

"Have you decided Granbury Court no longer warrants saving?" he asked, his mood no longer amenable to her concern. "Or am I not poor and down-trodden enough for your compassion? When are you going to quit drowning yourself and me in your self-reproach and grief? When are you going to quit blaming yourself for every damn thing that happens to anyone?"

"That isn't fair judgment of me. If anything, I have been your friend."

*"Friend?"*

"But I doubt you even know how to spell the word."

"L-O-V-E-R." His fingers found a wayward curl to torment. "As a general rule I have found women make notoriously poor friends."

She snatched back her curl. "You are right, of course. Friendship is too ambitious a term. The very insinuation implies respect and deep affection. With no secrets. You would be the absolute last man in this entire world I would ever allow myself to . . . to *feel* anything for."

"I have neither the time nor inclination to continuously defend myself or my actions to you, Winter." He swore, then looked away. "I can't, Winter."

"What about the countess? Was the gossip true about the two of you?"

His jaw tightened. "I don't intend to discuss her with you."

Winter thought the words would crush her. She knuckled away a tear. "Where did you go the night you went to London? When your grandfather was ill?"

"Can't you just bloody *trust* me, Winter?"

*"Trust?* How can you ask of me what you do not give back?" She swept around him. But before she could flee, Rory intercepted her at the door.

"Look at me, Winter. There are parts of my life I can never talk about."

"Does that include your relationship with the countess?"

"Past relationship," he said furiously. "Past, Winter, as in over with."

Winter drew in her breath, no longer interested in assessing his temper or her own. "Let go of me."

"Do you know what the real issue is?" he challenged her. "You're a coward. This is one more excuse for you to remain hidden away."

"Please, move aside, my lord."

When he obliged her, she stepped past him and into her cottage. Her sanctuary. The place she would always be safe. She turned with her hand on the door. Rory stood where she had left him.

"When you are ready to grow up and rejoin the real world again, let me know, Winter. And *maybe*, I'll let you know if I'm still interested."

"Winter?" Perry's small voice penetrated her fogged brain.

She lifted her head, and peered at her brother standing in the doorway of her bedroom. Except she wasn't in her bedroom. She was in Mam's room where she had gone last night rather than into her bedroom. She sat on the floor next to the bed, her cheek resting on her forearm. Squinting against the sunlight, she looked behind her at the window.

"What are you doing here, Perry?"

He shrugged and came to sit beside her. His trousers no longer reached his ankles. He'd grown at least two inches this summer. "You didn't come to Mrs. Kincaid's last night for supper like you always do. But I remembered you said I was to go with you to see Mam today."

She sighed and leaned with her back against the bed, resting her head on the mattress. One of her mam's dresses that she had been trying to alter lay on the ground where she had thrown it last night.

For the first time in her twenty-one years, she'd drowned herself in fermented drink. It had taken her longer to find the bottle of wine left over from the yuletide celebration last year than it had to consume it. Now she felt more miserable than she had yesterday.

Perry sat beside her and laid his head on her lap. "Are you angry because I'm late?"

"Perry . . ." She laid her hand on her brother's head. "You are not the cause of my upset."

He sat up. "Why are you in Mam's room?"

"It's cooler in here during the summer." She ruffled her brother's hair. "Find us some eggs for breakfast. Then we are going to see Mam."

After Perry left the room, Winter pushed herself to her feet. Pressing the heel of her palms against her temples, she waited for the throbbing to lessen. Then she gathered up the dress and stuffed it in the armoire.

For a moment as she stood in the doorway, she let her gaze touch the room, then she shut the door.

Twice during the next few days, Winter thought about swallowing her pride and riding to Granbury Court. Rory didn't come to her as she had secretly hoped he would. And by the end of the week, she knew he would not.

Rory had officially taken his place as the Marquess of Granbury. Along with his duties came other rumors that he had severed the baron's leases on his land. He had done what she had both hoped and feared he would. He had involved himself in the affairs of Granbury and sunk a substantial fortune into an estate he hadn't even wanted in the first place. And the shire had taken notice.

In time, his abrupt absence from her life finally bludgeoned her emotions into some semblance of acceptance, but not resignation. Instead, it had given her a new vision of herself. Trevor had once said she would never make an aristocrat's wife. She had never had a Season in London. She hadn't played the pianoforte in five years. Her needlepoint lacked any hint of precision and patience. She'd barely remembered how to waltz.

Indeed, for five years, she had allowed herself to drown in anger. She had let everything she was die in the mote of self-flagellation. Rory had been right about that. In deeming herself unworthy of love, she had opened the door of her soul to guilt, wearing it like a badge of honor, too long fighting from the shadows, putting others at risk, putting everyone else's problems ahead of her own because she had considered herself unworthy of their concern. She had allowed her uncle to win by default.

She'd been a complete and utter coward.

But the whirl of her hazy thoughts no longer left her confused. Indeed, they refocused her determination, imploring her to take care that these emotions were indeed sacred and belonged to the man who had awakened them.

Despite everything she did not know about Rory Jameson, the tenth Marquess of Granbury, there was far more she did know. He might have believed once he was rescuing her from her life. But wishing to marry her eluded the most basic logic, for a man like Rory did not act without reason or on nobility alone. He was too precise, his actions measured more by instinct than emotion. So for him to behave rashly meant he'd certainly cared for her.

For him to ask her to wed him knowing that the baron was her brother's and Mam's legal guardian meant that he had already arranged with her uncle some form of transfer, which meant contracts may have already been signed, which explained her uncle's unusual silence in the wake of Rory's recent lack of action concerning Lavinia.

If Rory had secrets, then maybe he had a reason to keep

them from her. Maybe he was protecting her in the same way she'd been trying to protect him.

Maybe, just maybe, she was not too late to salvage his heart.

It was a hazy late-summer afternoon three days later when Winter took Perry to Granbury Court. Astride her beautiful mare, with her brother in front of her, she held tight to the reins as she brought the horse to a stop.

Sunlight bathed the walls of the noble house stretching across the distant rise, reflected the heat of the day. She kept the mare out of sight near the grove of hawthorn trees. She could feel nervous anticipation budding in Perry's young body as he drew air into his lungs.

"Cooee, Winter, is that Granbury Court?"

"It is."

He fidgeted. "Why couldn't Robert come with us?"

"Robert is Mrs. Kincaid's family now. He won't be coming here to live."

Perry's head lowered. "But I want to live at Everleigh."

"I'm sorry, Perry. As much as I love Everleigh, too, our home is gone."

It was time to look toward their future. Winter steadied the mare and brought her attention back to the road leading to the house. A carriage jingled across the stone bridge toward the gatekeeper's cottage. She wondered who was visiting today. Nervously chewing her lower lip, she looked down at her flower-sprigged yellow muslin gown. But she was determined not to turn tail and flee. She had even brought an old calling card to hand to Smothers.

"I hope we're dressed properly for a visit," she said aloud.

"I'm wearing my socks today. And you're fixed up pretty."

"A different kind of dress, Perry. There are rules for such things."

"But won't his lordship be glad to see us even if we are undressed?"

For a moment, Perry's words made her smile, before she realized, she was no longer sure whether Rory wanted to see her ever again.

She had not seen him since he had left her that morning with the mare. But she had seen his sister and ten-year-old niece last Sunday when they'd attended service at the parish chapel.

Evelyn Macgruder had surprisingly come up to Winter after the service and spoken briefly. Rory's sister would be living at Granbury Court until the end of summer and issued Winter an open invitation to visit.

Perry grew pensive. Winter would not lie to herself. She'd brought him along as a shield, her first line of defense as a buffer between herself and the marquess. Yet, as she playfully nudged him in the ribs, she was surprised by how much she really wanted him to like Granbury Court. He had been six when she had taken him from Everleigh, and he remembered little of the life they had lived there. The feelings she so desperately tried to hide suddenly surfaced.

"It is all rather daunting, isn't it?"

A pair of fallow deer bolted from the grove, momentarily startling the horse. She brought the mare around and held tight to her brother as she studied the thicket of brambles and the distant dry streambed beyond.

"Winter . . ." Perry's small voice trailed. "Is that *girl* here, too?"

Winter laughed. "His lordship's niece? She seemed nice. Don't you think?"

He squirmed. "No."

A shadow crawled over the ground as the warm wind picked up. Winter peered up at the sky. It was now or never.

Smothers formally announced Winter and Master Perry to Eve. She had been entertaining guests in the salon but had *swished* at once to the foyer where Winter nervously waited, to tell her that Rory was currently not in residence.

"He is in London," Eve said.

"I see. I didn't know." Forcing a smile, Winter said, "We should be going. You have guests."

Eve's fingers encased in pale doeskin, touched Winter's arm. "Perhaps you would accept tea privately in the salon." Lowering her voice, she added in a secret whisper and leaning nearer, "Those are his guests I'm entertaining. You would save me, if only for a few minutes." She looked down at Perry. "My daughter has been terribly bored with only her dolls to play with. Perhaps you would allow Smothers to take you upstairs to the playroom."

"He would like that very much, thank you," Winter replied before Perry embarrassed her by blurting out something profane about girls.

After Perry was gone, Eve took her into the blue Delft drawing room next to the foyer as Mrs. Casselberry brought tea and informed Eve that their guests were entertaining themselves over the pianoforte.

"Mamas and their daughters come-a-calling," Eve informed Winter. Spreading her blue silk skirt over the white settee with practiced polish. "I have never seen so many giddy young females. I almost feel sorry for my brother.

I think that is why he escaped as quickly as he did. The coward." Eve smiled as she poured Winter tea.

Winter wrapped her palms around the cup but could think of nothing to say.

"You must know that my brother has put everything he has into this estate," Eve said. "You are important to him, Miss Ashburn, and I wish to understand. Not that my opinion would matter to him. He has always been one to follow his own mind since we were children, to blazes with consequences."

A dark spot of color burned her cheeks. "You must know we have not spoken in days."

Eve stirred sugar into her cup. "I suspected something might be amiss."

Outside, the wind picked up. But only seemed to agitate the heat.

"Why is my brother after Baron Richly?"

Winter looked away. But then she straightened and told Eve about the attack on Rory when he first came to Granbury Court. After a moment's hesitation, she also told Eve about the baron's attack on her when she was sixteen. Winter didn't know why she felt at ease opening up to this woman, but she was suddenly telling Rory's sister her life's story.

"Of course, he would protect you. But if he wanted to marry you, it is because he is in love with you, Miss Ashburn. A person would have to be blind not to have seen it at the ball. Are you in love with my brother?"

Winter set down the teacup with unsteady hands. "Yes. But I'm afraid I have involved him in something dangerous."

Eve sat forward. "Rory is connected to some powerful people who are helping him investigate the baron," she said, holding the lid of the pot as she poured Winter more tea.

"He hasn't told you because those particular people don't want their names bandied about even by him."

Winter dabbed at her eyes with her sleeve. "And yet *you* know."

"I know the people he works with because I used to work for them." Eve relaxed on the settee, reminding Winter of a blue-eyed feline. "How much do you know about my brother's life before he came here?"

"Very little," Winter said, hoping beyond hope to learn something.

"I told him he should tell you. But he is under the delusion that he should act first and explain later. It comes with the training you see. Hence, his reasons for wishing to wed you before you found out anything superfluous that might change your mind. But since we are going to be sisters-in-law, I will tell you that he works for our government. A specific part of it that deals with protecting our national interests."

"I don't understand."

"He is a spy, Miss Ashburn."

Winter choked on the tea.

"Or I should say, was a spy. He worked in counterintelligence. And because I have no doubt this will not change your mind about him, and because I do not suffer the same delusion that you should remain ignorant, I have elected to tell you." Rory's sister leaned forward and patted Winter heartily on the back. "Sometimes I, too, can act first and explain later. How can my dear brother counterbalance that logic when his is equally flawed?"

Numbly, Winter shook her head and set down her cup.

"It also helps"—Eve poured more tea—"that it is one of those tiny little secrets in our community that if you tell anyone else, he'll have to kill you."

*   *   *

The Granbury coach brought Winter and Perry as far as the narrow winding road leading to her cottage. Eve would have taken her farther, but the coach might have been unable to turn around on the narrow road.

Winter had stayed late at Granbury Court and had enjoyed supper as well as Eve's company. But the reality of what Eve had told Winter struck her fully as she watched the carriage amble down the winding road.

She now recognized why Rory seemed to have two sides, why he fit so easily into the night, and why they may not ever be together. He had lied for a living.

"Come on, Winter." Perry dragged her around by the hand and they walked up the drive.

And as she followed Perry, she wondered if it were possible to drown in one's own darkness. Lost in her thoughts, she almost missed seeing the lamp burning in the kitchen.

Snatching Perry back, she pulled him off the drive. "Wait."

Her eyes fell on the path. What she found was a hoof track so recent as to be easily discernible despite the dry soil and approaching night. Someone had recently come down this way. The sound of a horse pulled her attention to the stable. She walked to a place where she could see inside. A horse had been tied to the post. Only one person ever came to visit her on a horse.

"Hurry." She ran with Perry across the yard.

Her hand was on the door, the key in the lock when she saw the gray felt bowler on the table through the window. She opened the door.

She hung her cloak beside the door and walked into the kitchen. Her hand brushed the hat as she hurried into the parlor. And came to an abrupt stop in the doorway. The baron stood in front of the window.

His hands clasped behind his back, he stood with his back to the window waiting for her. Her hands tightened on Perry's shoulders and she edged her brother behind her. "What are you doing in here?"

He wore a mid-calf-link checked topcoat, hardly a suitable riding jacket. If he had not ridden the horse that was in the stable, then who had? Someone else was in the house, she realized. Winter's mouth went dry with fear.

"I want to know who Granbury is," he said.

Winter edged Perry against the stairway. "He is a toff, Uncle. Isn't that what you always wanted to be yourself?"

Advancing on her, the baron held up a paper crushed in his fist. "What business are my affairs to him?"

Alarmed she stared at the papers in his hand. "I don't kno—"

"Solicitors are crawling on my doorstep wanting *my* accounting records for the past five years. He has served papers on *my* bank. I want to bloody know what he thinks he is doing launching an investigation on *me*. Who has that kind of power to authorize such a search?"

Winter blinked in disbelief. A corner of her mouth turned up before she could stop herself. "Perhaps you finally extorted from the wrong person."

*"Extorted?* I had an agreement with the bastard. Ten thousand acres of Granbury land for your hand, sweet."

*Ten thousand acres?* Winter's fists clenched. "Perry," she kept her voice even. "Go upstairs and shut your door." Her eyes on her uncle, she said, "You don't mind if my brother does not have to witness this, do you? Go, Perry," Winter urged when he hesitated. *"Now."*

Perry ran up the stairs. She waited until she heard her brother's door slam. "Ten thousand acres?" she said in growing fury. "What did you do? Promise to remain silent about my past? About something that was not even my fault? Something for which I've felt nothing but shame for five years? *Extortion, Uncle*."

"As fascinating as you might be to me, you have been nothing but a thorn in my backside since the moment I ever laid eyes on you. But you are important to him, and he has something I want."

"You are attempting to swindle him out of his inheritance. Good luck. You finally entangled yourself with the wrong man. He'll destroy you."

His mouth flattened. "Call off Granbury, sweet." He advanced on her. "Or I swear you will learn exactly what I am capable of when provoked.

"Provoked? Oh this is *grand*." She laughed. "This is magnif—"

He backhanded her across the cheek. The blow sent her against the table in the hallway and overturned a chair as she hit the wall with her shoulder. Her vision blackened and she slid to the ground and sat there numb with pain.

"When I'm finished with you, no decent English woman will ever welcome you into her drawing room again."

Her hand came back with blood. "I hope he destroys you. You can't do any more to me than you already have."

"Think not? Ask yourself where your mother is."

Momentarily faint, she struggled to stand. "What have you done?"

"Oh, aye, girl. You forget I have legal guardianship over both your mother and that brat upstairs. I've been good to you letting you have them. I even tried to offer you a settlement, but that wasn't enough for you either."

"What have you *done*?"

"Something I should have done years ago. You and Granbury can *both* go to blazes. Beginning with you, my dear." He raised his hand and with a snap of his fingers, two men appeared from the kitchen. Her uncle's hand closed cruelly over her arm. "You're under arrest for robbery, larceny, attempted murder, *slander*." To one of the men, he said, "Get the boy."

*"No."* Winter kicked out at the man who would go after Perry. The blow connected against his hip. She screamed for Perry to get out of the house, fighting as hands lifted her. A gag was stuffed into her mouth and something that stank—*Oh God*—like ether. Her own scream was the last thing she heard.

# Chapter 19

In the heat and growing darkness of another dying day, Rory crushed the missive Smothers had just brought him. "Richly cannot remain hidden forever. When I find the worm, I'll kill him."

He threw the note at the refuse container near the desk in the library, realizing his sister held his arm. "Rory, please. You have hardly slept in days. You will do her no good like this."

Still wearing the riding clothes from his most recent search, which had taken him as far away as the river crossing in Henley, he turned from his sister, dismayed at the lack of news on Winter's whereabouts. Richly had not come back to Everleigh. Nor had his daughter yet returned from London.

The last four days had been naught but a nightmare.

Even now, Trevor was in Bisham seeking information from anyone who might have seen Richly's carriage days ago and the direction he might have traveled. Restell had gone farther north in search of one of his men who had also vanished the night Winter had been taken. Father Flannigan had contacts in London and nearby hamlets who were visiting the prisons and asylums looking for both Winter and her mam. Lord Ware was utilizing all of his resources. Rory could do nothing more but await word.

"I should have followed my instincts from the beginning and taken her family to live with me here, to hell with the consequences."

He would not make the same mistake twice.

And then he would hunt down Richly and kill the bastard.

"Where is her brother?" he asked.

"Upstairs in the playroom with my daughter and Robert. Mrs. Kincaid is with them. She thought it best to bring Robert here. Perry needs him."

It was because of Winter's brother any of them knew about the incident that had occurred at her cottage. Perry had escaped the baron's henchman and run through the dark of the night to Mrs. Kincaid.

But it had taken a full two days for Rory to receive Eve's desperate telegram and to return. Two days wasted while Richly's trail grew cold.

He strode out of the library. Upstairs in his chambers, he dismissed Smothers. In the darkness, Rory stood at the windows and looked across the grounds toward the placid lake bathed in a thin eerie mist. He despised inactivity. If he remained a second more within these walls, he would go mad.

Moonlight bathed the treetops by the time Rory rode out of the stable on Winter's white-stocking mare. Sensing his ruthless mood, the mare pulled at the bit. Rory's hand moved on the reins and he spurred the horse into a run, a bright three-quarter moon in the sky lighting his way. The hound greeted him at the gate. The dog had followed Perry and now lived at Granbury Court. For once, Rory welcomed the company. He skirted the edge of the woods and, with the wind in his face, rode like an avenging shadow to Everleigh. Only to come face-to-face with the sheriff and a dozen men on the road.

Rory brought the mare to a skidding halt in front of the group. They stared at each other in a clear standoff Rory had no patience in facing. "Move aside," he ordered, suppressed fury vibrating in his voice.

Derwood leaned his elbow against his knee. Clearly reading Rory's mind and the murderous intent in his heart, he said, "Richly isn't there. We'll know when he is. Unless you have another purpose being on this road, my lord."

"I said move aside."

Derwood edged his horse next to Rory's. "Miss Winter and her mam are one of us. If you stay in Granbury, you'll learn soon enough that we take care of our own, my lord. We'll find her, and you won't be doing her right if you go charging into Everleigh and get yourself arrested for murdering someone." Then Derwood quietly said in faint rebuke. "Go back to Granbury Court, my lord."

Some of the rage left Rory. His fists unclenched on the reins. Sanity returned to take hold of his actions. "Would you?" he asked. "Go back?"

"If I had me standing in your way as the voice of reason. We love her, too, my lord. I swear she will be found."

An hour later, the hound beside him, Rory was standing in front of Winter's cottage, soaked in moonlight. He tied his mount to a post, then walked past the gate into her garden. The lack of rain had left the watering trough empty, but someone had been here to feed the chickens, probably

Mrs. Kincaid. His gaze touched the silent woods, the empty stable, and finally the window of her room.

He opened the door into Winter's kitchen. Without lighting a lamp, he climbed the stairs to her chambers, and still booted and spurred, sat on her bed. For a long time, all he could do was stare about the room. Then he lay against her pillow and let her warm essence fill him with softness. His last thought was of Winter. And for the first time in days, he let oblivion claim him.

Only to come awake with a start.

Rays of morning sunlight spilled into the room. Someone was running up the stairway. Wide awake now, Rory came to his feet and moved with his back against the wall just as Sheriff Derwood filled the doorway.

"What is it?" Rory demanded.

"Angelique saw your horse when she came to feed the chickens this morning," Derwood said. "Mr. Jameson has been looking for you. Richly's daughter has returned to Everleigh."

Winter tore the mold from the bread before setting her teeth delicately on the crust and nibbling. Her sore jaw made it difficult to chew. Only after she had swallowed the first bite did she look down and see that the bread had worms.

Her stomach churned and, no matter her hunger, she dropped the bread back into a bowl of watery gruel sitting on the cot.

She drew her knees to her chest, covering her bare feet with her filthy skirt. Her cell reeked of an unemptied chamber pot. Straw littered the floor. Pressing her cheek to her knees in despair, she squeezed her eyes shut. She had no idea where she had been incarcerated or how many days she'd been here. She'd awakened on this hard cot with a sore cheek, no shoes, and torn stockings. Her tangled hair draped her shoulders. She didn't want to imagine what might be crawling on her scalp. Occasionally during the night, she heard fighting and disorder among other inmates through the grate in the door, and knew she was not alone in this place.

She'd been too angry to cry when she'd first awakened. Instead, she had shouted at the guards, demanding to be released. Now all she felt was fear. Did anyone even know she was missing? Had Perry escaped to tell what had befallen her? Had the baron put her little brother away in some cell as well?

Her gaze dropped to the bowl of gruel next to where she sat. She could not continue to starve herself. Dying would only give the baron his victory.

Winter lifted the bowl and stared at its contents. "You have made your very last mistake, *Uncle*." She choked down two bites of the bread.

Rory would find her.

No matter their differences, they shared the same side against the baron. He would not allow her to perish. He would search to the ends of the earth to find her. *"This world will not be big enough for you to hide."*

But as the days passed, Winter began to lose resolve. She took to pacing. She had yet to appear before the bench. And what of her family? Were they safe? She scrubbed the heel of a grimy hand across her cheek and glared at the heavy door, having beat on it earlier only to have water thrown on her. A single dwindling taper on the wall was all that kept this room from complete darkness. When the candle went out the rats would return. She threw herself back on the cot.

God, she hated the rats.

A key jiggled in the door and she shot to her feet. Tangled hair covered her face. Her clothes were torn, the hem of her skirt shredded, her bare feet unprotected against the chill of the cell.

As the door opened, she grabbed her battered food bowl off the cot and smashed it against the door. "Get out!" Truly she was as mad as the other inmates. Next, she threw the slop bucket.

She thought she heard someone call her name as she braced herself against the wall ready to hurl the tin water bowl. Lantern light cast a flickering shadow over the damp stone walls as someone stepped into the cell. "She be a wild one, my lord," a voice grumbled from behind the door. "Knocked poor Georgie clean out with her slop bucket yesterday when he come to refill it."

Rory ducked through the doorway. At the same time his eyes found hers, the tin bowl in her hand dropped to the floor. With a soundless cry, she pushed away from the wall and flew into his arms. "What *took* you so long, my lord?"

Her voice was muffled and weepy against the scented wool of his caped cloak as she murmured incoherently about rats and worms and smarmy, beetle-faced turnkeys. She wrapped herself around him.

He pressed his cheek against her hair and held her tightly. "Richly managed to vanish," he said. "We had to find you and your mam the hard way."

She pulled back and blinked into his eyes. "You've seen her? Is she safe? Did Perry make it out of the cottage?"

"They're both at Granbury Court awaiting your return." Placing a gloved finger alongside her cheek, he gently turned her face. She flinched when he touched the bruise on her cheek. "Would you like better accommodations, love?"

"Oh, please." She raised her arms to his neck as he lifted her against him.

Rory followed the guard through the dank bowels of the prison. Their boot steps rang in the cobbled stairway leading upward past flickering candles. His arms were strong around her. Forced to duck his head beneath the timbers, he stepped inside the common room housing a dozen or more women milling listlessly about on pallets of straw. Keys jangled on the guard's belt as he withdrew a large brass ring and paused at the last door.

Rory's eyes fell on the guard. "Open the bloody door."

The turnkey shifted nervously and peered up at Rory through greasy brown hair. "Th-the purse, my lord."

"When I am out of here you will be paid."

"Ye promised," the voice whined. "I can lose me position—"

Rory's hand shot out and grasped the man's collar. He shoved him hard against the stone wall. "You will lose far more than your position if you do not open the damn gate."

Nodding vigorously the man fumbled with the keys in his hands and shoved one into the lock. The door squealed on massive hinges and he cautiously peered through the crack that yielded only to the darkness.

Ducking out of the door, he carried Winter down the long narrow passageway that reeked of urine and finally up a stone stairwell, and past the nervous night watchman awaiting them at the top. Neither Rory nor Winter spoke until they stepped out into the cobbled courtyard separating the gaol from the iron gate and she saw the stars in the nighttime sky above them.

She held her cheek pressed against his shoulder. "Where am I?"

"Just north of London," he answered.

Without a word, Rory tossed out the bag of coins in his pocket as he swept past the gate and listened as it slammed shut behind him.

Two armed men met him and stood at his back as he walked toward a carriage sporting four nervous black horses. The driver released the step and opened the door. Rory stepped into the coach. Winter didn't loosen her grip around his neck and he kept her on his lap where she was wont to remain. "I must reek something terrible," he heard her say.

"We'll both need a bath after leaving this place."

Wiping the back of her filthy hand indelicately across her wet nose, she sniffed. "How did you get me out?"

*Sheer luck, connections that went all the way to the prime minister, and a hell of a lot of gold.* "The guards valued their lives," he said against her hair.

"Thank you," she murmured.

Soon she fell asleep in his arms, her head against his shoulder, and Rory's arms wrapped around her as if she might take flight and vanish forever from his life.


Winter came awake to the softest, silkiest sheets she had ever felt enshrouding her body. She opened her eyes and turned her head, her gaze touching the gilt-wood armchair where she knew Rory had spent a good part of the night. She lay in a half-tester bed draped in white Chinese silk.

She looked around at a huge, high-ceilinged room, its whitewashed walls trimmed in gilt. A sandalwood wardrobe and gilt metal cabinets lined the walls. Matching draperies had been drawn over French windows stretching half the room. She stretched like a tiger and sat up, suddenly wide awake and wondering exactly where in heavens she was.

Pressing a hand against her temple, she closed her eyes. She'd been asleep when she'd arrived here. She'd awakened long enough to eat and take a hot soak in a huge enameled bath as an older woman scrubbed the filth from her hair. Her hair was now dry but unmercifully tangled after its thorough washing.

A murmur of subdued voices in the adjoining dressing room pulled her attention to the door at the end of the opulent chamber. Something that had been asleep inside her awakened to the familiar voice.

Throwing off the covers, she climbed from the bed and looked down at herself. She wore a white cotton nightdress that could have passed for a shift, skimpy at best. But she didn't care.

Padding across the room, she made an effort at stealth as she stopped just to the side of the doorway to look inside. The dressing room itself was empty and the voices came from the tile and mosaic bathing chamber beyond. She eased past the dressing chamber and peered around the door.

Rory was talking to someone as he shaved at the basin, and she heard the scrape of the razor over his cheek. He wore no shirt and she stared at the flex of his back muscles and shoulders as he moved. A pair of dark trousers hung low at his waist. She stood at the door, attempting to hear to whom he spoke.

He still had not told her how he'd come to learn of her whereabouts. Now that she was clean and safe, a thousand questions filled her mind. He'd finished washing and was scrubbing a white towel over his face when he looked up just then to find her reflection in the glass.

Movement on the other side of the door startled her as the second voice in the room asked, "Is someone out there?"

Winter panicked. She whirled to run back into the bedroom and nearly slammed directly into the chest of another man casually leaning in the doorway.

"Miss Ashburn."

Looking into his stark blue eyes, she flushed a dozen shades of red. Clearly, he had been watching her while she'd been watching Rory. "I . . ."

He was a tall man and straightened with the same loose-limb movement that characterized Rory. With a gasp, she suddenly recognized him from the fair. He'd been one of the men standing with Rory in front of the Gypsy wagon that night. Dressed as he was in gentleman's attire, he didn't look Gypsy now.

"We've met," she said. "Not face-to-face. But I've seen you."

Rory was suddenly standing behind her and sliding a robe over her shoulders, a robe that smelled like him and that swallowed her within its fragrant folds. He'd shrugged into a shirt though it remained unbuttoned. "This is Restell Ryder," he said.

Winter dipped her head. She felt dwarfed in the company of such tall men and didn't like it. Behind her, the man with whom Rory had been conversing had moved through the doorway. Rory introduced him as Lord Ware.

She knew of this man. She almost fainted. "You are the former Foreign Affairs minister." She made a deep curtsy, flustered and more than a little awed that Rory appeared to be friends with someone so important.

Aware of her state of undress, she blushed in utter embarrassment feeling as if she'd made a cake of herself. "My lord. I was not aware Lord Granbury had guests when I awakened." Certainly not a former high-ranking minister in the government. "I didn't mean to interrupt."

Rory placed himself beside her like a stony sentinel and guided her out of the room. "What are you doing out of bed?" he asked her as if she were a child.

"She's awake now," Ware said.

"She isn't ready to discuss this," Rory said.

Winter came to an abrupt halt. "Discuss what?"

"Baron Richly has not been seen since your disappearance," Ware said. "We might not have found where he'd taken you if not for his daughter."

"Lavinia told you?"

"It seems Trevor Jameson convinced her to tell us anything she might know about her father's associates before Rory found her," Restell said, having moved behind Ware with a slow catlike grace.

"Through her, Granbury here found the orderly Richly hired to take you," Ware said. "It still took us two more days to find you and secure your release," Ware said. "No one would stop looking, Miss Ashburn."

She knew Rory was responsible for all of it. Her hands tightened against the silken fabric of the robe as she looked away. How could she ever repay him?

"My apologies that the baron got hold of you in the first place," Restell said. "The man I had at Everleigh . . ." Eyeing Rory, he scraped a big palm over his jaw. "Let's just say he regrets following the wrong coach that night."

Ware leaned on his cane. "We've built a substantial case

of embezzlement against the baron, going back through old records found in the home of your father's former solicitor." He suddenly looked uncomfortable.

"They need your deposition," Rory said quietly. "They need to know everything. If you—"

"Yes," Winter said.

Then grasping that she'd be telling her story to a room full of men, she realized it would not be as simple as she had thought.

Rory turned her slowly in his arms. "If you want me there it can be arranged. It would be my right as your husband to go into that room with you."

Winter experienced the brief panic that she'd married him in some hypnotic, drug-induced, or hysterical state and didn't remember. "Are you?"

"He will be before the day is out, Miss Ashburn," Lord Ware said. "We should be going now. Restell?"

"Bloody hell," Restell said from behind Ware. "I want to hear her reply."

Winter felt the almost imperceptible movement behind her and thought Rory might leap across Ware and lay the man low with a facer.

"Miss Ashburn," Ware said coolly, his voice incongruous with her racing heart and the sudden stifling heat in the room. "Lord Granbury has been apprised of the necessary procedures that need to take place before your deposition. Your testimony will be compromised once it is learned you two have . . ." Clearing his throat, he peered at her like a stern taskmaster, reminding her of Father Flannigan just before he launched into a lecture on the sins of immorality and properly fulfilling one's responsibilities. "You two have spent the night together in this room. If your character is brought into question, nothing you say will matter. Granbury has agreed to cooperate in this manner."

Winter found herself unable to meet Rory's eyes.

"In addition," Ware continued, "according to the provisions of your father's will, custody of your brother passes to your husband upon your wedding. It will be no trouble petitioning the bench for Lord Granbury to take charge of your mother." In a more grandfatherly voice, he added, "Richly will have no more power over your family after tomorrow, Miss Ashburn. And you will have the protection of Granbury's name against anything else with which he might try to hurt you. So you see, this is for the best. You can thank me later, Miss Ashburn."

The door shut, plunging the room into silence so loud it nearly deafened her. Neither she nor Rory made the first effort to move or say anything. Outside the window, she could hear traffic on the cobbles below, the warble of a constable's whistle, the sound of a distant steamer, and knew they were somewhere near the Thames. But none of the noise descending on her crowded out the thoughts that filled her head.

Finally, she looked up at Rory and found his expression notably blank. For all of her feelings and gratitude toward him, they had truly settled nothing between them. Now, to be forced into a situation that would have monumental consequences for each of them the rest of their lives? She looked away.

"Who conducted the investigation on my uncle?"

"Ware did."

Winter pulled the robe tighter about her body. "Why would Lord Ware do that?"

"Because I asked him to."

She shut her eyes. "I'm sorry," she said and shook her head. "This is an utter disaster."

"That is a fine statement to a man on his wedding day."

She tried to laugh only because he seemed to be taking everything in stride when she could not even walk two steps.

"Look at me, Winter." Tilting her head back, he spoke with polite authority. "We can come to some arrangement between us that will suit both our needs. I have no desire to rob you of your independence."

She didn't want independence. She wanted *him*. Forever.

She needed desperately to believe in him. And now that she knew who he was and what he did for the government, she was no longer sure if he planned to remain at Granbury Court.

A tap on the door interrupted them. "Your wedding dress has arrived, my love. Now, put on a cheery face. Let us get married and have done with this thing."

Winter married Rory on a hot late August morning at a chapel near St. James Park. She received from him a thin gold ring, which he removed from his pinky finger and which was too big for her. Afterward they signed the proper documents and the reverend's wife hugged her and called her Lady Granbury. Winter stared at her handsome prince bent over slightly as he spoke to the reverend, looking beautifully attired in morning gray and a crisp white shirt beneath his swallowtail coat, a startling contrast to his dark hair.

Her own wedding gown had an ethereal quality to it—white moiré-antique, draped in pearls and Brussels lace. It had fit her so perfectly that she could not imagine how Rory had accomplished its creation on so short a notice.

This entire morning felt surreal. A few days ago, she had been hidden in a dismal dungeon. Today she had married a peer of the realm.

As Rory finished his business and escorted her out of the chapel to their waiting carriage, she felt the distance between them, as if he, too, didn't know quite what to say. She settled against the leather seats, the upholstery feeling supple and rich beneath her palms. Rory sat next to her, dropping a worn satchel between his feet. He wore a hat low over his forehead and his eyes catching the reflection of the hot sunlight went over her face. The coach jerked forward.

She wanted to say anything to break the cool civility surrounding him. She'd already thanked him for the wedding gown. "Where have you been staying while in London?" she asked him.

"I use an apartment in Knightsbridge."

He looked out the opposite window, and her eyes slid longingly over his profile. "I thought you didn't have a place in London."

"On occasion I stay there when I have work in London."

Remembering everything his sister had told her, she asked, "Have you been in London working?"

His head turned her way. "I was at the Timber and West India Docks most of last week arranging for shipments of lumber to Granbury Court. I'll take you shopping along Bond Street," he said, changing the topic. "Would you like that?"

Winter couldn't remember the last time she'd shopped at a boutique. She brushed her palms over her wedding skirts. "That would be nice, thank you."

"Nice?" He sat forward and removed his hat. "As in 'thank you, you are very nice, Lord Granbury'?" Dropping the hat on the opposite bench, he sat back as if to say he was one of the *least* nice persons she would ever know.

Now they were at last broaching familiar ground. "I already know who and what you are, Rory."

"Is that a fact?"

"You're a spy."

He coughed abruptly into his gloved hand, then idly scratched his chin, his eyes filled with amusement. His reaction hurt her feelings, even if he had not meant it to do so. "I'm glad we have gotten all that out of the way so quickly. But don't romanticize. My sister exaggerated my importance. I was mostly a courier. The fact that I was couriering out someone else's information was incidental."

Her eyes subtly narrowed, and Rory felt as if he'd been spanked.

They arrived at the hotel shortly afterward. Rory had never noted the marbled opulence of the lobby until he saw it through Winter's eyes.

He'd never really noted much of anything, but he couldn't take his eyes off his bride. A vision to plunder a man's will, she wore a white gown of lavish fabric draped in pearls, the only dress in all of London he could find on short notice. He had guessed her measurements, and, clearly, he had guessed correctly. From the fullness of her perfect breasts, the gown narrowed to her waist and flared at her hips in a fall of lace.

She remained close to him, and he bumped into her twice. They stepped into a hydraulically operated lift. The lift operator smiled. "Top of the mornin' to ye, Lord Granbury. My lady."

The door closed and the cage ascended in a grinding start on its way to the topmost floor. Her fingers wrapped around his arm. He stared down at the small-gloved hand clutching his arm, the hand wearing his ring, and felt unprepared for the possessiveness that burned through him. That ring had belonged to his father. It was the closest thing he had to a personal possession that had meaning to him.

After ordering a hot bath and a meal, Rory found Winter standing at the window overlooking the London skyline. The sun had come out from behind gloomy clouds and spilled into the room, washing over them both. He looked around at the Chinese silk and white satin drapery, the Axminster carpet, all brilliant and beautiful, but nothing compared to his new wife standing with the sunlight behind her. She folded her arms and looked at him across her shoulder, as he moved beside her. "You seem to be well-known here," she said.

Indeed the staff knew him. He had stayed here on more than one occasion. "I've never had occasion to stay in this room. It's usually reserved for dignitaries." He raised his hand and cupped her nape.

She started to speak, but he covered her lips with his. He had held his desire for her in check for as long as he intended to.

He slipped his arm around her waist, bringing her closer to him. She kissed him back, but he tasted something akin to anger. He reveled in it because he felt it, too, inside himself. Her fisted hands opened and splayed over the crisp silk of his shirt and his heart pounded beneath her palms. He burrowed his own hands in her hair, tipping back her head so that he could probe her mouth with his tongue. The mating of their mouths was anything but gentle, and she let him know. She suckled his lower lip then bit him. Not hard, but sharp enough to make him pull back.

He scowled down at her. "Jesus, Winter."

"That's for lying and keeping secrets from me. For not *trusting* me. For daring to think you could give away ten thousand acres of Granbury Court to the baron for any reason. For making me suffer your politeness all morning."

"I missed you, too, my love."

"I'm not finished—"

"I think you are." He had already diagnosed his foul mood and recognized the cure.

He walked away from her and shut the dressing-room door where their bath was being delivered. He turned into the room, leaned against the door, and peered at his wife. He'd been exceedingly polite all morning, and he thought he'd been doing her a favor. He shoved off the door.

Winter stepped away from the window. Her gaze darted between the massive bridal bed and him. "We haven't finished discussing what we both know needs to be discussed."

He removed his blue silk tie and dropped it on the table. "Oh, but I have, my sweet."

Her eyes narrowed. "Short of saying 'I do' you've hardly spoken ten words of importance to me since this morning. I'm not ready for this. I need you to answer my questions." She tugged the ring off her finger and held it up to him. "I need to know what this means to you and, hence, about my future."

His waistcoat and shoes followed his tie while she watched. "What are you doing?" she demanded.

His own mood was no longer biddable. "I'm taking my wife to our marriage bed and doing what I've wanted to do for days."

"No," she said firmly. She sailed to the bedroom door but found it locked. She turned back into the room.

Rory leaned on the bedpost, holding up the key, nonplussed by her desire to escape him. He tossed her the key and she caught it reflexively. "If you would rather go, my love. If you would rather forgo what we both enjoy . . ."

Her chin lifted. Tears jeweled in her eyes. "I don't understand you."

"I don't understand myself either. I only know that I haven't slept in a week. Could we have this discussion later?"

As if having made up her mind, she laid his ring on the dressing table beside the bed and methodically removed her gloves.

"Put the ring back on, Winter," he said, his tone implacable.

She hesitated but did as he asked. Seeing the tremble in her fingers, he hated himself for his intemperate mood and his reluctance to open himself to her. He couldn't. Always something held him back. Even now, he found himself on the edge of something that resembled cold terror of that which was within him.

She began to remove the pins from her hair. It tumbled in a glorious silk cape over her shoulders. She kicked off her slippers, and he felt a primal recognition of his desire all the way to his gut, unsettling and revealing for what it exposed in him. She stopped in front of him and, lifting her thick hair, presented her back. He slid the tiny pearlescent buttons on her bodice from their moorings, his fingers unsteady. She unfastened the tapes around her waist and the entire thing slid to the floor in a billow of fragrant cloth. She turned to face him, her perfect breasts with their rosy peaks spilling over her corset. Tension arced inside him.

She raised a brow. "Well, my husband? Am I allowed to see you naked?"

It was not the first time he'd looked into her face that day, but it was the first time he saw another bruise on her cheek. He tilted her face. She'd been wearing rice powder. It must have rubbed off during the morning. Her fingers went to her cheek and she pulled away from his scrutiny. "Hasn't Richly's visit to me already cost you enough," she said. "Without dwelling on more?"

He cupped her nape with his hand. He stood on uncertain footing here and had no desire to talk about things he didn't comprehend. "Not nearly what it has cost you, my love."

She ducked away from his hand. "Answer my question. What does all of this mean to you? I need to know where I stand in your life."

His face hardened. "Bloody hell, Winter *Fuck!*" He walked a dozen steps and dropped onto the settee against the wall. "You don't give up." Suddenly so tired he just wanted to shut his eyes, he found himself contemplating the plaster on the ceiling, wondering where the hell to go from here.

She sat down beside him and placed a hand on his arm. "Rory . . ."

Even through his sleeve, he felt her to the marrow of his bones, as if she swam in his veins like a drug.

He sat forward and rested his forearms on his thighs. Scraping his hands through his hair, he turned his head and looked at her for long seconds. Then, through her flurry of protests, he dragged her into his arms and, in a breathless whisper, confronted her. "Can you get it through your head that I married you because I care about you? Enough that I want to protect you?"

She tried to turn her face away. He cradled her head with his palm, forcing her to look at him. "You've captivated me since . . . hell, since you stole my wallet," he said huskily. "What is not to love about a courtship that began as ours did?"

She blinked over a watery smile. "Now that you have nearly finished what you set out to accomplish at Granbury Court, will you be staying?"

"That is a fine thing to ask a man on his honeymoon," Rory murmured against her lips. "Are you inquiring whether I intend to remain in my home with you—a home, I remind you, I have just sunk every last shilling of my life into?" Rory peered at her from beneath his lashes. "I've staked my entire life at Granbury Court, Winter. I think you can trust that I will stay."

"You once told me you never trusted in anyone or anything."

"Marriage changes a man."

"Truly, my lord. You've only been a married man for ninety minutes."

"I adapt quickly, my love," he whispered, his lips only inches from hers. "Ours will be a real marriage, Winter. In every way imaginable."

In response, he laid his lips over hers. It was a kiss of intimate claiming, primal in intensity, and carnal in promise. Pleasure heated his blood and swam through his body and he drew her closer.

Pulling away, he looked at her, disheveled and wanton.

She slid her fingers into his hair. "Everyone in the other room will know what we are doing," she whispered.

He murmured something profane as his mouth drifted lower down her throat. "Of course they will. We are just married.

He adjusted her until she straddled his lap, making her sex more accessible to him. Her female scent came up to him and his nostrils flared like a wild animal's. He wanted what he wanted and at this moment had no interest in respectability. "This is mine forever," he hoarsely growled, cupping her sex. "I want to be buried inside you. I want you in every way possible. There will never be a time when I don't."

"My lord," she whimpered.

Her nipples coral and taut invited his mouth. He suckled her breasts spilling over her stays, at the same time using his fingers to stroke and tease and explore between her thighs, touching her as intimately as any man could. "Know that I love everything about you, Winter Jameson," he whispered hoarsely. "Your smell, your taste, your softness. Everything."

Though she had driven him insane with passion in the past, he had never been as aroused as he was now. She ran her palms beneath his shirt and over his waist. She slid her hands along his torso and between his thighs. He drew in a sharpened breath against her breast. Her fingers found his hardened length and he pressed himself into her hand, the fabric of his trousers an unwanted impediment between them. While she held him in the grip of one hand, she used the other to work his trouser buttons free. She pushed him back against the settee and found and coaxed his nipples to hardened buds beneath the hot lick of her tongue.

And then she found his erection and gripped him. He

was not proof against her touch. She touched the tip of his penis gingerly with her fingertips, while she worshiped his torso with her mouth, licking her way down his abdomen. Her eyes fell on his erection, extending thick and long past his foreskin. His penis jerked in her hand and a thick grunt came from his chest. His hips rose to her and her name escaped his lips. "Winter," he groaned.

A fire burned in her eyes like a brand. Something wholly primitive gripped him. Straddling her thighs across his hips, she guided herself onto the tip of his erection, her breath a warm ripple against his lips. His hands clamped her waist. He flexed upward, allowing her to sink onto his engorged length, touching her more deeply than he ever had. Heat flared anew. Time lost all meaning. She framed his face and kissed him. One of his hands slid beneath her veil of hair, his other splayed her bottom and they moved in perfect rhythm.

Rory was powerless to resist. He knew he should feel guilty consummating their wedding vows on a settee, copulating with his young wife like some ill-disciplined, lowbrow simpleton. But he did not.

He coveted her passion. He wanted to see himself in her eyes. He found her gaze locked with his. He let his lips relax. They were both floating on a plane of sensual awareness. And for a moment, they enjoyed giving and taking, enjoying the flux and flow of their bodies and he realized that what he felt was ecstasy. Her breathing grew ragged. Her fingers tangled in his hair, her mouth pressed to his. Her sultry groan burned through him.

He swallowed her cry and he felt his own release rumbling through him. He thrust one last time, spilling his seed unfettered inside her. And just that fast, the world around him righted itself; time began to flow again. He felt a loosening in his chest, as everything inside him opened.

He pressed his forehead to hers. "I think," he breathed, "you have sundered me from bollocks to brains, my love."

She collapsed against him and smiled against his lips. "I love you, too."

# Chapter 20

Winter stirred and opened her eyes and realized at once that she was naked and ensconced next to a warm naked body slumped heavily next to her. His arm draped her waist. She slept on her back with Rory's head next to hers on the pillow. The curtains were drawn, but she could tell by the lack of traffic outside the window that it was near dusk. The heat of the day had left a thin sheen of perspiration on her skin.

She turned her head and traced the angles and planes of Rory's jaw first with her gaze then the tip of her finger. Even in his sleep, his hands found her. Touched her. Held her. She'd recognized this about him from the beginning. His need for physical contact.

She knew when his body awakened. The air vibrated. Hummed. Giving birth to renewed feelings as he opened his eyes.

"Good evening." His voice was gravelly with sleep and desire.

"Good evening to you."

Their eyes touched and remained in the other's caress. Hers lingered. His smiled. Then hunted. He rose slightly on one elbow.

As if seeking the source of her mood, and discovering it was him.

Then he pulled the coverlet over them, softly cocooning her in their cave, and made love to her yet again. And they stayed there all night.

When Winter opened her eyes again it was morning, and Rory was no longer in bed. A tap on the dressing-room door sounded and a young girl entered, informing Winter that her bath was prepared. With the help of the maid, she dressed in the gown that Rory had delivered. She knew he would be meeting her at the deposition hearing; they had discussed the details yesterday. Restell arrived after breakfast to escort her to where Rory would be waiting, and Rory met them outside on the marble steps of a building just off the Thames in Westminster. As Restell delivered her from the carriage, Rory took her hands.

"How are you?"

She smiled tentatively for she recognized his dark mood. "I am ready to do this." She looked down at her mauve morning gown. "Thank you for the dress."

Nodding to Restell, Rory ushered her inside and, in a moment, took her down a narrow dimly lit corridor, turning her just as they reached two imposing doors. "You don't have to do this," he said.

She placed a finger against his lips then kissed him. "I do."

"I'll be behind a screen at the back of the room," he said. "If you will be more comfortable without me there . . ."

"I want you there, Rory."

He kissed her and she held tight to his arms. Then he opened the door into the chamber. Six bewigged men wearing black robes sat behind tables spread out in a half-moon before her, waiting for her to enter.

* * *

The next few days were the hardest Winter ever faced. More than once during the hours in front of the tribunal council, she knew Rory had wanted to stand and have done with the proceedings. But Winter wouldn't allow it. Lord Ware had gathered enough evidence to prosecute Richly on crimes such as fraud and embezzlement. Winter's father had not been the only account in Richly's bank to have been siphoned. But Ware considered her testimony an integral part in the inquest, for it laid down the foundation upon which Richly's character was built. Baron Richly was an important MP, his powerbase influential. Many of his friends were barristers. Every bit of evidence was crucial to maintain the integrity of the case.

Though in the end, it wasn't Winter's testimony that damned Richly, but his own daughter's that condemned him. Lavinia supplied evidence from her papa's papers of other blackmail schemes that spanned the realm of the political and economical landscape he had created. Many of the schemes revealed involved illegal and questionable moral activities by others of influence from the possible selling of classified secrets to crimping a horse race. Winter's father had been one such victim, paying blackmail money to keep an affair with a low-caste seamstress from his ailing wife. The extortion monies would go into the baron's financial institution of opulence and never come out.

"How long have you known about Angelique Kincaid and your father," Rory asked Winter as they were leaving the hall after the third day of depositions.

She had been quiet and stiff during the hearing proceedings, and her mood had nothing to do with the heat that had fallen upon London. Now in the carriage with only the lull of the wheels on cobbles to fill the silence, Winter felt an overwhelming need to share this part of her life, as if a dam had cracked and all the things she had held back rushed forth at once.

"I knew almost from the beginning," she replied. "I followed him one day. I remember feeling so betrayed, as if it had been my trust he had violated."

"He did violate your trust, Winter."

She lowered her head. Strange that he could feel so adamantly passionate in her defense when he'd also done so on numerous occasions.

"Mam had never been the same after Perry's birth. She wasn't . . . she wasn't Mam anymore. Papa had watched her fade for years."

Rory held her to him. "That is no excuse, Winter."

"Perhaps not. But he changed after he met Mrs. Kincaid. He became . . . he became happy again. She gave him back what he'd lost with Mam. But I was angry and hated him for what he was doing." She dabbed the corner of one eye with her thumb. "He had gone to her to break it off the night . . . the night the baron came to my room. I remember there had been a storm that evening. The baron had given me wine at supper." She drew in her breath. "Something must have been in it.

"I remember waking," she heard herself say. "Papa still had not returned. I ran away from Everleigh and went to Mrs. Kincaid's. Papa wept when he saw what had happened and blamed himself. Then he got into his buggy . . . and that was the last time I ever saw him alive. After that, Mam signed away the estate with Papa's solicitor as witness. He knew Mam was not in her right mind and allowed the transaction anyway."

Her small voice sighed. "Papa and I had argued earlier that night. It was my fault he'd left during that storm to go to Mrs. Kincaid's. If he had not been away to do what I had demanded that he do, I would never have been alone at supper that night with the baron, I'd never have drunk wine I was not supposed to drink. If I had not then gone to Mrs. Kincaid's . . . he would not have died."

"You understand the fallacy of that logic?"

She made a small sound of laughter. "Tell that to a sixteen-year-old. Afterward, I tried to find someone to listen to me. Most were horrified that I would make such accusations, and would have nothing to do with me. The baron finally allowed me to keep Mam and Perry in exchange for my silence; otherwise, he made it clear, I would never see either of them again. Hence, our arrangement. But he took Everleigh from me. From Perry. Papa made Everleigh."

"I wish I could tell you it is possible to get Everleigh back. But the baron did not declare your mother a ward until after the papers were signed. The solicitors involved would never admit to wrongdoing."

And after Lavinia's testimony against her own father today, Winter didn't think she could mount an expensive fight against her cousin to take Everleigh away, when she too had lost so much.

And as Rory held Winter, he thought of all the ways despair could kill a person as violently as any bullet. He knew then it took more courage to live and to remain among the human race than it did to hide within its shadows.

"I'm not some delicate flower," she said, her voice accusing him of thinking that very thing, which he was not, and his laugh told her so.

"What about his charges against me?" Winter asked. "They are all true."

"Says who, exactly?" Rory's tone was scandalized as he dragged his young wife unceremoniously across his lap. "Richly?"

"He could still hurt us."

"No one will ever believe anything he says again, Winter."

She settled her head against his chest as best as her new hat would allow. "It took courage for Lavinia to come forward and turn over all that evidence to condemn her own father."

"The authorities would have found most of it in time anyway."

But the entire ordeal with Lavinia Richland, when it came down to the bare bones of it all, made no sense to Rory, though he said nothing to Winter.

She brushed the hair off his brow, pulling his thoughts and all of his focus to the woman in his lap. "I have never known anyone like you in the whole of my life," she murmured.

"You aren't that old."

She smiled. "Perhaps not, I'm old enough to know I'll never meet anyone else who pleasures me the way you do."

"God forbid that you would. I'd have to kill him."

Laughing, she raised herself and straddled his lap, her gown rustling with her movement as their fingers busily worked the buttons of the other's attire. She kissed him thoroughly. "You are my passion, Rory Jameson."

"And you are my pleasure, Winter Morganna Constance Jameson."

"You know my entire name," she said softly.

He trailed his lips down the slim curve of her throat and back to her lips. "Do you doubt my ferreting skills, my sweet wife?" he said equally softly.

"Why does someone become a spy?" her rasp touched his lips. "You would truly have to believe in our way of life to risk yourself protecting it."

That was just it, the failed crux of his philosophy, he thought as he ran his palms beneath her skirts and up silk stockings to encompass the bare flesh beneath her garters. For Rory had never believed in anything—until now.

His breath fell on her lips and she seemed to forget that he did not answer and he soon forgot the question. "We are not so far from our rooms if you wish to wait, my lord." Her voice taunted in a medley that both challenged and defied.

His hands closed on the backs of her thighs. "Far enough when I want to see you naked now. If you haven't noticed, it is bloody hot in here."

Her eyes were as dark as her pupils in the sultry shadows. Pressing him back into the seat, she shoved off his jacket, entrapping his arms at his sides. Her breath came quickly atop his. "I am a vixen, my lord. And you are in my lair." She made a deep vibrating growl against his mouth. "Beneath my will."

And he groaned as she continued her manual exploration of his very hard body. Their gazes touched and locked briefly, his dark and searing, before her lips possessed his. City traffic was suddenly lost to them.

He made love to her. Or she to him. She pressed herself to him, the emotions, the physical need that came with their coupling drawing his hands to his body, and he invited her to touch. Freely. He traced the curve of her waist and eased

his hands to her hips over her bottom. He shifted her and settled his thighs more securely between her spread legs, then
slowly he penetrated and thrust more deeply as he parted her
for his pleasure.

He took, but so did she. Bliss was mutual. Her head fell
back, and he was no longer aware of anything but his own
driving hunger and the need for satiation that came when
he was with her. The rapture subsided too soon. Replete,
Winter sat unmoving against him.

She sighed. "Do you think your driver knows what we
are doing?"

He laughed softly. "Since we have been stopped in front
of our hotel for a good five minutes, I'd say so, love."

Horrified, she sat back and, pulling aside the curtain,
peered outside to see that he spoke the truth. She pressed
the back of her hand against her lips as her eyes met his in
mutual abandon and stifled a giggle, then he helped lift her
off him, though that was accomplished with less ease as he
slid past her swollen flesh. She sought to repair the mess
she'd made of her beautiful new gown.

Over the last few days after they'd left the hearings, he
had taken her shopping and for long walks along the banks
of the Thames, and at St. James and Hyde Parks. It had not
rained in weeks in this part of England, and the uncommon
heat made remaining inside even in the evenings nearly in-
tolerable. Except in the earliest hours of the morning when
he made love to her, and he could almost forget the rest of
the world existed around them. Almost.

The world did exist. And it came in the form of a letter
awaiting Rory and Winter inside the hotel lobby the next day
when they returned from the park. Rory opened the missive
from Eve and frowned. "What is it?" Winter asked.

"We're needed back at Granbury, love. I have an estate to save and you have a brother who needs you."

Winter took the letter from his hands.

Rory said, "It seems Perry has run away from Granbury Court and has gone back to live with Mrs. Kincaid and Robert."

The Marquess of Granbury's coach arrived in Granbury the next afternoon and detoured directly to Angelique Kincaid's cottage. It was not the homecoming that Winter anticipated, especially when Perry saw the coach coming and took off running. It was Rory who stopped the coach and went after both boys on foot.

Mrs. Kincaid came out of the house as the carriage moved around the bend and met Winter. They embraced and walked together in the garden. The shiny black Granbury coach and four remained just past the tall oak tree out of place in the simple country setting. A liveried footman stood waiting at the carriage step, taking in the hot summer eve that had baked the parched ground to dust these past weeks. And birdsong seemed incongruous with a mood that had cut short Winter's stay in London and brought her here.

"It has been difficult for your brother," Mrs. Kincaid said. "Much has changed for him and he is afraid. Look at you, *chère*." She gripped Winter's arms. "You are a bride. How does it feel to be a marchioness?"

A flutter of disconcertment wavered inside Winter as she found the tall figure of her husband standing near the pond in earnest conversation with Perry and Robert. "I love him," she said quietly. "I love them both."

"Do not fear." Angelique laid her hands atop the white picket fence. "His lordship will be good for Perry. The boy needs a stern taskmaster."

"The boys are close."

Angelique grew quiet. Winter placed her hand on Angelique's. "I won't take Robert from you."

Tears shone in the other woman's eyes. "I did not know how lonely I was before the children arrived. But I would not keep Robert for my own selfish reasons. I promise I will be a good mother to him."

On impulse, Winter hugged her. "I know you will. And he and Perry do not live so far from each other that they cannot still cause this town much grief."

Angelique laughed. "*Oui*, I fear that is so."

Their conversation diverged and Winter told Angelique about London and the last few days she had spent giving her deposition against the baron, but that he had yet to be found. "Rory has men still looking for him."

"The baron may be the least of our problems at the moment," Angelique said. "The heat and drought are killing off everyone's crops. Granbury Court is already all that stands between many of the people in this shire and going hungry. Trevor is building an irrigation system that will keep at least one field of crops alive longer than those from other estates surrounding us."

Winter had read the letter Rory's sister had sent him in London. The problem was one of the reasons Rory had returned. He hadn't told her he was worried, but Winter knew he was. "What about Everleigh?"

Angelique shook her head. "Everleigh has been hit the hardest."

Winter looked up as Rory returned with Perry and Robert at his side. Robert came to stand beside Angelique. Shamefaced, Perry apologized to Winter and gave her a hug, welcoming her back before climbing into the carriage.

"You will come see us often?" Rory asked Robert.

"Yes, sir, my lord," he said and ran to Winter with a hard hug. "His lordship is going to take Perry and me to Henley so we can pick out horses," Robert informed her, "and we can visit as much as we want."

Winter turned the force of her gaze on her husband. "You *bribed* them?" she asked in disbelief as they made their way to the carriage. "Stern taskmaster, indeed."

The line of his mouth unexpectedly tender, he leaned his lips against her ear. "I also told Perry if he ever ran off again, he was never too old to be turned over one's knee and paddled. The bribe was an afterthought."

Rory performed the same miracle the next morning with Mrs. Smythe when she'd balked at permanently moving into the dowager house with Winter's mother. Even the old spotted hound had taken to following him everywhere.

For someone who had once prided himself on his solitary existence, the Marquess of Granbury seemed to attract a world of strays to him, including Trevor, who had not been present when the Granbury coach rolled through the gates, but who had found Rory and Winter at the irrigation site the next evening.

He rode up to where Winter sat on her horse, watching Rory in the distance as he knelt in the dirt and scooped dry earth into his palm.

*"Cousin,"* Trevor said and took her hand, his eyes going over her new riding habit. "Or should I address you as Lady Granbury?"

Winter smiled. "I imagine you'll address me as you always have."

His expression sobered. "Are you all right? You had everyone worried."

"I am." Her gaze returned to Rory, standing with his back to her and looking out across the fields. "He won't say as much, but he's worried."

"It's bad, Winter. We could use more people digging at the site."

She would visit Sheriff Derwood tomorrow. "Thank you, for watching over your cousin while he has been gone."

"He has been trying to rescue Granbury Court from ruin. Something I never thought possible," he said quietly. "He has given me a stake in the outcome of my future. Do you think I would do any less?"

She looked up at the sky. Four years ago, these lands had suffered such a drought, and Winter remembered the fire. "Everleigh is suffering as well."

"We can't do anything about that, Winter. It's enough if we can save what we have here."

# Chapter 21

R ory stood near the huge churning waterwheel as it sent river water crashing into the ditches, spreading much needed moisture to the western field. He was pleased with Trevor's design and the speed in which it had been implemented. Two days ago, Winter had gone to Sheriff Derwood to ask for help, and thirty men had answered her call. Rory only needed another week before full harvest could begin. This morning Rory had sent Trevor and a score of men over to Everleigh to check on Lavinia and see what he could do to aid the people there.

"Done a fair job that young man did," the foreman said, standing next to the waterwheel, admiring the cogs and gears as if he had birthed the thing himself. He pointed up the hill. "The logs the men cut from this riverbank are up there waitin' fer me to load to the wagons. Mister Jameson wants to begin building the second wheel near the lake."

Or what was left of the lake. The water levels were low there as well. But Rory wanted to keep the orchard alive and the lake was the closest water source. He looked up at the sky. That morning Old Ben had told Rory his aching joints said there was rain in the air, but Rory had yet to feel change in the atmosphere.

The clatter of hooves drew his attention to the ridge and he saw Winter. Rory wiped the sweat from his brow with his forearm. He watched as she spoke to one of the workers. The man pointed in his direction.

She untied a picnic basket from behind her saddle and held it up to him. "I've come to bring you nourishment, my lord," she called down to him.

Rory took a step up the hill. "That depends on the nourishment, my lady."

She slid from the horse. "A surprise." A saucy hand went to her narrow waist. She was wearing one of the gowns he had bought her while in London. "But I have been assured that the dessert is your favorite, my lord."

"Ye best be doin' as Miss Winter says," the foreman replied, before flushing and correcting himself. "Lady Granbury, my lord. Is there anything else you need, my lord?"

Rory peered up the hill at the fair Lady Granbury. And for the first time he fully understood the enormity of love, its breadth and fullness. He was looking at what he needed. Seeing that Rory was distracted, the foreman hastily excused himself. Rory chuckled to himself as he watched the man leave, murmuring about the propensity of love to muddle a man's mind.

"Don't come down here," Rory called to his wife above the gurgitations of the waterwheel. "I'll come to you."

She returned to her horse. He started to walk down to the riverbank to wash the dirt from his hands and face. A splintering crack of wood broke the lull. He heard Winter scream his name, her warning too late.

To his horror, he glimpsed the logs barreling down the incline toward him. He saved himself by diving to the left into a narrowly spaced copse of trees as the load rumbled the ground beneath his feet and crashed into the river, barely missing the irrigation wheel. Men were already running across the field behind him and down the hill. He was sitting up when Winter dropped beside him, her incoherent babbling only coming to an abrupt stop when he took her hand.

"I'm all right, Winter."

"If you had acted any slower, guv'nor, you'd have been crushed beneath that load," he heard the foreman say. "Damn fool driver. Didn't put the stakes in the ground proper."

"Like hell," the man in question bellowed from his place atop the hill. "Ask the others. I secured the load afore I was called over to help at the ditch. The stakes are lying on the ground up there. Someone cut the ropes."

"Be ye all right, guv'nor?" the foreman asked.

Rory took the man's forearm and with Winter's aide came to his feet. He slipped his arm over her shoulder. "Get everyone back," he said to the men who had climbed down the hill.

He felt something warm seeping against his waistband. "You're injured," she said. "You're bleeding."

Winter helped him up the hill. The foreman walked to the place where the wagon had been and spoke to the men standing there. Taking pieces of rope, he looked up at Rory, a frown marring his face. "The rope chains may or may not have been cut. I don't know, my lord."

"It would only take the failure of one to snap the others," the driver said.

Rory limped over and took the rope from the man's hand. Turning it over, he recognized a knife-cut rope by the unique fray pattern. This one had been cut.

Winter's hands trembled as they touched his. "You don't think someone cut that rope, do you?"

"No, my love."

She had been responsible for most of the men hired on here and would blame herself. But Rory had long since come to a working arrangement with Sheriff Derwood. He trusted the man if only because Mrs. Kincaid seemed overly fond of the bloke. And Rory trusted Angelique Kincaid's judgment.

"What do you want me to do, my lord," the foreman's voice reached Rory.

Rory looked down at the waterwheel, then out across the field. "Keep the irrigation system running," he said. "Put men that you trust around the wheel and keep everyone else away."

"I need to get you back to Granbury Court," Winter said.

He put his arm back around Winter's shoulder and let her help him to his horse, listening to her worried ramblings. "Never fear," he quipped. "It must be a good omen. The wagon missed me *and* the waterwheel."

Father Flannigan arrived later that evening to check on Rory and pronounced that he would live. He'd bruised his ribs and the wound at his hip had been caused when he dived for cover and hit rocks. Trevor had come in just before supper, upset after he had heard about the accident. Rory didn't tell him about the cut rope or his suspicion that what had occurred was no accident. He and Trevor had finally reached an accord in their lives that offered some manner of peace between them, and, like Winter, Rory didn't want to believe Trevor wanted him dead.

Pampered in bed by his wife, Rory now looked at her as she sat on the mattress. "You are quiet," he said.

"I won't lose you," she said so passionately that her tone startled him. "I swear I will not."

Rory's voice was hoarse as he murmured against her lips. "I married a Valkyrie."

A sudden fierceness entered her eyes. "I am not as patient to watch events unfold as you are."

"No you aren't." Though he was sufficiently moved by her passion, his eyes when they narrowed on hers were deadly serious. "But I have been playing at this sort of game far longer than you have. I need you at my back, Winter. Not forging ahead of me where your distraction will get me killed." His hands were on her waist, turning her beneath him in their very large bed. "There is only one place I want to be distracted by you."

She cupped his face with her palms as his open, hungry kiss parted her lips. His hand slipped downward over her breasts. The kiss was heady. Fused with heat, she slid her arms around his shoulders and he tasted her hunger. When he pulled away, she looked into his eyes.

"Why is it that when we are the most happy we are also the most afraid?" she said. "It is as if one must counterbalance the other to even everything out."

"Do you think I am never afraid? Being here is more daunting to me than anything I've ever done. Everything is different when people depend on you."

"But didn't people depend on you before?"

"It wasn't the same. I've never had anything that was mine before, Winter."

He made love to her slow and easy. Later he fell asleep with his head cushioned against her breast.

Winter didn't sleep as she circled her arms protectively around Rory, but she must have shut her eyes, for she awakened later to the grumble of distant thunder. She turned her head. The windows were opened.

The wind had picked up ahead of an approaching storm and billowed the curtains. But along with hope of rain, came something else. She noticed, not the smell of a storm in the air but smoke. An odd light flickered in the glass as if it were reflecting a distant sunset. Rory stirred.

"Something is burning," she said.

He shoved himself out of bed first and padded naked to the window. Winter pulled on her wrapper and joined him. A faint red glow lit the horizon.

The blood seemed to leave her heart and drain out of her body, for she was remembering the last time a fire had swept across Granbury lands.

"The crops," he said. "Someone has set fire to the fields."

Rory turned on his heel. He dragged on his clothes. Winter met him in the hallway already dressed. "I'm going with you."

The air was full of smoke as they rode closer to the source of the flames. The distant fields were definitely burning, but the wind had pushed the fire into the surrounding woods, igniting tinderbox-dry trees and underbrush. The sky looked as if it was filled with thousands of fireflies.

Her gaze followed the sparks carried by the wind and saw them land in the grove of trees behind them. Her attention turned to the thousand acres of woods surrounding Granbury Court and to the old marquess's fruit orchard. The trees would be like tinder. Rory too had followed the movement and his eyes took in Granbury Court gleaming in silhouette on the far distant hill. Their concern was no longer the fields.

"It may miss us," he said.

There was a lake between the house and the woods, but

the wind was already carrying sparks and the ground was dry. She turned her head and met Rory's gaze.

"I will get everyone out," she said.

"Eve has probably already begun the process" he said, "but I need for you to make sure."

She knew his request was more than that. He thought he was sending her to safety. She wanted to stay with him. She didn't know what he could possibly do. But she had a need to make sure her family was accounted for in the chaos that must be taking place right now. She would try to save what she could. Rory wrapped his hand around her nape and pulled her into a kiss that was too short.

"This fire is going to hit Everleigh land as well. There are tenants there. I need to make sure everyone is out," he said.

She understood. She didn't tell him to be careful. It was in her eyes, and she already knew that he would. They both turned their horses. The hound ran out of the darkness and followed Rory. Winter stopped at the top of the rise to search for her husband. She could just glimpse his shape in the distance before the shadows and the darkness took him away from her, then she swung her horse around and ran the mare toward Granbury Court.

Rory followed the streambed. He kept to the path because it was the safest route in the near darkness. The light from the fire cast a pale glow and provided the only illumination to guide him. The hound had stayed with him. He rode for two miles and then, striking off in a tangent, cut through a glade until he reached the old gristmill where he and Winter had come that warm day in June. He reined in the horse just at the edge of the woods.

He could see the glow of a lantern on the stone wall just

across the millpond. Two people were arguing in what remained of the ancient courtyard filled with dry grass and scrub and surrounded by trees. It took Rory an instant to realize one of the pair was Trevor. A hot spark landed on Rory's arm. The wind was driving the fire in all directions at an alarming speed. A family of whitetail deer bolted past him for the river. His horse nervously sidestepped and Rory gripped the reins in an attempt to steady him. The air had grown hot.

He turned his attention back to the gristmill and realized on second glance, the woman with Trevor was Lavinia Richland. Rory spurred the horse through the shallow riverbed and sloshed across the millpond to the edge of stone that bordered the ancient structure. He dismounted and tied the reins of his horse to an old iron gate. He could hear Trevor shouting now, could make out the words "why" and "how could you" and something about murder. As Rory moved closer, he could hear their words.

". . . goddamn told you what would bloody happen!" Trevor was shouting.

"I didn't know. I swear it. One of us had to do something."

"What does destroying Granbury Court get you, Lavinia? What does it get us? We had Everleigh."

"For how long, Trevor?"

Making no more sound than a shadow, Rory walked into the courtyard. Lavinia saw him first and froze. Trevor spun around. As one, they both stared into Rory's blazing eyes.

"Rory." He heard Trevor say his name, and his face was suddenly bleak.

The distant scream of a horse pulled Rory's head around. On the other side of the old stone tower that had once served as a grain storage, Rory saw the stallion. *His* stallion.

*Apollo.*

Tethered to a post, the horse fought the restraint holding him.

At the same time, Rory heard the cock of a revolver. "That is as far as you best be going, guv'nor," a cold voice said from behind him.

He recognized the owner of that voice as belonging to the bastard riding the gray mare that he'd been hunting all summer. "At least until you hand me that gun I know you be carrying."

"I'm not carrying a weapon."

"Bloody hell you aren't."

With his arms raised, Rory turned. He wore no jacket. He had no place to conceal a weapon. He'd left too fast that evening to take the time to secure one to his ankle. "You've been on Granbury land the entire summer?" Rory asked Stronghold.

Stronghold's teeth flashed. "Ask your cousin about all the tunnels and places a man and horse can hide."

Rory turned his furious gaze on Trevor. He remembered everything Trevor had once said about Granbury Court's growing stable. All this time he'd had Apollo. *In another few years, we have a chance to bring in huge purses at the Ascot and Manning Downs.* "You're a fool."

"God, I am so sorry about everything," Trevor said, raking his hands through his hair. "It was Lavinia and Stronghold who started the bloody fire."

Rory's eyes impaled Lavinia. "It was never the baron behind the attacks on me, was it? Where is he?"

"The baron is dead," Trevor said. "Murdered."

In front of them, the fire was no longer a distant crackling but a steadily growing roar, and Rory knew if they didn't leave soon they would be trapped.

"We will we all be dead in fifteen minutes," Lavinia shouted over the growing din. "We have to leave!"

"I'm not going with you," Trevor said.

"How terribly heroic of you. As if you could." She viciously slapped Trevor's face. "Burn to death. I hate you! You could have had it all if you had just done it right the first time." Lavinia stopped in front of Rory, but not so close that he could grab the little bitch. "I'll thank you for your horse."

Stronghold backed up a step. "'Fraid she be correct, guv'nor. The other horses slipped their reins. Yers be the only one here. Enough to take two people. Though you can try to ride that killer stallion if you can loosen him from the post."

"You aren't leaving them alive!" Lavinia shouted. "Kill them!"

Rory didn't give Stronghold a chance to decide whether to obey the girl. He charged and hit Stronghold in the chest. The backward momentum pushed them both down the incline and into the millpond. The gun discharged next to Rory's ear. The measure of emotion that swept through Rory lent strength to his body and he took Stronghold down beneath the water, gripping him by his shirtfront. Two hands came out of the water like boar tusks into Rory's injured chest, and Stronghold dislodged the death grip, sending Rory stumbling back onto the bank. From the corner of his eye, he glimpsed Lavinia mounting his horse. Stronghold was suddenly out of the water. A bear of a man and Rory kicked out, connecting the heel of his boot to the man's knees. Stronghold still did not go down. Then a flash of black and white streaked past as the hound leapt from the bank in a growling ferocious snarl and attacked Stronghold.

Trevor smashed a tree limb across the back of the man's head and laid the man out unconscious. Trevor bent over panting. His eyes burned wet with the smoke. A tree on the other side of the millpond suddenly ignited.

Rory could hear Apollo's terrified struggle. "Take the knife," Trevor said. "Get your horse free."

Rory struggled to his feet breathing hard. He saw the stain growing on Trevor's chest and remembered the gunshot from Stronghold's gun.

"I'm so sorry," Trevor said.

But Rory wasn't going to let his cousin die so easily. "Damn you!" He shoved his shoulder beneath Trevor's. "I'm bloody not leaving you here."

He hobbled with Trevor across the open courtyard to where Apollo was tethered to a post, tearing rabidly at his lead. Blood and foam bubbled around the bit. Eyes wide with terror, the horse reared and flailed, clipping Rory in the shoulder as he tried to loosen the rope. The stallion's fight had tangled the rope into an impenetrable knot, and Rory barely had the strength to saw through the strands. Then the stallion was suddenly free.

Rory held the rope, but Apollo reared and ripped the rope from Rory's hands. The horse crashed his front forelegs down, his mane flying, his hooves striking blue sparks on the rocks, then bolted. He leapt the stone wall and splashed across the river.

All around Rory, the sky was an orange pall as sparks shot into the darkness and caught the surrounding trees. The trees in the glade were already burning like an inferno and the fire had jumped the river to the western fields.

Trevor sat bent over his knees. "Go!"

Rory thrust his shoulder beneath Trevor's and pushed him to his feet. "Like hell. Get up."

The river and millpond were too shallow to protect them. Rory felt the first drops of rain on his face, but the rain was coming too late.

They weren't going to outrun the inferno.

# Chapter 22

**T**he rains came that night.

Like teardrops at first, the rain fell light then unbelievably a storm opened up. Winter held her face to the sky and let the rain fall upon her. They had not yet all made it out of the house. The fire had reached the lake's edge, but even as Winter watched, the downpour began to extinguish the blaze. The red pall dimmed and soon there was only the night and the smell of cindered wood and ash. It still rained when dawn broke, and Winter and Eve went outside to take stock of the damage. Much of the woods around Granbury Court had been destroyed, the fields where the fire had originated two miles away were lost, but miraculously no one perished, Sheriff Derwood reported.

Rory still had not returned by noontime, and Winter began to worry, especially with Trevor now also unaccounted for.

Sheriff Derwood returned after a search and said Rory never made it to any of the tenants' homes on Everleigh last night. The wind had picked up with the rain, and Winter stood in the stable looking out as the rain fell over her husband's land.

"Is Everleigh still standing?"

"Yes, Miss Winter," Derwood said. "But the servants haven't returned yet."

"Find my husband. Please. Trevor might be with him."

After Sheriff Derwood left with six of his men, she changed her clothes and ordered a horse saddled. Old Ben and the grooms were startled by her request but did as she asked. Heavy gray clouds raced across the sky, and for an hour the rain didn't stop.

She didn't know what prompted her to ride to Everleigh. Perhaps it was a need to learn for herself if the house stood empty. What if Rory was injured and had gone there? Where was Lavinia?

The fire had burned to the hill. The same place Rory had let her off that day in June when he'd returned her to Everleigh the first time they ever made love. She could see Everleigh Hall and the surrounding trees as if nothing whatsoever had happened last night.

But someone was there. She saw a horse on the drive.

Rory's horse. The one he'd been riding last night.

Winter nudged her horse down the slippery slope now wet with mud and ash. She rode up the drive. The wind in the trees masked the sound of her approach. Rory's horse looked in poor shape. She dismounted. She ran her hands along the gelding's white-flecked flanks, cooing softly as her gaze went to the front door that stood wide open to the rain.

She entered the house. No lamps lit the corridor. The walls of the house creaked in the gusts. Somewhere a door slammed and she heard a crash. Winter did not call out Rory's name. Instead, she followed the sound of breaking glass down the corridor toward the massive library where Winter and her father used to spend evenings reading. She stopped in the doorway.

The beautiful room had not changed in the years since she had last been in here. Lavinia stood on the other side of the room in front of a safe. Winter would not have recognized the bedraggled woman if she did not know Lavinia. Her cousin's fair hair was a blackened soot-colored mess. Her dress torn.

Her fists slammed against the safe. Unless the baron had replaced the safe, Winter could have told her the combination.

Why was Lavinia riding Rory's horse? Fear and confusion lanced Winter.

Lavinia pounded her fists on the safe again. With a cry of rage, she whirled. Halfway to the door, she saw Winter.

For a moment neither moved. Then they both reacted at once. Lavinia ran toward the fireplace, her intent clear as she leapt for a poker. But Winter was already on top of her before she reached the hearth, pulling her around.

"Where is my husband?"

Lavinia blanched and pulled away.

And Winter knew something horrible had happened. Something terrible.

"Where is my husband?" she demanded again, her voice a low growl, giving her cousin a vicious shake. "Answer me, Lavinia. You are riding his horse. Where did you get it?"

Lavinia struck out at Winter and screamed. "Let go of me! I don't know where I got it. I found it. I found it last night."

Winter grabbed a handful of Lavinia's gown and spun the girl around. "Where? Where did you find it?"

"I don't know," she screamed and covered her ears. "I don't know. Trevor was with us. Trevor . . . !"

"Who started the fire?"

"Get out of my way."

But Winter was finished standing still while everything and everyone she loved was destroyed in front of her. "Who started the fire, Lavinia?"

Lavinia shoved against Winter and ran for the door, but

Winter was faster. She grabbed her cousin by the hair and
yanked her back, sending them both crashing over an end
table and to the floor. "Where is my husband?"

"He's dead," Lavinia cried when Winter straddled her
back. "He was with Trevor at the gristmill when the fire
overtook them. They couldn't get away. The fire overtook
them. I saw the whole place go up in flames." She sobbed
and sobbed. "They burned to death."

Winter rose to her feet and took a stunned step backward.

"He's dead." Lavinia buried her face in the crook of her
arm. "Stronghold was there. *He* started the fire. He and
Trevor. They started the fire, just like before. Just like before.
It is Trevor's fault. Always Trevor." Lavinia buried her face
in her palms. "Always Trevor."

"It was you from the beginning," Winter whispered, her
throat tight with agony. "It was you from the beginning.
Always *you*, Lavinia."

"It was Trevor," she sobbed. "He was supposed to be the
marquess, not his cousin. He was supposed to marry *me*. I
was supposed to be the marchioness. Not you."

With tears blinding her, Winter grabbed Lavinia by her
filthy hair and dragged her cousin to her feet and screaming through the house. She pulled her downstairs struggling
and fighting into the pantry where she shoved Lavinia into
the darkened room. Winter knew where the cook kept the
key and reached above the ledge. She locked the door, as
Lavinia slammed against it and started beating it with her
fists. Winter left the kitchen amid Lavinia's screams and
started running for her horse.

Winter met Sheriff Derwood halfway to the gristmill. A
dozen more men had joined in the search for the marquess.

"We were there earlier," Sheriff Derwood said. "Nothing is left of the place, Winter. Just charred stone."

She shook her head. Rory wasn't dead. She would know it. She would feel it in her soul. "That is just it. The place is made of stone. Underground tunnels lace that entire hillside. If Trevor was with him, he would know where to go."

"It will be dark soon."

"He's alive. I know he's alive." Winter swung the horse around.

She would not allow herself to believe otherwise.

The once beautiful glade surrounding the gristmill was gone and in its place a blackened wasteland that stretched for as far as she could see from Granbury land. The fire had crossed what was left of the riverbed but had died about two hundred yards on the other side. Winter slid off her horse and, for a moment, could only stare in horror at the desolation.

"Winter," Sheriff Derwood said, his voice pulling her around. "Look."

Winter stared into the old courtyard surrounding the gristmill.

Rory's stallion stood near the blackened wall. A rope dragged on the ground from the stallion's halter. Winter slogged across what remained of the millpond and climbed the incline into the courtyard. She turned to look into the shadowed entryway that led below the ancient structure.

She moved into the crumbling building that had survived centuries. The walls were blackened with soot that came off on her hands. Halfway down the stairs, Winter stared into the dark pit below them. A dank musty odor wafted against her nostrils from the offending darkness. She stared into the rank vat of darkness, started to turn, and stopped. She'd heard something, a noise, the distant, hollow reverberation of a dog barking. The sound had been so faint and so brief, it could have been the wind or—as she and Trevor used to imagine when they would explore these old tunnels—a banshee. A breeze pushed against her face, and she heard it again. The sound was coming from somewhere below her.

"Hurry," she called up the stairs. "Someone is down here." She couldn't see in the darkness. "We need a torch. Anything."

Rory heard the faint faraway shouts as if from a great distance and raised his head. The darkness was pitch. He'd heard the dog barking earlier and had attempted to call out. Trevor was propped in the wet darkness next to him. He was no longer conscious and Rory didn't know for sure if he still lived. He didn't know how long they'd been standing in the deep well water, but it had been steadily rising and had reached his chest.

The voices above him sounded like angels. He heard Winter call his name. Then suddenly her face peered at him over the stone rim. Someone held a torchlight and it shone down in his eyes and forced him to momentarily look away. Then Winter was calling his name and he was smiling up at her.

"It's about damn time, my love."

Winter and Rory were standing outside Trevor's room as Father Flannigan opened the door and gently closed it behind him. Rory saw the solemn expression in the old priest's eyes and knew what it meant before he spoke.

"I am surprised he has lived this long," Father Flannigan said. "But he is conscious and wants to see both of you."

Rory looked into Winter's face and saw the shimmer in her eyes. But she nodded. He braced his arm around her shoulder and together they entered Trevor's chambers. His cousin's eyes opened. Winter sat on the chair next to the bed and took his hand.

"I'm sorry." He said the softly spoken words to Winter, but when his gaze lifted, Rory knew the words were also meant for him. "I didn't know how to undo everything I had done. I allowed myself to be talked into a criminal act of lunacy. Winter . . . the boys . . . they were never supposed to have come into town that night. Lavinia . . . Is she still alive?"

Winter nodded. "She is not well. I don't know if she will be able to stand before a tribunal. We may never know for sure what happened to her father."

"Stronghold killed him. He—" Trevor coughed. Blood-tinged spittle formed on his lips. "Richly was buried somewhere in the field that burned. I . . . I signed a confession," he said. "I take responsibility for everything that has happened. Father Flannigan has the paper." He looked at Rory. "I want you to see that the authorities get it. She is not well. I don't want her to go to prison. Will you swear?"

Rory's mouth tightened. But he swore to see Trevor's last wishes fulfilled.

"The night in the glade . . . the night we came upon you. I had every intention of killing you," Trevor said. "But it's different when the gun is actually in your hand and you're looking into someone's eyes. I had never killed a man. I couldn't do it. Stronghold is the one who shot you. Your . . . bullet hit me. Lavinia and I concocted the story about the duel. I knew who you were months ago."

Trevor coughed again. His eyes closed. "I found the letters Lord Granbury wrote to your sister. Lavinia hired Stronghold to follow the posts and find you."

Winter pressed her palms against her face. "Trevor, how could you?"

"I don't know. God . . . honestly, I don't know. Something just took over when I was around her, Winter. She was beautiful and needy . . . you never needed me. You could always take care of yourself. But Lavinia. She was like a child sometimes. She loved me. I would have done anything for her." Tears welled in his eyes. "I did do anything for her."

Winter wiped the corners of his eyes and the blood from his lips. "Don't talk anymore."

He took her hand, but his eyes were on Rory's. "I wish I could have known you," he said. "Before . . . before I ever met the baron. I wish I could have been more like you in Lord Granbury's eyes. But I am glad you are the marquess, my lord. *Coz.*" His last word turned into a cough. "This place will survive now." He smiled at Winter. "And you make a beautiful marchioness."

That night in the library, Rory sat in a tall chair, his legs stretched out in front of him, and peered into the flames. Winter had gone to their room and Rory had not seen her since they'd left Trevor. He was sitting there alone when Father Flannigan came down later to tell Rory that Trevor's body would soon be ready to be moved to the guardroom. Rory came to his feet.

"Where is the confession he signed?" Rory asked Father Flannigan.

The priest removed it from his jacket pocket and gave it to Rory. "He condemns himself," Father Flannigan said. "And this will free Lavinia. I imagine he made you swear to give it to the authorities."

After Father Flannigan left, Rory stood alone in the library aware of the weight on his shoulders. Strange that he could spend so much of his life living in and out of one lie or another. Now he was bound by an oath he did not want to keep. He looked up to see Winter standing across the room. She wore yellow and looked like a beam of sunlight in the dour shadows of the room.

She walked over to him, her dress a soft inviting rustle, and quietly took the paper and the decision from him. "He did not make *me* swear an oath, my love."

And she ripped the paper in half, throwing its remains into the flames.

# Epilogue

F rost etched the glass in a myriad of patterns reflected
in the light. Christmas was upon Granbury Court
and the ice and the cold of December had set in. But in the
master's bedchamber, another kind of winter had taken hold
of Rory, one far warmer and much more pleasant than the
weather outside. His wife remained ensconced in his arms
with her back to him and her face warmed by the blazing
fire in the hearth.

"Truly you can come up with a better name than Boy,"
his wife said.

"I like Boy. It fits," Rory said stubbornly.

The hound sat on a rope carpet in front of the fireplace,
oblivious to the fact that he was the topic of much debate
going on in the bed above him.

Naming the spotted hound had been Winter's mission for
four months. But nothing seemed to fit the dog better than
Boy. It was the only name to which the hound responded.

Rory's hand slid to Winter's abdomen. He held his palm
to her flesh. "I promise I'll be more diligent in naming our
own son, madam. We'll call him Rory."

Winter turned in his arms. "Naturally. As homage to his
father's conceit."

"Naturally." He laid his lips to her perfect cleavage in a homage of his own. "And to his mother's beauty."

Her grin matched his. "You could have a girl."

"Then may she be born hairless and toothless. Or I will have to guard her with big a stick."

Winter laughed and slid her arms around his neck. He loved her laugh. "I can most certainly guarantee she will be born toothless at the very least."

He pressed his lips against the fragrant curve of her throat, loving the way she smelled, too. "Ugly. Beautiful. Boy. Girl." He smoothed her hair off her neck to give him better access. "Whatever we have will be ours, Winter."

She ran her hand over his shoulder, but already she'd begun to purr in his arms. "I love you," she said.

His answering grin was pure seduction. Their kiss passionate.

Unlike the imperfect world outside their window, theirs was a perfect joining.

And when Winter finally lay asleep in his arms, Rory held her protectively tucked against him and placed his hand possessively on her belly. Emotion closed his throat.

She was four months gone with their first child, a son or a daughter that would be born sometime around the first of June. He smiled to himself. Almost a year to the day from his arrival in Granbury.

He had not told her about Everleigh yet. He had secured the estate for the back taxes owed. Purchased it for her and for Perry. Granbury and Everleigh would at last be joined. The deed would go into her Christmas stocking on the morrow, and he was confident she would reward him very well for his thoughtfulness. She always did.

He loved her.

He would buy her the moon if he thought it would add to her happiness. But she seemed to have found her own special brand of peace and contentment in this home and with him, and did not need anything so elaborate. Their life was simple. Nothing guaranteed. A beginning.

The world where he now lived was still so foreign to him in many ways. But like the great oaks that sprang from Granbury land, his seed would also take root and grow and he would leave his own mark and his own legacy, a heady reality for a man who never wanted responsibilities or a place to call home.

Rory found that he rather liked both.